Peter Harrold thinks he's a very lucky guy. He lives in one of the best cities (Sydney) in one of the best countries (Australia). He has a wonderful wife (Caren), three great kids (Caitlyn, Lydia & Cameron), and now a very kind company (Austin Macauley) wants to publish his first novel.

To Caren, for all your love and support.

Peter Harrold

MARIA AND THE GHOSTS OF BARRENGARRY

AUSTIN MACAULEY
PUBLISHERS LTD.

A CIP catalogue record for this title is available from the British Library.

ISBN 9781786122537 (Paperback)
ISBN 9781786122544 (Hardback)
ISBN 9781786122551 (E-Book)

www.austinmacauley.com

First Published (2016)
Austin Macauley Publishers Ltd.
25 Canada Square
Canary Wharf
London
E14 5LQ

Acknowledgments

Thanks to everyone who supported and encouraged me in this endeavour but extra special thanks to Jenny, Yolanda, Mark, John, Ben and Ron.

In addition, I would like to pay my respect and acknowledge the traditional custodians of the land on which this book was written and where the story is set, and also to pay my respect to Elders both past and present.

Part 1

The Present Day

Chapter 1

Deep down Maria had always suspected that she was special. Or rather, that there was something special about her. Not in the way someone like Lady Gaga or Adele was special. It wasn't that sort of in your face, obvious to everyone specialness that was bound to lead you to fame and fortune. She often wondered about the moment people like Lady Gaga or Adele realised that they were special. But were they special or talented? Talent, of course, was a much more obvious thing. Everyone could see if you played the piano or flute brilliantly, or if you could do perfect pirouettes or cartwheels.

Special was something else, more of an inside thing. For Maria it was a kind of feeling that there was going to be something in her life that she would *do* better than most people, maybe better than anyone else. Somewhat frustratingly, even though she was approaching 12, she still hadn't worked out what it was.

She was pretty good at school work, without being the brightest in the class. Secretly, she was happy about this. As far as she could see, being really good at school work generally increased the amount of school work that you had to do, which didn't seem quite right to her. In year four one of her best friends, Genevieve, had to miss out on loads of stuff so that she could do extra tutoring to prepare her for the exam for the opportunity class. And much worse, once she'd taken it, and of course passed with flying colours, her parents had made her change schools. Now she was at a school where the idea of fun was an extra maths test. Yes, there were definitely benefits to doing just well enough to make your parents think there were no issues academically, but not so well that they started to consider opportunity classes or selective high schools.

What Maria would have really liked to be special at was dancing. For as long as she could remember she had never been able to stay still for long. In her mind any supposedly spare moment was an opportunity to be practising a dance move or perfecting her cartwheel. Maria didn't see why people couldn't talk to her while she was in a handstand or cartwheeling around the room. But for some reason other people, and especially her dad, found it pretty annoying. When she thought about it, this may well have been a big part of the reason her parents had allowed Maria to take on so many dance classes, hoping that she might burn off some of that kinetic energy.

Whatever the reason, Maria was now doing 10 hours a week of various dance classes, and mostly loving every minute of it. Though she could have done without her ballet teacher's shouting, which always increased in both frequency and volume as the annual grade exams approached. But much as she loved the dancing, and as much as she enjoyed the positive feedback about how well she was doing, Maria also knew, and not that deep down, that she was probably not going to be good enough to be a dancer. When she watched her classmate Anna glide effortlessly across the floor, Maria knew that Anna had 'it'. That natural talent that maybe, just maybe, might lead her to being a dancer when she got older.

Maria often looked at the other members of her family to see if they might offer some clues as to what her specialness might be. When she'd watched the Olympics on TV she remembered seeing a kayaker or canoeist – she could never remember which was which – win a medal in an event in which both her dad and mum had previously won Olympic medals. How cool was that? Surely they must have passed on of some very special genes? And now she'd attended a couple of the sex education classes at school she had a much better idea of what that actually involved.

And in films and books families often had similar qualities or powers, like the family in *The Incredibles*, who were all superheroes. Maria had always thought that the girl's powers – being able to make herself invisible and generate force fields - were especially useful ones for an eleven year old.

However, whilst her mum, dad, sister and brother all had their special qualities and interests, it didn't appear to Maria that there was any sort of theme to them. People did say that her little brother, Bobby, was 'incredibly good at soccer for a six year old'. Maria put this down to him sleeping with a soccer ball and with his boots on the night before a game. With that sort of commitment how could he not be good at it?

And her sister, Lizzie, was 'a fantastic goal shooter'. In Maria's mind this was mostly due to her height, Lizzie was a good 10 centimetres taller than Maria, even though she was 17 months younger. Apparently her dad had been shorter than his younger brother at the same age she was at now, but after his teenage growth spurt he ended up being taller than him. Even though she outwardly made out that she didn't mind, Maria desperately wanted the same to be true for her, as she was more than a little tired of people thinking that Lizzie was the eldest. But Maria herself disproved any chance of a sporty type theme of specialness by being at best an average performer on the sports field.

Her dad was, well, a dad. Maria knew he worked with computers, and was a manager (whatever that meant) but he didn't seem to enjoy it enough to be special at it. Maria was sure that anything you were really special at you had to love. Apart from that he seemed to do and know a bit about everything, just like you'd expect a dad should.

Mum, on the other hand, was a teacher and absolutely loved her work. However, Maria didn't know if she was particularly special at it. She regularly talked at the dinner table about not having enough hands, or there not being enough hours in the day, and that she didn't know if she would survive to the end of term. But somehow she always did.

People, especially her relatives, always said that Maria took after her mum, and that Lizzie was more like her dad's side of the family. Maria was okay with this, apart from the comments and jokes about her mum being a white witch. Apparently, in the past her mum had had some supposedly supernatural experiences. When she'd relayed them to Dad soon after they'd started going out, he'd dubbed her the "white witch".

Added to this Mum did seem to have an uncanny ability to put people at ease. Dad would often say that Mum only had to say 'Hello' to someone for them to immediately tell her their whole life story. Maria wasn't sure how true this was, but she did remember a time when everyone had been waiting in the car while Mum paid for something or other. When she'd returned she said that the reason she'd taken so long was because the salesperson had wanted to tell her about his marriage break-up and his drinking problems.

Despite this Maria certainly didn't think of herself as the daughter of a witch, or that she would inherit some mystical or supernatural powers. Her specialness, she feared, wasn't going to be anything nearly as exciting or interesting as that. She'd probably just end up being really good at balancing a spoon on the end of her nose or able to put her whole fist into her mouth, just like her Aunty Wendy could.

Chapter 2

Maria and her best friend Liv often talked about what they were going to do or be when they grew up, assuming that is that they weren't going to be famous dancers, actors or singers.

She and Liv had been best friends from the moment they met each other, which was on their first day at pre-school six years before. At first sight they looked like a bit of an odd couple. Maria was small and wiry with sandy coloured hair, while Liv was tall and stocky with very dark hair. Dad once described them as 'looking a bit like Laurel and Hardy'. Having no idea who they were, Maria thought at the time that it probably wasn't a compliment. When she eventually got to see a scene from one of their old black and white movies on some TV show, she'd made a mental note to give her dad a good telling off when he came home from work.

From the very beginning Maria and Liv looked at the world, people, and things in the same way. They'd lost count of amount times one of them had started to say something, maybe an observation about someone or something, and exactly the same thought had been going through the other one's head. 'That's just what I was thinking' the other one would say, and then they'd burst out laughing, touch fingertips and say 'spooooky'.

Of course there'd been a few fallings out over the years. Normally these were about one of them thinking the other was ignoring them in favour of somebody else in the class. But they rarely lasted more than a day or two.

And now they were in year six, their last year at primary school. They'd vowed that they were going to make it a really special year, as it was looking increasingly unlikely that they would be going to the same high school the following year. Only one of the schools on Maria's current high school shortlist was on Liv's too, and it wasn't the preferred one for either of them.

The year had got off to a great start though, as on the first day back it was confirmed that they would be having their favourite teacher, Mister Andrews, for their final year at school. And then a few days later, Mr A had informed them that their school had been one of only a very few primary schools chosen to trial the use of iPads in the classroom, and it's been decided that this class should be the one to get them. Maria reckoned everyone in the school had heard the cheer that followed that announcement.

She and Liv both had an iPod Touch, which they used all the time at home. But you could do so much more with iPads. And Mr A was great at finding ways of using them for their schoolwork. The only down side was that they weren't allowed to take them home, and so most of the homework still had to be done with a boring old pencil or pen. When Maria had complained about this at home one afternoon, she'd been surprised about how defensive her mum had got about it.

"Well, you can't do everything on an iPad," she'd said. "You still need to be able to write. I mean, what happens when you get to exams? You have to write then."

At this point Lizzie chipped in, "But Mum that's so old fashioned. In a few years I bet everyone will be doing their exams on computers. That's what my teacher thinks."

"Hmm, I'm not so sure about that. But in the meantime it's pencils, so let me see you using them to finish off this homework."

Maria had recalled that discussion a few weeks later when Dad had given her mum an iPad for her birthday. Within in a few days Mum was doing everything on it, and didn't know how she'd 'ever been able to manage without one'. Most nights now, as Maria was going off to sleep, she could hear her mum's nails tap, tapping away on the iPad as she entered another item on the shopping list, or set an alarm to remind her of something to do the following day. Pencils don't seem to be getting much of a look-in nowadays, she thought to herself smiling.

Chapter 3

It was breakfast time when Maria first heard that she was going to visit Kangaroo Valley. Even at the best of times breakfast was not a lively affair in Maria's household. Especially so on the days that Mum had to get out to work as well. Maria, Lizzie and Bobby were all head down in their bowls of assorted cereals when Dad, who was busy preparing the school lunches, made the announcement.

"Hey you guys, been meaning to mention, next weekend we're going to be getting out of Sydney for a few days. An old friend of mine has a house in a place called Kangaroo Valley that he rents out, and he does really good mate's rates. It's been ages since we got away somewhere all together. It'll be really fun to get into the country, do a bit of bush walking, and sit beside a big log fire."

He paused momentarily to see if his own obvious excitement was going to be even remotely picked-up on. As it wasn't, he decided to push on.

"Pete, the guy who has the house, says that there are loads of kangaroos down there, and sometimes they come right up to the house."

This was enough to spark some interest from Bobby, albeit in keeping with his current favourite topic of conversation.

"Does that mean that there will be kangaroo poo all over the gardens?"

Though not quite the type of response that Dad had hoped for, he saw it as a possible opening to generate some broader interest.

"Sure. And there might even be wombat poo, and echidna poo, in fact I'm sure we will see all sorts of animals. Hey, girls what do you think? Fancy getting up close and personal with some kangaroos and wombats?"

Lizzie, who had just finished her Weet-Bix, grunted a, "Maybe," as she carried her bowl over to the sink.

It was then that Dad realised that Maria's lack of contribution was related to her close attention to her iPod which had been strategically placed behind a yoghurt pot.

"Maria, how many times have I told you not to play with that before you're completely ready for school? Please switch it off right now or you won't see it again for the rest of the week."

Maria ignored the question and went straight on the counter-attack.

"Dad, I'm not *playing* on it, I'm just asking Liv about what homework we need to bring into school today. Why do you always assume that all I do is play on it?"

"I don't care what you're doing on it, you know fine well that it doesn't get switched on before you're ready." However, the fact that from what he could see it wasn't actually a game seemed to mollify him a bit and he decided to at least use the fact he'd finally got Maria's attention to his advantage.

"Anyway, what do you think about what I was saying before about getting out of Sydney and seeing lots of kangaroos?"

Realising that she'd seemed to have gotten away with the iPod at breakfast thing, Maria decided she should probably placate her dad by trying to show some interest. "Oh, I thought that was you and Bobby and having one of your boysie chats about poo again. When are we going? In the next school holidays?"

"No, like I said, next weekend. And as the Monday's a public holiday it means we can go for three nights."

Maria was suddenly a lot more interested. "How can it be three nights? If we leave after my dance classes on Saturday, and come back on Monday, that's just two nights." The look on her face which accompanied the 'that's just two nights' statement was fully intended to leave her dad in no doubt as to what her thoughts on this topic were.

But Dad was obviously prepared for this reaction, and played the 'I've already spoken to Mum' card.

"I've already spoken to Mum about it, and she and I have agreed that as it's been so long since we've had a break together as a family, and because it's such a good deal, especially over a long weekend, that we should make the most of it. And we have spoken to you before about how we might occasionally ask you to miss a day of dancing. And this is the first time we've done it this year …" Dad knew that there were several more 'Ands' but thought better of it, and decided to finish with a "Well?"

"Well, what?" Maria responded as brusquely as she could manage.

"Well, do you think you'll be okay about missing dance, and joining in with having some fun with the rest of your family?"

"Well, it doesn't sound like I've got much of choice, does it?" Maria's volume switch had definitely gone up a couple of levels. "I thought the idea was that you'd ask me first to see if it's okay for me to miss it. And Miss Leora said last Saturday that we're going to start learning a new dance for the end of year concert over the next couple of weeks. And if I miss out at the beginning it's always very hard to catch-up. And …"

21

Maria's dad sensed that there were probably going to be quite a few more 'ands' and so he bravely decided to interject. "That's a fair point, we did say that we would talk to you first, but there were quite a few people interested in Pete's house, and so I had to say we'd take it pretty quickly. And as it's a long weekend he was looking to rent it out for all three nights." He sensed that this wasn't really making much of an impression on Maria and so he added "If you think it would help, Mum or I could come in and talk to Miss Leora this week, to let her know that it's our fault, not yours, that you're missing the classes. And that you're really keen to get a big part in the show."

Maria picked up her bowl and walked over to the dishwasher. "Dad, it's not a play, you know. There aren't parts."

Her mum walked in just as the dishwasher tray took the impact of a half-rammed cereal bowl. "Everything okay in here?" she said to the room in general.

"I was just telling the kids about our trip to Kangaroo Valley, and Maria's not very happy about missing her dance classes on the Saturday," said Dad. And then a thought struck him which he decided – foolishly as it turned out – to share with everyone. "It's not just you who'll be missing out, you know, Maria. Bobby's going to miss his soccer practice on that Saturday morning, and …"

Maria's mum interrupted him. "Actually he won't be. As it's a long weekend they've decided not to have the soccer practice."

The fact that Bobby was not going to miss out on something didn't appear to be any consolation to Maria. "So I'm the only one who has to miss out, that's great."

Without even realising it was happening Maria's mum's voice switched to its most soothing and conciliatory tone. "Look Maria, I'm sure Miss Leora will understand. There's still six months to go before the concert, and people can't be expected to attend every class. If you were sick you wouldn't be expected to go, would you?"

Maria looked at her mum and then her dad, and realised that she only had one course of action left to her. "*Whatever*," she exclaimed in the most disdainful voice she could muster as she stomped up the stairs to her bedroom.

Mum looked at Dad. "It's a control thing," she said. "If you'd asked her if she was okay about missing dance sometime in the next few weeks, then let her know in a day or so that we were thinking about the long weekend, she would probably have said fine without blinking."

Dad realised that he was getting another of his frequent lessons in bringing up pre-teen girls. In a resigned 'I'm out of my depth here' voice he responded with "Whatever." And then he carried the lunchboxes out to the waiting backpacks beside the front door.

Chapter 4

Maria sat in the back of the car doing her best to not watch the DVD that was causing both Lizzie and (especially) Bobby to regularly convulse into fits of laughter. Whilst she had a firm view of the type of movie they should watch on a Friday night drive out of Sydney, she also eventually had to concede that it was Bobby's turn to choose. This of course meant that it was an animated one, and that they had all seen it at least 12 times before. Maria had tried very hard during the walk home from school to convince Bobby of the merits of a *High School Musical* movie. But since he'd started school he was much harder to sway. He had his own opinions for goodness sake. And firm ones at that.

Despite not winning the movie debate, Maria reluctantly admitted to feeling excited about the coming weekend. The previous Saturday her mum had spoken to Miss Leora about Maria missing the following day's dance classes and rather unexpectedly Miss Leora had been absolutely fine about it. In fact, during one of the breaks she had shared with Maria the story of a romantic weekend she'd had in Kangaroo Valley, and that it was still one of the most beautiful places she'd ever been to. Maria felt that Miss Leora had gone into a little too much detail about some aspects of her trip there – the word 'lingerie' sparked images that Maria preferred to forget. But on the other hand prompting Miss Leora to think about her time there had put her into such a good mood that she'd barely raised her voice for the rest of the afternoon. And as Maria left the class Miss Leora called out to her to have a great time the following weekend and, rather unnecessarily in Maria's mind, she had added with a conspiratorial look in her eye that "maybe *you* will meet someone special there?"

Packing for the weekend had been fun. She and Lizzie had started getting their stuff together on Tuesday or Wednesday, but somehow they both still had things to grab as Dad was trying to lock the front door of their house. When it came down to it, Maria thought that as long as she had Pink Bear, who had been her constant sleep companion for the last 10 years, and her iPod then she could probably survive anything the weekend might throw at her. Of course having Wi-Fi in the house would be a distinct bonus so that she could keep in touch with Liv and her other school friends. Dad had been ridiculously vague about whether or not his friend's house had Wi-Fi, but very excited about the prospect of there being a wood pile and an axe.

At last the movie ended, but this only brought short relief for Maria, as about three minutes later Bobby wanted to know if they were over halfway there yet? For some reason Mum and Dad always found this very cute – to start with.

"Yes, we're way over halfway there, Bobby, in fact I'd say we're probably three-quarters of the way by now," said Dad.

Bobby considered this for at least few seconds and then asked, "So how long is it before we get there?"

"About 30 minutes," replied Dad.

Again Bobby gave this some deep consideration before enquiring, "How long is 30 minutes?"

Mum must have recognised a slight tensing of Dad's shoulders because at this point she stepped into the exchange. "Thirty minutes is about the length of a 'Star

Wars the Clone Wars' episode, Bobby. And you know how short they always seem, don't you?"

Sensing that this would only lead into a discussion about that's because Clone Wars are so good and being in the car isn't, Maria decided that would she try and change the topic under discussion.

"Dad, how many times have you been to Kangaroo Valley?"

"I used to go quite there quite a lot," he responded. "Before you lot were born – in fact, even before I met your mum – I used to come here with Pete. You know the guy who owns the house we're going to be staying in. We would come down and stay in different holiday houses, or sometimes we'd camp there. It really is a fantastic place with lots to do."

He stopped for a moment as if to allow the memories to return. "I remember that there was a great swim hole on the river, which was such a beautiful spot. And there's a great pub there too, which we spent way too much time in." He smiled and glanced at Maria's mum.

"You mean you used to go there to get drunk," Lizzie said rather indignantly. Ever since a presentation they'd attended at school, both Maria and Lizzie (but especially Lizzie) felt it was their dutiful responsibility to monitor and comment on their parents' drinking habits. Even if they were habits from over 10 years ago. The way Lizzie saw it, it was best never to miss an opportunity to let them know that she was watching.

Dad cleverly sidestepped the insinuation by responding with "Actually, I seem to remember that we had a fantastic night there on one of our first dates, didn't we dear?" He then reached over and touched Maria's mum's knee.

Maria recalled Miss Leora's story from the previous Saturday about her romantic trip there, and felt herself cringe at the thought of spending the weekend in a place filled with couples walking around hand-in-hand and kissing everywhere you looked. *Yuk.*

Bobby decided it was his turn again for a question, "Daaad, what's a valley?"

"That's a very good question," Dad responded. To Maria's mind, Dad thought all of Bobby's questions were good ones, even when they were obviously stupid. But at least this one wasn't related to 'how far' or 'how long'. "Hmm, how should I put it, valleys are areas of land that have steep hills or mountains on each side. I think they're usually formed by a river eroding …"

Mum chipped in with a quick translation, "Eroding is wearing away, Bobby."

Dad continued, "… yep, a river erodes, or wears away, the ground over millions of years. I'm pretty sure that's what happened in Kangaroo Valley. The Kangaroo River has been gradually wearing away the rock. But what makes it so spectacular is that all the erosion has left behind a big area of flat land surrounded by these sheer (Mum said "very steep") cliffs that have all these amazing colours in them. During the day when it's sunny they look yellow, maybe even gold-ish, and then in the evening when the sun is setting they can look really red."

"Oh, I'd forgotten about that," said Mum. "Do you think we'll be there in time to see it this evening?"

"Don't think so. I think it's going to be just too late," replied Dad. "That's definitely something to look forward to tomorrow night though."

Everybody was quiet for a moment. "You know," said Mum, "the other day when I was driving home from work I'm sure they were talking about Kangaroo Valley on the radio, which was a bit of a coincidence. Anyway, the speaker said that it was one of the largest – maybe they said it was the largest – proper valleys in the world."

"What do you mean by proper valley, Mum?" asked Lizzie.

"Actually I'm not sure that's the word they used, but I think it was to do with the fact that the valley is completely surrounded by cliffs and escarpments."

"That's right," said Dad. "There are only two or three roads in or out of the valley, and they're all really steep and windy. Just like the ones in the Tour de France, guys." He glanced in the mirror to see if the kids understood the reference.

"Arrghh, I completely forgot about that," said Mum. "We should have given Bobby one of those travel sickness pills before we left. I don't suppose we were clever enough to leave some in the car for emergencies ..." as she opened the glove box door and started to rummage around amongst the maps, tissue packets and various chargers that lived in there.

"Nope, we weren't that clever," she announced to the car in general a few moments later.

Maria wasn't really sure why the thought suddenly came into her head, but it did, and almost without knowing it popped out as a question, "How long have people lived in the valley?"

Assuming it was mostly directed at him, Dad decided to have a go at responding to it. "Some of the buildings in the village are pretty old, and I'm pretty sure the bridge over the river is over 100 years old. So I'd guess there have been people there since at least the late 1800s."

As well as monitoring her parents' drinking habits, Lizzie also saw herself as responsible for ensuring that Australia's indigenous population were never left out of the reckoning in any family discussion or decision making. "How about the aboriginals? Do you think they ever lived in the valley?"

"That's a good question," said Dad. Maria briefly wondered why her last question hadn't received the 'that's a good question' award as well. Maybe, she thought, it's something to do with Dad's ability to answer them. "I don't know for sure, but you would have to think that they at least knew about it. I think the aboriginal tribes were mostly pretty nomadic. That is, they moved about and didn't stay in one place for very long," he quickly added in an attempt to pre-empt the need for Mum to add a translation. "You know, I'm pretty sure there's a little museum in the valley, near the bridge. That might be a good place to visit, especially if it looks like it's going to rain."

"Urgh, that sounds really boring," moaned Bobby. "I thought we were going to go canoeing."

"Hey guys, we're just about to start the drive down into the valley," said Dad excitedly. "Unfortunately I think it's going to be a bit too dark to really see much, but you'll definitely get an idea of steep the walls of the valley are as we start going round all the hairpin bends."

"I do hope Bobby is going to be alright," said Mum looking back at him.

However, as soon as they exited the first slight bend in the road Bobby indicated that he wasn't likely to be. "I feel siiick, Mum."

"Try looking forward," and "I'll open his window," said Mum and Dad simultaneously. This seemed to do the trick for a couple of bends. But after the first real hairpin Bobby exclaimed, "I feel reaalllly sick Mum."

"Do you mean you feel sick or you're going to be sick?" asked Mum.

"Urrrggh, he better not be sick in the car," shrieked Lizzie.

The bubble containing Lizzie's words was still hanging in the air above her head when Bobby started to visibly turn a pale shade of grey.

"Quick, pass him that plastic bag, Lizzie," said Mum.

"Pull over, Dad, pull over!" screamed Lizzie.

"Don't do it this way! Put your head out of the window," demanded Maria.

Just as the plastic bag was being placed below Bobby's chin, his shoulders heaved and he was sick. To his credit he got most of it into the bag.

"Good boy," said Mum.

"Gross," said Lizzie. "Argghhh, some of it's gone on my best jeans." She started to slide across her seat away from Bobby and onto Maria's seat.

Maria put her arms up to try and push Lizzie back the way she was coming from, and said "Phew, it smells really bad."

"Dad will pull over as soon as he can," said Mum.

"I don't think I'll be able to pull over while we're still on the hilly part of the road," Dad responded. "We're almost at the bottom, and once we are it's only five more minutes until we get to the house. Do you think you can hang on until then, Bobby?"

There was a non-committal grunt from the plastic bag.

Not a great start to the weekend, Maria thought to herself. But just as she did the road started to flatten and straighten out a bit. Even though the sun was completely gone, it had been a very sunny day and there was a sort of reddish purple glow to the sky. The glow allowed her to become aware of the cliffs that Dad had talked about off in the distance on either side of the car. And when she angled herself to look between Mum and Dad she could see more cliffs further off in the distance in front of the car. There were lots of trees, especially over near the cliffs, but as they drove there also seemed to be fields on both sides. The road started to dip and climb and she also became aware of creeks and streams criss-crossing their way across the valley floor.

Maria thought she saw an animal, but she wasn't sure, maybe it was a bush or some grass? But then she was certain she'd seen one. "Hey, I just saw an animal in that field we just passed."

"Was it a cow?" asked Lizzie.

"Where's a cow?" asked Bobby excitedly. Now that he'd been sick the colour was beginning to return to his face. Though in truth, he would've had to be very sick to not join in a discussion about his favourite animal. Maria thought that it wasn't cows he was really interested in, more the size of their poos.

"It was too small to be a cow," said Maria, "though it was kind of that shape."

"It was probably a wombat," said Dad. "This is exactly the time of day that they come out. How cool is that? We've only been in Kangaroo Valley for a few minutes and we've already started to see the local wildlife."

"I think that's the first time I've seen a wombat in the wild," declared Maria, mostly to herself. That's pretty cool, she thought.

And as Dad signalled to turn left off the road, she also got a strange sensation, a bit like 'having been here before' or déjà vu, but not exactly either of those. Whatever it was, as the car started to drive up the side road, the hairs on her skin stood up just like they did when Mum brushed her hair after it had been washed.

Chapter 5

They soon turned off the sealed road and went through some gates on to a dirt drive. There were trees to their right, which Maria guessed correctly were hiding their view of the house. After about 150 metres the drive swept up and to the right and directly in front of them the headlights illuminated the most fantastic looking wooden house.

"Welcome to Grevillia Cottage," said Dad, "also known as Pete's house."

Dad parked the car parallel to the front of the house, with the boot close to the steps that led up to the veranda. Maria and Lizzie escaped from the car as soon as it came to a stop. Bobby was keen to follow but couldn't quite release the seat belt whilst holding the plastic bag full of sick.

Mum was immediately into 'operation clean-up' mode. "Now, Bobby, don't you move just yet. Here, pass me the bag," she said as she swivelled round in her seat and on to her knees so that she could reach over to see how much damage Bobby had inflicted on his surroundings. "Lizzie can you try and find some plastic bags from somewhere. There might be some stuffed in that crate in the boot that your dad keeps the jump leads and tools in. Maria, you go with Dad and see if you can get a bucket and some rags from the house. Oh, and don't forget to put some water in the bucket."

Lizzie was standing beside the car trying to flick pieces of - she didn't really know what, and didn't want to think too much about – off her new mustard coloured jeans. "If only I'd warn my black ones," she muttered as she moved to look in the boot, which Dad had just opened.

Maria was standing a few metres away from the car doing a slow 360 degree turn taking in both the house and the view. Even though it was almost completely dark now, as she stared out and her eyes adjusted to the light, she could sense that this was going to be a pretty amazing view come the morning. She was jolted back to the now when her mum called out again.

"Maria, buckets, rags and water, please."

Maria turned and jogged over to the steps, getting to the front door just as her dad was opening it. He switched on the lights and Maria followed him in. As she went through the front door she let out a little "wow" and then said, "What an amazing house, Dad."

On the left-hand side was a dining table with benches on both sides which looked like it could accommodate 20 people – well 20 kids maybe. Beyond that was a large breakfast bar with wooden high stools pushed under the bar bit. And past the breakfast bar was the kitchen area which had one of those cutting block tables in the middle of the floor. Mum always wanted one of those, Maria thought to herself. Dad always pointed out that first she was going to have get a kitchen big enough to have one. And before that they'd have to have a house big enough for that sized kitchen.

Above the cutting table, hanging from the ceiling, was a frame with loads of pots and kitchen utensils attached to it by hooks. "Oooh, Mum is going to be so envious when she sees this," Maria whispered to herself.

On the right was the living area. There were four, no five huge lounges. Between two of the lounges that had their backs to the front of the house was a table with a telescope on it. Maria thought that it would give great views of the valley, and made a mental note to be first up in the morning to have a look through it. On the far wall to her right was a very large black firewood thingy. Maria couldn't remember what they were called, maybe it was a stove? And beside the stove, stacked up against the wall was a huge pile of firewood. Dad had been very excited about the prospect of getting it lit and 'sitting beside the fire reading books, playing cards and falling asleep'. Maria could see why now, it all looked really welcoming and cosy.

Maria's reverie was disturbed by a call from outside. "Maria, what are you doing? Have you found that bucket yet?"

"Not yet, Mum, I'm looking for it," she shouted back. "Hey, Dad, do you know where they might keep a bucket?" she said more quietly.

Dad had gone straight down the central corridor which led to the bedrooms and bathroom in the back of the house. As he came out of one of the bedrooms he called back, "Try under the sink in the kitchen, and if it's not there then try the laundry, which is down here beside the bathroom."

"Okay, thanks," said Maria as she slid across the floorboards and into the kitchen. Thankfully, along with all manner of cleaning products, tea towels and rubber gloves there was indeed a bucket under the kitchen sink. And it had a blue cleaning cloth neatly folded over the rim. "Yes," Maria said and she lifted it out and into the sink. After filling it half full of water, she lifted the bucket out of the sink and carefully carried it out of the house and down the steps to the car.

By now Mum had removed Bobby from the car and stripped him down to his underwear. "Thanks for that, Maria, put it down beside the car, just there," pointing to a spot beside the door where Bobby had been sitting. "How does the house look?"

Not much got past Mum Maria realised. "I just had a quick look. I haven't seen the bedrooms yet. But from what I saw it looks amazing. There's a big – what do you call them – is it a stove?"

"I think they call them wood heaters or just fires," said Mum.

"Anyway there's a big one, and there's loads of wood beside it. And there's a fantastic kitchen, which I think you're going to love. And there's a telescope as well, which …"

"I'm just about done here," interrupted Mum. "Do you think you could take Bobby inside and see if Dad can find him a blanket, or maybe he should just get the fire on, while I take a look at the damage in the car. Thanks."

"Okay, not a problem," Maria said and walked over to take Bobby's hand.

"Do you know where I'm sleeping?" asked Bobby as they started up the stairs. The allocation of bedrooms and beds was always a bid deal when they went away anywhere. Who got the top bunk, who got the room nearest to Mum and Dad, or the one furthest away from the adults.

"I don't know I haven't seen the bedrooms yet. Should we go in and look, and then *we* can decide?"

Even though Bobby wasn't quite six yet, he recognised the very slight conspiratorial tone in Maria's voice. 'We' meant before Mum and Dad get a chance to look and decide for us, and, much more significantly, before Lizzie.

"Yes, good idea, let's go," he said and he sprinted up the last couple of steps.

"Hang on a sec," said Maria. She was beginning to get that feeling again. The one that caused the hairs on her arms and the back of her neck to stand up. She wondered what was causing it. It wasn't exactly unpleasant, but it normally only happened when someone was doing something like brushing her hair or scratching her back. But there certainly wasn't anyone or anything touching her here on the stairs. She had a sudden thought that maybe it was to do with the pangs of guilt she'd been feeling during the week about making such a fuss about missing the dance classes.

"Hey Mum, MUM."

"Yes, Maria," replied Mum as she removed her head from the foot well of the car and angled her body so that she could see round the car door.

"I just wanted to say that I'm really glad that you and Dad booked this house and that we've come away for the weekend. I think it's going to great." She paused for a moment and then added, "And I'm sorry I gave you such a hard time about missing dancing tomorrow."

Mum smiled, "Thank you for saying that. I do think it's what we all need. And we will have lots of fun. Though before I can start having any fun I will need to get the smell of vomit out of my nostrils." She said this last bit as she started to turn herself back towards the foot well. Then she quickly turned back and called out to Maria, "It was good that you said that to me, Maria, but don't forget to say it to Dad as well. He's done most of the organising of this weekend. It'll mean a lot to him."

"Okay, I will," Maria shouted as she pulled open the front door and ushered Bobby through. "Come on Bobster, let's go and see what the beds we're going to have."

***

Although it took three attempts to start it, and several mild expletives, Dad did finally get the fire going, and the heat from it quickly filled the front part of the house. While he was doing that, Mum *oohed* and *aahed* her way round the kitchen as she moved the food from the cool box into the enormous fridge, and started to heat up the spaghetti bolognaise that she'd prepared the night before.

They had dinner at the big dining table. It felt very odd to Maria – at home they seemed to fill their table, but here the five of them only took up one end. After clearing up, despite the kids' protestations, it was decided that there wasn't going to be a card game beside the fire tonight. Mum and Dad ran through the usual 'it's late', 'it's been a long week' and 'Mum and Dad need some time for themselves'. However, the negotiations did result in the kids not having to have a bath before bed, just a quick wash and teeth clean, leaving time to read before lights out.

The bedroom allocation question hadn't been hard to resolve. The kids could have had a bedroom each but both Maria and Lizzie had decided that, for the first night at least, in a strange house, they would prefer to share the room with two single beds in it. Whilst Bobby had been delighted to take the top bunk in one of those bunk beds which had a double bed on the bottom. Mum thought this would be okay because he wouldn't hurt himself as much if for some reason he fell off the top bunk during the night. Whereas Bobby thought jumping from the top bunk on to the bed below looked like his idea of fun.

When he came in to say goodnight to them, Dad said that the girls could read for a bit longer "just make sure the light is off by 10." Maria suspected this was probably because they felt bad about not allowing the cards.

As he leaned over to kiss her forehead, Maria whispered "I'm really pleased we've come away to the house, Dad. And I'm really sorry for making so much of a fuss about missing dancing."

Dad smiled, and whispered back, "Thanks for saying that, Maria, I really appreciate it. I think it's going to be great weekend. And so make sure you have a good sleep so that you're ready for action tomorrow. I reckon we should get the weekend kicked off with a big cooked breakfast, what do you think? And I could definitely do with your help doing the poached eggs."

"Urgh, I hate poached eggs," said Lizzie from her bed on the other side of the bedroom.

"We can do some scrambled eggs for those people with peculiar tastes," said Dad without turning his head, and smiling at Maria.

"Sure Dad, I'd be happy to help."

Dad got up and walked to the door. As he pulled it closed behind him he said "And make sure you don't forget to switch the lights off by 10."

Maria heard his footsteps on the wooden floorboards as he walked down the hallway to join Mum beside the fire. They seemed very loud, much louder than footsteps sounded on their floorboards in their own house back in Sydney. Maria wondered why that might be. Maybe it was something to do with being in the country? She reached over and picked up her book from the bedside table. She was about halfway through the fourth book in the *Ranger's Apprentice* series, and had thoroughly enjoyed all of them, including this one. But having examined the picture on the front cover, and re-read the text on the back cover (for about the tenth time) she decided she was probably a bit too tired to read. She put the book back on the table, and reached over to switch off her light.

"Hey, Lizzie, how long are you going to read for, do you think?"

"Not very long" replied Lizzie. "I'm feeling pretty tired after school sports and that drive down. What about you?"

"I'm switching my light off now." And she did.

Maria pummelled her pillow into the required shape (Mum always said that it reminded her of a cat pawing at a cushion before it settled down for a snooze) and rolled over on to her left side facing the wall, just as she did every night. As she closed her eyes and settled for sleep, Maria's thoughts were filled with images of what they would be doing over the next few days. Little did she know that the following three days, or more precisely the following three nights, were going to change her life forever.

Chapter 6

Maria felt herself becoming awake. Or at least she thought she was. Something didn't feel quite right.

She heard a noise. And a few seconds later heard it again. That must be what had woken me, she thought.

Maria lay very still waiting for it to occur again. It was a much longer wait but there it was. This time she could make it out much more clearly. It sounded like a creaking noise and it was coming from outside. Her bed was the one which was closer to the outside wall and hence to the window.

She realised that the hairs on her arms and the back of her neck were standing up again, like they had earlier on in the car, and again on the steps to the house. But this time it was different. She couldn't really feel it – it was more like she was observing it.

She heard the creaking sound again. She realised that it was getting closer and – causing her to breathe in sharply – that it was footsteps. Someone, or something, was walking very slowly along the porch that ran round the front and sides of the house. She remembered that Dad had said that wombats and possums would be out at night and might come into the garden or, in the case of possums, even get on to the roof. "And so don't be surprised if you heard strange noises on the tin roof. That's just the possums," he'd told them.

That made her feel better, and she thought about getting up on to her knees and taking a peek behind the curtains to see if she could spot whatever animal it was. But before she could she heard the footstep again, and this time it was a lot closer, almost right outside the window. And there something about the sound, it was very soft and deep, not at all like the padding or scratching sounds that she'd imagine small animals would make on wooden boards.

She decided that she wasn't brave enough to get up and look. She'd just wait and hopefully in time it would go away.

Almost as soon as Maria had that thought there was another footstep, and this time she knew it was right outside the window. Without consciously doing it or being aware of it, Maria held her breath.

The tap on the window pane caused her to let out a muffled yelp, and start breathing again, but now very rapidly. She doubted that wombats or possums went around tapping on windows.

"Who's there?" she shouted in a whisper. She waited for a few seconds and then added "Go away, whoever you are."

She waited for a few seconds. And then for the first time wondered if Lizzie might have heard the sounds and woken up too. All this time she had been lying on her side facing the wall, facing away from Lizzie's bed. She started to very slowly roll over under the quilt, as she didn't want to give whoever or whatever was outside the window any indication that anyone was awake in the room. As Maria turned the hairs on her skin felt like they were literally standing up straight, and she had the strangest sensation that the quilt was really heavy.

Once she'd rolled all the way over Maria put the sensation to one side and peered across the room towards Lizzie's bed. The curtains did a very good job of keeping the room dark, and so it was difficult to make out if she was awake or not. She decided to risk a whisper.

"Lizzie, Lizzie, are you awake?" There was no response.

She wondered about waking her up, and as she did there was a second tap on the window. That made her mind up for her. "Lizzie," she whispered again, but this time much more forcefully. Still no response.

What should she do? What on earth did the person outside want? Maybe it's a burglar, who's seen that somebody is staying at the house and has come up to see if there's anything worth taking? But why would they tap on the window and risk waking people up? But then again maybe they were checking to see if anyone was awake before they tried coming into the house. Maria's thoughts raced – What to do, what to do?

After a few seconds Maria narrowed it down to two options. Go and wake up Dad, so that he can take a look outside. Or just put the bedside lamp on, and hopefully that might startle whoever is outside and cause them to go away. She started to consider the pluses and minuses of the two options (just like they did in the school debating team) but realised that it would take much too long. She took a deep breath and whispered to herself 'okay, I'll just do both'.

Maria carefully moved her arm up and out from under the quilt, and started to fold it back. Or at least she tried to. For some reason she couldn't get a good hold on it. What on earth is going on? she thought to herself. Maria wondered if it was possible that she was so tense, so scared, that it was affecting her nerves and hence her fingers? She tried to calm herself by taking some longer deeper breaths (just like Mum said told her to do before starting a dance routine). Eventually she managed to move the quilt back a foot or so, but she really had to push it, and her fingers didn't contribute very much at all.

Maria swung her legs up and around and then put her feet on the floor. She paused for a second and took an extra deep breath in. Just as she started to raise her arm towards the lamp there was another tap on the window. This caused her to jump up and at the same time reach under the lamp shade to press the switch on. She moved her hand up the neck of the lamp and her fingers found the switch but, just like with the quilt, she couldn't get any purchase on it in order to slide it into the on position. Maria moved her hand down slightly and flexed her fingers. Then she tried again. Still couldn't do it. "Blast," she whispered. "What is going on?"

Maria decided to leave the lamp and to just wake up Dad. She half-walked, half-jogged on her tip-toes across the rug that lay between the two beds. The door was ajar, so she slipped out into the corridor without moving it. Which bedroom were Mum and Dad sleeping in? Once she orientated herself Maria turned to her right and went about five steps up the hallway towards the front of the house. Thankfully their bedroom door was ajar too. Mum always worried about there not being enough air in the room, so most nights before she went to bed she checked that all the doors were open. Maria tip-toed into the room and around the bed so that she was beside her dad. She leaned over and whispered "Dad, wake-up … wake-up, I think there's someone outside the house." Although she was whispering, Maria thought that it ought to have been loud enough to wake him. She tried again, just a little louder (she really didn't want to wake up Mum and get her all agitated). "Dad, dad, please wake-up, there's someone outside my bedroom window, and they're tapping on it." For the first time she felt herself getting upset and tears began to form in her eyes.

As Dad wasn't showing any signs of waking, Maria decided to give him a little shake. She placed her hand on his shoulder and realised that she could barely feel his t-shirt. She tried pressing harder and moved her arm forward and back in a rocking motion. But she could see that he was barely moving at all. This was all too weird. She stopped trying to shake him and stood up. "Dad" she said in a voice that was as close as a whisper can get to a shout. But there was still no reaction.

Maria's legs started to feel wobbly, and so she moved a couple of steps back from the bed and put her hand on top of the chest of drawers to give herself some support. A feeling of desperation rose up within her. What was happening? Something's not right. Should she just scream at the top of her voice and wake everyone up (and hopefully scare whoever it was outside away at the same time)? Or maybe she should just go back to bed. Maybe she was imagining the footsteps and the tapping. Maybe she was coming down with something, a virus or something like that. Yes, that would explain the vivid dreams and the lack of energy in her fingers. "Yes, that must be it," she whispered to the room in general. She'd go back to bed, ignore anything she thought she was hearing, and try her best to get back to sleep.

Feeling a little better, Maria walked as quietly as she could out of her parents' bedroom and back down the corridor. She slipped through the gap between her bedroom door and the frame and on to the rug. This room was a lot darker than her parents' and it took a moment for her eyes to adjust. When they did, she became aware of a shape in her bed, under her quilt. She froze and waited for her eyes to become more adjusted to the darkness. She noticed that the quilt was folded back just as she had left it when she got out of the bed a few minutes earlier. And there was definitely someone in the bed. They were lying on their side facing away from her towards the wall. Who could it be? She checked behind her to see if Lizzie was still in her bed. Again it took a moment for her eyes to adjust, but she saw that Lizzie was in her bed – in fact, she was now mostly hanging out of it (which she often did). Was it Bobby, had he woken up and crept in for a cuddle (which he often did at home)?

She leaned forward to try and get a better view, but as she did she suddenly thought about whoever it had been outside – had they somehow got into the house and for some reason got into her bed? This thought made her stand back up with a start. Her legs suddenly felt even more wobbly than they had in her parents' bedroom. She began to feel very weak, like she was going to fall or faint. However, and she wasn't sure why, Maria also felt like she had to move forward and see who was in the bed. She took a deep breath and clenched her fists, and took a small step towards the bed. And then another one. One more and she should be able to lean forward and see the person's face. She paused for a second and glanced down at the shape of the body. It didn't appear big enough to be an adult. But it also seemed too big to be Bobby.

Maria took a breath and moved another step forward. As she leaned over she started to make out the features. It definitely wasn't Bobby. But she did recognise who it was. She felt her knees buckle, and she half fell on to the bed, right beside the serenely sleeping form of herself. She closed her eyes and either passed out or fell asleep immediately.

Chapter 7

Maria felt herself becoming awake. There was no doubt about it this time because Lizzie was shouting, "Wakey, wakey sleepy head," as she stomped across the room. And just as Maria opened her eyes, Lizzie threw open the curtains to reveal a beautiful sunny blue sky day. This caused Maria to pull the quilt up over her head.

"Hey, watch out, that's very bright," she protested to Lizzie.

"Well that's what happens if you sleep in," retorted Lizzie. "Everyone else has been up for ages. Me and Bobby have already been outside to explore the garden, and Dad's been out to get a paper, and we've all had a look through the telescope. It's sooo cool. There's a house on the other side of the valley and you can see right inside their living room. And …"

"So what time is it?" interrupted Maria, who wasn't that keen to hear about any more things that had been done without her.

"About half past nine, I think," said Lizzie, and she walked over to her bedside table to check the time on her iPod. "Nine thirty seven actually. And just so you know, Dad is about to start cooking breakfast and wants to know if you're going to help him, like you said you would last night?"

"Oh, I forgot about that. Tell him I'm just coming," she added as Lizzie started to walk towards the door. Just as Lizzie was about to go out into the hallway she had a sudden and strong recollection of what happened during the night. "Hey, Lizzie, hang on a sec. How did you sleep last night, did you wake up at all?"

Lizzie made a show of grabbing on to the door frame and pulling herself back into the doorway. "Nope, not that I remember. I felt like I slept like a log. That is until I heard Bobby shouting and screaming as he was jumping off the bunk on to the bed. I can't believe you slept through that."

"So you didn't hear any noises at all?" asked Maria.

"What, before I went to sleep?"

"No, during the night."

"How could I if I was asleep?" said Lizzie with just a hint of sarcasm. Then she noticed the concerned look on her sister's face and said, "Why, did you?"

"I dunno. I thought I did. But then ..." she paused.

"Then what?" said Lizzie stepping back into the room.

Maria thought for a moment and then said, "I think it must have been a dream. But it was sooo real. And a bit weird too. And right at the end of it ..." she paused again.

"Yes, yes ..." said Lizzie who was becoming quite intrigued.

Maria didn't know what to say. Although she felt like she remembered everything that had happened, she wasn't really sure what had happened. And she certainly didn't how she should describe it to Lizzie without coming across as a bit crazy. In the end she decided to go with, "Oh nothing, I think it was just a bad dream. First night in a new house, and a new bed, you know. And I did eat a lot of cheese last night," she added, remembering one of her mum's favourite old wives' tales.

"I told you that you were," said Lizzie.

Maria walked over to her bag and started to pull out some clothes, which she hoped would indicate to Lizzie that the discussion was over. Lizzie clearly already thought it was, because when Maria glanced over her shoulder Lizzie was nowhere to be seen. "It must've been a dream," Maria repeated to herself. *What else could it have been?* she thought.

She quickly pulled on her jeans and the first t-shirt she found in the bag and headed out of the bedroom and down to the front of the house. As she walked into the living area she got her first sight of the view the house gave of the valley. She paused to try and take it in, though it was actually quite difficult to do as there was just so much for her eyes to take in. It was like the house was situated half way up the side of a huge bowl. A patchwork of fields and trees filled the bottom of the bowl. Where the bottom of the bowl ended and the sides started there were more trees of all different types and shades of green. As the sides of the bowl got steeper the trees gave way to cliffs which were a striking mix of yellows and oranges. "Wow, what an amazing view," she said to the room.

Dad looked up from the chopping board. "Hey, finally she emerges. Must have needed a good sleep? Bet you feel better now, eh?"

"Err, kind of, I had a very strange dream. And I'm feeling a bit tired from it this morning," Maria replied.

"Great," said Dad, who was clearly very busy with the preparation of their breakfast, and hence not really listening. "I'm almost ready for the eggs, are you okay to get started on them?"

"Yeah, sure," said Maria, and headed over to the fridge. "Does everyone want them poached, Dad?"

"Urghh, not me," said Lizzie, who Maria hadn't noticed was lying on one of the lounges on the far side of the room.

"I hate how the whites of the egg go when they're poached."

"Okay, we'll scramble one for you," said Dad. "I'm sure everyone else will have a poached one though. What was your dream about, Maria?"

So he had heard, Maria thought to herself. "Well ..." She wasn't really sure how much to say or even where to start. After a moment she continued "Well, I was sure that I woke up and could hear something moving on the porch outside my window." On the spur of the moment she decided to leave out the whole bit about getting up and trying to wake him up, and moved straight to "but later on I realised that I must have been dreaming the whole thing. It was just so real though."

"Does sound a bit strange," said Dad. "Did it make you wake up with a bit of a jump? I don't like it when that happens."

Maria realised what he was asking. After most bad dreams you woke up, usually feeling pretty bad. But that hadn't happened to her. In fact, it was kind of the opposite. After seeing herself in the bed she didn't really remember anything else until being woken up by Lizzie. And so, she thought, she must've just carried on sleeping.

"Err, no, I don't think so," she replied to her dad.

"Well, it was your first night in a new house and in a new bed," said Dad. Maria smiled to herself when he said this. "And it was a pretty full on day. Probably not very surprising that you didn't sleep as well, or as ... you know, as peacefully as you normally do in your own bed. I bet you sleep much better tonight."

"Hope so," said Maria. And just as she did Mum and Bobby started to come in through the front door.

"Bobby, take your boots off outside," Maria heard her mum say. And then as she came into the house "I can't believe how he does it. If there's poo to be found, he'll find

49

it. Is breakfast almost ready? I'm starving. Don't know why after eating so much last night, must be to do with breathing in all that fresh air first thing in the morning." Mum came over and picked a mushroom out of a saucepan on the stove.

"It'll be ready in just a couple of minutes," said Dad as he tried to swot Mum's hand out of the saucepan with the tongs he'd been using to turn the bacon.

Bobby burst through the front door, ran a few steps and then slid to a stop in front of the breakfast bar. The floorboards in this house had clearly been polished much more recently than the ones in their house in Sydney, Maria thought to herself. It would probably end in disaster though, as she knew Bobby wouldn't be able to resist trying faster and faster and longer and longer slides. She turned her attention back to the eggs, which were now cooking in a saucepan on the hob.

"Dad, Dad, you should see how much poo there is in the garden! It's all over the place."

"Well, I did tell you that Pete told me that they regularly get kangaroos and wombats in the garden. So it's probably from them."

"There's even some on the deck thingy, you know that runs around the outside of the house," Bobby said with a huge smile, obviously very excited about the prospect of animals coming so close to the house to do their business.

Maria, who had only been half listening to the exchange, suddenly became interested. "Hey, Bobster, where on the porch, um deck thingy, did you see the poo?"

Bobby, clearly delighted that someone else should be showing some interest in his favourite topic, ran into the kitchen area and pointed out of the window and to the right. "Down along there, almost at the end. I can show you it, if you like."

Maria realised that would put it pretty close to her bedroom window. Maybe I did hear something? she thought to herself. But then she remembered the tapping on the window pane, surely an animal couldn't have done that? Maybe I was half awake and half asleep. Maybe I was awake when I heard the steps on the boards, and then went back to sleep and dreamt the rest.

Her thoughts were interrupted by Bobby, who was still standing expectantly beside her. "Well, do you want me to show you or not?"

"Don't worry, that won't be necessary," said Maria. Bobby was clearly disappointed. Then she had a thought and added, "But if you can check it out and let me know what sort of animal you think did it, then that would be really great."

"Sure," he replied bursting into a smile. "I can do that." He turned and called over to Dad, who was in the process of transferring plates and pans from the breakfast bar to the table. "Hey, Dad, can you come and look at the animal poo with me?"

"Let's have breakfast first, shall we?" he replied. "Breakfast is ready everyone," he called out so that even Mum would hear it in the bedroom. And, glancing at Bobby he added, "And make sure your hands are washed before you sit down."

As she walked over to the table with the pan of poached eggs Maria did feel a little better about the previous night and her dream, that there was a reasonably rational explanation for it. But right on the edge of her thoughts there was still a lingering doubt. Getting up and shaking her dad and then, weirdest of all, seeing herself in her bed had all felt so real. After she'd placed the pan on the table she shrugged her shoulders a couple of times and shook out her arms in an attempt to change her focus.

"You okay, Maria?" asked her mum as she came up to the table.

"Yeah, I'm good," she said. "And I am really ready for this breakfast. Thanks so much for doing it, Dad."

"Well, you did the eggs – so it wasn't all me," he said smiling at her. "So what are we going to do on our first day in Kangaroo Valley?" he asked the table in general.

As the suggestions and counter suggestions bounced around the table, the doubts Maria felt gradually started to fade into the background, and by the time they cleared the table the events of the night had been filed away in a segment of her brain labelled 'weird dreams'. For now, anyway …

***

By the end of breakfast (which took well over an hour) the only thing that had definitely been decided about the day was that they would head into the village and try to find a café with Wi-Fi. This served the dual purpose of allowing Mum and Dad to get their coffee fix for the day, and Maria and Lizzie an opportunity to check various things on their iPods, and of course to let their friends know about the house and the valley.

After a café there were a number of options, and so before departing they packed walking boots, various types of footballs, and their swimmers and towels into the back of the car. Even though it was a very sunny day, Dad thought that the river would be too cold for anything but a quick paddle at this time of year. But this didn't deter Bobby in the slightest, who was adamant that he would be jumping straight in without even feeling it first. And so in went all the swimmers and towels, 'just in case'.

They had only been driving towards the village for a few minutes when they came across a very old looking building, which as they got closer they could see was named the Barrengarry [Old] Store. However, what caught Dad's eye was the sign 'The World's Best Pies'.

"Wow, I'd forgotten about this place," he said as he suddenly turned off the road to the left, and the car slightly skidded to halt on the gravel. "You've got to see this place, guys. It's just like one of those general stores that you see in cowboy films."

"Why are we stopping here?" complained Lizzie at the same time. "I thought we were going to a Wi-Fi café."

Dad ignored this and continued. "… and the pies are amazing. Maybe we could get some for dinner tonight?" he said over his shoulder as he opened the car door and got out.

Bobby, who was just getting into reading at school, and hence liked to read every sign they passed on the road, had just spotted and taken in the meaning of the 'The World's Best Pies' sign. "Dad's right, this shop sells the best pies in the world. I want to go in too and choose one," he said as he unclipped his seat belt and started to clamber over Lizzie to get to the door.

"Well, I'm not sure they are actually necessarily the best in the …" Mum started to say. But it was too late, Bobby was already out of the door. "Hang on, Bobby, that's a busy road. I'm coming with you." She got out of the car and caught up with Bobby just as he made it round to the front of the car.

"I guess we might as well go in too," Maria said to Lizzie with just a hint of a sigh, and she opened her door. "Hey, hang on Mum, I'll come with you."

"Well, I'm not going," replied Lizzie. She leaned forward to check and said, "Which given Dad has left the keys behind is probably not such a bad thing."

"Okay, see you in a minute," said Maria, and she closed the door and jogged over to join her mum and Bobby crossing the road.

The three of them climbed the steps up to the porch and the front door, and Mum held the door open for them to go in. As she entered Maria saw that her dad was standing towards the back of the shop beside a huge fridge with a pie in each hand. She thought about going straight over to join him (she loved pies almost as much as her dad did) but as she looked around she was distracted by the huge variety of stuff that was available in the shop. She turned to the right and saw jars of pickled veggies and fruit, hats, boots and tools. Dad was right, it was just like one of those general stores that you saw in westerns. As she walked up an alcove on the right side of the store, Maria had a thought that the store probably hadn't changed much for a long time. And that it was probably very old. She remembered that she'd seen a date on the front of the shop as she crossed the road. She couldn't remember exactly what it had said, but she was sure it had started with '18'. Which made it well over one hundred years old – Pretty old, she thought to herself.

At the end of the alcove Maria turned to her left and saw her dad a few steps in front of her, still checking out the pies. As she walked towards him she started to say "Hey, Dad, do you know how old ..." when she suddenly felt the hairs on her arms and the back of the neck stand up, just as they had a couple of times the previous day. But this time it was so quick it was almost if she'd been subjected to a blast of static electricity.

"Whoa, that's weird," she said shaking her shoulders and arms.

"What is?" said Dad without taking his eyes off the two pies he was holding.

"The hairs on my arms just stood up on end, really quickly, as I walked over towards you. Actually, come to think of it, it's happened a couple of times just recently."

"Probably someone was walking over your grave ... or whatever the phrase is."

"What do you mean by that?" said Maria with just a hint of concern in her voice.

Dad took his eyes off of the pies and looked at Maria. "Don't worry, it's nothing sinister. It's just something people say when that sort of thing happens. You know when your hairs stand up on end, or you get a shiver down your spine." Dad could see that even though he was smiling, Maria wasn't. "Look, it's just a saying, it doesn't mean anything. It doesn't mean that you're about to die or a ghost is about to jump out in front of you."

Maria looked a little more comfortable, but Dad decided that a change of subject was probably the safest bet. "So, what do you think, Maria, Thai curry chicken or beef and mushroom for tonight?" He held up the two very impressive looking pies.

She smiled, "Who for? Me or you?"

"Well, I was thinking for everyone," replied Dad. "You always have a good sense of which filling is best."

"Well, in that case I think it has to be the Thai curry chicken," said Maria pointing to the one in her dad's left hand.

"Good call. I was definitely leaning that way myself."

Dad put the other pie back, and as they started to walk back down to the front of the shop he turned to Maria and asked, "Weren't you about to ask me something back there, about how old something was?"

"Oh yeah, I was wondering how old the store is? I think I saw a year on the front as we walked in, which I think started with an '18'. Does that sound right to you?"

"Oh yes, definitely. I think the year is 1880."

By now they had reached the counter, and as he put the pie down he said to the assistant "Hi, how you going? We'll take this one please. And we're wondering ..." he gestured to Maria and then himself, "... how old is this store?"

The assistant, who was a very friendly looking woman (and who Maria guessed was a bit older than Mum and Dad), put the pie into a paper bag. "Well, there's been a building on this site since 1880," she explained, "but it's been added to and developed quite a bit over the years. I'm pretty sure there was a homestead here, or pretty close by before that, but I don't think there's anything left of that." She entered the price of the pie into the register, and also for some postcards that Maria's mum had added to the pile, and continued, "If you're interested, the Pioneer Museum which is down the road on the right, just before you get to the bridge, has lots of information and photos of what life was like for the first settlers."

Maria wasn't quite sure where it came from (usually it was Lizzie's job to ask this sort of question). She said, "Excuse me, do you know if they have any information about the aboriginal people who lived in the valley before the white people came here?"

"I'm not really sure. I think so," responded the woman. "But even if they don't, I'm sure they'd be able to tell you where to go to get some. Why do you ask? Is it for a school project or something like that?"

Maria blushed slightly, she really didn't know where the question had come from. "Err, no, I'm just interested that's all." She decided it was time to move away from the counter and so she added 'thank-you for your help' and walked behind her dad towards the front door of the store. As she did she got the distinct impression that the thing with her arm and neck hairs was about to start again, and so she hurried her pace and pushed her way through the door. Exiting the store seemed to stop it, and so she stood and checked out the view from the porch. Although the store was much lower in the valley than the house they were staying in, it still had a spectacular view. The thought occurred to Maria that anywhere you went in the valley probably had an amazing view.

She looked down at her arm and thought about the sensations she'd been experiencing. Maria suddenly wondered if it might be anything to do with her age and the physical changes that she knew would be going through in the next few years. She hadn't been expecting it to happen to her so soon, but then again Mum had told her that she'd been 12 when it happened to her. *Maybe that was it,* she thought to herself, and she made a mental note to discuss it with her mum the next time they had some time together.

Chapter 8

After leaving the store, they drove on towards Kangaroo Valley village. Within only a minute or so, the fields that stretched away on either side of the road across the bottom of the valley gave way to some houses and then some shops, including one where you could hire bikes and canoes. And just as the lady in the store had said, on the right hand side of the road they saw a sign for the Pioneer Museum.

"Hey, Maria," said Dad, "there it is. Would you like to go in and have a look around?"

Before Maria could respond Lizzie wailed, "Noooo, don't stop again. I thought we were going to a café? We're never going to get there if we keep stopping."

"Don't worry, Dad," Maria replied. "We've got plenty of time to go there. Maybe we can go this afternoon, or tomorrow morning."

Just as they were passing the museum, the cars in front of them slowed to a stop, and Dad did likewise. Unaware of the traffic, Lizzie thought her dad was slowing to turn in. "Daadd, Maria said not to go in there now."

"I know, Lizzie, chill out. I'm not stopping for that," said Dad. "We're just about to go over a bridge, and it only has one lane. And so you have to take turns in giving way to the traffic coming from the other direction. Hey, Bobby, take a look at this bridge, the ends look a bit like castles."

Bobby leaned forward so he could look through the front windscreen. "Wow, it does," he said excitedly as they moved forward and drove under the first castle looking structure that stood at the near end of the bridge. Then looking forward he noticed something that clearly concerned him and he exclaimed, "Whooaa, Dad, this bridge is made of wood. Do you think it's strong enough to hold all these cars at the same time?"

Dad chuckled, "I think it'll be okay." He paused for a moment and then, with the car situated pretty much in the middle of the bridge, he added, "Mind you, it has been here a long time, so maybe it is getting a bit old and tired and …"

"Stop! Don't say that, Dad," said Maria. "Jinx, jinx, jinx …" said Lizzie at the same time.

"Only jokin'" said Dad. "Hey, look down there, that's the Kangaroo River. Is there anyone swimming?"

"Can't see anyone in the water," said Lizzie, who was sitting on the passenger window side with the best view of the river.

Maria strained against her seat belt to try and get a view. "It doesn't really look deep enough for swimming. Are you sure you can, Dad?"

By now they were off the bridge and passing what looked to be a campsite on their left hand side. "Did you see the bend in the river, it's actually pretty deep there," said Dad. "Maybe we can check it out later, on the way back to the house."

"Maybe we can just see how the day goes," said Mum. "We don't have to do everything on the first day. I thought the idea of getting away was to relax and not to rush around like we do all the time at home."

"Good point," said Dad, and for the next few seconds they drove along in silence.

Then Bobby spotted some tennis courts. "Hey, Dad, there's a park with some tennis courts … and a basketball hoop. Can we go there later? Can we?"

"We'll see," said Mum and Dad together and with exactly the same slightly exasperated tone, which caused them, and Maria and Lizzie to start laughing.

"What is it? What is it?" demanded Bobby, who suspected that he was the cause of the laughter, but didn't know why, as he hadn't said anything funny.

A few moments later they had clearly arrived in the main part of the village. There were shops and cafes on both sides, and quite a few cars parked on the road. And there were lots of people walking along or milling around the shops, or sitting at tables outside the cafes.

"It's a lot busier than I thought it would be," said Maria.

"Well, that's because it's a Saturday morning and there are lots of people like us staying in the valley for the weekend," said Mum, as Dad stopped the car and began reversing into a vacant spot. "During the week I expect it's really quiet."

"Do you think that the people that live here get annoyed by having all these people coming at the weekends?" asked Lizzie.

"Maybe," said Mum "but, then again, the people who run the shops and cafes probably rely on the weekends to make enough money to get by."

"So they're very busy just at weekends, while we're very busy during the week, that doesn't sound like a bad deal," said Maria, and then to clarify added 'for them'.

"That's one of the reasons why so many people think about leaving the city and moving to the coast or the country," said Dad. "They call it doing a sea change."

"Or a tree change when you move to the country" added Mum smiling.

"A tree change? I like the sound of that," said Maria. "I think it would be cool to live in the country for a while."

"Not me," said Lizzie as she opened the car door. "There are no big shopping centres around here. What do you do if you need to go to a Smiggle or Typo?"

"Well, I guess when people make that sort of change, they must be prepared to make a few big sacrifices, like not going to Smiggle or Typo as often," said Mum with more than a hint of sarcasm in her voice. Then looked at Dad and smiled. And he nodded and smiled back.

Maria saw the exchange and said, "What are you two smiling about?" They didn't respond and moved to get out of the car. Maria decided to ask again. "Come on, what is it? Is it to do with us?"

Mum relented and turned and put her head back in the car. "I guess we just find it a little bit funny how you kids can be so similar in some things, and so different in others. That's all."

"What do you mean by that?" said Maria.

"Well, for example, how you like the idea of maybe one day living in the country. Whereas for Lizzie, that would be her idea of a nightmare." Mum smiled at Maria. "It just reinforces this feeling that Dad and I have that you're our earth girl and Lizzie is our city girl."

Before Maria could respond, Dad, who now was now standing on the pavement along with Lizzie and Bobby, called out to them. "Come on you two, you can finish whatever it is you're talking about in the café. We're all waiting for you."

"Come on, we better go," said Mum. "It appears that Dad is determined to fit as many things as possible into our supposedly laid-back, relaxing weekend."

Maria and her Mum shared a conspiratorial smile. Then they got out of the car and started to follow the others, who were already heading towards a café that had several tables outside.

***

It was about five o'clock when they returned to the house. As they drove up the driveway Maria could see that the sun was just about to drop below the line of cliffs that stood in the distance behind the house. For about the last hour the late afternoon sun had filled the valley with a special glow, but now as the sun got really low in the sky it gave the valley an almost surreal, magical feel. Dad turned the car so it was parallel to the house, and when Maria looked out to her right across the valley, she could see that the rocks high on the cliffs appeared to have changed colour. They were now a stunning mixture of gold, dark orange and reds.

She got out of the car and walked a few steps away from it so that should take it all in properly. A mist or fog seemed to be forming in some parts of the floor of the valley. And she could see that as the sun got lower it was causing huge shadows to form over some parts of fields, whilst other parts were still sitting in bright sunshine. As she stood there a group of kookaburras started up a loud and what sounded like, to human ears at least, heated discussion. Maria smiled. There was something about the sound kookaburras made that to her mind sounded like laughing. And she liked the idea that one of them might have just cracked a really good kookaburra joke.

It really is an amazing place, she thought to herself. Just as she did she became aware of someone walking up behind her. She turned and saw it was her dad. He stood right beside her, but didn't say anything. For a few moments they stood there, staring out across the valley. Then her dad said, "It's a pretty amazing place, isn't it?"

Maria chuckled and said, "That's a bit spooky. I just had exactly the same thought."

"Oooh, white witch stuff," said Dad, and they both laughed.

They were silent again for a while. "What do you think it was like for the first person who ever came across the valley and looked down into it?" asked Maria.

"It would have been pretty mind blowing, don't you think?" Dad paused. "Actually it might have looked quite a bit different to how it looks today, as I'm sure there would have been a whole lot more trees. The white settlers, when they got here, cut downs loads of trees to make the land ready for cattle and farming."

"I wonder what the aboriginal people who were here made of that?" said Maria.

"Not a lot, I reckon," said Dad, and as he did he turned to head back to the house. "Come on let's go in and get the fire going."

"That sounds good," said Maria, and she turned and walked with her dad.

After a few steps her Dad smiled and said, "It's been a good day, hasn't it?"

"Sure has," said Maria. It was definitely one of the best days that they'd had as a family in a long time. And that was despite the near disaster of having to visit three cafes before finding one that offered Wi-Fi access for its customers. But once they had, and Mum and Dad had had their coffee fixes (that they said were 'just as good as the ones they get from their local café in Sydney'), and she and Lizzie and Bobby had had their hot chocolates (with lovely little cookies on the side), things just seemed to get better and better.

After the café they'd gone for a stroll around the village shops. Dad thought the second-hand book and record shop was fantastic, whilst Mum loved the art gallery. Maria, Lizzie and Bobby's favourite shop was without question the lolly shop, which sold the widest range of old-style lollies Maria had ever seen. After the shops they'd walked up to the far end of the village and gone into a playground. Maria and Lizzie had invented an obstacle course for all the kids to time themselves on, and Mum and Dad had sat on the bench and read the newspaper. After a while Dad had decided he would try the obstacle course, but had got stuck trying to go over the top of the hanging net thingy. Lizzie and Bobby had climbed up on either side to rescue him, and everyone had been laughing so much (even though Maria thought her dad had only been pretending to be stuck). As a result of getting stuck (supposedly), Dad decided that he wanted to do something else and so he had gone back to the car to get a ball, and after much pleading Mum finally agreed to join in with a game of touch footie on the oval. That had been great fun. And they were so hot afterwards that Mum and Dad had said that they should go back to the lolly shop to get some ice creams without the kids even suggesting it first (which Maria couldn't remember happening in a very long time).

The ice creams did help cool them down a bit, but when Dad had asked about what they should do next, and Bobby had said he wanted to swim in the river, they were all still hot enough to think that would be worth a go. And so they'd driven back out of the village and parked near the bridge with castles on either end. Bobby and Lizzie had wanted to go straight to the river, and so Mum had gone with them.

Maria had gone with her dad to take a closer look at the bridge. Dad had used his phone to look up the history of the bridge, and they discovered that it was called Hampden Bridge and was over 100 years old. They had taken a few photos of the bridge, including a timed one with the two of them standing in front of it. Their first attempt only got their heads in, and it had looked so funny that they both burst out laughing. It had taken them quite a while to calm down enough to have a second go. Again Maria couldn't really remember the last time that had happened with her and Dad, or with her mum come to that.

Maria and her dad had then walked down the path to join the others at the river. Bobby was already stripped down to just his board shorts and splashing around in the water. However, Mum and Lizzie had had one feel of the water and decided it was too cold for them. After dipping her foot in, Maria had decided they were right. But in the end everyone had paddled at least once across the small weir that stretched across the river just before it turned under the bridge. And there was general agreement that the water wasn't that cold once you got used to it. Dad had skipped a stone which appeared to bounce about twenty times on the water, and had led to him giving everyone lessons on how to get the stone to spin and skim. By the time they'd finished, the sun had gone below the level of the trees, and the temperature seemed to drop rapidly. This led quickly to Mum suggesting that it was time to head back to the house, put the kettle on and get the fire started.

Maria followed her dad into the house, and flopped down beside Lizzie on one of the lounges.

"You okay?" asked Lizzie.

"Yeah, good ... in fact, really good. That was such a fun day." Maria remembered the photo of her and her dad, and pulled her iPod out of her pocket. She found the photo and handed the iPod over to Lizzie. "Have a look at this photo of me and Dad."

Lizzie looked and immediately burst out laughing. "That is sooo funny," she managed to get out. "It looks like Dad's head is part of the bridge."

Lizzie's laughing caused Maria to find it funny all over again, and soon she was laughing uncontrollably. Bobby, Mum and Dad came over and the photo was passed around causing everyone to join in with the laughing.

Eventually, after a few attempts, they calmed, and Dad said, "Let's try and get the fire going. Who wants to help me get some kindling from outside?"

"Me, I will," said Bobby, and he jumped up and ran over to the door.

"Hey, girls, what about you come and help me with dinner?" suggested Mum as she got up from the lounge and headed towards the kitchen.

Chapter 9

About an hour later the fire was roaring (only two attempts this time), and they were all sat at one end of the big table eating the pie chosen by Maria and Dad earlier in the day. As they ate they discussed what they'd done during the day and what they should do the next day. Dad suggested visiting the Pioneer Museum, and this caused Maria to think about the early settlers, and the valley, and about her dad telling her about all the trees being cut down. This in turn had reminded her of what her dad had called the 'white witch moment'.

Maria waited for a break in the conversation and then said, "Hey Dad, can you tell us again why you think Mum is a white witch?"

"Nooo, not that again," said Mum leaning back in her seat and shaking her head.

"Yes, tell us Dad, tell us," said Bobby who loved hearing or talking about anything to do with witches or wizards or monsters, or in fact anything that could be deemed spooky or scary.

After Lizzie also joined in the call for the story, Mum relented and nodded to Dad. "Okay, if you have to."

Dad made a show of making himself comfortable in his seat and said, "Well, as you know, your mum likes to cook a big roast dinner on a Sunday." There were nods around the table. "Soon after we started going out she invited me round to her flat on a Sunday afternoon – no, it must have been an evening because it was definitely dark – to have dinner with her and a few of her friends who I hadn't met before." A mischievous smile came on to his face and he went on. "I took this to be a good sign, that I was making headway, because I figured she wouldn't be getting me to meet her friends if she wasn't interested, a least a little bit." Dad paused and looked at Maria and Lizzie and saw that they were smiling. He knew that they loved to hear about how he and their mum had first met and their first dates together.

Bobby, who wasn't at all bothered about that sort of stuff, urged him to continue, "Go on Dad, tell us what happened ... and why you think Mum is a witch!"

"He doesn't really think I'm a witch, Bobby," said Mum shaking her head again. "I can't believe that you're filling their heads with this stuff."

"Now where was I?" said Dad, ignoring Mum. "Oh yeah, Mum invited me over for dinner. And during the dinner Mum told this story about something that had happened to her while she'd been living in that flat, and I remember that everyone around the table, including me, thought that it was a really spooky story. You know one of those stories that give you a chill down your spine, or cause the hairs on the back of your neck to stand up." When he said this he looked at Maria, remembering their discussion in the store that morning. Maria widened her eyes very slightly in acknowledgement.

"Anyway, sometime after that when we were with some of my friends, Mum told the story again, and I thought it was even spookier the second time. And you know my friend, Ryan, he was *really* spooked by it. I don't think he's ever forgotten it. Do you remember that, love?" he said looking at Mum. She nodded and smiled. "And so that was sort of the start of it. But there have been all sorts of other things since then. You all know how Mum manages to get people to tell her their life story as soon as they meet her. It's all part of her witchiness. But she's obviously not an old, ugly, bad witch, so I like to think of her as a white witch. You know, like the beautiful white witch in *The Wizard of Oz*."

"Eurgh, not her, Mum is much prettier than her," said Lizzie.

"Yes, of course she is, I was just trying to give you an example," responded Dad very quickly. And then he suddenly thought of a better one. "What I meant to say is that she's like the character that Cate Blanchett played in *The Hobbit* movies."

"Hmm, Cate Blanchett, I like that example a lot better," said Mum.

"Mum, have you ever told us what the spooky thing was that happened in your flat?" said Maria. "I don't think you have."

"Yeah, tell us what it was Mum," said Bobby.

"Yes, please, please tell us," Lizzie said joining in the chorus.

"Ooh, I'm not sure I should, especially just before you go to bed. I don't want to give anyone any bad dreams."

"We won't get nightmares, Mum, promise we won't," pleaded Bobby. "Please tell us the story."

"Okay, okay, but don't blame me if you do," and then as an afterthought "and if you do, and you wake up and can't get back to sleep, make sure it's your dad that you wake up."

Hmm, I would if I could? thought Maria remembering what had happened last night. Or what she had dreamt last night she quickly reminded herself.

"Well, where to start?" said Mum sitting up very straight in her seat. "Okay, I know … Like Dad said I was living in a flat, with my friend Katie. But she wasn't in when it happened. I was in the kitchen doing something or other, but I had the radio on in the living room. All of a sudden I heard this weird noise in the living room, and then the music stopped, and came on again but *really* loud. Of course, the first thing I thought was that Katie had come in and turned the music up. And so I carried on doing what I was doing. But then, when she didn't come into the kitchen, and the music was so loud, I thought I'd go into the living room and see her. As I walked through I remember thinking that she'd probably had a bad day at work and I'd find her slumped on our lounge."

She paused and looked around the table. Whilst Dad had the faintest smile on his face, the kids all had very serious looking faces and their eyes were wide with expectation. "Are you okay?" she asked them, mostly to try and break the tension that she sensed had built up.

'Yes, yes' and 'we're fine' they chorused back.

"Go on, Mum, what did you find when you into the room?" said Lizzie. "Was Katie there?"

"Well, no, she wasn't. In fact, no one was there. But what I saw was pretty strange – all of the CDs and cassette tapes that Katie and I usually had …"

"Mummm, what are cassette tapes?" asked Bobby.

"Never mind" and "they're music things like CDs and records," said Lizzie and Maria simultaneously.

And Maria added, "We'll show you one later, Bobby. Go on Mum."

"Yep, okay, so where was I? … All the CDs and tapes that were usually piled up on the coffee table and the cabinet where the music player was, and even most of the ones that were in the CD rack were now spread all across the floor. The first thing I thought was that Katie must had done it and then gone straight into her bedroom, which was near the front door. And so I went to see if she was there. But she wasn't, and so I quickly checked the bathroom but she wasn't there either. Then I thought that someone must've somehow got into the house and done it, and then gone out again. And as you can imagine, by this time I was starting to feel pretty freaked out. I checked the front door but it was definitely locked. And so I went back into the living room to take another look, and I noticed that the window was open. But we normally did have it open a few inches to let some air in, and when I checked it was bolted into position," and she moved her hands to show what she meant by that.

At this point she paused and took sip from her glass of wine, which she knew would allow the questions that were always asked whenever she related the story to be asked.

Lizzie started them. "So Mum, do you think that weird noise that you said you heard was the CDs falling on the floor?"

"Probably," said Mum, "but you know, when I came back into the room and looked a bit more closely at what happened, I noticed that nearly all the CD boxes and tape boxes were facing upwards. And hardly any of CD boxes had opened up either. If they'd fallen, or been thrown by someone, then I don't think that would have happened, do you?" Everyone was silent for a while they considered this new piece of the puzzle. Then Mum went on, "You know, a long time after it happened I heard a sound that I realised was the same, or at least very, very similar to the one I'd heard that day."

"What was it?" Maria asked, probably unnecessarily as her mum was clearly about to tell them.

"It was on the TV," said Mum, "in a documentary about an attempt to break the world record for the number of dominoes knocked over in one go." She used her hands to show dominoes falling one on to another and another. "The sound I heard was just like lots of dominoes falling

71

over. But it only lasted for a second or two." Again they were all silent again for a few moments.

Bobby asked the next question, "Was the music very loud, Mummy?"

"That's a good question, Bobby," said Dad. (What a surprise, Maria thought to herself.)

"That is a good question, Bobby," echoed Mum. "You know I was so freaked out by it all that it was quite a while before I realised that the music was even on, let alone how loud it was. But eventually I sort of became aware of it again, and once I did I realised it was very loud indeed. The neighbours were probably wondering what we were doing having a party at that time of day. And so I went over to turn it down. And that's when I thought about the song that was playing. It wasn't one from the CD that I thought we'd last been playing, which was only the night before. Anyway I switched the music off and checked the CD, and it was one of Katie's that I had never played. Later, when Katie actually did come home, I asked her about it and she said she hadn't put that CD on for ages, months maybe."

"Mum, did you tell Katie about what had happened?" asked Lizzie. "What did she think?"

"Of course I did. In fact, I left the CDs and tapes and everything just as they were until she got home so that she could see it. We talked about it for ages. By the end of the evening I think she was just as freaked out about it as I was. If I remember rightly, after we'd been talking about it for a while – an hour maybe – we decided we clear it all up and go out to get some Thai take-away, as neither of us felt like cooking."

Again there was a short period of silence as the kids mulled over what they'd heard. Then Maria asked the question that they were all thinking, "So, Mum, do you think it was a ghost or something like that?"

Before her mum could respond, Maria's dad interjected, "Don't forget, love, that's not the whole story. Tell them what happened when you called your sister and told her about it."

"Oh yes, thanks, I had forgotten about that," said Mum.

Maria wondered how much spookier the story was going to get. Only a little while ago Mum had been worried about scaring them before they went to sleep, and now she was about to add more spookiness to what was already a pretty freaky story. But as she wanted to hear whatever it was that had happened with Aunty Wendy, she didn't air her concerns.

Mum continued. "Like Dad says, I called Aunty Wendy. I think it was the next morning to tell her what had happened. And as I did she kept saying, 'that's so weird, that's sooo weird'. At first I thought she was just freaked out by what had happened to me, but then her reaction seemed, you know, just a bit too much. Anyway, when I finished telling her, she said it again '*that's sooo weird*'. And then she explained that a very similar thing had happened to her as well. And I asked her when, and she said the day before – same as me. And it turned out, that as far as we could tell, it happened either at the same time, or within a few minutes. To me in my flat in Sydney, and to her in her house in Melbourne."

This time the silence lasted considerably longer than a few seconds.

Eventually Lizzie said, "Wow, that's amazing … and very spooky."

Bobby followed up with "I liked that story, Mum. Do you know any more spooky stories?"

Then Maria repeated her earlier question. "So Mum, what do you think about it now? Do you think it was a ghost or something else, something supernatural?"

"Well, that is *the* question, isn't it?" said Dad. (Maria noted that it still wasn't worthy of a 'good question' status, but took some comfort in the fact that she seemed to be making progress.) "I guess it kind of depends on whether you believe in ghosts or not. If you do, then that would seem to be the most logical explanation for what happened. But, if you don't, then I guess you just keep trying to find some other logical or rational explanation."

Maria nodded at her dad and said, "I think I understand what you're saying." And then she turned again towards her mum, "So, Mum, what do you think it was? Do you believe in ghosts?"

Mum sat back in her chair and took a deep breath in. "You know …" she said, and then seemed to change her mind about what she was going to say next, and paused for a moment. "You know, yes, I do. I do think that there are things – ghosts or spirits, call them what you will – that can't be explained by science or physics or whatever."

She paused again and shrugged her shoulders. "Now I can't say that I absolutely one hundred per cent know that it was a ghost that came into mine and Katie's flat that day …"

"And Aunt Wendy's," said Lizzie.

"Yes and Aunt Wendy's. But, what I feel in my gut is that somebody, or something, tried to make contact with me – and probably Aunt Wendy – that day."

"Why do you think they were trying to contact you, Mum?" asked Maria.

"I really don't know. I thought about it lot afterwards. Was it a sort of message? Was that particular song meant to mean something? Was it from someone who used to live in that flat or the building? But if that was the case, why did it happen to me and Wendy at the same time? Did that mean it was someone that we both knew – a family member, maybe – who was trying to tell us something? Who knows?" she said, shrugging her shoulders.

"Well, I don't think it was a ghost," said Lizzie. "I don't believe in them at all."

"Is that right?" said Maria. "Well, how come you still believed in Santa up until …" she tried do the calculation, but then just said, "well, quite, very recently?"

Lizzie folded her arms and turned away from Maria making a sort of 'hmph' sound.

"What do you mean?" said Bobby. "Santa's real, isn't he Mum?"

"Absolutely," she responded smiling at Bobby before throwing a quick glare at Maria. "Look, we don't have to argue about it …"

"I wasn't arguing," said Maria, "I was just pointing out that …"

"Never mind," said Dad, cutting Maria off before her not arguing developed into an argument between her and Lizzie. "Look, the way I see it is … it's a bit like the chicken and egg thing. Well maybe not that exactly. But, anyway, if you are open – you know, have an open mind – to these sorts of things, then they are probably more likely to happen to you. Which, when it does, makes you believe in it even more. Does that make any sense?"

He paused to see if was making any sense. Despite the vague looks he was getting, he decided to press on. "I've always been the sort of person who needs to see some evidence, first hand evidence, before I can start really believing in something like ghosts, or UFOs, or anything like that. Which I guess makes me pretty closed."

"I think I see what you're saying, Dad," said Maria. "Because Mum is open minded …"

"Open to this sort of stuff," he interjected.

"Okay, open minded to the idea of ghosts and spirits, which makes it more likely that she'll have these types of …" Maria thought about the right word, "experiences."

"Yes, that's exactly right," said Dad nodding.

"And maybe it's not just the ghosts who can pick up on it," Maria continued. "Maybe people can too, which is why they feel so …" again she thought carefully about the word she wanted to use, "… so comfortable talking to her about all those personal things as soon as they meet her."

"Hmmm, I've never really made that direct connection before," said her dad. "But now that you've said it, I think you might be right," he added, this time holding his chin and smiling at her. "Another piece of the white witchiness puzzle falls into place."

Maria turned and looked at her mum. She was smiling too, which was good. But it quickly changed to mock serious when she decided it was time to finish the discussion. "Okay everyone, that's quite enough of all that. It's getting late, and we need to clear the table, and you lot need to have showers, and …"

"Ohhh, Mum, do we have to have showers tonight, we are on holiday you know?" said Bobby.

"And we did get wet in the river?" added Lizzie.

"Are we still going to be able to toast marshmallows tonight?" threw in Maria.

"Hmm, I'm not sure that getting wet in that water really amounts to getting clean, in fact probably quite the opposite," said Mum. "Well, at the very least I want to see some good washing going on. If you do that, and you're quick, then I suppose we could do a few marshmallows." All the kids immediately stood up and started clearing the table.

Jobs done, everyone gathered round the fire to toast marshmallows. They each chose a stick from the basket containing the kindling, and squashed a pink or white marshmallow on to one end. Bobby went first, but held his marshmallow over the fire for too long, and it caught light before slipping off into the fire in a gooey mess. It sizzled and caused a burnt toffee smell to spread through the room. Eventually they all managed to toast at least one to their preferred level of brownness and crispness, and it was time for bed.

Maria felt very tired as she walked into her room. Dad had said that she and Lizzie could read for a while, but Maria told him that she didn't think she'd be able to keep her eyes open for long once she got into bed.

"It's been a big day, that's for sure," said Dad.

And that's after a pretty weird night, Maria thought to herself. But all she said was, "Sure has."

"Sleep well," Dad said as he switched off the main light and left the room.

"You too," and "Thanks," called out Maria and Lizzie in response.

"Are you going to read for a while, Lizzie?" asked Maria.

"Yep, just for a bit. What about you?"

"Nah, I'm ready to go to sleep." Maria rolled over on to her left side and pulled up the quilt so that it was over her shoulder.

"Okay," said Lizzie, and then added, "I hope you don't have any of those weird dreams tonight."

"Me too," she said with a little laugh. Maria closed her eyes and within a couple of minutes was asleep.

Chapter 10

Maria felt herself becoming awake. She opened her eyes but lay completely still. The room was very dark, so it definitely wasn't morning yet.

The tap on the window made her jump, and instinctively she tried to pull the quilt up higher so that it would cover her head. For some reason the quilt felt very heavy, and it took all her strength to pull it up just a few centimetres. Maria remembered the same experience from the night before. And the hairs on her arms were standing up, just as they had done several times over the last couple of days.

"Not again," she whispered to herself. And she tried to flatten the hairs on her left forearm with her right hand. As she did there was another tap on the window. This time, Maria decided, she was just going to stay in bed and ignore it. Instead of pulling the quilt up, this time she tried to wriggle her whole body down underneath it. This proved to be a little easier, and when she was satisfied she was far enough down she covered her ears with her hands.

"Please don't tap again, please don't, please don't …" she mouthed to herself. But no more than five seconds later there was another tap. Despite being under the quilt, and pressing her hands tight against her ears she heard it just as clearly as she had done the previous time. They must be tapping louder, Maria thought. But why would they do that? How can they possibly know where I am or what I'm doing?

She waited, pressing her hands even tighter against the sides of her head. The gap was a little longer this time, maybe 15 seconds, and for a moment Maria thought that it wasn't going to happen again, and allowed herself to relax a little. When the tap came it made her jump, and she instinctively tensed and brought her knees up towards her chest.

"Why is this happening to me?" she whispered to herself. "Why me? Why not Lizzie?" This thought reminded her that Lizzie was in the room too.

I should wake up Lizzie. She can help me decide what to do. She started to roll over but, just as before, the quilt felt like a lead weight. What is going on? This is so weird. She forced herself to roll over and as she moved on to her right shoulder she also pushed her head out from under the quilt so that she could see across the room to Lizzie's bed.

"Lizzie … Lizzie … Lizzie wake up," Maria whispered. No response. She tried again this time in a loud whisper, "Lizzie … Lizzie, please wake up." Maria couldn't believe that Lizzie was sleeping so heavily that she wasn't able to hear that. Normally she was the lighter sleeper of the two. "Lizzie!" she called out in her normal voice. And then a few seconds later, at a level just below a shout, "Lizzie wake up … wake up now … please wake up!" Still there was no response from Lizzie.

I can't believe, it thought Maria. Maybe I should throw something at her, surely that would do it. But what to throw? Something heavy enough to wake her but not so heavy it hurts her. She thought for a second, and then her slippers came to mind. Yep, one of those ought to be enough.

Maria was just about to lean forward to see if she could reach one of them when there was another tap at the window. She froze. And then she heard a voice. It came from just outside of the window. She couldn't make out exactly what it said, but it sounded something like 'Leeze'. She stayed completely still and waited. She heard it again, this time it sounded like 'Lizz'.

Her mind raced, what were they saying? 'Leeze'. 'Lizz'. Maria replayed them over in her mind. Suddenly she thought she knew what it was. Whoever was outside had heard her calling out to Lizzie, and they were trying to repeat it. But why were they finding it so hard? It was almost like someone who doesn't speak English was trying to get their mouth and tongue around the word. She remembered students from Japan visiting their school earlier in the year. Their attempts to say Maria and her friends' names in English had sounded very similar. Actually, now she thought of it, Maria's own attempt to say the Japanese students' names was even more like it.

Her thoughts were interrupted by hearing the voice and the word again. But this time it was different, there was a harder sound at the beginning. This time is sounded like 'plizz'. She waited and a few seconds later she heard the sound again. 'Pleeze'. Now she realised what the person outside was saying, and she whispered it to herself, "Please."

Immediately Maria felt much less tense. Someone was outside her window struggling to say the word 'please'. Sure it was the middle of the night and they'd tapped on her window, but really not one of the taps had been in any way loud or angry. And then she thought about the taps she'd heard the previous night, none of them had been loud either. Maria's thoughts raced even quicker. Of course, it had happened last night as well. Was it the same person last night? It had to be. Why would different people come up to the house on different nights to tap on the window? Maybe it was part of some elaborate practical joke. Maria quickly dismissed this idea. She considered the voice itself, it was gentle and almost apologetic. And there was something else about it …

Just then Maria heard the voice and word again. This time it was much clearer. "Please." Then it came to her. The voice belonged to someone old. Definitely older than her mum or her dad. A lot older.

Suddenly Maria knew what she had to do. And, having decided, her fear vanished. She started to push the quilt back down the bed. It felt incredibly heavy (what *was* that about?), but her new focus gave her extra energy and she managed to push and then kick it down the bed. She pulled her legs up under her and twisted at the same time so that she ended up kneeling in front of the window. Maria paused for a second and then lifted her arms so that she could grasp an edge of each of the curtains in each of her hands. Again she paused, and this time took a deep breath.

Very slowly she began to part the curtains. It was a clear night and the moon was almost full. As she opened the curtains she was aware that she was going to be able to clearly see whoever (or whatever) was out there. Still it took her eyes a moment to adjust. After opening the curtains about thirty centimetres, Maria stopped and tried to make sense of what she was seeing.

Standing on the deck about two metres away from her was a very old aboriginal man. Maria sensed that he had moved away from the window – probably once he'd realised that she was going to open the curtains – because as she looked at him he was very slowly moving his right leg back a few centimetres. Eventually he stopped moving it and then stood very still.

Maria noticed then that he was wearing hardly any clothes. He had on what looked to Maria a bit like a nappy. Even though the moonlight made his outline very clear, she had to strain her eyes to pick up detail. After a few moments she realised that the nappy thing was made of animal fur. Apart from that he had a number of necklaces around his neck and a bracelet around his right wrist. In his left hand he held a stick which was pretty much the same height as him. Maria guessed that he'd used it to tap on the window. As her eyes became more accustomed to the light, Maria could make out that he was indeed very old. His skin was dark and very wrinkled, especially on his face. And his hair was wispy and grey, almost white.

For a few seconds Maria stared at the man and he stared back. After taking in what, or who, she was seeing, Maria tried to make sense of what was going on here. As far she knew there were no aboriginal people left living in the valley, at least not ones who went around dressed like this. She felt sure if there were her dad, or the lady at the store, or someone somewhere would have mentioned it. So what is he doing here? And why on earth is he tapping on my window?

As these thoughts raced through Maria's mind, the man slowly raised his right arm and then proceeded to make an even slower beckoning gesture with his hand. Maria could see that his fingers were very thin and gnarled.

Maria's immediate thought was, is that meant for me? And she raised her own right hand and pointed at her chest. Almost as immediately she realised that it could only be meant for her and she dropped her arm to the side and felt herself blush ever so slightly. To her amazement the man seemed to pick up on it – surely he couldn't have noticed that, she thought to herself – as a small smile appeared on his face. And then he repeated the beckoning gesture. Maria's mind raced. What to do? What to do?

The sensible thing to do was to run straight to her parents' bedroom and wake them, to let them know that there was a strange, almost naked, and very old aboriginal man standing on the porch outside their house. But ... and Maria thought, how can there really be a 'but' in a situation like this? BUT the truth was, that somewhere inside her, somewhere very deep down inside her, that didn't feel like the right thing to do. As she considered these conflicting feelings, the man made the beckoning gesture for a third time, and this time she could see him mouth the word 'please'. Still she didn't move.

The man started to turn to his right. As he did so he beckoned again, this time more quickly. He gestured two more times and then started to walk away from Maria's window, and along the porch towards the front of the house. Maria leaned forward and rested her forehead on the window pane so that she could see him at the far end of the porch. A thought flashed through her brain - That's strange, I would have expected the window pane to be cold, but it's not. In fact, I can barely feel it at all. Her thoughts quickly moved on, because just as he was about to turn to the left and along the front of the house, the man stopped and looked back at Maria. To her total astonishment he raised both his arms and did what appeared to be an enormous shrug. As if to say, 'What's keeping you?'

Maria stopped thinking about the most sensible action. She turned and scrambled off the bed, and half-stepped, half-skipped across the rug and out of the bedroom door into the hallway. She headed towards the front of the house, but paused when she reached her parents' bedroom door.

I really should wake them, she thought to herself, that's the right thing to do. The thought bounced to and fro in her head, and whilst it did she moved forward a step so that she was standing in the doorway to the front part of the house. She looked out across the breakfast bar and the dining table and through the windows expecting to see the man on that part of the porch. But he wasn't there.

Maria forgot all about waking her parents and ran forward past the table. She slid to a stop about a metre from one of the large front windows and peered out into the moonlight. He definitely wasn't on this front part of the porch. She turned to her left to see if he had already passed the front door and was somewhere on the other side of the house. But she couldn't see him there either. She stepped forward so that she was only a few centimetres from the window pane and looked out through the rails of the fence that ran around outside the porch. And then she saw him again, standing on the grass a few metres beyond the steps that led up to the house. Wow, he moves very quickly for an old man, Maria thought to herself.

Maria realised that he was looking straight at her, as if he'd known exactly where she was going to be even if she hadn't had a clue where he was. And he was smiling at her, a big warm friendly smile. Even though she had no idea what was going on, and her insides were feeling all churned up, Maria couldn't help but smile back. Seeing this, the man repeated the beckoning gesture, though this time he used his whole arm rather than just his hand and forearm. Clearly he wanted Maria to follow him outside.

"Outside," Maria whispered to herself. Her mind raced and she felt herself getting very anxious. He wants me to go outside. There's no way I'm going to do that, she thought. I really should just go and wake up Dad and Mum and let them know what's going on.

She realised that her heart was beating very fast, and that she was starting to get that sensation where the heart beats feel like they are moving up into your throat. Maria closed her eyes and tried to slow her breathing and hence her heart beat. She probably only had her eyes closed for a second or two, but when she opened them Maria was stunned to see the man standing right in front of her on the other side of the window, no more than a metre separating them. Instinctively she jumped backwards, but was stopped from moving too far back by a chair. Maria felt like she was going to lose her balance and so she put her hands behind her to grab the sides of the chair. For some reason she found it very difficult to get a grip on the chair, almost like it was slippery. But after a moment she managed to get some traction on it. This allowed her to steady herself, which also allowed her to gather her thoughts.

How on earth had he managed to climb back up the stairs so fast? He's an old man for goodness sake. And he isn't smiling anymore, in fact, he looks very sad. Now he was so close Maria could clearly see his eyes. They were very dark brown, almost black. And they were very moist, like your eyes get just before you cry.

Maria felt very confused. Obviously he wanted her to follow him for some reason, most likely he needed help with something. And she got the strongest sense that he meant her no harm. But on the other hand it was the middle of the night, why didn't he just come to the house during the day and ask her parents for help? *And* he had just given her the biggest shock by appearing in front of her like that. And almost without meaning to, Maria found herself saying in a very low voice, "You scared me just then." And after a pause she added, "Why do you want me to follow you? What do you need me to do?"

He nodded very slightly, seemingly acknowledging the fact that he'd scared her. Then he repeated the word 'please', and at the same time turned and used his stick to point out into the middle of the valley.

Maria suddenly had the thought that he might not be able to tell her. She remembered the first few times he had tried to say the word 'please', maybe he didn't know much English? Maybe that was the only word he knew? She had an idea. Maria raised her right hand and in an exaggerated fashion pointed at her chest. She then pointed at the man. He looked at her intently. She then raised her left hand and did her best to imitate two people walking away from the house and out into the middle of the valley. She looked at him and saw that he was nodding and that his eyes now didn't look quite so sad.

Maria felt better that they had successfully communicated with each other, but had to push her heart beats back down her throat when she realised that she was actually considering going outside in the middle of the night with this strange old man. She let go of the chair and stepped forward. She had been hanging on to the chair in a sort of semi crouch (probably as a result of the shock of finding him so close). She extended her leg and back muscles so that she was standing straight, and was surprised to discover that the man wasn't actually that much taller than her. She thought that Lizzie would definitely be taller than him.

Their similar(ish) heights meant that Maria felt like she was able to look him right in the eyes, and she was convinced she saw no bad intentions in them. She nodded at him, turned to her left and walked over to the front door. As she did she kept her head turned to the right and she saw the old man follow her along the porch. When she got to the door she raised her hand and took hold of the handle. She pushed it down. Or at least she tried to. For some reason she couldn't move it at all. What was this? What was going on?

As she tried harder to push it down, she recalled how weird it had been trying to roll over in her bed and how hard it had been to push back her quilt. Yes, it was the same thing. Like she had no energy. No, that wasn't quite it. She actually felt fine (considering it was the middle of night, and presumably she'd only had a few hours of sleep). It was more like she had no weight, or no force. She put her other hand on the handle and stepped closer to the door so that she could bring more of her body weight to bear on the handle. Eventually she felt it move slightly and then it slipped down far enough to allow the latch to be released. The door swung back, almost carrying Maria with it. She let go of the handle and stepped away to let it go past her.

She could see that the man was standing out on the porch a little to the right of the front door, but between him and her was another barrier, the screen door. She looked at the latch which was much smaller but higher up than the one on the other door. Maria sighed and stepped forward. *Hopefully this one will be a bit easier,* she thought to herself.

It wasn't. Whatever Maria tried, she just couldn't budge the latch. She looked out and saw the man staring back at her. His eyes were wide, almost imploring her to open it. "I'm trying," she said more to herself than to him. She took a deep breath and grasped the latch with both hands. As far she could tell she was applying all of her strength to it, which, even though she wasn't the biggest 11 (almost 12) year old in the world, ought to be more than enough to turn the latch. There was definitely something very odd going on. Maria stopped to look at the old man. The look in his eyes seemed to have changed, from imploring to what Maria thought was a sort of resigned. He broke eye contact with her and looked down at the floor. Maria closed her eyes. It was just for a moment, to allow herself time to regroup and think about what she should do next. When she opened her eyes the old man had disappeared.

Maria leaned forward to look up and down the porch, but she couldn't see him. "What is going on?" Maria said out loud. And then realising how loud it had come out she said in a much quieter voice, "He couldn't have got around the corner that fast." She ran to the side of the house where her bedroom was and looked out of the window and down the porch. No sign of him. She moved back to the front door and looked out of the screen door and down the steps into the garden. She stood very still so as well as looking she could listen out for any sounds he might make while moving away. Nothing. In fact, completely nothing. For the first time Maria realised just how quiet it was. She knew it was night time and so she wasn't likely to hear any birds, but she was sure that even at night time the country would be making some sort of noise.

And then she thought about the sounds she would expect to hear in a house at night. Maria remembered getting up at home up during the middle of the night a few months before and having a desperate urge for a drink of milk. When she had gone downstairs to the kitchen she had been shocked by how loud the fridge had sounded. 'Was it always like that?' she'd wondered. And she'd guessed it was, but during the day it was drowned out by all the other sounds. Maria turned round and looked over towards the kitchen to check out the huge fridge (which her mum had been so envious of). And yes it was definitely there, and it was definitely on, because she could see a blue glow coming from the water dispenser in the front. But she couldn't hear it at all.

She started to walk towards it, but even getting closer she couldn't hear any noise coming from it. Or anything else, come to that … except for the sound of her feet padding across the floorboards. That's very odd, she thought, realising that it felt like the hundredth time she'd had that same thought in the last few minutes. Or however long it had been since she'd been woken by the tapping on the window. All of a sudden she felt totally exhausted by the number of times she'd thought things were weird or odd.

As soon as Maria felt the exhaustion come on, she felt like it was going to cause her to fall over or faint. Part of her was tempted just to fall gently to the floor and go to sleep. But another part of her imagined Mum or Dad, or Lizzie or Bobby, finding her there in the morning, and all the questions they'd ask, none of which she would be able to answer, even if she wanted to. She summoned all her willpower and started to walk towards the entrance to the hall. She really didn't know how she managed it, part of her brain felt it like it was already asleep and weirdly (what a surprise) already dreaming, whilst another part was doing its best to guide her down the hallway and back to bed. By the time she made it into her bedroom the former part of her brain had virtually won, and she took the last few steps with her eyes closed. She was only vaguely aware of falling forward, and the sensation of collapsing on to her mattress. One second later she was asleep.

Chapter 11

Maria did not wake up gradually. Before she woke she was aware of nothing at all. Then her eyes were wide open and she was immediately aware of the detail in the paint on the wall in front of her. She thought she could make out a pattern, but she stopped thinking about it when she started to get the strange sensation that she was not lying on a flat bed. She felt that somehow it was sloping and she was about to roll out of it backwards. She decided to turn over and see what was going on. As she did she realised that the quilt was a lot lighter than she remembered it. But that thought disappeared in a flash as she found her mum sitting right beside her on the bed smiling at her.

Her mum's smile turned into a chuckle as she realised that how startled Maria was to find her there. "Sorry," she said, "didn't mean to startle you." Her mum leaned forward and kissed her on the forehead. "Wow that was an amazing sleep, even by your standards."

Maria brought her hands up from under the quilt and rubbed her eyes, "Why, what time is it?"

Her mum looked at her watch and then turned her wrist so that Maria could see it and at the same time said, "It's just gone 11.15. By my reckoning you've been asleep for 14 hours. Nothing wrong with that of course, clearly your body thinks you need it."

Her mum stood up and pulled the curtains apart. Sunlight spilled into the room. It was another beautifully sunny day in the valley. Her mum sat down again and continued, "It's not really surprising given how busy you've been at school just lately and how much dancing you've been doing. All those competitions and extra practice, it's bound to take its toll." She stopped and looked at Maria.

Maria got the distinct impression that her mum didn't quite believe that was necessarily the whole story. And so she was pausing to let Maria add anything else that she felt she needed to. In the back of her mind Maria was already starting to process what had happened during the night. It was so real; it couldn't have been a dream … could it? For some reason her mum opening the curtains had sparked a thought in her mind. Yes, that was it … I opened the curtains during the night. Or at least I thought I did, because they were completely closed just then before Mum opened them. She closed her eyes and let her thoughts race for a few seconds. What should I say to Mum? Should I say anything about the tapping, or the old man? Or about the front door? Or the fridge not making any sound? Taken all together it did sound pretty nuts, very much like a weird, very weird, dream. And, if she does happen to think or believe it wasn't a dream, then what is she going to think or do about a man walking around our house at night? And as for me trying to get outside to go off into the valley with him … Maria had a little shudder inside at how that discussion might go. Probably best not to say anything about any of it she finally decided.

Maria re-opened her eyes and saw that Mum was still looking at her, and was clearly waiting for her to say something. Suddenly she remembered the mental note that she'd made the day before when she'd come out of the old store. But she didn't want to raise that topic if Lizzie or Bobby were going to walk in on them. Then she became aware of how quiet the house had been for the few minutes that had passed since she'd woken up. "Where are Lizzie and Bobby? What are they doing?"

"Oh, they've already gone out to the village with Dad to buy a paper and get some coffees, and some stuff so that we can make up a picnic lunch. Dad did wonder about waking you so that you could go too, but I thought it would be better to just let you sleep." She paused and briefly looked out the window, and then turned back to look at Maria again. "It really interests me, you know, how long we would sleep for if we didn't have alarm clocks? Do our bodies or brains know exactly how much sleep we need, and so they will just automatically wake us up when we've had enough? Sleep is pretty a weird thing, don't you think?" she said chuckling again.

"Sure is," Maria replied, smiling back at her. *It sure is,* she thought to herself. And then she said, "Mum, you know, how we went to that talk at the school last term, the one about puberty and how we're going to start feeling different and all that?"

"Yes, I remember it."

"Well, I was wondering … you know, when you were my age … and you were going through the changes … you know, when you started to get periods, and you know, hair and boobs and all that … did you ever get strange feelings?"

"What sort of feelings do you mean? About boys?"

"No, not boys, nothing like that," Maria said very quickly. "No, I mean feelings in your body, you know, sort of physical things."

Her Mum smiled "Of course. It's a very big thing when your body starts changing. Some days I felt really good about it, looking forward to growing up and being a woman and … And other days, well, I felt awful. I hated getting hair here …" she lifted her arm to point at her armpit, "…

and I hated getting spots. When I was 13 I was covered in spots. Well, at least I thought I was. I probably wasn't. I think I tended to exaggerate things a bit. Actually, I seem to remember that I got pretty over-emotional about lots of things back then." She paused, and Maria could sense that she was transporting herself back to those days in her mind. After a few seconds she went on, "Anyway, that was me. I take that you're feeling something? Something different?"

Maria nodded. "I'm not really sure how to explain it. It only started in the last few days." She ran the finger tips on her right hand down the top of her left forearm, which caused her to recall waking up last night and the old man and … She pushed the thoughts away. "You know that feeling you get when someone brushes your hair or scratches your back, how it causes the hairs on the back of your neck and on your arms to stand up?"

"Yep, sure do," Mum said smiling.

"Well, I've been feeling my hairs standing up along here and around here," said Maria first pointing to her arms and then to the back of her neck, "and no one is doing anything to me. In fact, yesterday it happened when I was walking around in that old store we went to." She stopped for a moment to think about what she was going to say next, and then went on, "and during the night I woke up and it was happening again."

"Hmm, can't say I ever had anything like that" said her mum. "Does it bother you at all? Is it itchy or anything like that?" And as an afterthought, "How long does it last for?"

"Nope, it doesn't itch at all. And it only lasts for a short time, maybe a few seconds. Why do you ask that?"

"Well, I was wondering if you might be having an allergic reaction to something." Mum repositioned herself on the bed to make herself more comfortable. "When you go to new places, sleep in new beds, eat different food and things like that, it's possible that you might come across something that you're going to have a reaction to. In fact, that's why Dad always brings one of those inhalers away with him. Sometimes, depending on the time of year, he can get pretty bad hay fever in the country. Sometimes even the smoke from fires or wood burners can set him off. I remember I told him once that I couldn't understand why he likes the country so much because he's allergic to it." She laughed.

"So do you think I might be allergic to something around here?" Maria said. "Actually, now that you've said that, I'm pretty sure that the first time I remember feeling it was when we were driving into the valley on Friday night. Do you think it could come on that fast? Maybe it's something in the air?" she said excitedly.

"I really don't know," said Mum raising her hands in a calm-down motion. "It may not be an allergy thing at all. It might be an anxiety thing. It could be any number of things."

"What's an anxiety thing?" asked Maria quickly.

"Well, it's probably not that. But … when people get a bit stressed or tense … or anxious … about something, then their bodies react in some way. Some people, who got very stressed or tired, say through doing long hours at work, get things called ulcers, usually in their stomachs, which are not very nice at all. Other people get twitches, some get headaches."

Maria thought that this sounded like a better and more likely explanation than the allergy stuff. "Do you get something?" she asked. "Or Dad? Does he?"

"Sure, pretty much everyone does. But it's different from person to person." Mum paused to think for a second and then continued, "For me it's headaches. When I start to feel one of my migraines coming on then I know I'm over doing it, or getting a bit stressed. My body is telling me to slow down, calm down."

"And for Dad, is it his neck and back thing?" asked Maria.

"Yes, that probably is it. Though, of course, he also has his grumbly stomach. And let's not forget about the bubbly vein in his eye …" Mum said smiling.

Maria smiled back. "So you think that *might* be what this is?" she said pointing at her forearm.

"*Maybe.*"

Maria thought for a second, and then asked, "And what about dreams, you know bad dreams – no, not bad dreams, weird dreams – do you think they could be caused by anxiety?"

"Ah," said Mum, feeling that they might be getting a bit closer to the reason for Maria's long sleeps. "Yes definitely. Sleep, or rather not sleeping well, is one of the most common things brought on by being anxious or stressed." A quizzical look came across her face, "Have you been having some bad or strange dreams, then?"

"Well, actually, just for the last couple of nights. They're not bad, not what you'd call nightmares, or anything like that. They're just *soo* real. It's almost like I'm not dreaming at all, it's like they're actually happening. And …" Maria paused. She really wasn't sure where or how far she should go.

"And?" repeated her mum.

"Er … and maybe … maybe that's why I'm sleeping in later? It's almost like I'm using up actual energy in the dreams. Do you think that's possible?"

Mum was pretty sure that that wasn't what was originally going to come after the 'and', but she decided that she'd let Maria tell her in her own time. "Sure it's possible. I think there's a name for those sorts of dreams." She looked up to the ceiling as she tried to recall it. "Yes, I know. I think they're actually called 'anxiety dreams'. I have one about being late for school. I keep trying to leave, to be on time, but something always stops me. And when I wake up I usually feel pretty awful, like I haven't slept at all. And, like I said before, when they happen I think it's just your body, or your brain, trying to tell you something. Like slow down. *Or* get more sleep." And as she said this Mum turned her palms over, clearly indicating that Maria still being in bed at 11.15 was a pretty good example of it.

Maria thought for a second, taking in everything that they'd discussed. Then she smiled and sat up and held out her arms. "Thanks for that Mum," she said as her mum leaned forward and they give each other a hug. "Just having a bit of a chat about it makes me feel much better about it all."

"Well, I'm glad to hear that," said Mum. You know that you can talk to me anytime, about anything … anything at all."

"I know that Mum, and I will," Maria replied. Though I'm not sure I'm quite ready to discuss dreams about old aboriginal men inviting me on moonlight walks through Kangaroo Valley, she thought to herself.

Mum stood up and away from the bed and said, "Probably about time you got up, what do you think?"

"Yep, probably is," replied Maria laughing, as she threw back the quilt and swung her legs over the side of the bed.

"Are you hungry at all?" asked Mum. "I'll make you some breakfast, if you like?"

The mention of food made Maria realise that she was actually feeling very hungry. "I would definitely like something," Maria replied as she dug into her bag to try and find something to wear. "I'll be there in a minute, when I'm dressed," she added over her shoulder. And she heard her mum walk out of the room.

Hmm, anxiety dreams, she thought to herself. Not sure what I'm so anxious about that it could be causing me to have dreams like I've had the last two nights. But if I guess if I knew then I'd be doing something about it, and then I wouldn't be having the dreams. She smiled to herself. That sounded a bit like Dad logic. She pulled on her denim shorts and grabbed a brush off the bedside table as she walked out of the room.

***

As she headed down the hallway towards the front of the house she heard Lizzie and Bobby's voices outside. They must be back from the village, she thought. By the time she made it into the kitchen the two of them and Dad were coming up the steps and into the house carrying a selection of bags and boxes.

"Ah, sleeping beauty has awoken," said Dad smiling as he made his way through the front door. "What time did you get up? Did Mum tell you that we were going to wake you, but she thought it was better to let you sleep?"

"Yes, she did," said Maria, "and I've been up for a while." She glanced at Mum, who looked back and widened her eyes but said nothing. Maria smiled at her and put a couple of slices of bread into the toaster. Dad started to busy himself getting the various bits and pieces that he'd bought for the picnic out of the paper bags that he'd just put down on the table.

"Well, if you've been up for a while, why are you just having your breakfast now?" asked Lizzie, who had sat herself at the breakfast bar and was thumbing through a magazine which she'd just bought in the village.

"Because me and Mum were talking for ages after I got up, woke up, whatever. Anyway what's it got to do with you what time I get up?"

Before Lizzie could respond, Dad stopped emptying the bags and looked up at everyone. "Sorry to interrupt your *discussion* girls ... I forgot to mention it before we went out, but coming in just now reminded me of it. When I got up and came in to put the kettle on this morning, I found the front door wide open."

Maria stopped looking for the jam in the fridge and turned to look at her dad.

Her dad went on, "The screen door was still closed, so it wasn't like anything, you know any animals, could have got in. But I think we should just double check that the latch is properly closed before we go to bed, or before we go out."

"That's strange," said Mum looking at Dad, "because I thought I did check it last night, just before you and I went to bed."

"Yeah, I thought you did, but maybe it's just a bit temperamental? Anyway, all I'm saying is let's just double-check it to make sure. Okay ... everyone?"

"Yesss, Dad," said Lizzie.

"Yes, but I don't know how it could have happened," said Mum.

Maria's mind raced. Either the door had somehow come open by itself, and she had very coincidentally had a dream about opening it, or ... she had got up in the middle of the night and opened it. And if that was the case then ...

"Hey, Maria, are you okay?" asked her dad. "You look like you're a million miles away. Did you hear what I said about double checking the door?"

"Oh, yes, yeah I'm fine. Make sure we check the door is properly locked okay before we go out," she said and walked over to the breakfast bar. And if that is the case, she thought to herself again as she sat down, then ... the old aboriginal man is real. I really did see him outside my window, and follow him round to the front of the house. He's real. But how could he be? And what about all those other weird things, like the heavy quilt, and it being so quiet? Maybe the door did just unlatch itself, and I heard it, and that's what made me dream about it.

Suddenly a new thought started to take shape in her head, something that her mum had said earlier. No something she'd done. Oh yes, that's it, the curtains. In her dream, or whatever, she'd opened the curtains. But after she'd woken up, Mum had opened them, which meant that they were closed. Hmm, that would seem to suggest that the door being open was just a coincidence. Unless …

"Hey, Lizzie, when you woke up this morning, did you notice anything odd about the curtains in our room?"

Lizzie looked up at her, "Huh, if by odd you mean that they were wide open, and so the sun shone right through on to my face, and I got woken up at about 6.30 or something. Then yeah, I did. I got up and closed them, but I couldn't get back to sleep, and so in the end I just got up." Lizzie started looking at her magazine again, but then paused and looked up at Maria. "Why? Did you know they were open? Why didn't you close them? They're just above your bed?"

Maria had already started processing the implications of what Lizzie had said and so she was slightly taken aback by the follow-up question. "Er, no, I was just …" What should I say? What should I say? "Ah, I think, I think I must have somehow been aware of you closing them."

"Oh. You looked absolutely out of it to me," said Lizzie.

"Well, you must have got on the end of my bed to close them, and so even though I looked like I was totally asleep, I must have felt you climbing onto my bed."

Lizzie seemed happy with this response, and made a 'hmmph' sound and went back to reading her magazine.

Maria stood up and walked over to the toaster as if she was in auto pilot mode. A bit of her brain was looking after the job of putting margarine and jam on the toast, but the vast majority of it was trying to make sense of what these two pieces of information meant. The front door and the curtains. They couldn't *both* be coincidences, could they? And, even if the door somehow wasn't latched properly and had sprung open by itself, how could the curtains open themselves? That's not possible.

She took the plate with her toast and a glass of water over to the table and sat down. So, if I opened them, both of them, does that means that I definitely woke up? And that I definitely did see the man. Surely it does. And, if it does, does that mean he'll come back again tonight? Well, I'm pretty sure he's been at my window for the past two nights. And it seems pretty clear that he wants me, just me, to help him with something. And so the answer is probably, yes. What should I do? What should I do?

Maria's train of thoughts were broken for a moment by her dad's voice calling out, "Okay, everyone, time to start helping."

She stood up and at the same time put the last piece of toast into her mouth. As she took her plate and glass over to the dishwasher, she could hear Dad issuing instructions to Lizzie and Bobby. "Lizzie, can you please fill all the water bottles. Bobby, can you please get all the beach towels together …" But she was so deep in thought that it sounded like it was happening in the background, rather than just a few feet away from her. She opened the dishwasher, but as she battled with the question of whether or not to speak to Dad and Mum about the man, she slowly stopped moving and turned into a statue with one hand on the dishwasher door and the other holding her plate in mid-air.

"Maria … Mariaaaa … Planet earth paging Mariaaa … *Maria.*" Her dad said the last 'Maria' so loud and so close to her ear that she jumped and dropped the plate into the dishwasher. Luckily it pretty much fell where she was intending it to go and so it didn't break, or break anything else. "Maria, are you okay?" said her dad as he leaned over and repositioned the plate to a new spot. (At home her dad was known as the dishwasher policeman, because he had to check it before it got put on to make sure everything was properly packed. And clearly he wasn't any less relaxed about it even when he was supposed to be on holiday.) "For a second there it looked like you'd fallen asleep standing up, but then I saw that your eyes were open. But you were miles away ... again. Is everything okay?"

"Yes, no, yes. I mean I'm good. I wasn't asleep. I was just thinking about something." As she spoke another part of her brain decided that she wouldn't mention anything right then about the man or the door. She needed more time to work out what she was going to do, and how she should explain it. "What would you like me to do, Dad?"

"Okay, good, how about you come and help me with the rolls?" replied Dad, moving back to the breakfast bar where he had already laid out lots of fillings and several jars of sauces and dressings.

Maria moved over to the breakfast bar and had a look at the fillings. "Would you like me to put these into the rolls?" she asked her dad whilst holding up some ham and cheese slices.

"Yeah, that would be great. And then I can add the salad stuff afterwards. But you'll need to cut the rolls first, and then could you please spread a bit of marg onto one side of each of them."

"Sure ... but where are the rolls?" said Maria looking all over the breakfast bar.

"They're in that brown paper bag over there," he said pointing with the sharp knife he was using to cut the tomatoes.

"Aha, I wasn't expecting that. I was looking for a plastic bag."

"It's because Kangaroo Valley – well, the village of Kangaroo Valley – has decided to do away with plastic bags in the shops. It's to help the environment, you know, by not having so many plastic bags go into landfill." He paused, and then added, "Actually, I think Kangaroo Valley was either the first or second place in Australia to do it."

"Does that mean we shouldn't have put that plastic bin liner in the bin when we arrived?" asked Maria.

"Nah, I'm pretty sure that's okay. It's not like it's illegal to bring plastic bags into the valley," he said smiling. "And there are some things that they're just much better for, like the inside of bins. But for things like shopping, why not try to use something that can be recycled? I think it's a great idea. Especially for somewhere like here, which has so much natural - you know - beauty." As he said this Dad pointed the knife towards the windows and then moved it round the almost 180 degree view. "What do you think, Maria, do you reckon it's something that more places should be trying to do?"

"Definitely, I think that anything which is trying to help the environment is a good idea. Although sometimes, when you hear about things like the rainforests being cut down and people starving in places like Africa, I wonder how anything we do here can make any difference to that?"

"Hmm, I know what you mean," said Dad nodding, "I often think exactly the same thing. I guess you just have to believe that it has to start somewhere, and if lots of people do little things then that eventually adds up to a big thing. And, if you do believe that, then you … not you *you* … I mean each person or each community has to decide how they want to respond. Do you want to be the sort of person who tries to recycle, or to not waste water, or throw away food?"

At this point Mum walked through the doorway from the back of the house and came over to the breakfast bar. "Hmm, this sounds like a pretty deep conversation for a Sunday morning. How's the picnic coming along? I think Lizzie and Bobby have done their things, and I've got all the swimmers," and she held up a beach bag. "And so when you're done, we're ready to go."

"That's great," said Dad. "We're almost done. I'll just pack the rolls into this container, and Maria can you please grab the apples out of the fridge and put them in that backpack."

"Okay, sure," said Maria. There was a bustle of activity as Mum called for Lizzie and Bobby to come out to get into the car, and Dad and Maria filled the backpacks.

As they walked over to the front door Maria said, "Dad, if people back a hundred years ago, or two hundred years ago had known what we know now, you know about the environment and global warming and all that stuff, do you think they would have still cut down all the trees in the valley?"

"Wow, that's a big question?" said Dad as he held the front door open for Maria. After he'd gone though he pulled it shut with a very firm tug, and then leaned against it to make sure it was definitely shut. "I don't think that's going to open by itself anytime soon," he said smiling at Maria.

Maria felt herself starting to blush and so quickly changed the subject. "So, what do you think? Would they have cut down the trees?"

"Hmm, I have to say I think they probably would have done it anyway. You have to remember that it was done in a particular time in history. If you assume that Captain Cook would still have come to Australia when he did, and Britain would still have sent people - convicts - here to populate the place, then they would have still needed wood

103

for houses and wagons and tables and the like. And they would still have had to clear land for crops and farming."

They reached the car, and put the back packs in the boot. As they walked round to their seats Dad added, "But maybe they would have not cut down quite as many as they did. And ..." he paused as he opened the driver's door, and looked over the top of the car at Maria, "you'd like to think that if they had known more about the environment, then just maybe they might have interacted a bit differently with the aboriginal people."

"Why do you say that?"

"Because ... if they had been thinking about the environment at all back then, then they might have also recognised that the aboriginals had lived here for thousands of years without having to cut down millions of trees. Maybe they would have been better able to share their knowledge with each other. And maybe even live together a lot better than how it turned out."

"That would have been good," said Maria as she ducked into the car, "... very good."

Maria tried to imagine what it must have been like for the aboriginals when the settlers arrived, and how strange it would have been for them, how quickly the world they'd known for thousands of years was turned upside down by their arrival. She found it hard to think of anything at all that might have been good about it.

Chapter 12

"What would have been good?" said Lizzie, as Maria sidled into the car beside her.

"Where are we going today?" asked Bobby almost at the same time.

Maria was about to try and reply to Lizzie, but before she could, Dad answered Bobby. "Well now," he said, as he started the engine, "I thought we'd start by going to the Pioneer Museum."

"Urgh, not a museum," responded Bobby immediately, "that sounds really boring."

"Well, apparently there's a really good bush walk that starts just behind it. I thought we could do that first, and hopefully we can find a good spot to have our lunch on the way. And you never know, we might even be able to find a place to have a swim in the river. But if we don't, then as soon as we've finished the walk and had a quick look round the museum, we can go back to the swimming place we went to yesterday. It's literally just across the road …"

This seemed to placate Bobby and as the car headed down the drive he grunted an, "Okay, I s'pose."

About 45 minutes later, Bobby was feeling much better about being at a museum. First, rather than being a single building or hall with lots of glass cabinets or tables containing exhibits, the museum was made up of a number of replica houses or rooms each of which showed a particular aspect of settler life. They popped into a couple of them on the way to the bush walk, and in the first there had been some jars containing some pretty gruesome looking snakes. And the second room turned out to be a reproduction of a settler toilet, which Bobby thought was very cool.

And now they were on a rope suspension bridge that led to the start of the bush walk. It spanned a deep creek and looked very similar to the one that Indy had been trapped on at the end of *Indiana Jones and the Temple of Doom*. Bobby and Dad were re-enacting the scene where Indy is stuck in the middle and ends up cutting the ropes to get away from the baddies.

Mum was not at all impressed by the way Dad and Bobby's movements were causing the bridge to swing from side to side, and so along with Maria and Lizzie, she made her way swiftly past the sword fight and up on to the ground on the far side of the bridge.

"Apparently there's some markers to show us the way," said Mum as she looked at the map that the man at museum reception had given her.

"Do you think the yellow arrow on that post is one of them?" asked Lizzie pointing at a post about 10 metres away to their left.

"I'd say so," replied Mum.

"I'll find the next one," Lizzie said excitedly as she ran forward. Lizzie always liked to be at the front of their walks or expeditions, though normally with Bobby in close pursuit.

"Don't go too far in front of us Lizzie," Mum called after her.

Maria and her mum turned at the same time to see where her dad and Bobby were, which was just in time to see Bobby (aka 'Indy') thrust a sword stick into the midriff of Dad (aka 'The Baddie'), which he neatly deflected under his armpit. He screamed in pretend agony and then began to collapse against the ropes that made up the side of the bridge. Bobby pulled out his sword and thwacked it against Dad's leg.

"Take that," he shouted, and Maria and Mum started laughing.

"Be careful, Bobby" called out Mum, "Dad is going to need his leg for this bush walk. On the topic of which, Lizzie has already started on it, and we should probably catch-up with her."

"I'm coming," said Bobby and he turned away from Dad ran up the bridge to join Mum and Maria. "Which way did she go?" he asked as he approached.

"That way," said Maria pointing to her right. "We've got to follow those yellow arrows." Without reducing speed at all Bobby hurtled passed them and on towards the post.

"Lizzieeee, wait for me," he called out as he disappeared into the bush. A few seconds later Dad joined them and they turned and started along the track.

"How's your leg?" asked Mum with a big smile on her face.

"I'll survive," he said smiling back at her. "How good is this?" he exclaimed raising his arms to indicate that he was referring to what was all around them. "You wouldn't have guessed from the road that there was bush like this only a couple of hundred metres away."

"Do you think that the whole valley would have been like this, before the settlers came?" Maria asked.

"I guess so. Pretty hard to imagine now, isn't it?"

After a few minutes they turned to their right and Maria realised that they must have been climbing, because through the trees she could see a river quite a way down below them. Maria wondered if it was the same river that they swam in yesterday, under the bridge. She stopped for a moment to get her bearings, and then decided that it must be the same one. They continued on. A bit further up the path they came across Lizzie and Bobby waiting for them.

"There's two arrows here and we didn't know which one to follow," said Lizzie.

"I think it's this one," said Bobby, who was holding on to a post that had an arrow pointing down a steep path to their left.

Mum pulled the map out of her back pocket and opened it up so that she, Bobby and Lizzie could all see it. "I think you're right Bobby," she said after a few moments. Bobby immediately let go of the post and headed for the path, clearly in an attempt to beat Lizzie to the front position.

"Slow down," Mum and Dad called out at the same time. "It's very steep, and some of the rocks look pretty slippery," added Mum.

At the bottom of the steep section they came to a little stream, and the track turned to the right to follow it. The trees seemed thicker here and as Maria looked ahead she could see sunbeams filtering through the branches. The water in the stream seemed to be sparkling, and Maria wondered if the sunbeams had anything to do with that. She also noticed that the moss on the rocks beside the stream looked very green, almost like it was glowing. *What a magical spot,* she thought to herself.

The thought was still in her head when Dad stopped walking and said, "Hey guys, I think this would be a good spot to have our picnic. What do you think?"

"Great idea," said Mum, and she pulled a back pack off her shoulders and put it down on a flattish rock away from the stream.

"Yes," agreed Maria, "it's a beautiful spot." She looked at her dad and he winked at her, almost as if he'd known what she'd been thinking about.

Dad called out to Lizzie and Bobby that they were stopping for lunch, and Maria moved over to sit down on a rock that was beside the stream. As she did so she felt just the merest sensation of the hairs on her forearm starting to move. She stopped and looked down at them. Maria thought that she could almost see the hairs starting to tense, to stand up. She wondered if something physical could be causing it, and she looked up and around her. There didn't appear to be any wind – in fact, none of the branches or plants around them seemed to be moving at all. And she wasn't in the sun, so that seemed to rule out it being caused by a change of temperature, or anything like that.

As she sat down Maria placed her right hand on her left wrist and then moved her palm up along her left forearm, as if to flatten the hairs. This seemed to make the sensation go away, on her left arm at least, and so she repeated it on her right arm. By the time she'd done the brushing twice on each forearm the feeling had completely gone.

"Everything okay, Maria?" her mum asked from behind her. Maria was a little startled by the question and she turned round a little too quickly, so that she had to stop herself sliding off the rock and into the stream.

"Er, yes … hmm, no. Well, what I mean is … actually, I just had another of those weird moments where it feels like the hairs on my arms are all standing up. Well in this case, about to stand up, because before they did stand up all the way I stopped it happening by stroking them. Did you see me doing that?"

"Yes, I did," said her mum. "What were you doing when it started?"

"Nothing," she quickly replied. Then, looking at her mum, she realised that her mum's question wasn't at all an accusatory one. "Well, what I mean is, I was just walking over to this rock to sit on it, and as I did I felt the feeling start. And so I sat down and for some reason had the idea to rub my arms. And so that's what I did, and the feeling went away. That's it. Weird, eh?"

"Hmm, that is a bit weird," agreed her mum. She thought for a few seconds and then asked, "You're not feeling tired or out of breath or anything like that, are you?" Maria shook her head. "Or very hungry or thirsty?"

"Well, I'm ready to have lunch and a drink, but I wouldn't say I'm especially, you know, tummy rumblingly hungry … or especially thirsty. Why, what do you think it might be?"

"To be honest, Maria, I have no idea. I think I was just trying to rule some obvious things out."

At that moment Lizzie and Bobby returned from their advance scouting, and they were obviously very excitedly about something. Bobby could hardly get the words out quick enough, "Over that hill there's a river, and it looks like there's a place where you can swim, and maybe some rocks that you can jump in from, and we felt the water and it's really warm, and do you think we can swim there, Dad?"

"Why don't we go there now? We could have our lunch there," added Lizzie.

"We can definitely take a look at it, but let's have lunch here first. There's lots of shade and, look there, there's some great rocks for you guys to sit on while you eat." Dad held up his hands which contained a bread roll for each of them. Lizzie thought for a second and then clearly decided that she wanted to eat more than she wanted to continue discussing it. She stepped forward and took a roll from her dad, and then went to sit on one of the rocks that Dad had pointed out. Bobby scuffed the ground with his shoe in a moment of protest, but then decided he too was ready to eat, and so took the other roll on offer and headed over to the rocks.

As Bobby did, Mum leaned forward and in a very soft voice said to Maria, "Just to finish what we were talking about before ... the next time it starts to happen please tell me. As soon as it starts."

Maria nodded, and then took a big bite out of her ham salad role. She had no idea what was causing it, but if she'd found a way to stop it, or control it a bit, then that did seem at least to be a step in the right direction.

As soon as lunch was finished Lizzie and Bobby ensured that they very quickly made their way over the hill to the river. As it turned out the swim hole they'd found had too many rocks in it to be safe for jumping into, and wasn't really deep enough for a proper swim. But, in the process of finding this out, Dad started a water splashing fight which meant that everyone got pretty wet. Once they'd dried off a bit they continued with the bush walk, which followed the river for a while before heading up a steep slope and then passing through a very dense part of bush.

Eventually they got back to the bridge, but as Bobby was by now desperate for a number two, there was no repeat of the battle on the bridge. Instead he went ahead with Mum to find where the real toilets – as opposed to the reproduction settler version – were located.

Meanwhile Maria, Lizzie and Dad started to take a closer look at the various buildings and huts. Maria loved it all. In fact, even Lizzie, who had pretty much shared Bobby's view that it would be 'really borrring', ended up really enjoying it.

Maria was fascinated by the family tree that was drawn up on a blackboard outside of the homestead. She and Dad stood in front of it for ages as he explained how it worked. Maria thought that it was amazing that it included so many generations and that it went right back to the middle of the

1800s. And she couldn't believe how big some of the families were. How could anyone have 12 children?

Maria and Lizzie both really liked the school room. They sat at some very old looking desks and listened to a lesson that was supposed to be replicate one from back in the 1800s. On the way out of the room they discussed how much better school was today. Then Dad showed them an article that indicated that because there used to be so many schools in the valley and not enough teachers, kids only had to go to school every other day. Lizzie thought that was fantastic, and that she would even have been able to endure the old style lessons if she only had to go to school for half the amount of time.

After the school room Lizzie went off to see what Mum and Bobby were up to, and so Maria walked with her dad over to the hall which contained the jars of pickled snakes, and lots of general exhibits like clothes and tools. After they'd been walking round for a few minutes, Dad came over to Maria and said, "Given what the lady told us at the general store yesterday, I've been keeping an eye out for any information they have on the aboriginal people who lived in the valley. But I can't say I've seen very much, in fact anything really. What about you?"

"I haven't either," said Maria. "It's pretty much all about the white settlers, isn't it?"

"Maybe we should go and ask the man at the museum shop. What do you think?"

Maria hadn't really been sure at the time where the question about the aborigines had come from, and she had just been thinking of asking her dad if it was about time to go to the river for a proper swim. But for a reason that she couldn't really explain, Maria felt like she should do it. So she said, "Sure, let's go and ask. And after we've done that can we find the others and go to the river for a swim?"

"Sounds like a plan to me," said Dad. "I'm sure we won't get any complaints from Lizzie or Bobby about going to the river."

They headed out of the hall and over to the office. The man who had given them their tickets a couple of hours before was still there. When they entered he looked up from his magazine and said, "G'day, how was your walk?"

"Great," said Dad. "We had a picnic by a small stream, a really beautiful spot."

"And then we had a paddle in a river, and Dad started splashing us, and we all got very wet," added Maria.

The man looked at Maria and smiled. "Sounds like a lot of fun, especially on a hot day like this. Have you had a chance to look at the museum as well?"

"Yep, I like it. It's really interesting," replied Maria. She paused and looked up at Dad, who nodded back to her. "But we were wondering if you have any information about the aboriginal people who lived in the valley when the settlers arrived?"

"That's a good question," said the man, his smile turning into a much more serious, studious look. "I have to be honest with you. I've not been doing this for very long and so I'm probably not the best person to ask. Is it for a school project or something like that? Because if it is I could arrange for someone from the Historical Society to contact you, or your school."

"No, it's not for a project, I'm just interested that's all." As she said it Maria had a sense of déjà vu, remembering that the woman in the store had asked pretty much the same thing the day before. Maria wondered if all adults thought that kids only asked questions about 'serious' stuff when they had a project to do for school.

The man nodded, and put his hand on his chin. "I see. Hmm, let me think." After a few seconds he slipped off his stool and walked around the counter. As he did he pointed down a corridor that ran away from the office and said, "You know what, we have a collection of old photographs along here, and I'm pretty sure that a few of them include some of the aboriginal people who stayed in the valley while the settlers were ..." He thought for a moment, obviously trying to find the right word. And then said, "... settling." He smiled, and then added, "Would you like to see them?"

Maria was about to say that she didn't want to put him to any trouble when her dad quickly said, "Thanks, that would be great."

The man turned and headed off down the corridor, and Dad put his hands on Maria's shoulders and steered her through the doorway after him. They passed by a room which had a lot of different objects laid out on several tables, and then turned into a room where a large square table was covered with boxes of photographs. The man walked round the table and pointed at some boxes sitting on the corner furthest away from where Maria and her dad were standing in the doorway.

"I think these are the ones. They're very old and so please don't handle them too much. In fact, probably best not to take them out of the boxes at all if you can help it, just flick through them." And he gave them a little demonstration of what he meant. "And while you're doing that I'll go back to the desk and call someone who will know a lot better than me what info or artefacts we have." And with that he walked back around the table and slipped by them into the corridor.

Dad tapped Maria on the arm and said, "I think I better go and let Mum and the others know where we are, in case they start looking for us. If they can't find us they might think we've already gone to the river. Will you be okay here on your own for a few minutes? I'll come straight back after I've seen them."

"Of course, I'll be fine," she said.

Dad nodded and then turned to walk back along the corridor. Maria walked slowly round the table looking at the boxes. The photos at the front of the first few she passed looked like they were taken pretty recently, well in the 1960s or 70s she thought, judging by the clothes. But as she passed the corner of the table the photographs became noticeably older. She reached the boxes which the man had pointed to and looked at the front photos. They all looked very old and grainy, and all three of them depicted people standing in front of a house or, in the case of one of them, what could only be described as a large hut. Considering how rough and unsafe that building looked, Maria thought that the people in front of it looked quite well dressed.

She carefully pulled the photo up a few centimetres so that she could see the whole image. On the bottom left hand corner of the plastic sleeve enclosing the photo there was a sticker labelled 'Kangaroo River – c.1870'. Maria scanned the picture. Behind the shack there were lots of trees, so this was probably taken before the tree cutting really got going, at least in that part of the valley. There were a lot of big logs lying on the ground in front of the building, and some leaning up against it. After a few seconds she realised that these were probably there to help prop up the structure. They looked very heavy, and Maria suddenly had a sense of how difficult life must have been for these people trying to make a home for themselves in a new land.

She let that photo slip back into the box, and then leaned it forward so that she could see the second one, and then the third, and the fourth. These were very similar to the first one. People standing very rigidly in front of a building, either their houses (she assumed) or a shed. She remembered then something that they'd been told at school about how with old cameras people had to stand really still for a long time in order for the image to work properly.

That would explain why everyone looked so stiff and no-one was smiling.

Then she came across one of the Kangaroo Valley Public School taken in 1872. The school actually looked pretty good. The walls were made out of thick, tall timbers and there was a proper roof. And how many children were there? She started counting. There were about 20 in the front row alone, so there must have been about 50 altogether. She was very surprised that were so many as far back as that.

Maria flicked through a few more, and then came across one which was quite creased and very grainy. It showed a group of people sitting in front of what looked like a cross between a hut and a tent. She pulled it up out of the box and held it in front of her, but it was still difficult to make it out properly. As she studied it Maria realised that it was a picture of an aboriginal family. But they were wearing the same sort of clothes as the settlers. She wasn't expecting that to be the case at all.

Maria counted – there were five adults and seven, no eight children. One of the women had a small baby in her arms. She held the photo up a bit higher and moved it to the right so that it had more light on it. She started to scan the faces, and then stopped, and blinked, and looked again. She felt her heart start to race. It couldn't be.

She blinked again but for longer, and then moved the photo closer to her eyes. The man standing furthest to the right of the group looked just like the old man who she'd seen outside her window the night before. Or that she had dreamed she'd seen outside of her window, she reminded herself. She looked at him again, he was dressed very differently to the man she'd 'seen'. He had a heavy dark jacket on, and light coloured long trousers, and a hat that looked a bit like a beanie. Maria thought that must be why she hadn't recognised him sooner. She looked closely at him, and it was definitely him. Though maybe he was a bit younger in this photo than he had appeared to be last night.

What could it mean? This morning, after Dad had mentioned finding the front door open, and Lizzie had complained about being woken up by the open curtains, she'd been pretty much convinced that it wasn't a dream. That she actually had been woken up by, and spoken to by an old aboriginal man wearing little more than a nappy. But now … if this was him, in this photo from – she couldn't see a date on the front so she turned the photo over, and saw written in pencil 'Aborigine family 1860' – from 1860, then how could she have possibly seen him for real?

But then, she thought, if it wasn't real, and I did dream it, then why would I, how could I dream of him the night before I see him in a photograph? Maria's mind raced. What was going on? What was happening here? What was happening to her? She suddenly realised that her heart was still beating very fast, and it was almost like the beating was in her throat.

She felt anxious, almost panicky, and her knees started to go a bit rubbery. With the hand that wasn't holding the photograph Maria grabbed the corner of the table to try and steady herself. That helped, but her heart was still racing. She decided that she should put both hands on the table, and so she brought her other arm round to put the photo down on top of the closest box of photos. But as she did the photo slipped from her fingers and started to glide down and under the table. Maria thought about bending down to pick it up, but very quickly decided that wasn't such a good idea, and so completed her plan to hold on to the table with both hands.

At this moment Maria's Mum appeared in the doorway. She took one look at Maria and then rushed into the room. "My god, Maria, are you okay? You look very pale." And she put her arm around her waist to give her some support.

"I'm fine Mum," said Maria, even though she clearly wasn't. Mum twisted Maria's shoulders round so that she could look into Maria's face. The look on her mum's face made it very clear that she didn't believe that response at all.

"Okay, I'm not. Or at least I wasn't a few moments ago. I'm feeling a lot better now." This was reasonably true as just having her mum in the room with her had caused her heart beat to slow down dramatically, and the rubbery feeling in her legs had virtually gone. "I was looking at these photos and all of a sudden I felt … kinda … you know …" There was a word that her mum used sometimes, what was it? Oh yeah, that's it … "I felt all giddy, like I was about to fall over. And so I grabbed hold of the table, and that's when you came in. And now I feel okay again."

Mum looked at her. Maria sensed that she knew that she wasn't hearing the whole story, but then she put her arms around her shoulder and gave her a hug. "Well, that's good," she said. "But I am a bit worried that it might be connected to those feelings you've been having in your arms. I think it would be a good idea to see a doctor when we get back to Sydney, have a bit of a check-up, just to make sure that everything's okay. What do you think?"

Maria could tell by Mum's tone of voice that there was only one possible answer to that question. And so she nodded and said, "Sure, I think that would be a good idea." And then she smiled and added, "Better safe than sorry, as you always say."

Mum smiled back. "Yes I do, don't I?" She looked around the room and then asked, "Are you finished here? Only Lizzie and Bobby are desperate to go to the river for a swim. I told them I'd stay with you if wanted stay here longer."

"No, no, that's fine, I don't want to look at any more photos," said Maria, and started to walk out of the room.

She wondered whether, if her mum hadn't been around, she might have 'borrowed' the photo that was now sitting under the table, and then thought about whether it might still be possible. But in the end, she concluded that apart from the fact that taking the photo would actually be stealing, it really wasn't worth the risk of bringing any attention to it, and then having to try and explain it all.

And so she and her mum left the room and walked down the corridor. The man at the reception asked her if she'd found anything interesting or useful, and when Maria told him she had, he insisted on giving her a phone number of someone who would be happy to talk about the aboriginals who had lived in the valley. Apparently there were some sites where you could still see aboriginal art and other stuff that they'd used or made.

Thankfully, at this point, Mum stepped in and said that they were running late for something and so they had to go. They both thanked him very much for all his help, and then headed out to the car. Maria's door was open and so she got straight into her seat alongside Lizzie.

"Where have you been?" Lizzie asked, "We've been waiting ages for you."

Maria thought this was a bit of an exaggeration, but decided not to enter into a 'discussion' about it. And so she just said, "Sorry about that, I was looking at some really interesting photos and I guess I lost track of time."

Lizzie started to respond, but Maria realised that Mum and Dad were talking to each other at the back of the car, and so she decided to ignore what Lizzie was saying and instead try to hear what they were saying. As she was pretty certain that it would be about what had just happened. The door was still open and so she leaned to her left and concentrated on their voices. It took a few moments but eventually she was able to tune into the conversation, and the first thing she heard was her mum saying …

Chapter 13

The words – or rather *the* word – entered Maria's brain like a tiny explosion. Her mum and dad had carried on talking for a while longer, but Maria wasn't listening any more. If you'd asked her later how long they'd talked for, or how they'd got from the museum to the car park beside the river, she wouldn't have been able to recall it at all.

And the fact that her mum had only been referring to an old saying was completely lost on Maria. The word 'ghost' had triggered a multitude of new thoughts and questions in her head. Until now she had thought that basically one of two things had been happening to her. Either she was having the most unbelievably real feelings and incredibly weird dreams in which an aboriginal man wanted her to go with him out into the valley – or she actually was waking up and truly had seen the aboriginal man.

The problem was that both of these explanations had their ... well, problems. If it was all a dream then who had opened the curtains? And the front door opening, that just seemed too unlikely a coincidence. But if it really did happen, then why hadn't she been able to open the screen door? And what about all those other things like the quilt feeling so heavy, and being unable to wake Lizzie or Dad the night before?

And now, just to make things even more complicated, she'd seen the same aboriginal man who had stood outside her window the night before – either in a dream or for real – standing in a photograph that was well over 100 years old. If it really was him in the photo, then he couldn't have been standing outside last night, not for real. That meant she'd dreamed it all. But somewhere inside, somewhere deep down, she didn't think that was what was happening.

What about ... what if ... her mum had been partly right? It wasn't that Maria had 'just seen a ghost', rather it was that she had just realised that she'd seen a ghost the night before. Could that be it? But do ghosts normally carry things like sticks? she thought to herself, and can they use them to tap on windows? Maria didn't know the answer, but she thought that it sounded a bit unlikely. And the way that the man had spoken to her, like he was practising or relearning a word that he'd just heard, surely ghosts didn't do that?

These thoughts and what-if questions raced around Maria's brain so fast that she had absolutely no awareness of anything else. And so when her dad put his head into the car beside her and said in a loud voice, "Hey, Maria, are you coming for a swim with us, or what? You seemed pretty keen a few minutes ago," she almost jumped out of her skin. "Oops, sorry, I didn't mean to startle you. Well, not that much anyway. Are you okay?" he added.

Maria's slowly re-focussed and saw that she was only one left in the car. Realising this she looked out and saw that Mum, Lizzie and Bobby were already walking towards the path that led down to the river. It was almost as though she'd been sleeping, but she knew she hadn't.

"I'm okay, Dad, I was just thinking about something."

"Was it what happened back at the museum just now? Mum told me you looked pretty ..." he wasn't quite sure what word he should use. "Umm ... you know, a bit bothered about something. You do know you can talk to me about it, about anything. If you want to."

Maria got out of the car, and gave her dad a quick hug. "Yes, I know. But, really, I'm fine." And as if to show this was the case she stepped away from her dad and did a cartwheel along the side of the car. It felt good, and she realised that it had been a few days since she'd done one, which was pretty unusual for her. She did another one back and finished up about half a metre from her dad.

"Okay, I get it. You're okay," said her dad laughing. "In fact, if you're that okay come here and help me with this bag."

Maria smiled and took the bag from his hand. They closed the car doors and walked after the others. The water in the river was very refreshing after the bush walk, and this time they all managed at least a quick dip in the water. And after a while Maria was able to think about things other than the photo, the aboriginal man, plus open doors and curtains.

***

When they'd finished at the river there was a family vote on where they should go for dinner and, due to its huge garden, the pub in the village won easily. They popped back to the house to get changed, and for Mum and Dad to have a nice cup of tea, then headed back out to the village.

When they got to the garden they found a man and a woman singing and playing guitars, with lots of people gathered round. For a while the kids sat with Mum and Dad listening to the music. But when the singers announced a 10-minute break, Bobby suggested a game of tag, and Maria and Lizzie were more than ready to have a run around. Mum said that they could go anywhere as long as they were still in view. But as the garden stretched out for about 200 metres before the grass turned into bushes and then trees, this still left them with plenty of room.

The three of them skipped and walked away from the area with the tables, and then Bobby decided it was time for the game to start. He prodded Maria in the back and shouted 'you're it' before sprinting off further away from the tables. Within a couple of minutes the tag game had taken them about three-quarters of the way to where the bushes and trees started.

After a particularly long chase, which had ended up with them all running around in smaller and smaller circles, Maria fell to the grass to catch her breath. As she sat there looking around, she realised that from this location the walls of the valley were visible from every direction. The sun had long since passed below the walls, and it was beginning to get dark, but you could still see enough to be wowed by it.

Maria turned and saw that Lizzie and Bobby's last chase had ended up in them wrestling on the grass, about half way between her and the trees. And so she stood up, aiming to separate them before it all got out of hand. As she started to walk towards them she began to feel the merest sensation of her hairs tingling on her arms and whispered to herself, "Oh no, not this again."

Remembering what she'd done earlier, she started to rub her forearms, smoothing down the hairs as she walked. But this time it made no difference, and now she could also feel the back of her neck starting to tingle. As she walked closer to Lizzie and Bobby, she could feel the sensation growing stronger and stronger. Until, when she was about five metres away from them, the tingle seemed to transform itself into a kind of shiver which seemed to pass through her whole body. She let out a "whoa" sound and dropped to her knees. For a few seconds she could feel her whole body shivering just like it did when you got really cold. Then, as quickly as it had come on, it started to ease. By now she was on all fours looking down at the grass. She looked up to see Lizzie and Bobby staring at her, both with their mouths wide open.

"Wow," exclaimed Bobby.

"What was that?" said Lizzie.

"Do it again," said Bobby.

"Err, actually, I'd rather not," said Maria, as she pushed herself back into a kneeling position.

"Is that the same thing that happened to you in the museum?" asked Lizzie. "I heard Mum and Dad talking about it when we were getting changed back at the house."

"No, no, that's not what happened." Maria paused and then realised what Lizzie had said. "You shouldn't have been listening into their private conversations, Lizzie." And then, after an even shorter pause, "Well, what did they say?"

"Oh, I didn't hear much, really, it's just what I heard as I was walking into the kitchen. Dad said something like, 'what do you think it was?' then Mum said that she'd been talking to you about being anxious, and something about 'having a panic attack', whatever they are, and then they saw me and stopped talking about it."

Maria's shoulders dropped a bit. She suddenly felt overwhelmed by everything that was happening to her, and also a desperate need to talk to someone about it. She just had no idea where to start. She saw that Lizzie was still looking at her, but Bobby was already up and off on another run. All Maria could manage in response to her was a sigh and an, "Oh."

Lizzie crawled forward so that she ended up sitting about a metre away from Maria. "So do you know what a panic attack is?"

"Hmm, something to do with being very panicky, or getting anxious, I guess," replied Maria, remembering what

125

she'd discussed with her mum earlier that day. That felt like a long time ago now.

"Is that what happened just now?" asked Lizzie, in a genuinely concerned voice.

"You know, I really don't know what that was," said Maria. "Ever since we came to the valley I've been getting these strange feelings on my arms and on the back of my neck. You know when someone brushes your hair, or rubs your back, how that makes your hairs stand-up, and get a bit goosebumpy?" Lizzie nodded.

"Well, that's a bit what the feeling I get is like," Maria continued. "But, up until just now, it had only been on my arms and my neck. This time it started on my arms, then the back of my neck, and then spread all the way down my back and onto my legs." Maria used her hands to show Lizzie how it had progressed around her body. "It didn't hurt at all. It's just very weird, you know." She paused for a moment, and then went on. "I spoke to Mum about it this morning and to start with she thought it might be an allergy thing. But she also wondered about it being something to do with me being a bit anxious or stressed. I don't think it's that – I mean, do you think I'm stressed?" Lizzie shrugged. "Problem is I have no idea what else might be making it happen."

They were both silent for a while. Then Lizzie asked, "Well, if what happened just now wasn't what happened in the museum, what did happen there? Mum and Dad sounded very serious when they were talking about it."

Maria opened her mouth. She really wanted to tell someone, but she was really struggling with how or where to start. She managed a "Well ..." when Bobby came running over to them.

"Hey, guys, Dad's waving at us. I think our meals are ready. Come on, let's go." And with that he rushed off back towards the tables.

Maria started to get up, but Lizzie put her hand on her arm and said, "Well, what?"

Maria looked down at her. "Well … well, it's a long story, and I'm too hungry to tell it now." She smiled and bent over and tapped Lizzie on the head. "You're it," she shouted and started to run after Bobby. Lizzie leapt up to give chase.

Before they reached the table Maria slowed. When Lizzie got to about three metres from her she said, "Hey Lizzie, thanks for being interested. There is something I'd like to talk to you about, but can we do it tonight when we're in bed?"

Lizzie nodded and said, "Sure, no *problemo*." And as she passed, she tapped Maria on the arm and said, "You're it!" before running the last few steps to the table.

Chapter 14

By the time they had finished their meals it was completely dark. As a consequence, Mum and Dad had said no to another game of tag, but yes to ice-creams for dessert and to staying for a while longer to listen to the singers.

It was about eight o'clock when they got back to the house. The warmth of the day still hadn't disappeared, and so there was a discussion about whether or not to light the fire, but 'as it would start to get cold very quickly and it was their last night staying there', Mum thought that they should. And so Dad got started on that while Mum supervised the kids showering and getting ready for bed. After that was done the family sat on the lounges surrounding the fire to read or be read to.

A bit after nine, Mum decided that it was time for the kids to get to bed, and so Maria, Lizzie and Bobby marched off to the bathroom to do their teeth and then go to their respective rooms. By the time Mum and Dad had been in to say goodnight, it was nine thirty. As Dad left the room, Maria and Lizzie shared a knowing glance and nodded at each other. They waited a few minutes for Mum and Dad to be satisfied that they had settled, and then Maria crept out of her bed and over to Lizzie's.

"Move over a bit so I can get under the quilt with you," Maria said in a whispered voice. Lizzie did and Maria got in. "You have to promise not to tell anyone else about this."

"What, about you getting into bed with me?" replied Lizzie.

"No stupid. Well yes, don't say anything about that. But what I meant is, don't say anything about what I'm going to tell you now. To anyone. Okay? You promise?"

"Yes, okay, I promise," said Lizzie.

Maria had looked like she'd been reading earlier when they'd sat around the fire, but in truth she'd really been trying to work out what she should tell Lizzie. She knew it would be good to be able to share at least some of what she'd experienced over the last couple of nights, but there were also some parts, some of her own ideas about what might be going on, that she felt it would be better not to mention.

"Okay, that's good. So … you know how I've slept in pretty late the last couple of mornings?"

Lizzie whispered, "Yep."

"Well, both nights we've been here I have had the weirdest dreams. But as well as being weird, they've felt so real I've not been sure if they're dreams at all."

"Why were they so weird? What were they about?" said Lizzie.

"Hold on, I'll get to that," replied Maria, in a slightly exasperated tone. "What's been making me wonder if they've even been dreams is that things I think I've dreamt doing, when I've got up, or later on in the day, I've found that they're real, that they've actually happened."

Maria realised that she hadn't said that quite as she'd intended, and Lizzie's forehead was starting to furrow. "What I mean is … you remember this morning I asked you about the curtains? You said that they had been open when you woke up. In fact, it was them being open that caused you to wake up, coz the sun shone on your face." Lizzie nodded. "Well, last night I dreamt that I opened them. And

I'm pretty sure that they were closed before we went to sleep – Mum and Dad always check that sort of thing."

"They do," agreed Lizzie.

"And the other thing I dreamt was opening the front door. And you remember how Dad said he found …"

"Oh, yeah," whispered Lizzie before Maria could finish her sentence, and then, "wow, that is weird." Lizzie paused to think and then said, "Maybe you've been sleepwalking? There's a girl in my class – you know, Hannah D – who sleepwalks. I'm not really supposed to know about it, but Nikki's been to her house for sleepovers and told me. Her mum has to lock her bedroom door every night, so that she doesn't go anywhere. Apparently, one time when it first started, she went out of the house and started bouncing on their trampoline." Maria's eyes widened and Lizzie thought that meant she didn't believe it. "It's true, Hannah's mum told Nikki all about it."

"I believe you," said Maria. "I'm just thinking about what you said about me sleepwalking. I hadn't thought about that, and I'm not sure why because it's a very good thought." Maria closed her eyes for a moment and tried to see how this new potential explanation fitted with what had happened. Of course it could explain her opening the curtains and then getting up to open the front door. But what about her not being able to wake her dad, or Lizzie? And then there was the aboriginal man and, of course, the photograph – how would her sleepwalking explain that?

Somewhere in the back of her mind she remembered a book she'd read a while back in which someone had been a sleepwalker. There was something in that book … something about sleepwalking. Ah yes, that was it, sleepwalkers have no memory of what they've done when they wake up. She didn't know if that was true or just something that the book had made up. But it certainly wasn't the case with her over the last two nights. She remembered vividly everything that had happened. But she had to be careful what she said to Lizzie, because clearly she hadn't told her a lot of what she'd just been thinking about.

She opened her eyes and looked straight into Lizzie's. "That's a great idea, Lizzie, but I'm not sure it's really what's been happening to me. I mean for one thing, why would I suddenly start doing it here, in Kangaroo Valley, in this house?"

"Hmm, I don't know." Lizzie thought for a second and then said, "Well, everyone has to start doing it somewhere, you know do it for the first time. And maybe there's something about this house that brought it on. Helped it to start happening."

Maria was very impressed by Lizzie's thought process. Whilst she was pretty convinced that she wasn't sleepwalking in the way most people thought of it, the idea that perhaps there was 'something about this house' was a very interesting one.

"Maybe there's some way we could check it, you know, to see if you are getting up," said Lizzie.

"What do you mean?" replied Maria a bit uncertainly.

"Well, we could put something somewhere, and if it's moved or changed by the morning then we'd know if you've got up during the night. Like …"

Now she understood what Lizzie meant, Maria thought this was a very good plan. Even if it wasn't sleepwalking it would help confirm whether or not she was dreaming it all, or really getting up. "Like maybe putting some tissues on the floor beside my bed," she suggested. She thought for a second about how to do it. "If I get back into bed, then maybe you could lay some out between my bed and the door. If I do get up and walk around then I'd have to step on them, and they'd get moved around or all scrunched up."

"Yeah, that's a great idea," said Lizzie. "Let's do it."

Maria smiled and started to turn over to get out of the bed. But then she stopped and rolled back. "Hey, Lizzie, thanks for this. You don't how much better it makes me feel to be able to talk to someone about it." And she leaned forward and kissed her sister on the cheek.

"Well, I don't know why you didn't talk to me about it yesterday. I knew *something* was up, it was so unlike you to sleep in when we'd only just arrived at a new place."

Maria shrugged. "I should have done. I guess I didn't know what to say about it. And, anyway, it was only this morning, today, that I found out about the curtains and the door. The first night was just a weird dream," she said, and quickly rolled over and got out of the bed. And as she walked back over to her bed, she murmured to herself, "Well, mostly just a weird dream."

Lizzie followed her over, picking up the box of tissues off the chest of drawers as she did. Maria jumped into her bed, and then Lizzie carefully placed the tissues on the rug that lay between their two beds. Maria watched her intently and when she finished said quietly, "Perfect, Lizzie. Thank you so much for your help."

"No worries," Lizzie whispered back as she stood up and reviewed her work. "I don't think you'll be able to get anywhere without moving at least some of them." She paused for a second and then added, "Unless you're sleep flying rather than sleepwalking, that is." After considering this thought for a second or two they both started to laugh, and Lizzie had to stuff her hand into her mouth to stop it getting too loud.

She got back into bed, and they were both quiet for a few moments. However, if someone had entered the room just then, they would probably have been able to hear both their brains ticking over with their respective thoughts. Just as Maria felt she was about to drop off to sleep, she heard Lizzie whisper, "Hey Maria, are you still awake?"

"Yes, but I was almost asleep."

"Oops, sorry about that. Only I was wondering ... let's just say that you were sort of sleepwalking last night, and it was you that opened the front door, why do you think you did that? Do you remember if you were going somewhere, you know, in particular?"

Wow, Maria thought to herself, Lizzie doesn't miss anything. How do I respond to that? She thought for a second, then said, "Actually, I just remember wanting to be outside. I opened the front door, but for some reason I couldn't open the screen door. And then ... well, I can't remember anything after that until I woke up and Mum was sitting at the end of my bed looking at me."

"Oh, I see," said Lizzie. "Well, I hope you have good dreams tonight."

"Me too ... me too. Night Lizzie."

"Yeah, good night."

Maria thought about those words for a while as she settled herself down to get to sleep. What would be a *good* night for her? Her first thought was for a night without any dreams or visits or wanderings. But there was part of her that wanted to find out what was going on. And nothing about the two nights had actually been *bad*, had it? It was more that it had been unexpected and weird. Very weird. Very, very weird. And with that she went off to sleep ...

***

Maria felt herself becoming awake. This time she wasn't at all surprised that the room was still dark. She waited for a few moments to see if things were going to follow the same course as the previous two nights. But this time there weren't any footsteps or taps on the window. She turned her head and looked across the room. After her eyes had adjusted to the darkness she saw that Lizzie was sound asleep. She also looked down and could just about make out the tissues on the floor.

As Maria turned her head back she felt the merest sensation that the hairs on her arms were beginning to stand up. She wasn't sure where the next thought came from, but it came nevertheless. He's coming. And this time I'm going to be ready, so there won't be any need for taps on the window causing me to jump out of my skin.

Just as it had done for the last two nights, the quilt felt very heavy, but this time Maria was ready for it. Rather than just pulling and heaving it, she tried a bit of pulling and, instinctively, a bit of wishing it would move. It still didn't feel quite right, but after a few seconds it did move much more easily than the night before.

Maria sat up, and then moved on to her knees. She decided against pulling the curtains apart, and instead leaned forward and brought her head and shoulders up on the other side of the curtains, so that her face was only a few centimetres away from the window pane. Maria was surprised by how light it looked. It must be a full moon, or almost one, she thought. The posts and rails that ran around the deck cast almost perfect shadows on the deck itself.

Maria pushed herself up so that she could look over and past the fence out into the garden and fields beyond. And almost immediately she caught sight of a figure walking across the field towards the house. Because the moonlight was behind the figure she couldn't make out any features, but from the outline Maria was pretty sure that it was the old aboriginal man. And when she saw that the person was carrying a stick, she was certain of it.

Maria glanced down at her arms. She had sensed that the hairs on her forearms were about to stand up again, and somewhere in the back of her mind a thought or maybe a question started to take shape. *Is that feeling I'm getting somehow related to what's going on now?* She would have to think about that later. But now the figure was approaching a fence, about 75 metres away, which separated the house's garden from the surrounding fields. Maria wondered if there was a gate, she couldn't remember seeing one anywhere near there. But all of a sudden the man was past the fence walking in the garden. Maria wondered if she'd somehow blinked and missed him climbing, or maybe jumping over the fence. Wow, whether it was climbing or jumping, it was pretty good for someone of his age.

When the figure got to about 30 metres away Maria could see that it was definitely the same old aboriginal man that she had met the night before. But unlike the night before, she felt completely calm about what was happening. It was almost like she was looking forward to seeing him again, and realised that a smile had formed on her face.

The man walked purposefully up the steps that led to the deck, then turned to his left and stopped. Maria saw that he was smiling too, and she got the distinct impression that he knew she would be waiting for him. For a few seconds they stared at each other. Then the man turned to his right and started to walk around the deck just as he had done the previous night. Clearly he is expecting me to follow him, thought Maria. And that means following him out of the house.

These thoughts made Maria feel a little less calm. All of a sudden she remembered the photo that she'd seen in the museum. If only she'd picked it up. Was it the same person? In the museum she'd been certain it was. Now she was less so. Argh, she wished she had it with her to show him. Maybe he would have been able to explain somehow what it meant.

While Maria was processing these thoughts, she became aware that the man had reached the far end of the deck and had turned to the left to walk along the front of the house. Time to decide, Maria thought. This is our last night here. If I lay back down and go back to sleep I'll probably never know what this is all about, why this has been happening to me. Maybe that would be a good thing. But just as she had been the night before, Maria was convinced that the man meant her no harm. But then again, even if he meant her no harm, that didn't mean that no harm would come to her.

After a few seconds Maria realised that all these considerations were pointless, because deep down she had already made her decision. And, in the instant that she touched or tapped into that deep down place, she got the faintest sense that this was something she had to do. Okay then, let's do this.

She got off the bed and walked across the room. She stopped when she got to the door and looked down at Lizzie. For a moment she thought about waking her to let her know that the weird 'dream' thing was happening again. And that she was awake, and it definitely wasn't a dream – or sleepwalking come to that. But then Maria knew that Lizzie would want to come along with her, and she'd have to say no, and there'd be a *discussion*, and … And anyway, Maria remembered, I've tried waking you (and Dad) before, and I couldn't manage it. And so I probably wouldn't be able to do it now.

Maria was about to turn and walk out of the room, when thinking about Lizzie reminded her about the tissues she'd put on the floor. She looked down at them, but it being so dark in the room she couldn't really make them out. She squatted down, which allowed her to see them much better. To her surprise they looked completely untouched. She must have stepped on loads of them as she'd walked across the room, surely some of them would have been disturbed. Yet another *weird* thing. How many times had she thought or said that word over the last few days?

"Oh well," Maria whispered to herself as she stood up. She turned and headed out of the room, and then walked quickly down the hallway to the living area. As she approached the front door she could see the man standing at the bottom of the main steps leading from the deck down to the garden. He nodded to her and she smiled back. Again Maria sensed that he was expecting her to follow him. And this time she found that thought quite comforting. She wasn't entirely sure why but she felt it was related to that sense she'd had in the bedroom that all of this was supposed to be happening.

With this thought Maria took hold of the handle for the front door. She tried pushing it down, but like the night before she wasn't able to move it. She recalled it had taken all of her strength to open it, but then also remembered what had happened with her quilt a few minutes before. She tried pushing down and at the same time concentrated on it moving. This time she felt it start to move straight away. It still took quite a bit of physical effort, but a moment later the latch had released and the door swung open. One down, one to go.

She took hold of the screen door latch, while at the same time thinking, or rather wishing, that this time it would open for her. And it did. Almost without any effort or force at all. She let out a gasp, and realised that she'd been holding her breath.

As the door swung away from her she looked down the steps and saw that the man had a huge grin on his face. She couldn't help but let out a laugh and she instinctively put her hands over her mouth to smother the sound. The man raised his stick and pointed it out across the valley. Maria knew that he was indicating the direction that he wanted them to head in. She felt her heart beginning to beat faster.

Even though she'd started to get the feeling that this was somehow supposed to be happening, the idea that she would start walking away from the house in the middle of the night with a complete stranger was a pretty daunting one.

The man turned and started to walk down the driveway. Maria hurried down the steps and ran after him. Once she'd passed him she turned and stopped so that she was standing right in front of him, blocking his way forward. He stopped and looked questioningly at her. Maria shook her head and raised her hands on each side making what she hoped was the universal, 'what's going on here?' sign.

"I'm sorry, but before I go any further I need to know where we're going? And why?" She paused for a moment and then said, "And I'd like to know who you are? And why you don't come to the house during the day?" She paused slightly again, "And how is it that earlier on today I saw you in a photo that was taken way back in the 1800s? How is that possible?"

Finally Maria took a breath, and as she did quickly realised from the look on his face that he hadn't understood any of what she'd just asked him. She sighed and looked down at the ground between them.

"Look, I think I know that you need my help with something. Why it's me and why it has to be in the middle of night I'm a little less sure about. But you've got to understand, I shouldn't really be doing this. If my mum and dad knew I was here, outside the house, with you, a complete stranger, at this time, they would go absolutely … absolutely … mental." As Maria said this she looked up, and saw that the man was again pointing his stick out into the valley.

"I know; I know you want me to come with you. But why? Please tell me *why*?" Maria said with a desperate tone in her voice.

Maria noticed a change in the look in the man's eyes. He lowered his stick and started to look around on the ground. Maria moved back a few steps, very uncertain about what was going on. After about a minute he stopped and looked up at Maria. He made the slightest of gestures with his hand, which Maria took to mean she was to come closer. As she took one hesitant step forward he started to scratch at the ground with his stick. What was he doing?

Her first thought was that he was digging for something, but after moving a couple of steps closer she realised he was drawing. Ahh, she thought, he was looking for a patch of dirt. She moved forward until she was standing on his right side about a metre away and saw that he had drawn what looked to be … she leaned forward and put her hands on her knees so that she could see better. Even though the moonlight was very bright, it was still night time. Yes, it was … he'd drawn three stick figures. Two were standing together on the left, and a third was about 20 centimetres away to the right. The man used his stick to point to the first of the figures on the left and then, as Maria looked up at him, he touched his chest with his left hand.

It took a moment for it to register, but then Maria realised, "Okay, I get it, that's you." And she pointed at him.

He looked down again and saw that he was already moving his stick to the second shorter figure on the left. She nodded and looked up to see his left hand pointing straight at her. "And that's me. Okay, okay." She quickly looked down again and re-examined the figures. She knew she shouldn't, but she couldn't help herself. A thought along the lines of 'you're not that much taller than me' passed through her mind.

As it did, the end of the stick came into her line of vision, and Maria saw that the man was now pointing at the third figure, the one out to the right. She looked back up at him, and he raised his left hand to point in the same direction that he'd done a few minutes before. Maria stood up, continuing to look at him as she did. Very deliberately he pointed at himself again, then at Maria, and then at the third stick figure. After this he raised both his stick and his left arm in the direction that he clearly wanted them to go in. Maria nodded her head.

"I think I get it," she said, and realised then that the man must've understood the word 'why'. "You want me, to go with you, to see, or meet, with someone, who is out there." And as she spoke she used her hands to describe what she was saying. After she'd finished he moved his head ever so slightly forward, which Maria took to be a nod of agreement.

"Yes," she said, "now we're getting somewhere." But then, more to herself than to the old man she added, "Of course, who that is, how far it is, why I need to go to them … and why they just don't come here, is all still a complete mystery."

Maria shrugged her shoulders. At least he has tried to explain something to me, she thought. She put her hands on her hips, and looked back up at the house. She then turned her head through almost 180 degrees and in the direction the man wanted them to go in. In doing so, she suddenly realised that she was standing there in just her pyjamas, and with no shoes or slippers on. What on earth am I doing? What am I thinking about? How can I go anywhere dressed like this?

But hang on a moment, I'm not actually cold at all. In fact, she looked down, even though I've got bare feet, I'm not even aware that I'm standing on grass. She looked back along the ground she just walked across – most of it was grass, but part of it was the driveway which was made of gravel and stones. She couldn't recall walking over anything as rough as that at all. How weird was that? She rolled her eyes, I'm going to have to think of another word, she thought to herself.

"Okay, let's go," she said in the direction of the man. "I know I shouldn't but ... but ... I know that you're not going to hurt me. That's right, isn't it?" He didn't respond at all, but she couldn't see anything bad his in eyes, and so she decided to take that as a 'yes'.

"And, you know what ... well, obviously you don't, as you don't understand anything I'm saying, but anyway ... for some crazy reason I've got a feeling that I'm supposed to go with you. And ... and ... and it seems to me that I'm going to find out more about what's happened to me over the last few days out there," she said, pointing out into the valley, "than I am back there," and she turned her head to the left to indicate the house. And with that she started walking.

Chapter 15

The man, who had patiently stood and listened without understanding a word, was clearly caught a little by surprise, and it took him a moment to react and to start walking after her. Maria dutifully slowed down to let him catch up, and to walk slightly in front of her.

After about a minute of walking they came to the fence that surrounded the house's garden. Maria looked to the right and left for a gate or some other way to get over it. By the time she looked back to see what the man was going to do about it, he was already on the other side beginning to walk across the field. "Wow!" exclaimed Maria. "How did you do that?" She looked to see if there was a step or a gap that she'd missed, but there wasn't.

The man didn't stop walking, and so Maria called out, "Hang on, wait for me." She then squeezed herself between two of the wires that made up the fence. There's no way he could have done that, she thought, as she got to her feet on the other side. She started to jog to catch up with him and noticed that the ground was a lot rougher than in the garden, but it didn't seem to bother her feet in the slightest. That's ... she started to think to herself, but then settled on that's very odd, and smiled.

They walked for about 200 metres and came to a small ridge where the ground started to slope down. Maria paused and looked out across the field. Even though the night was very clear and the moon almost full, she was very surprised at how well she could see. It really didn't feel that much different from the daytime. She saw that the field they were in was huge, and that if they continued in this direction they would eventually come to some trees. And clearly that was the direction they were heading, because even though she had paused the old man hadn't, and he was now 30 to 40 metres further on towards the trees. Maria jogged after him again, and then fell into step just behind him on his right hand side.

As they approached the trees Maria found herself having to skip to the right and left to avoid small bushes and pieces of wood, but noticed that the man didn't appear to need to. He seemed to almost glide around or over everything in his path. Maria tried to watch what he was doing, but a combination of having to keep an eye on where her own feet were going and, for some strange reason, being unable to properly focus on what was he was doing, meant she couldn't work out how he was doing it. When they entered the tree area itself, Maria gave up trying. She needed to concentrate on where she was going just to keep up with him.

They walked through the trees for what Maria thought was only a couple of minutes and then the man stopped, but only briefly. He waited for Maria to catch up and come to stop beside him, and then he immediately started to scramble down a small but quite steep slope. Maria looked down and saw that the slope was actually the bank of a river. That's where … Odd, she thought to herself, it's running quite fast, I wonder why I didn't hear it. And then, like the night before, she was struck by how quiet everything was. Sure it was the middle of the night but, now she came to think of it, she couldn't recall hearing any significant sounds on their walk to this point. Maria realised that the man had got to the bottom of the slope and was waiting for her to follow.

"Okay, okay, I'm coming," she muttered to herself as she started down the slope.

At the bottom there was a flattish piece of ground about two to three metres wide before you got to the river itself. As soon as Maria reached it the man raised his stick and pointed it across the river. It took her a second to realise what she thought he was proposing.

"You've got to be joking," Maria almost spat out the words. "You think we're going to cross the river. There's no way I'm going to do that." Maria looked out across the water. She couldn't really tell how deep it was, but it was easily ten metres wide and surprisingly fast flowing given how calm the river they had swum in during the day had been. The man continued to hold his stick up and point it directly across the river. Maria shook her head and said, "Look, I've come all this way with you, which I shouldn't have done, and if my parents ever find out I'll be in so much trouble ... but, I'm sorry, there's just no way I'm going to go into that water. I'm sorry, but that's it."

Maria looked at the man to see if he understood anything of what she'd just said, but neither his expression nor his stance seemed to have changed at all. She was just about to try again when she realised that he wasn't just pointing across the river, but was trying to focus on wherever it was he was pointing at. And as she looked at his face she saw the corners of his lips slowly turn up to form a warm looking smile. Maria turned and tried to follow his line of sight. She didn't see anything for a few seconds, but then she did. To her complete and utter amazement, on the other side of the river, half hidden by some bushes, stood a young aboriginal girl.

It was hard to tell from this distance, and in the shadows formed by the moonlight, but Maria guessed she was probably about her age. She looked to be about the same height as Maria, but she had much longer hair, which was black and curly. And, Maria noticed, she wasn't wearing anything, or at least not on the top half of her body.

The girl raised her arm and waved at them, and without thinking Maria started to raise her hand to wave back. What am I doing? She thought, and came out of the trance like state she'd been in for the last few seconds.

"What is going on here?" Maria said quietly, and turned to look back at the old man. She was quite taken aback to find the man pointing his stick directly at her, which meant that the end of it was only about a metre away from her face.

Maria let out a 'Whoa' and stepped back a couple of paces. When she had resettled herself, the old man slowly moved the stick to the left until it was pointing across the river at the girl again. When Maria didn't move or say anything, he started to repeat the process. As the stick moved from Maria towards where the girl was, Maria stepped forward and said, "Okay, I think I get it."

"For some reason you want me to go across the river to where the girl is," and she used her hands to indicate firstly herself, then her going across the river, and finally her being with the girl. The man gave one of his almost imperceptible nods. Maria had a very quick thought that it was almost like he was too cool, or too proud to nod properly. She started to shake her head and turned to face the river. "Like I said, that's just not going to happen. There is no way I'm getting in that water. Apart from everything else." and she threw hands into the air as she repeated "... *everything* else. Just look at what I'm wearing. I'm not going in that water with my pyjamas on. And, as a matter of interest, even if I did do it, how do you think I'm going to get dry afterwards?" She paused and turned back around to see if any of what she'd said had registered with the man.

Maria realised that even if he didn't understand the words, he did at least understand that she didn't want to do what he was asking of her. He had lowered the stick so the end of it was now touching the ground, and his smile had now been replaced by a very forlorn look. He lowered his eyes and for the first time this night he spoke. "P-liss," he said in a very hesitant voice.

Maria felt her heart start to beat faster. Two competing emotions were welling up inside her. She was convinced that the man, or the girl, or maybe both of them, needed her help with something, and she was sad that it looked like she wasn't going to be able to provide it. But at the same time she was getting very frustrated, bordering on angry, about what was being asked of her. She felt that it had been incredibly good, no, *fantastic of her* to do what she'd already done. Walking across the valley, in the middle of the night, with an almost complete stranger. No one, she was convinced of it, would be prepared to get in the river and walk or swim across to the girl. For goodness sake, she didn't even know why it was so important for her to do it. She felt tears forming in the corner of her eyes.

"Look, I am really very, *very* sorry, but I'm not going to go across that river. Is there anything else I can do to help you, or her?" and she turned to look in her direction. But she wasn't standing where she had been before. Maria scanned the trees and bushes assuming she had just moved to a new spot, but couldn't see her anywhere. Maria turned back to the old man, but he too had gone. It had only been a few seconds that she'd been looking the other way. There's no way he could have walked out of sight in that time. But for some reason she wasn't that surprised. She remembered how quickly he had disappeared the night before after she hadn't been able to open the screen door.

Maria might not have been that surprised, but she was definitely angry, very angry. It was one thing to have someone disappear on you when you were standing in your

146

own living room ... well, Dad's friend Pete's living room. But quite another to have them disappear on you when you were standing in ... she looked around ... in the middle of a wood, god knows how far away from your house. With this thought large tears started to roll down her cheeks.

Suddenly, like a switch had been pressed, Maria felt incredibly overwhelmed by it all, and incredibly tired. She had a very strong urge to fall to the ground and lie down. And, again, she remembered that the night before she'd had a similar feeling, just after the man had disappeared, and had only just made it back to her bed. She sensed that even if she just sat down that she would be asleep within seconds. And then what would happen, if she wasn't in her bed when everyone woke in the morning? Maria clenched her fists and decided that she wasn't going to give in to the urge, and almost immediately she felt it begin to weaken.

"Right, come on Maria," she said, as if she was a personal trainer standing beside her, "You can do this." She walked over to the bank and started to scramble up it. Her mind was diverted for a moment by the fact she could see her toes squashing into the soft grass and earth, yet was only barely aware of them touching anything. So many weird things, so many questions – Maria wondered if she would ever really know what had been going on the last few days.

When she reached the top of the bank Maria decided that she needed to stop wondering about all that sort of stuff, and just concentrate on getting back to the house. She gritted her teeth and started to walk. Once she got out of the wood and looked out across the field and up the slope, she was pretty sure she could make out the top of the house. And this made her feel a *lot* better. In fact, better enough to think she should start jogging across the grass. She started very slowly, worried that it might bring back the urge to lie down. But quite the reverse happened. After jogging about 30 metres Maria felt even better, as if the exercise was

147

giving her energy as opposed to sapping it. She decided to try going a bit faster and it felt even better, in fact it was quite exhilarating.

Maria didn't consider herself to be a runner. Sure she could cover short distances, for things like netball or softball, but she wasn't keen on anything over about 50 metres, not all in one go anyway. But here she was getting faster and faster *and*, she suddenly realised, she was now going up a pretty reasonable incline. This was amazing. And I think I can l go even faster, she thought to herself. And she did. It felt so good, and so easy, that it was as if her feet were barely touching the ground.

Within a few minutes Maria reached the fence that bordered their house. She slowed and stopped, and was amazed to find that she didn't feel that out of breath. Her heart rate had gone up a bit, but within a few seconds her breathing was almost back to normal. She wondered what people would think if she ran like that in the next school cross country race, and smiled as she imagined the looks of surprise on their faces.

Maria turned and looked out across the valley. There was just the slightest hint of dawn approaching. With a start she realised that dawn meant morning, and morning meant people would be waking up. Especially Bobby, who usually started to stir as soon as daylight hit his window, no matter how thick the curtains. And once he was up, others would soon have no choice, at least about being woken up, if not actually getting up.

Maria hurried up to the fence and slithered through the wires again. She sprinted up the garden, but slowed when she got to the steps so that she could tip-toe up them. At the top she was surprised to find both the screen door and the front door wide open, and it took a second for her to realise that it was her who had opened them. She stepped through the doorway and pulled the screen door closed behind her. For an instant it felt heavy, but rather than resorting to tugging at it, she remembered what she'd done earlier and concentrated on wanting it to move. After that it swung shut quite easily. As did the front door.

She turned and started to walk across the living area to the hallway that led to the bedrooms. By the time Maria got to the doorway, she had started to get an uneasy feeling. She couldn't really hear anything (then again she'd heard very little sound the whole time she'd been up), but she just had a feeling that something or someone was moving about. Blast, she thought to herself, I hope it's not Mum or Dad getting up. She waited for a few seconds, and then started to move forward up the hallway.

She was just passing her Mum and Dad's bedroom when she realised that someone was up, and the change of light in the hallway told her that it was her and Lizzie's bedroom door that was slowly opening. She let out a sigh. Having Lizzie get up and find her was the best it could have been. In fact, after all that had happened Maria was quite relieved that she was about to see a familiar, friendly face.

She tip-toed forward a couple of steps so that she could meet Lizzie closer to their bedroom door, and not right outside Mum and Dad's. Lizzie slowly stepped into the hallway with her hands out in front of her. Maria thought she looked pretty funny, a bit like a person pretending to be a zombie, but then realised that her eyes hadn't had a chance to get accustomed to the darkness like hers had. Maria saw that Lizzie's lips were moving but it was almost like she was miming because she couldn't hear what she was saying, even though she was only two to three metres away.

"Hey, Lizzie, I'm here," Maria whispered. But Lizzie's expression didn't change at all. In fact, she continued to move forward slowly, her lips still forming words that Maria still couldn't make out even though she was by now very close to her.

"Hey, Lizzie, I'm *here*," Maria whispered again, this time a little more urgently. Still Lizzie's face showed no signs that she'd heard Maria, or even that she was aware of anybody else's presence in the hallway. By now Lizzie was literally right in front of Maria, and if she'd wanted to she could have reached up and touched her face. But something told her that wouldn't be a very good idea, and just as Lizzie was about to walk into her, Maria stepped to the side and pushed herself back against the wall. Lizzie continued on, and as she passed her Maria looked closely at her lips.

She wasn't normally a very good lip reader, but she was certain that Lizzie was saying her name, "Maria. Maria. Maria are you there?"

"I'm here, I'm here," Maria whispered after her. But Lizzie didn't turn, and she walked slowly on into the living area. What the hell is going on now? Maria thought to herself.

Suddenly the thrill of running so quickly across the field felt a long way away. So many weird things had happened over the last few days, she was almost … No, she was now officially completely weirded out. And in many ways what had just happened was as weird as any of them, which was saying something.

Lizzie hadn't seen her, or even felt her presence, even though she'd passed within a few centimetres of her. Some thoughts started to form in her brain about other things now making a bit more sense, like not being able to wake up Lizzie the night before. Or her dad the night before that. At the same time, she started to feel unbelievably tired and heavy. Her knees began to buckle and her back slid down the wall so that her thighs rested on her calves.

She tried as hard as she could to push herself back up but quickly realised that she wasn't going to be able to. What could she do? For a moment Maria was certain she was going to pass out, but she willed herself not to. And as the fainting feeling passed she felt like she had a tiny bit more energy. She decided that if she wasn't going to walk back to her bed, she'd just have to crawl there. Maria allowed herself to slide down to the right and then twisted her shoulders so that she ended up on her hands and knees. She moved her right hand, and then her left, and then her right knee. As she started to move very slowly forward a song or rhyme popped into her head from somewhere deep in the back of her brain: "Just keep moving, just keep moving, just keep moving." What on earth is that from? she thought to herself. She knew she knew it, and she wracked her brain to think of the answer. Which definitely helped her avoid thinking about how heavy her limbs, body, and eyelids, in fact every bit of her, was now feeling. "Just keep moving, just keep moving ..."

Almost without any awareness of how she'd managed it, she realised that she'd reached the side of her bed. Maria reached up, took a hold of the quilt and started to pull herself up, praying that the quilt just didn't slip straight off the bed and send her falling backwards. But this time the heaviness of the quilt seemed to act in her favour. With her last tiny speck of resolve, she pulled her legs up on to the bed, and precisely one nanosecond later was asleep.

Part 2

The 1830s

Chapter 16

Just as she always did, Leena woke up as soon as the sun started to shine into the valley. For a few minutes she lay listening to the sounds made by the stream that ran a few body lengths away from their camp; and then to the birds as they too started their day. And, of course, in the background she could also hear her grandfather's snoring. Leena thought about getting up and prodding him with a stick. Normally though she only did that if she wanted to get back to sleep, but today she was too excited to do that.

She threw off her animal skin cover and sat up. Rubbing her eyes, she looked around the camp area. Leena and her family had slept here many times before, in the sandy earth beneath the large overhang that had formed in the bend of the creek. Her grandfather had told her that when he was young the stream that ran through the creek was much bigger and deeper, more like a river. And that most of the time water had filled the area that they now used as a camp. Now it only filled after a big storm, or if it rained for many days in a row. At this time of year neither of those things was likely to happen, and so it was a very safe and comfortable place for them to sleep.

As well as her grandfather, the camp included her father and mother, and her three brothers and one sister, all of whom were younger than her. There were also two other families, which meant that altogether there were 18 people sleeping beneath the overhang. They had been together as a group for some time, but today they were starting the walk out of the valley to the next gathering of the tribe, up beside the lake. And Leena knew that after gatherings the make-up of their group might change. One of the other families might join another group, or a new family would join theirs. She didn't really understand why it happened, but at the gatherings the men spent a lot of time together talking and, she guessed, part of that was working out who should be with who.

Leena had only been to a few of the gatherings. Normally they happened after 10 or 12 full moons, but sometimes it was sooner than that, other times longer. At first she'd been wary of them, travelling away from the valley, and meeting lots of new people. But now she really looked forward to them, getting an opportunity to see other children her own age and to watch the ceremonies that were always part of the gatherings. As well as that she loved the food that was prepared at the gatherings. All the different clans and groups that made up their tribe were expected to bring food, which was then shared out during the big evening meals. This meant that Leena got to eat things that you couldn't get in the valley, like shellfish and turtles from the groups who lived closer to the sea, and the big juicy fruits that were usually only found in the lowlands to the north.

Leena got up and walked over to the stream. She squatted down, cupped her hands and scooped up some water, which she drank down quickly. The water was cool and refreshing. Her throat was always dry in the mornings when they camped here – it must be sleeping in the sand that does it, Leena thought. After three more scoops she stood up and started to walk along the bank of the stream following the flow of the water. She hadn't gone that far when she realised that she hadn't picked up one of the dried palm leaves which they used to carry things around. She quickly turned back and retrieved it from beside her mother's still sleeping form.

After walking for a while she turned right, away from the stream and up a bank into the trees. Leena knew exactly where she was going. I just hope that the birds and possums haven't found out about it yet, she thought to herself. After about ten minutes of walking, Leena paused for a moment to get her bearings. She saw the tree that she was looking for, the one that had a large branch broken off, and she turned a quarter turn to her left before continuing on her walk. About five minutes later she was there and, given the lack of half-eaten fruit or droppings on the ground, she was sure that she was going to get a good feed for her family and the rest of the group.

One of Leena's main jobs, alongside helping to keeping the other children entertained, was to find their first meal of the day. In the evenings, they would cook and eat whatever the men brought back from their hunting, usually something like a wallaby or a goanna. However, in the mornings they usually ate fruit or seeds. Leena had spotted these plum trees the day before when she and the other kids in their group had gone exploring. She had thought about picking them then, but she had been worried that they wouldn't have made it back to the camp, as the little kids would have begged her to let them eat them there and then. And, anyway, they always tasted better when they'd been freshly picked. Fifteen minutes later she was on her way back to the camp carrying a palm leaf tray full of succulent blue plums.

***

154

After eating, the group gathered together their belongings. Given that they never stayed in one place for very long this, by necessity, did not amount to very much. The men carried their hunting tools and weapons, and the women carried a collection of skins, tools and pouches, which contained seeds to snack on and leaves that they used for cooking and treating wounds.

Leena wasn't yet expected to carry anything other than her own skins, but she knew that the time when she would wasn't far off. Her mother and her aunts had already begun to speak to her about the things that would soon start happening to her body. When it did she'd start her initiation into the tribe, which would be completed in a ceremony at a gathering. And once that was done, she knew it wouldn't be long before she was matched with her future husband. Even though Leena knew that this is what her mother and her mother's mother, and all her aunts and all their mothers had gone through, it somehow didn't make it sit any easier with her. On the outside she was always very careful to listen and to agree, but on the inside she couldn't help feeling that she wished she could follow a different path. But she had no idea what it might be or how it could ever happen.

The sun had just appeared above the walls of the valley when they started their journey. Last time it had taken them seven nights to reach the site of the gathering, but Leena knew that many things could impact that, not least the weather. It was much harder to travel in the rain, especially if it was heavy or lasted for a few days. And added to that, their group now included two very young babies. However, initially at least, they made good progress. First they followed the stream until it reached the main river that ran through the valley, and then they turned to the left to follow the river upstream. After about an hour of walking the river started to bend round to left, at which point they turned right to start walking up the slopes that would eventually lead them to the top of the valley walls.

As they climbed up through the trees, Leena walked alongside the other children. She was the oldest one in the group, and the others, especially the younger ones, continually asked her questions about what would happen at the gathering and what things they might get to eat. There was lots of excitement and giggling as Leena talked about the things she'd seen or eaten at previous gatherings. Occasionally she would tell them a made-up story – like how one time the men had caught and cooked a huge fish the size of a tree that had fed everyone at the gathering for several days – and she would watch as their eyes got wider and wider. And when she eventually told them it wasn't true, they'd pretend to be annoyed before they all burst out laughing.

About halfway up the slope they stopped for a rest. However, the men did not sit for long, as they wanted to take the opportunity to hunt for some smaller animals to catch and carry with them for their evening meal. Once the men had left, Leena's grandfather came over and sat beside her. Leena loved spending time with him, and she knew that she was his favourite amongst the children, even though he was very careful not to make it too obvious.

"Are you looking forward to the gathering?" he asked, even though he already knew that she was.

"You know I am," Leena replied smiling at him.

"The other children seem to be excited about it too. Mainly due, of course, to all the stories you've been telling them." He paused for a moment and then said, "I hope at least some of them are true, so they aren't too disappointed when they get there." And they both laughed.

After a few moments he went on. "You know, Leena, this will probably be the last time you'll walk to a gathering with the children. By the time the next one comes around it may well be time for your initiation ceremony." The grandfather noticed that as he said this Leena broke eye contact with him and looked instead at the ground. He had thought for some time that Leena wasn't completely happy, and suspected that her impending initiation was at least part of the reason. He decided to try and see if she wanted to talk about it. "How do you feel about that?"

"Good, I'm happy about it," replied Leena quickly and without looking up.

"Okay, that's good," he responded just as quickly.

After a few moments of silence, he held up his left hand and said, "Look Leena, I've made you something. Something for you to wear at the gathering."

Leena looked up and saw that her grandfather was holding a necklace made of white shells and coloured stones. As the necklace swung ever so slightly from side-to-side, and the shells and stones caught the sunlight, it looked as if they were sparkling. It was the most beautiful thing that Leena had ever seen. She couldn't believe it was for her.

"For me, but why?" she gasped.

"Why does there have to be a why?" her grandfather responded. But then he relented and he said, "Well, let's just say that I wanted to make something special for a very special person. Is that okay?"

"Yes, that's okay," said Leena, and she put her arms around her grandfather's chest and back in a big hug. "Thank you, grandfather."

"Here, let me put it on you," and he leaned back so he could put the leather loop over her head and rested it on her shoulders. "There you go. It looks good on you, even if I do say so myself."

Chapter 17

By the time they reached the top of the climb the sun was just about at its highest point. Leena was relieved when the men decided that it was time to find a camping spot. After a short search they selected a huge fig tree. Its low branches and thick roots would provide protect them from the heat of the afternoon sun and any winds that came their way later in the day. Leena was pretty sure that she'd slept here before, on one of their previous trips to a gathering.

Everyone lay down to rest or sleep through the hottest part of the day, but Leena, too excited about her necklace, found she couldn't sleep. She kept feeling the shells and stones, and then taking it off to look at it. All the other children had loved it too, and some of them had asked her grandfather to make them one as well. After a while she decided to go for a walk on her own. She headed back the way they had come. After a couple of minutes, she emerged from the trees and walked out onto an outcrop of rock that gave her a view out across the valley.

Apart from a few small wispy clouds over to the south the sky was completely clear and very blue. And Leena noticed that she had virtually no shadow, which meant that the sun was almost directly over her head. She guessed that it was the combination of the bright sun and blue sky that helped give the green of the trees a blue haze, in much the same way the sea looked so blue on a sunny day. Trees filled the valley as far as she could see, but if she looked carefully she could see where the rivers ran. From up here the gaps they made in the forest looked like wavy lines, or snakes slithering across the tops of the trees. It was an amazing view, and it's an amazing place to live, thought Leena. Though sometimes she did wish that they could spend more time near the sea, as she'd always loved being in or around the water.

When she was much younger Leena had once asked her father why their group of families spent so much time in the valley, when they could be living much closer to the sea. He had told her that he'd asked his father the very same question when he was a child, and that his father had told him it was because the animals couldn't get out of the valley, and so there was good hunting all year round.

"And he was right Leena," said her dad. "We always find something to eat, don't we?"

"We do. But in that case, why don't more families or groups come here too?" asked Leena.

"Well, some do. Another group sometimes hunts in the valley to the south, about two days walk away," her father pointed in that direction. "But what do you think would happen if lots of people came here to live and hunt?"

Leena thought for a second before replying, "All the animals would get hunted, and then there wouldn't be anything left for us to eat."

"Good, that's right. And that's why we come here, and others stay at the lake, and others go west or south. That way we don't over hunt any one area."

Leena thought for a second and then asked another question, "But why is it always us who come here? Why don't we get a turn of living near the beach?"

Her father smiled. Leena did like to ask 'why' questions. Lots of them. "That's a good question," he said. "It's mostly because your mother and I, and your uncles and aunts, all know the valley so well. We know where the goanna nests are, where the kangaroos graze at different times of the year, where the fruit trees are ... where the best places to set the traps in the river are. If someone new came here they would have to learn all that."

"I see," said Leena. "And by the time I become an adult I will know all that too."

"That's right," said her dad smiling.

A big smile formed on Leena's now much older face as she remembered that conversation. Her thoughts were interrupted, however, by the sound of voices coming from the direction of their camp. She turned and walked off the rock back into the shade of the trees. That feels better she thought to herself, it was very hot out on that rock. As she approached the tree she could see that her father and uncles were engaged in a discussion which involved a lot of pointing, most of which was in the direction she knew they'd be heading in tomorrow. Leena went back to the spot where she'd tried to get to sleep earlier, behind one of the largest roots, and sat down to listen to what was going on.

While the group had been resting, one of her uncles had gone ahead to check their route for the following day. Leena knew that this was pretty normal, especially if the men were at all concerned about something, say a particular river crossing. From what she could make out the uncle had been surprised to come across a group heading in this direction, into the valley. Yes, that would be odd, thought Leena, all the families and groups in their tribe should be heading towards the gathering. And then she heard some words that caused her to catch her breath. Had she heard her uncle correctly? That couldn't be what he'd said, could it? But she had heard him correctly, as there he said them again. It was a group of pale people.

Leena, of course, knew that the pale people existed. Her grandfather had first seen them a long time before she was born. And occasionally she overheard the adults talking about them and what they're coming might mean to the tribe. But as she understood it, there were only a few of them, and they mostly camped around a large bay many days walk away to the north. But Leena herself had never seen one. And now that it was possibly going to happen, she might actually see a pale person, she found herself excited and terrified in equal measure. She tried to calm herself down, and listen in again to what her father and uncles were discussing.

The main point seemed to be about whether or not they should go out and meet them. The uncle who'd seen the pale people said that they had a guide with them. The guide wasn't from their tribe, but the uncle was sure he recognised him from a big gathering of tribes that had occurred sometime back. Leena had heard of these but had never attended one. After a few minutes it was decided that they should go and meet the group, so they could ask if they were intending to stay in the valley or just passing through. Leena heard the men stand up and get ready to depart. What should she do? Part of her wanted to go with them, but another part thought that after waiting this long to see one, she could easily wait a bit longer. In the end excitement won out over fear, and she stood up abruptly.

The men were just about to leave, but one of her uncles caught sight of her and touched her father's shoulder whilst angling his head in Leena's direction. Her father turned and looked at Leena. He started to shake his head, and opened his mouth to say something. But before any words came out he stopped and looked slightly to Leena's right. She turned to follow his gaze, and saw her grandfather walking up behind her. He was nodding his head, and as he passed by her he used his stick to gently tap Leena on the back, clearly indicating that she should start walking with him.

Leena's father shrugged his shoulders, and he and the two uncles turned to follow the grandfather and Leena away from their campground.

The uncle who had seen the pale people quickly found his way to the front of their little group, so that he could lead them. Having completed the climb in the morning, they were now on an area of high, relatively flat land that separated the valley from the lowlands that bordered the sea. Leena knew that there were a few different routes the men used to cross the high land, and which one they chose depended on things like the time of year and the weather. As they walked she supposed that the guide travelling with the pale people must be aware of the routes too. That's why he'd made the same decision as her father and uncles about which one to take and, she guessed, why the two groups were just about to pass each other.

They hadn't been walking for long when the uncle at the front signalled for them to slow down. They had come to a point where the path they were following started to slope downwards. From his gestures it was clear that he had spotted the oncoming group. However, from where she was standing at the back of their group, Leena couldn't see anything.

After her father and the two uncles had a short discussion, Leena's father indicated that the three of them would go on, but he wanted Leena and her grandfather to stay where they were. This time her grandfather nodded his agreement. Although she probably wouldn't have admitted it, inside Leena felt quite relieved by this. As the three men moved on and down the path between the trees, Leena and her grandfather walked slowly forward until they reached the point where the path sloped away.

From there Leena could see that the path went into a rocky hollow, where the trees weren't quite as thick. She scanned the far side of the hollow to see if she could see the other group, but she couldn't see any movement at all. But then her grandfather tapped her on the shoulder and she saw that he was pointing his stick to the left of where she had been looking. As she focussed on the spot a tall and definitely not pale man emerged from behind some large rocks. He was quickly followed by a large brown animal which had an assortment of bags tied on to its back. Leena saw that the man was leading the animal by means of a rope which was attached to its neck. Wow, that must be a horse she thought to herself. She had heard stories about them at the gatherings. Leena turned to ask her grandfather whether it was a horse, but before she could speak he used his hands to turn her shoulders back around.

Two more horses had appeared from the behind the rocks, and in front of each of them was a pale person. The first was a pale man who had the largest belly Leena had ever seen, and the second was a small pale woman. They were both wearing – Leena didn't really know how to describe it – more skins than she'd ever seen anyone wearing before. As well as their bodies, the skins covered their arms and legs, and they even had some skins on their feet. If it was all made from animal skins, thought Leena, they must be very hot walking at this time of day in this sun.

Leena was so focussed on these first two pale people that it took her a few seconds to realise that another horse had appeared, and that this one was being led by a third much shorter pale person. As well as skins covering the body, this pale person had a skin thing on their head, making it difficult to see their face. But as she watched, the group came to a halt, and the shorter pale person removed the thing from their head, and used the skin on their arm to wipe the sweat off of their face. Now Leena could see that it was a boy. A boy with skin so pale that Leena thought it might be as white as the shell on her grandfather's necklace. And, Leena had to blink to check she wasn't

164

mistaken. He had red hair! As red as the valley walls at sunset.

Leena suddenly realised that the reason that the group had stopped was because her father and two uncles were talking to the man at the front of the group, and so for the moment she turned her attention to that. That must be their guide, Leena thought, the one that my uncle recognised from the tribal gathering. Judging by their gestures and stance she thought the discussion must be a friendly one.

But it didn't take long for her gaze to return to the pale people and in particular the boy. It was a bit hard to tell, but Leena thought that he might be a similar age to her, or perhaps a little younger. As she watched him he became very agitated by the flies, continually flapping at them with the skin thing he'd had on his head. She wondered if the pale people knew about the leaves from the kallara tree, and how they helped to keep insects away. Probably not, she concluded, as she noticed that the pale man and pale woman were also struggling with the flies. Leena started to wonder about where the pale people had come from, and why they had decided to come here, to the valley. She'd heard the uncles and aunts talk about how some of them had arrived in huge canoes, so she guessed that they had come from somewhere up or down the coast, or maybe a nearby island. Maybe they've heard about how good the hunting is in the valley and have come to try it for themselves.

Leena's thoughts were interrupted by her grandfather tapping her on the arm. She turned to look at him, and he beckoned her to move away from where they were standing. She started to follow, at the same time glancing back at the group. Leena saw that her father and uncles had stepped aside and were waving as the guide and pale people started to urge their horses forward. She followed her grandfather up to and behind a rock and then stood close beside him as the group came up the slope towards them.

165

The guide and the horse he was leading passed no more than two body lengths in front of where they were standing. The guide looked over at them, and nodded towards her grandfather. Leena looked up and saw her grandfather nod ever so slightly in response. Leena quickly turned back so that she could take a good look at the horse. She couldn't believe how big it was, and how strong it must be to carry such a large load on its back. And then she wondered why the horse was prepared to do it. She thought about trying to tie something on the back of a kangaroo, especially one of the big males, and smiled to herself. After the guide came the large pale man, and then the pale woman. Neither of them looked towards Leena and her grandfather. Leena thought they looked tired, and perhaps a little frightened.

After the woman's horse there was a small gap before the boy appeared. Leena noticed that as he walked he was looking from side to side, and hence moving a little slower than the others. When he was almost directly in front of Leena and her grandfather he turned his head to the right and looked straight at them. His eyes widened and his mouth fell open at the same time. Leena couldn't help but smile. Suddenly it hit her that all the feelings that she had about seeing a pale person for the first time – excitement, wonder, doubt, fear – he would probably be experiencing too about seeing her and her people. And he was doing it in a strange land as well.

As the boy passed by he didn't take his eyes off Leena and her grandfather, and he ended up walking and straining to look back over his right shoulder. Just when it looked like he would either have to turn away or start walking backwards, he stepped in a pile of poo that had just been deposited on the ground by the horse in front of him. It caused him to slip and almost fall over. Leena tried very hard not to, but she couldn't hold it in, she let out one of those laughs that almost spray out between your closed teeth. Her grandfather immediately placed his hand on her shoulder, and Leena did her best to remove the smile from her face. At the same time the boy did his best to pretend it hadn't happened. He straightened himself up and turned to walk purposefully forward. Without turning her head, Leena watched him move away up the path. But just as he was about to disappear behind some rocks she saw him look over his shoulder directly at her. She couldn't really see his mouth, but there was something about his eyes that made her think that he was smiling.

Chapter 18

After Leena's father and the two uncles re-joined them, they started to walk back towards their camp. They must have gone a different way back because they didn't catch up with or even see the pale people again.

As they walked Leena's father and uncles explained to her grandfather what the guide had told them, and Leena listened intently. Several times she desperately wanted to join in or ask a question, but she knew that it wasn't her place to do so and that she was very lucky just to have been allowed to come along at all.

The guide was leading the pale people into the valley in order for them to join up with some other pale people who were already there. Leena was very surprised to hear this, as she had no idea at all that pale people had already visited the valley let alone were staying there. Well, it is a very big valley, she reasoned, and so it was not that surprising that pale people could be there without them knowing about it. But she did notice that neither her grandfather nor the men seemed to be as surprised as she was by this news.

From what she could make out it seemed that the pale people had come to see if it was possible to bring animals into the valley. Leena's first thought was that this must be to provide more animals for hunting, for the pale people and for them. But as the discussion went on she realised that this was not the case. She sensed that all the men, including her grandfather, were quite anxious about what it would mean for them. Though Leena didn't really understand what it actually was that they were worried about.

Whatever it meant, it did appear that the pale people would be staying in the valley for some time, and that all the boxes and bags on the horses were to help them set up some sort of camp. With all that stuff they won't be able to move their camp very easily, thought Leena, which will really limit what they can hunt for. As she thought about it, about them, Leena realised that she was actually quite pleased that the pale people were going to be staying in the valley for a while. Whilst the prospect of seeing pale people had initially made her feel a mixture of excited and scared, now that it had happened she just had an overwhelming feeling of ... of ... of wanting to know more about them. Where they came from, why they had come to the valley, what they ate, why they wore so many skins? She wondered about where they would set up their camp, and if there was any chance that she would see them again.

When they returned to the fig tree the men called out that they were back, though Leena wasn't sure that many, if any, of the others had known where they'd been. Within a few minutes the camp was full of activity as everyone got on with their chores for the evening meal. Leena and the other older children went out to look for berries and any extra leaves that could be eaten with the meat the women were preparing.

As she searched Leena had a thought that it was quite strange how quickly things returned to normal. Only an hour before she'd seen pale people for the very first time. And, she couldn't believe that she'd almost forgot, she'd seen *horses* for the first time as well. And now here she was collecting fruit and leaves with the other children, just as she did every evening. She wondered about what she'd expected would happen, that somehow things would be changed. But how? Even if something big happened to her or the others, they still had to eat, find a camp each night, and go out hunting. That wouldn't ever change, how could it? But despite the logic of this, deep down inside, Leena did have a feeling that things had changed for her. That somehow her life would be different because of what had occurred that afternoon.

Over the next few days, as she and the other members of the group walked first east to the lowlands and then north to the lake, she spent a lot of time thinking about her encounter with the pale people and whether or not she'd see them again, or any other pale people come to that. In fact, it distracted her so much that it started to affect her chores. On several occasions, when she was out looking for fruit or seeds she'd suddenly look around and wonder where she was, or even how she came to be there. Then on the day before they were due to reach the place where the gathering was to be held, her grandfather came over during the afternoon rest time and sat beside her. As usual he didn't say anything straight away. Leena often wondered about why he did that, why he waited for a while before speaking. It was almost as if he was waiting for the air he'd moved by his arrival to settle down. Like waiting for the water on a lake to calm down after you throw a rock in.

Once he was satisfied all was calm he asked, "How are you Leena?"

"I'm good, grandfather. Why do you ask?"

"Well, I'm not exactly sure what it is, but I've just had a feeling for the last few days that you've not been your normal self." Leena immediately broke eye contact with him and looked down at the ground, and he knew then that he was right, something was bothering her.

"No, I'm fine" said Leena "but I am interested in why you think that?"

"Hmm, let me see ... Maybe it's something to do with how many times people have to call your name at the moment before you respond to them. Or it could be because I haven't heard the other kids laughing as much as they normally do during the walks. Or maybe it's because that was the smallest collection of fruit you've brought back for our morning meal since you were this size." And he put out his hand to indicate that it was when she was very small.

Leena looked at his hand, and then up into his face. He was smiling at her, and she knew that he was just trying to help. She smiled back at him, and felt her face blush a little as a result of being found out.

"Okay, you're right. I have been feeling a bit weird lately. Ever since ..." and she paused.

"Ever since we saw the pale people coming into the valley," continued her grandfather.

She looked up at him again. "That's right. How did you know?"

"Just a hunch," he replied quietly. "Being old and seeing lots of things has to count for something, you know."

"Well, yes, I agree. Anyway, ever since we saw the pale people I haven't been able to think about anything else. Normally all I think about on the way to the gathering is the gathering, who I'm going to see, what all the news will be, whose ceremonies will be taking place there," explained Leena.

"But this time, since we saw the pale people, I've hardly thought about that at all. I just keep thinking about why the pale people have come, and what it will mean for us – for father and mother, and you, and me. What it will mean for all of us really," and she swept her right arm around to indicate everyone in their group.

"They are really good questions Leena. And they're also very big questions." He paused to consider what he would say next. "You know, some of the men think that the pale people won't be around for long because they don't know how to live in this country, how to hunt, what to pick to eat," and he tilted his head in the direction of Leena's father and uncles. "Others think that they've come here because they've run out of food in their own lands. And so they will stay, but they will need our help, lots of our help, in order to survive here. And others say that as there are so few of them it doesn't matter whether they stay or go."

Leena was fascinated by what her grandfather was saying, but when he paused momentarily she couldn't help but ask a question. "But what do you think, grandfather? Do you think they're going to stay? And do you think they will stay in the valley?"

"Hmm, what do I think? Well I think they're here to stay, for a good while at least. I don't know about the valley though, in my mind there's not enough animals to support a lot more people camping and hunting in there. I do have a feeling though, maybe even a hunch," he said looking sideways at her, "that things are going to change for us, all of us. Do you remember the guide who was leading the pale people into the valley?" Leena nodded. Her grandfather continued, "He was wearing pale people skins on his feet. And the uncles told me that he is able to speak some of their language. It's the way of things that when people come together that they share ideas. Some of them will be for the better, and others won't be. But nevertheless it will mean changes."

He paused briefly again. "But Leena there is something else I think … Actually it's more than that, there's something I know will be the case. We – you and I, them – aren't going to be able to answer all these questions. In fact, we might not be able to answer any of them. And so we shouldn't spend all our time thinking about or worrying about them. We'll just have to deal with things when they occur, if they occur. And at the moment that means the gathering, which unless we've been very badly informed starts tomorrow. So put all this stuff out of your head for the next few days, and try to enjoy it as much as you can. You know …"

Leena knew exactly what he was about to say and so she finished the words for him, "Yes, I know, this might be the last one before my initiation ceremony."

"How did you know I was going to say that?" he said, pretending to be hurt.

"Oh, it was just a hunch," she replied with a knowing look. "Being this old and having sat and listened to my grandfather lots of times has to count for something, you know."

And with that they both started laughing. After a few moments Leena leant across and hugged her grandfather around the neck, and whispered *thank you* into his ear.

Chapter 19

Following the chat with her grandfather Leena went to sleep that night feeling much more excited about the gathering. He was right, of course, about what she should be spending her time thinking or worrying about, and what she shouldn't.

On waking the next morning, Leena immediately got up and headed out to look for fruit for the morning meal. She remembered that just before the last gathering she had found some fantastic cherries, and although they hadn't camped in exactly the same place this time, she was hoping she'd find them again. And after only a little searching she was delighted to come across a bunch of trees full of the pink coloured fruits. And, as if that wasn't lucky enough, the first tree she walked up to had some very low branches which meant she could easily scramble up to collect it. There was so much ripe fruit that in the end she decided that she would bring a first lot back to the camp and then return for some more.

It was just as she tipped the second lot of fruit onto the grass that her grandfather opened his eyes, and so looked straight into the large pile of cherries that was no more than a body length away from his face. He rubbed his eyes as if he couldn't believe what he'd seen, and then looked up at Leena with a big smile on his face. She smiled back, and skipped off to get some water.

After they had eaten Leena and the rest of her group started the last leg of their walk to the lake where the gathering was going to take place. The day before, when they had climbed over a ridge, they had seen the lake blue and sparkling in the distance, and so they knew that they only had a relatively short distance to go this morning. All of the children were getting very excited, and the younger ones were barely able to walk in a straight line. On a couple of occasions, Leena's mother and aunts had called out for them to keep up. Each time Leena did her best to round them up and calm them down. But it didn't take long for somebody – and it wasn't always Leena – to say or do something that would cause the children to burst out laughing and lose focus on the walk.

Eventually they came to the southern edge of the lake, at which point they knew they were getting very close. A little further on, as they walked along the western edge, they started to smell smoke. Leena knew what this meant, a family or group who had already arrived had started to heat the rocks and sand pits they would use to cook the animals and fish for that evening's first big meal. Just the thought of it made Leena feel hungry even though it was still morning. When they reached the gathering site they found that they were one of the last groups to arrive, and that some had already been there for two nights. However, the formal part of the gathering, the ceremonies, hadn't started yet and so they hadn't really missed anything.

Leena spotted some other children she'd met at previous gatherings and ran straight over to greet them. They spent the afternoon catching up on all the things that had happened within their various groups and families since the last one, and every so often they'd run into the lake for a swim and a cool down. Leena told them about her encounter with the pale people. She was a little surprised to discover that many of the other children had already seen pale people, and horses, and that a few had pretty regular contact with them. One of them, a boy about the same age as Leena, even claimed to know some of their language. He said a few of the words, and they sounded so strange that everyone burst out laughing. However, Leena thought that she would like to learn some of them as well.

From what Leena could make out, it was the groups and families who lived along the coast and to the north of the lake that had the most contact with the pale people. Those who lived in the high lands – like her group – or further to the south had generally seen much less of them. The boy who claimed to know their words said that some uncles in his group had travelled north to the bay where the pale people had their main camp. They had returned saying it covered a huge area, and that hundreds of pale people lived there. The boy thought that was why the pale people had started travelling down the coast, because the camp couldn't support them and they were looking for new places to set up camps and to hunt. Leena was fascinated by it all and was quite disappointed when they had to stop to go and help with preparations for the big meal.

***

The gathering lasted for three nights and, although she enjoyed it, when the time came to leave Leena was ready to get back to their valley and their normal routine. On their final morning there, after they'd eaten their morning meal, everyone said their goodbyes. The one that she was saddest to leave was the boy who had talked about the pale people on the first afternoon. She had ended up spending a lot of time with him, though always within a large group of children. She had made him repeat the pale people words over and over again, and as they were parting she tried one last time to say them back to him. Some of the sounds were completely new to her, and she found it really hard to get her tongue into the right shape.

"Huh ... huh ... huh-low," was her final attempt at what the boy had said was the pale people greeting word. They both laughed, and then both waved as they walked away from each other.

Later on that morning, when the lake was already some distance behind them, they all sat down for a break and rest. Leena's grandfather came and sat beside her. After his customary pause he got straight to the point.

"I see you made a new friend."

Leena was a bit slow on the uptake. "What do you mean?" she said looking at him with a puzzled look. Her grandfather looked back at her with his eyebrows raised. Then she realised what, or rather *who* he was referring to. "Oh, you mean the boy I was talking to just before we left."

"And who you were talking to yesterday, and the day before that," interjected her grandfather.

Leena blushed. "Is that all you do at the gatherings, keep an eye on who I'm talking to?"

"That's right," he said smiling. "It's one of the most important responsibilities of a grandfather, keeping an eye on his grandchildren. Not just you of course, I have to look out for all of them. It's a very time consuming job."

"Hmm, I suppose," said Leena clearly not that convinced. "Anyway, the reason why I talked to him so much was because he knew a lot about the pale people. He even knew some of their words, and I so asked him to teach me."

"Ah, I see," replied her grandfather, just a little disappointed that the topic of their conservation had so quickly returned to the pale people. But he knew that it was important to Leena and so he asked, "And what did he have to say about them?"

177

Leena told him about the trip the boy's uncles had made north and grandfather had to admit it was very interesting, assuming of course it was true. And she also ran through the pale people words that she'd learned from the boy, and tried to get her grandfather to repeat them after her. But after attempting the first two, he decided that was enough.

"I'm too old to learn new things like this," he said shaking his head.

"I thought you told me that you're never too old to stop learning," responded Leena as she gave him a friendly nudge on the arm.

"Well this is different. For a start I don't think I have enough teeth left to make those sorts of sounds," and he opened his mouth wide to show Leena all the gaps.

At that point her father and uncles indicated that it was time to get going again, and so Leena helped her grandfather up and they continued their trek back to the valley. Apart from some particularly heavy rain on one day during which they decided to shelter in a cave, the journey back was uneventful. As they crossed the high strip of land where two weeks earlier they'd passed the group of pale people, Leena couldn't help but think about whether or not they might see them again. It was, she knew, very unlikely that they would see them up here. That would probably only happen if they had already decided the valley wasn't for them, and that they should return to the big camp to the north. Leena really hoped that wouldn't be the case, not yet anyway.

On their last night before they walked back down into the valley, they camped beside the same fig tree that they had camped beside on their first night. Leena took the opportunity to walk back out on to the same outcrop of rock she'd stood on just before she'd found out that the pale people were coming their way. Hmm, a lot has happened since I last stood here she thought. And it's only been ... she counted silently on her fingers ... fifteen nights. It's not just that we've seen or done lots of things, a lot has changed in my head as well. The world somehow feels like a much bigger, more complicated place now.

Leena sat down and looked out over the trees. There were more clouds than there had been the last time she was there, and a strong breeze was coming in from the direction of the sea. This meant it was nowhere near as hot, which was a good thing. After a while, as she sat sorting through her thoughts, she noticed that feeling again, the one about not being happy about the path she must take in the not very distant future. She knew that one of the things her father and uncles would have discussed with the other men at the gathering was who she should be married to after her initiation into womanhood. She knew that this was how it was always done. That her father and mother had been brought together this way, and that they seemed pretty happy. Well, most of the time anyway. But what about if she didn't like the person they chose? For a start he'd probably be a lot older than her, that's normally how it worked. Why couldn't she have a say in who she married? Supposing she liked someone, someone closer to her own age?

At this point an image of the boy she'd met at the gathering flashed into her mind, and immediately she remembered the question that her grandfather had asked her just after they'd left. Even though she was on her own she felt herself blush ever so slightly, and smiled. This helped quell the sense of unfairness that had started to well up inside her, and she allowed her eyes to refocus on the view, the trees and the valley walls.

It was then that she spotted a tiny wisp of smoke emerging from the tops of the trees way off in the distance. She stood up to try and get a better sense of where it was, and how far away. There was no way of really knowing, but she guessed that it was at least a full day's walk away, maybe two. From this distance it was hard to spot the course of the river by the gaps in the tops of the trees, but she guessed that it was fairly close to the main river. She immediately wondered if that was where the pale people have made their camp.

Leena did her best to position where the smoke was coming from in relation to the valley walls, but as she was doing so the wisps started to fade and then disappeared altogether. Still, she thought she had a pretty good idea where it had been. Of course, she didn't really have any say about where they made their camps, and there was only so far she could travel away from them, especially if she had to bring the other children along with her. But, if we did end up camping at that end of the valley, and if the opportunity arose … She felt a little tingle of excitement at the thought of maybe seeing the pale people again. But, she then thought, what an earth would I do if I did see them?

She shrugged her shoulders and turned to walk off the rock, back to where the others were resting. As she did she whispered to herself, "I'm sure I'll think of something."

Chapter 20

They descended back into the valley the following morning. Leena was a little disappointed when they then proceeded to head in almost the opposite direction to where the smoke had been. But she figured that they rarely camped in the same spot for too long, and so they would probably head that way at some stage.

It was always a bit strange, she thought, coming back into the valley and getting into their normal routine after they'd been away for any reason, but especially after a gathering. And not just for her; she could sense that everyone felt like that. There wasn't the usual chatter at meal times, and the children didn't seem as enthusiastic about the things they normally did together after their chores were finished. She knew that this was because everything seemed a bit mundane after the excitement of the gathering.

After they'd been back for three nights the mood still hadn't noticeably improved. So during the morning meal Leena suggested that after their chores were done she and the other children should go to find some water to play in. The initial reaction wasn't that enthusiastic, but when the time came it had turned into such a hot day that everyone decided that they should go, if only to cool down a bit. They were currently camped very close to a stream, which gave them water for drinking and washing, but it wasn't deep enough anywhere for them to be able to jump in or swim. And so Leena led the other children on the walk down to where this stream joined a much larger one, which she knew had a good swim hole.

There were a few moans from the younger ones on the way, and Leena ended up carrying two of them, one on her shoulders and the other in her arms. By the time they got there her shoulders ached and her arms were burning, and she was wondering why she had even suggested doing this. But after they'd been in the water for a while she knew it had been a good idea. Everyone was smiling and laughing, and it definitely felt like the post gathering mood had been lifted. They stayed in and around the water well into the afternoon, and when Leena suggested it might be time to return to their camp there were cries of, "no, not yet," and "please, can we stay longer." She said that they could, just for a while. But when she noticed that the shadows from the trees on the other side of the stream were now reaching over to their side, she announced it was time to go.

They all climbed out of the water and started to rub and shake themselves dry. As they did Leena thought she heard the noise of a branch or twig snapping somewhere in the trees on the other side of the stream. Probably a kangaroo or wombat she though, as she used a large leaf to rub the water off of the back of her youngest brother. Though it is a bit early for them to be out and about. They were just about ready to leave when Leena felt sure she heard another sound, again coming from the other side of the stream. But this time it wasn't a distinct one like a snap, more like whisper or murmur. It was probably the wind and the trees playing tricks on her, but she was intrigued. And so she told her oldest brother to start walking the other children back towards the camp, and that she would catch them up very quickly.

As they walked noisily away, Leena took a few steps along the side of the stream to see if she could make out what, if anything, had made the sounds. She reached some rocks that jutted out into the water and scrambled up them to give her a better view into the trees. She stood very still and listened for a few seconds and then turned her head from left to right to scan as best as she could into the dense bush and trees on the other side. Nothing.

Leena was just about to give up and jump down off the rock when she heard what sounded like a human voice. It came from her right, way down the stream. She listened and heard it again – yes, it was definitely someone speaking. And from the tone it sounded like they were speaking quite loudly, and so they must still be some distance away, she thought to herself. She didn't hear anything for some time and then all of a sudden she heard the voice very clearly. It meant that they had got a lot closer, but much more disconcerting than that was the fact that she didn't recognise any of the words. On occasions members of other tribes did come to the valley, and they spoke different versions of their language, but there were generally enough commons words for Leena's people to communicate with them. But she hadn't recognised any of these words.

Leena jumped down off the rock and then leaned herself against the side of it so that she could just see over the top and hence back down the stream. Some time went by and she didn't hear or see anything. But then there was a whole lot of noise at once and she realised that someone was emerging from the trees on the other side of the stream no more than five body lengths away from her. Even though they were in the shade of the trees, Leena could tell straight away that it was a pale person. None of her people would be covered in skins on a hot day like today. The person continued to move forward and then stepped out from the shade. Leena realised that it was the boy. The same boy who they had seen coming into the valley when they had been travelling out to the gathering. The same boy who had almost fallen over after slipping in the horse poo.

Having pushed his way through some low and particularly thick branches the boy brushed himself off and started to look around. First to his left downstream, and then to his right upstream. Just as he turned to the right Leena dropped down, she wasn't at all sure that she wanted to be seen here now. Having spent so much time thinking that she would like to see the pale people again, she was now having second thoughts. This was just so unexpected; she didn't feel ready for it. What to do, what to do, her mind raced. Then she heard a voice calling out. She didn't understand any of the words, but she was certain that it was him, the boy, saying them. And she was equally certain that they were aimed at her. How could he have seen her? She was sure that she'd hidden herself well before he'd turned around. He called out again, and this time Leena thought she recognised one of the words. There, he said it again, the greeting word.

Very slowly Leena started to stand up until she could see the boy and she saw that he was looking straight at her. Clearly he had known that she was there. She wasn't really sure why, but Leena felt that it wasn't right to stay behind the rock, and so she scrambled back up on top of it, all the time maintaining eye contact with the boy. For a while they both stood motionless, looking at each other.

Leena was absolutely fascinated by his red hair. All of her people had either black or very dark brown hair. And now that she seeing him close-up, she could hardly believe how pale his skin was. As she stared at him Leena got the distinct impression that he was just as anxious and wary and curious as she was. She decided that one of them had to do something and so she decided to try saying the greeting word back to him.

"Huh … huh … huh-low," she stammered, only realising then how nervous she was.

The boy smiled and immediately said *hello* back to her.

In response to his smile Leena let out a little nervous laugh, and with that he started laughing too. In a matter of seconds the tension and wariness had almost completely lifted. However, when they stopped laughing they both found it difficult to maintain eye contact. Leena looked down at the stream and then back up at the boy only to find him looking up at the treetops. The moment of awkwardness was broken by the sound of a single word being called out. The boy immediately turned round to face in the direction of the voice. Initially he didn't respond, but when the word was called out again even louder, he cupped his hands and called back. Leena didn't understand any of the words, but it occurred to her that the single word being called out was most likely the boy's name. She tried to remember the sounds and then began to very quietly recreate the sounds. The boy was still facing away from her down the stream.

She thought she had it and so tried it a little louder. "Rub-bett." The boy turned back round to face her. She tried again. "Rub-bert." And this time she pointed at him at the same time.

He smiled and nodded. He raised his right hand to his chest and then said a few words, the last of which was "Robert."

Leena smiled back and tried it again "Ro-bert … Robert."

Robert nodded excitedly, and they said the name together several times. When they'd finished Robert pointed at Leena with a questioning look on his face.

Leena knew straightaway what he was asking. "Leena," she said quickly and then again more slowly.

Robert smiled, licked his lips, and then said "Lee-ner."

Leena was surprised but also delighted at how well he'd said it. She nodded and smiled, and gestured with her hand for him to try it again.

"Lee-na, Leena, Leena ..." repeated Robert. As he did he took a couple of steps along the bank of the stream towards where Leena was still standing on the rock. However, he stopped when he heard the voice behind him call out again. This time it sounded a lot closer.

As Robert responded to the call, Leena scrambled back down behind the rock. She felt exhilarated by her exchange with Robert, but she didn't feel like she could meet any more pale people today. Not on her own. She popped her head back above the rock and saw Robert looking around to see where she had gone. When he spotted her he waved, and then pointed first at himself and then back along the stream. Leena nodded that she understood, and then raised her hand and waved back at him. He smiled and turned away, and started to walk along the side of the stream. After a while he turned to his left so that he could head back into the trees. Just before he was about to disappear from sight he paused and turned. Leena saw him scanning the stream and rocks to see if she was still there. She was about to stand up and wave when noticed that another figure about to emerge from the trees, and so she ducked down behind her rock. She waited a few moments and then very slowly looked over the top of the rock. Neither Robert and nor the other person were anywhere to be seen.

Leena waited a while longer just to be certain, then jumped up and started running back along the side of the stream. When she got to the swim hole she turned to the left and made her way up between the trees and rocks. She wondered how far her brother and the other children might have got. She really had no idea how much time had passed since she'd sent them off back to their camp. This panicked her a bit, and she hoped that they were okay. She quickened her pace and started to look from side to side just in case they'd wandered off the path that had led them down to the stream.

As it turned out she needn't have worried, because just after completing a short uphill stretch Leena rounded a large rock and to discover them all sitting in the shade of a huge tree. A number of them were happily dozing on each other's laps. Her brother explained that two of the smaller ones had complained of being too tired after going up the big hill, and as he wasn't able to carry them by himself he decided to wait for her to catch up with them. Leena wasn't overjoyed at the prospect of carrying a couple of kids the remainder of the way back to camp, as she was feeling pretty exhausted herself. But being so pleased to see them all, she didn't say anything.

As they walked slowly back to camp, Leena was only half listening to the chatter of the children. She kept replaying the encounter with Robert over and over, and practiced repeating his name in her head. However, as soon as they got back to camp, she and the other older children had to help prepare for the evening meal, and so she was forced to take a break from thinking about him. But it only lasted a while. As soon as the meal was over and everyone settled down to sleep, Leena started to think about when she might see Robert again. She wondered how close his camp was to the place they'd met that day. And whether or not he might go back to that same spot. Well, that's what I'd do Leena thought. She decided that after she'd finished her chores in the morning she'd go back to the swim hole, and if he didn't show up she'd explore along the stream. And with that she closed her eyes, and a few seconds later she was fast asleep.

***

Leena did see Robert the following day. In fact he was waiting for her, sitting on the same rock that she'd stood on when they'd met the day before. As she approached he was using a knife to sharpen a stick. He was concentrating so hard on it that Leena was able to walk up quite close to the rock without him noticing.

When she was about five body lengths away she stopped and said, "Huh-low Ru-bert."

He was so taken by surprise that he dropped the knife. He blushed and smiled at the same time, and as he retrieved the knife he replied, "Hello Lee-na."

Leena walked over and sat on another rock that was about two body lengths away from Robert's. They looked at each other for a while and then Leena pointed at the knife. She'd never seen one before. Her people used sharpened rocks to make the points on their spears. Robert held up the knife, and when Leena nodded he passed it over to her and said, "Knife."

"Knife," she quickly repeated, and almost perfectly.

Robert nodded, clearly impressed, and said, "Yes, knife."

"Ye-ess," said Leena. And they smiled at each other.

Leena looked around and then reached over to her left to pick up a small piece of wood. She ran the blade along the wood as she'd seen Robert do. She couldn't believe how easily the bark came away from the wood.

She passed the knife back to Robert and then held up the wood and said 'wood' in her language.

Robert repeated the word, and after his fourth attempt Leena nodded and smiled to indicate she was satisfied with it. He then said what the word was in his language, and Leena was very pleased when he nodded after just her second attempt. They spent the whole afternoon exchanging words and, by the time they got up to go their separate ways, the sun was so low in the sky that the stream and their rocks were completely in shadow.

Over the next couple of weeks they met up most days, on the same rocks beside the stream. Robert wasn't always able to make it, as sometimes his father needed his help for the whole day. Each time they met the number of words they exchanged increased. Leena hadn't been counting, but after two weeks she guessed that the total would have to be well over a hundred.

Then one day Leena's mother and aunts insisted that she take the other children with her to the swim hole. At first Leena protested, but knew that one day this was going to happen and so she quickly relented. It wasn't that Leena wanted to keep her meetings with Robert a secret, in fact she didn't want them to be a secret thing at all. She just knew that once everyone found out it would cause, at the very least, lots of questions. But more than that she was a bit worried about how Robert would react to all these new people turning up without any warning. Of course it was very difficult to judge as she'd never seen him with anyone else but her. But her instincts said that he would be quite reserved, maybe even shy around other people.

As she and all the other children walked out to the swim hole, Leena thought about nothing else than how best to handle it. Eventually a plan formed in her mind, and just before they reached the swim hole Leena asked all the children to stop and stand still.

"We're going to play a game," she said. "I need you to wait here until you hear me call out your name. And when you hear it, I want you to run through that gap in the bushes over there," and she pointed to a spot about five body lengths away from where they were. "And then I want you to run up to the swim hole and do your very best jump into it. Do you all understand?" They all nodded. "Does it sound like fun?" They all nodded.

The youngest member of the group, a four year old girl, looked up at Leena and asked, "Will you tell us who does the best jump?"

"Of course I will," said Leena smiling. "Okay, I'm going to go through and sit by the swim hole now, and when I'm ready I will call out a name. Nobody comes out before I call, okay?" she said as she looked around the group. They all nodded again.

Leena jogged through the gap in the bushes and once she got to the stream she immediately turned to the right to see if Robert was there. He was, and so she continued her jog down to where he was sat. He heard her approaching, and looked up and smiled. Leena smiled back, but as she came to a stop put her right hand to her mouth to indicate that he should be quiet, and with her left hand she gestured for him to get up. He did and started to say something, but Leena reached forward and put her hand over his mouth. This startled him a bit, but he saw that Leena was still smiling, and indeed that her eyes were sparkling. And so he immediately relaxed, and brought his own hand up to his mouth to indicate that he wouldn't speak until he was allowed to.

Leena indicated that they needed to move upstream, and Robert followed as they walked quickly up to the side of the swim hole. She then directed him to sit, and by moving her flat hands up and down she hoped was conveying that he should stay seated. He nodded and smiled back at her. I hope you're still smiling in a few minutes, thought Leena. She sat down beside him, took a deep breath, and then called out the name of the youngest girl. She'd agonised over who to call out first, but had eventually decided to leave the oldest ones until last because they'd be better on their own on the other side of the bushes. Less than a second after Leena had called a tiny figure sped out from the gap in the bushes and hurled itself into the water in a jumble of arms and legs.

Leena sensed that Robert had tensed when the figure first appeared, but when he realised how small the person was he relaxed again. The girl surfaced and looked excitedly at Leena. Leena smiled and clapped, and as she did she turned to Robert clearly expecting him to do the same, which he dutifully did. Leena looked back at the girl and saw that she was staring at Robert with her mouth wide open. Leena told her to come up and sit beside her and, when she had, she introduced her to Robert, and then Robert to her. Okay then, Leena thought, that went as well as I could have hoped for. Just nine more to go. And then she called out the name of the next child, who was four also and her youngest brother.

About ten minutes later all of the children in their group were sitting in a line to the right of Leena. Every one of them had their eyes and mouths wide open, and they were all staring at Robert. Robert sat to Leena's left, staring back at the line of kids. He was obviously just as surprised as they had been, thought Leena, but he at least was managing to keep his mouth closed. He handled it all really well.

She called out to the children that it was okay for them to go and play in the swim hole, but none of them moved. And so she stood up and shooed them up and into the water. Eventually they all managed to take their eyes off Robert long enough to do as she asked. Then she went back and sat down back beside Robert. He was watching intently as the children jumped and splashed around in the water.

Leena wished she knew the words to ask what he was thinking. But in the end she settled for just saying, "My family." And she used her hands to indicate firstly all of the children in the water, and then herself. Robert repeated the word back to her a couple of times, and then smiled and nodded. Leena then used her hands to suggest that they should go and join them in the water. At first Robert seemed reluctant to, but after a few beckons from Leena he

191

got up and came and stood in the water just deep enough to cover his feet. As soon as he did a couple of the younger children came up behind him and started splashing him. And they were delighted when he used his feet to splash them back.

On the walk back to their camp later that afternoon Leena was not at all surprised to be asked countless questions by the other children about Robert. How long had she been meeting him? Why did he never take off the skins that he was wearing even when he was playing in the water? What words had he taught her? Why was his hair such a strange colour? Leena didn't really mind; in fact, she took it as sign that the other children were generally okay with it. She was actually a bit more concerned about the reaction she would get from her father and mother, uncles and aunts, as she was in no doubt that the other children would be telling the grown-ups all about it when they got back to camp. And she was right.

As soon as she and the other older children started to help the women prepare for the evening meal the topic of Robert came up, and Leena had to respond to a whole host of questions from the women, many of which were the same as the ones the children had asked. But none of the questions or comments made her feel as if they disapproved in any way. In fact, quite the contrary, it seemed to Leena that the women rather liked having a new thing to talk about.

However, the opinion that Leena was most interested in was her grandfather's. And just before the evening meal was about to commence, he came over and joined her while she was washing her hands in the stream.

Leena decided not to wait through his customary pause and immediately said, "So, I take it you've heard about Robert?"

Her grandfather didn't say anything for a while, then replied, "How could I not have? It's the only thing that anyone in the group is talking about."

"So?" said Leena.

"So what?" replied her grandfather.

Leena sighed and turned to look at him. "So, what do you think about it?" She paused before adding, "You know that I really value your opinion."

He smiled and turned to face her. "I'm not really sure what it is you're after from me. It's not up to me to say who you spend your time with." Leena opened her mouth to respond, but her grandfather raised his hand to stop her, and then he continued. "But, yes, I know this is a pale person, and that's different." He paused, and this time Leena didn't attempt to jump in.

"You remember how I told you a while back that I thought the arrival of the pale people would mean change, big change for all of us?" Leena nodded. "Well, I think this is just part of that change. And I'm not all surprised that it's you who's helping to make the change happen." He said this with a big smile on his face. Leena couldn't help but smile herself and blush a little as well.

"Thank you for saying that grandfather," said Leena. She looked to her left around the camp, and saw that the others were beginning to sit for the evening meal. "Do you think everyone else in the group thinks the same as you?" Leena remembered what her grandfather had said to her about the differing views that the people in their tribe had about the pale people. "What about my father, what does he think about it?"

Her grandfather turned and started to walk to where the meal was laid out. "Maybe you should ask him yourself Leena." He'd only done a few steps when he stopped and turned towards Leena again. This time he leaned forward so that he could lower his voice, and Leena instinctively copied him. "But just so you know," her grandfather went on, "your father, uncles and I already knew about you spending time with the pale boy." Leena's eyes widened, she hadn't expected him to say that. "The men came across the pale people's camp on one of their hunting trips soon after we returned from the gathering. And on occasions they have followed the pale people when they've left the camp to see what it is they're doing."

Her grandfather paused for a moment, as if to give Leena time to process the information. Then he continued in an even quieter voice, "Your father and I might not agree about how long the pale people will be around for, or what impact they will have on us, but he is a very practical man. For instance, I know that he thinks it will be very useful for someone in our group to understand the pale people's language." He nodded once to indicate that he'd imparted all the information that he wished to at this time. Before Leena could even think about what to say in response he turned and marched over to join the others. "Are you coming?" he called over his shoulder. "It's time to eat and I'm very hungry."

Chapter 21

Over the next few days Leena was asked fewer and fewer questions about Robert or the pale people. She continued to meet with him most afternoons, and occasionally brought the other children along. Robert seemed to genuinely enjoy these times and joined in enthusiastically with their games, except the ones in the swim hole. Leena was amused by Robert's competitive relationship with her oldest brother, who was a couple of years younger than her but big for his age. He and Robert clearly enjoyed out-running or out-climbing each other.

When the weather started to cool, Leena and her group changed the location of their camp to be closer to better hunting sites. This meant that she had further to travel to the stream and swim hole, but in time they realised that the new location meant that they both arrived from the same direction. And so at the end of one afternoon they walked together to Robert's camp, before Leena headed on back to hers. Leena got to see Robert's camp for the first time, and to meet his mother.

As she and Robert walked up to the camp his mother was on her knees tending to some plants. She was smaller than Leena remembered from the brief encounter they'd had a few months before. Of course, back then she hadn't known that the small woman was Robert's mother, and the man with the large stomach was his father. When Robert called out she got up and wiped her forehead with the sleeve of her dress, causing dirt to smear across her face. It looked pretty funny, and Leena and Robert tried to hide their smiles. The mother realised that something was up and asked Robert a question that Leena didn't understand. Robert responded and pointed at her face. For a second she seemed a bit flustered and rubbed her face with the back of her hand. When she realised that this was, if anything, making it worse she stopped and smiled.

Leena thought she had the most amazing eyes. Robert's were quite dark, but hers were blue like the sky, and when she smiled they seemed to sparkle. After a few moments where the three of them just stood and smiled at each other, the mother thrust her arm out in the direction of Leena. Leena didn't know how to respond to this, but Robert came to her rescue by walking forward and grasping his mother's hand with his and then shaking it up and down. He then stepped back and gestured for Leena to do the same.

Leena now realised that this must be a pale people greeting ceremony, and so as she took the woman's hand she said, "Hello."

"Hello Leena," she replied with a big smile on her face.

Leena was a little surprised that she had used her name but then again, she thought to herself, everyone in my group knows Robert's name. As she was thinking this the mother turned and directed Leena and Robert to follow her into the camp.

Leena could hardly believe how many things Robert and his family had in and around their camp. But she was even more surprised by the structure that they were heading towards. A number of thick trees had been cut down, stripped of their branches, and then dug into the ground. Thinner trees were attached cross ways to the tops of the upright trees, and pulled over all of this there was the biggest animal skin that Leena had ever seen. She wondered how long it would take them to pack it all up when they moved to a new location. And, now she came to think of it, she couldn't imagine how they would be able to carry it all to a new location. Leena told herself to ask Robert these questions the next time they met at the swim hole.

Over the next few months as their understanding of each other's language developed further, they asked each other many such questions. Leena discovered that Robert's camp was not intended to be movable. When the time came for them to move on they would load as much as they could on to the backs of their horses, and leave the rest behind. However, they had no plans to move on anytime soon, which Leena was very pleased to hear.

Robert had explained that this was because his father still had a lot of things to do here. Other pale people were planning to bring some animals called cows into the valley. Although it was possible to eat these animals they weren't hunted, rather they were kept in spaces called fields and grown to provide large quantities of their milk. Robert said it was good to drink and could be used to make other things which were very nice to eat. Leena knew that she had drunk milk from her mother when she was a baby, but she couldn't imagine what drinking milk from an animal would be like. The pale people with the cows had asked Robert's father to find some good places for these fields to be prepared. As far as Leena could make out this mostly involved cutting down and removing trees, so the grasses and bushes the cows fed on would grow better, and to make it easier to keep the cows together.

Leena was interested in everything to do with the pale people, but she was especially fascinated about where they came from and why they had come to this land. During Robert's story about the long journey he and his parents had made, in a giant canoe called a ship, she had barely blinked. And she found it almost impossible to imagine the cities and towns where huge numbers of pale people lived together in things called houses. Robert said that his family had come from a city called Edinburgh. He'd been quite young when they'd left so didn't remember a lot about it. Leena wondered whether she'd ever be able to see these places for herself.

Robert, on the other hand, wanted to know all about the various animals and plants that lived and grew in the valley. As the days started to get shorter and the sun cooler, there wasn't such a need to be by the water, and so they started to go on walks through the valley. Leena would point out what plants and fruit were good to eat and what should be avoided, where the different animals made their nests or burrows, and how to recognise them from their tracks or droppings. Robert was generally keen to try everything that Leena said was good to eat, but absolutely refused to eat some huge grubs they came across one day in a decaying tree. However, it turned out not to be the type of grub Leena thought it was. And when she had to spit it out and run around looking for something to take away the taste, Robert could not stop laughing.

***

Once the colder months passed, the men and women in Leena's group started to talk about the next gathering. Leena wondered if this might be the one where she would be initiated into womanhood. She assumed not, as she hadn't yet started to experience the changes described by her mother and aunts. But she thought she should check, and so one morning while the women and children were collecting berries she manoeuvred herself close to her favourite aunt and asked her about it.

She smiled and shook her head. "Not yet Leena, you still have some growing to do," and as she said it she glanced down at her own breasts and then at Leena's still flat chest.

Leena nodded and blushed, "I thought that would be the case."

"Hopefully next time, eh?" her aunt said kindly.

However, Leena definitely wasn't disappointed to hear what her aunt had said. Inside she was struggling even more with the idea that, if not at this one, then most likely at the next gathering she would be initiated, and then not long after that married. And that would almost certainly mean she'd have to leave her group and the valley. And, of course, she'd no longer be able to see Robert, which she was coming to realise would be the most upsetting thing of all.

As the time approached to depart for the gathering, Leena sought out her grandfather. She wanted to know if he'd heard anything at all about them not returning to the valley after the gathering was over.

"As far as I know we're coming back here," he replied. "Why do you ask?"

"Well it's just that sometimes we don't come straight back here. I remember one time when I was quite small we spent some time camping by the sea before we came back into the valley. And if that was to be the case again ..." she paused.

"Then you'd like to let Robert know," said her grandfather.

Leena hesitated, as if she was thinking of denying it, but then realised there was little point. "Yes, that's right," she sighed. "I'm just worried that if we're away for a long time then there's more chance that he and his family will have moved away before we return, and I won't know where he's gone. And if that happens I'd probably never see him again."

"I understand that Leena, but I think you just have to accept that whatever happens, it's for a reason. I said that *as far as I know* we're coming back to the valley, but I don't know that for certain. These things usually get decided at the gathering itself. If groups get changed, or asked to move to a new area it's because the elders of the tribe think there's a good reason to do it."

Leena could feel the frustration building up inside her, but she really didn't want to take it out on her grandfather. She took a couple of deep breaths and then said in as calm a voice as she could manage. "I know all that. But sometimes … just sometimes I want to feel like what I would like to happen, what I would like to do, matters." She felt tears forming in the corner of her eyes, and tried to brush them away without her grandfather noticing.

Clearly it didn't work because he immediately came over to her and put his arm around her shoulders. "Leena. Leena. What are we going to do with you?" He held her for a few seconds and then said, "You know how special I think you are. I've always had a feeling that you would take a different path, and I've tried to do my best to help you follow it."

"I know you have grandfather and you know how grateful I am," said Leena between sobs.

He took Leena's face in his hands and turned her head so that they were looking into each other's eyes. "There are some things that even I can't control or change," he said smiling. And Leena smiled back and sobbed at the same time. He continued, "Yes, I know you thought there was nothing that I couldn't do or couldn't get done. But what I can tell you, in fact what I can promise you, is that I will always be there for you if you need me. Do you understand?" Leena nodded. Her grandfather started to turn away, but then thought of something else. "And can I suggest that in the meantime, before we head off to the gathering, you do your best to cheer up and enjoy the time you know you have with your friend." He half turned again before making a show of stopping to add one more thing. "I can't believe that I need to tell my Leena to go off and have fun. Who would have thought it?" And this time he turned and walked away.

The next morning Leena made sure that her grandfather got the biggest and juiciest figs for his morning meal.

***

Over the next couple of days Leena thought a lot about a fun thing that she and Robert might do before she left for the gathering. Then at their evening meal, one of her uncles mentioned a place in the valley that she had been to only once before due to it being some distance away from their usual camping and hunting grounds. It was a swim hole formed by a big bend in the main river that flowed through the valley. But what made it special was an area of flat rocks that the river cascaded over straight after the swim hole. Leena remembered how good it had felt to lie on the rocks in the sun looking up at the trees and the clouds, listening to the sounds of the water.

Where they were currently camped was about as close as they ever got to that part of the valley, and so it should be relatively easy to walk there and back in a day. But it would need to be a full day. She'd have to miss her usual morning chores, and hope that Robert's parents wouldn't need him. In the end they came up with the plan to tell their respective families that the other one needed their help with something important that would require them to be away for the morning.

And so just two sleeps before her group was due to depart for the gathering Leena met Robert at a pre-arranged spot just after sunrise and they started their walk to the swim hole and the flat rocks. On the way to meet Robert,

Leena had taken a small detour to collect some bush apples, and they ate them as they walked. They headed south for a short time until they reached a stream which Leena knew would eventually take them to the main river. The stream ran to the west which meant they would have the early morning sun on their backs as they walked. Leena looked up and saw that there was still a lot of mist and cloud in the valley, especially close to the valley walls. But more and more patches of blue were appearing, and she could tell that it was going to be another hot, sunny day.

As they walked Robert asked Leena questions about the gathering, many of which they'd discussed before, some several times. It was as if he was making sure it was all clear in his mind. Yes, it was held beside a lake to the north. Robert was pretty sure they had passed by it on their own trip down to the valley. Yes, it would take about seven days to get there, maybe a few more if the weather was bad. No, there was no chance that it had been cancelled and people had forgotten to tell Leena's group. Yes, the gathering itself usually lasted for three to four days. Yes, if nothing untoward happened she would be back in around 20 days. And no, definitely no, she wasn't going to be married when she returned.

Leena hadn't told Robert about the possibility, albeit a pretty remote one, that her group might not come back directly to the valley. And she had already decided that she wouldn't tell him today because didn't want to risk spoiling the happy mood.

The sun was well above the valley walls when they reached the point where the stream joined the main river. Leena was surprised by how high the water was, given the lack of rain over the past few weeks. From the number of broken branches and twigs spread along both banks it was clear that the river would rise much higher than this when there was heavy rain. They turned to their right and started following the river upstream. The banks of the river were quite steep and rough, and so they walked through the trees above the bank. Although this slowed their progress it did mean that they were mostly walking in shade, which was a good thing given how hot the day was becoming.

They had to cross a number of small streams that fed into the main river, and as they stepped out of one of them Leena was excited to spot a particular type of cherry tree, still laden with ripe fruit. They stopped for a few minutes to pick and eat some, and then Robert filled a small pouch that he had brought with him. Leena had told Robert how strange she found the number of boxes and bags that the pale people had with them, since in her mind it only encouraged them to keep and carry things that they mostly didn't need. But on occasions, she had to admit, they did come in useful.

As they followed the river the distance to the valley walls on either side of them started to lessen significantly. Robert remarked that it was beginning to feel more like a canyon than a valley, and then had to explain the word canyon to Leena. Once she understood she agreed, and she told Robert that further up the river there was a waterfall which had sheer cliffs on both sides that were impossible to climb. She had never seen it herself, but several of the men in her group had been there and spoken to the rest of them about it. Robert responded by saying that one day the two of them should go there. Leena thought that was a great idea, and they both laughed.

Eventually the flat land to the sides of the river almost disappeared. Instead steep and heavily wooded slopes led straight up to the base of the golden cliffs that formed the valley walls here. Leena had noticed that the river seemed a lot shallower now, and so she suggested that they continue their walk in the water. At first Robert wasn't very keen, but when he saw that the water was only just over Leena's ankles, and she assured him that they didn't have far to go, he came down into the water with her. And he had to admit that it was very refreshing now that the hot sun was almost directly overhead.

Not long after they'd started walking in the river it started to widen, and there was also a series of bends. Leena smiled and said, "I think I remember this part, I think we're almost there. Yes, I'm sure we are."

Sure enough as they came out of the next bend, they came to a much more open area. They both stood still for a moment to take in the scene. To their left was a large area of almost flat rock which was dotted with small bushes and ferns that had somehow managed to root themselves in the thin strips of soil that had formed between the slabs of rock. The river ran towards them on the right hand side, and as it came across the expanse of rock it formed a sparkling cascade. Past the cascade there was a large area of almost still water formed by a long slow bend to the right. At the bend the valley narrowed considerably and slopes got even steeper. Trees came right up to the edge of the riverbanks, and their branches of green and yellow leaves stretched out across the water.

"What a fantastic place," said Robert quietly.

"Really? You like it?" Leena replied, and looked over at him. She saw he was smiling and nodding, and she smiled back, "Come on let's find a place to have a rest, that was a long walk." She walked up on to the rocks and stopped by a small tree that had grown up close to the cascading water.

"This looks like a good spot," she said and lay down on the rocks in the shade of the tree. The rocks felt very warm on her back.

Robert joined her and for a while they lay in silence. Leena could see the tops of the trees swaying in a breeze. Pity we can't get some of that down here she thought to herself. But then she thought that she was being a bit greedy, because everything else was so good. She turned to face Robert and rested her head on her arm.

"Robert."

"Yes?"

"I was just wondering … if something happened while I was away at the gathering and it meant that you and your family had to move away, how would I know where you'd gone?"

Robert turned to his left so that he was facing Leena. "What sort of thing?"

"Oh, I don't know. Something like …" she paused to think. "How about if the people who own the cows decide that they want your father to build fields somewhere else?"

"Ah, I see. Well I don't think that is going to happen. But, if it did, I would find some way to let you know where we'd gone. And, anyway, I'd know where you are, and so I could always come back to tell you where we'd moved to."

"You would do that?"

Robert could see in Leena's eyes that this was a serious question. And so he tried to make his face as serious as possible and said, "Yes, of course I would." However, as soon as he said the words he couldn't hold the look and he started to laugh, which caused Leena to burst out laughing as well.

Once they'd stopped Leena jumped up, "Come on let's get in the water, I need to cool down."

She ran over to the river and half-stepped, half-jumped into the water. It immediately came up to her waist. She turned and called out to Robert, "Come on! It's really good."

Robert walked slowly over and looked down at the water suspiciously. Leena often wondered what it was with Robert and water, but she had just put it down to pale people's reluctance to take off their clothes even when it was very hot. She turned and leant forward, and then glided forward under the water. The water felt so good on her skin.

Often, and especially after rain, the river would be brown and cloudy, and you wouldn't be able to see anything. But today, with the sun directly overhead, she could see pretty well. Over by the bank she could see sunbeams in the water that had managed to make their way through the branches and leaves above. They looked like golden poles. As she approached the far bank she came up for a breath and turned to see Robert walking gingerly through the water towards her. Leena could hardly believe it; he'd actually taken his shirt off. His skin looked so white in the sun it was almost blinding.

She was so lost in thought that she hadn't noticed how far out from the bank he'd come. Suddenly she realised that he must almost be at the ledge.

She called over to him. "Watch out, Robert, it gets deep just …" The words were still hanging in the air when he took one more step and fell forward into the water. Leena couldn't help but laugh. Robert came up to the surface with his arms flapping, which made her laugh even more. But then he went under the water again, and she started to feel uneasy.

"Robert, are you okay?" she shouted across the water, and at the same time she moved her legs behind her. It was probably only a few seconds, but she was sure that it was too long. She screamed his name and kicked out towards the middle of the swim hole. She was about half way to him when he came back to the surface, but this time he barely got his face and mouth out of the water. And he immediately dropped down again. She ducked under the water and stroked and kicked furiously towards him. It seemed to take forever but eventually she reached him, put her hands on either side of his back and immediately kicked upwards.

She managed to get him to the surface and heard him take a huge breath, but he was a lot heavier than her and despite her kicking she didn't think she could hold him up above the water. They started to sink again, and Leena let it happen so that she could move her body round and hopefully start moving them both back to the ledge, which couldn't be that far away. As they went under Robert tried to get a better hold on Leena and put his arms around her neck. She kicked as hard as she could and used her arms to push him towards the ledge. It seemed to work and Leena thought that she could make out the ledge only a body length or so away from them. She pushed him as hard as she could towards it, and as he moved away from her she felt him grab and then tug on her necklace. And then she felt it come away from her neck.

Even though she was fighting to save a life, she became intensely aware of the fact that she'd been parted from her most treasured possession, the necklace that her grandfather had given her just before last year's gathering. As Robert managed to put one of his feet on the ledge, she saw her necklace floating down towards the bottom of the river. She decided that she wasn't going to risk losing sight of it, and so in one movement she gave Robert a final push on to the ledge and then kicked downwards. Leena could see the necklace falling ever so slowly towards the bottom of the river. She desperately wanted to try and reach it before it got to the bottom which she could see was quite rocky. But, as hard as she stroked and kicked, Leena realised that she wasn't quite going to make it.

At the same time, Robert was just starting to think that maybe he wasn't going to die today. He'd managed to get one knee and a foot on to the ledge, but was very worried about falling off backwards. He used his arms like oars to try and bring his body weight forward, and very slowly he managed to do it. As he felt his torso move in front of his knees he leaned forward with his arms out in front of him.

Unfortunately, the water here was deeper than his arms and so as his palms reached the rock his face went under the water, which caused him to panic again. He started to crawl forward on his knees so he could get away from the ledge and stand up, and in doing so his left foot make contact with a rock which was sat right on the edge of the ledge. He screamed as a sharp pain shot through his foot and up his leg, and as a result he only had the vaguest awareness that the rock was dislodged and fell to the bottom.

Leena could feel her lungs beginning to strain but she was sure that she could make it to the necklace. She could see that it had fallen in a little crevice between two rocks but it was only about a foot's length deep, so she would have no problem reaching between them to get it. As she kicked one more time and opened her fingers of her left hand to grasp the necklace she had just the vaguest awareness of the rock that had been dislodged by Robert passing by her right ear and falling straight into the gap between the rocks, and right over her hand. She felt a sudden pain in her hand and desperately wanted to let out a wail of pain but some mechanism in her brain stopped her from doing it. She'd worry about her hand later she needed to get to the surface and to breathe, and she needed to do it now.

Leena pulled backwards, but her hand wouldn't budge. She pulled again, but still it didn't move. The sudden realisation of her situation hit her like a huge ocean wave. Her lungs were bursting she had to get air now. She managed to bring her right hand down to try and push the rock away, but she very quickly realised that the rock had fallen very neatly into the gap and was wedged tight. She knew then that she wasn't going to make it to the surface in time. Leena turned her head as far she could to the right to examine the water between her and the ledge. There was no sign of Robert. He was safe at least. She smiled to herself, closed her eyes and opened her mouth.

Part 3

The Present Day

Chapter 22

Maria awoke but wasn't quite ready to open her eyes. An important thought was forming in her head, and she needed to concentrate. Was it something she had wanted to remember to do today? No, that wasn't it. I know, she thought, it's a line from a song and I need to know what the song is. It was something that she'd heard recently or maybe that she'd been singing. But it was still very vague. She focussed on it and started to feel a rhythm, and sensed some words that you repeated over and over again. But for the moment she couldn't recall any more than that, and so she put it to one side. As soon as she did the events of the last few days and, in particular, the previous night flooded into her head. The old man, the photo, the walk across the fields, the river, the girl, the run back and Lizzie. Oh my god, she thought, Lizzie didn't see me even though I was standing right in front of her. What was that about? It was almost as if I was invisible to her, but that's not possible … except in movies.

Maria became aware of a sound that seemed to be coming from far away. She tried focusing on it and realised that it was someone calling her name. She listened to it for a while. It was gradually getting louder. And then all of a sudden she heard it properly.

"Maria. Maria. Mariaaa, wake up."

Maria opened her eyes and saw Lizzie standing right in front of her.

"There you are at last," said Lizzie. "It's almost impossible to wake you up at the moment."

"Tell me about it," responded Maria as she sat up. "By the way, what time is it? Is it late? Have I slept in again?"

"Don't worry; it's not that late. Dad asked me to come and wake you up because we're just about to have breakfast. And then he wants us all to help with the packing up, cleaning and stuff."

There was a couple of seconds of silence as they both thought about what they wanted to say next, and then Lizzie said "Maria ..." at exactly the same time as Maria said "Lizzie ..." They both laughed, which helped relieve the tension caused by the not-knowing-how-to-say-it pause.

"You first," said Maria.

"Okay. Did you dream about getting up again last night?"

Maria was about to say "Why do you ask that?" but then decided she should just be as open as she could with Lizzie.

"I did, and I'm as sure as I can be that I got up and went ..." she paused immediately wondering about how open she should actually be.

"Went where?" said Lizzie.

"Out of the bedroom and along the hallway to the front of the house," Maria answered, deciding that she wasn't ready yet to tell Lizzie that she'd spent a big chunk of the night wandering around the valley.

"I knew it," exclaimed Lizzie. "For a while there I thought I was going mad. I reckon Dad thinks I am for sure."

"Why Dad does think that? What have you said to him? This is meant to be our secret."

"I haven't said anything to him about it, honestly. Only last night ... well, this morning really ... I woke up and looked over to check that you were in bed. And you weren't. Well, it really looked to me like you weren't there. And because I thought you weren't, I decided to get up and see if I could find you, and maybe see if you were sleepwalking or not."

Maria nodded, "That was a good idea."

Lizzie smiled, "Thanks. I do have them sometimes, you know." She stepped forward and then sat on the side of the bed. "Anyway, I went out of the room and down the hallway to the front of the house, but I couldn't find you anywhere. As I was coming back along the hallway, Dad called out to me. I think he'd been to the toilet and was still awake and obviously he heard me go by."

He didn't hear me, Maria realised, and I must've made a lot more noise than Lizzie, crawling along the floor. Or, maybe just like I couldn't hear what Lizzie was saying, she and Dad couldn't hear anything I said or any noise I made. What could cause that to happen? She put the question to one side as Lizzie went on.

"Of course he wanted to know what I was doing so early, and so I said to him that I'd thought you'd got up to watch TV, and was getting up to join you. But when I realised you hadn't done that I thought I'd go back to bed. Then he got all worried about where you might be if you weren't in bed, and so he got up to look for you. But first he said he'd take me back to bed, and of course when we walked into the room there you were asleep in your bed."

"What did he say then?" asked Maria.

"Nothing. He just gave me one of those looks. You know the one …" and Lizzie did it. Maria couldn't help but laugh, Lizzie was really good at recreating Dad's expressions.

"Anyway, it was only then that I remembered about the tissues. And so when I was sure that Dad was back in bed I got up to check them out. And none of them had moved at all. I was so sure that you'd got up, and that some of the tissues would be crumpled up to prove it. And so then I thought I must have dreamed it, you know about you not being in bed. But now you tell me that you're sure that you did get up. But if you did, how come you didn't move any of the tissues?" Lizzie paused to take a breath. "This is all really weird."

Maria couldn't help but let out a chuckle. "You don't how many times I've said or thought that word over the last few days." Maria decided then that even if she didn't feel ready to tell Lizzie about the aboriginal man and girl and her trip into the valley, she should tell her about their close encounter in the hallway. "And I'm going to tell you something now that I'm pretty sure will make you say it again." On hearing this Lizzie leaned forward, and her eyes opened even wider than they already were.

Maria smiled at her obvious eagerness to hear the next part of the mystery. "Are you really sure you want to know?" said Maria, "I'm a bit worried about freaking you out."

"Yes, yes, of course," replied Lizzie immediately. "Tell me. Tell me now."

"Okay, okay, I was just winding you up" said Maria with a smile. But the smile disappeared as Lizzie picked up a cushion and threw it at Maria's head.

"Alright I get it, no more joking," and Maria's face quickly became much more serious looking. She went on, "I don't think you were dreaming last night when you saw that I wasn't in my bed. I'm as sure as I can be that I did get up. Though I have to admit that I have no explanation for why the tissues didn't get moved about when I walked on them. *And* I already knew that you got up and went to the front of the house to look for me." Maria saw Lizzie start to say something but raised her hand to indicate that she was about to answer the question she knew she was going to ask. "And the reason I know that is because I was standing at the other end of the hallway when you came out of the bedroom. I saw you come out with your hands out like this, and then start walking very slowly towards the front of the house. And as you went I'm pretty sure you were saying, 'Maria, Maria, are you there?' And I said to you, 'Lizzie, I'm here.' In fact I think said it three times." Maria paused for a moment to let Lizzie take it in. She was clearly very surprised, maybe even a bit shocked, and for a while she didn't seem to blink let alone move or speak.

Eventually she said, "So where were you? Why didn't I see you?"

"I really don't know Lizzie. But for some reason you couldn't see me at all, and I could see you as clearly as I can now. I was standing right in the middle of the hallway as you walked up. At one point I was about this far away from you," and Maria sat up and moved forward to show Lizzie how close their faces had been. "When I thought you were about to walk straight into me I moved to the right and stood with my back straight against the wall. You went past me and your arm would have been that far away from me," and Maria lifted her hands to indicate a gap of about 20 to 30 centimetres. "You walked on into the living area, and I suddenly felt incredibly tired. I mean completely and utterly couldn't even walk tired."

"So what did you do?" asked Lizzie.

"Well actually I ended up crawling most of the way to my bed ..."

And at the same time they both looked down at the tissues laid out on the floor. Some of them had been moved, where Lizzie had walked over to the bed to wake Maria up. But most of them were still lying just as they had been after Lizzie had finished putting them out the night before. Neither of them said anything, but both of them knew what the other was thinking. How could someone possibly crawl across the tissues and not move them at all?

Their thoughts were interrupted by the sound of Dad's voice calling them to come for breakfast.

Lizzie stood up and as she did she smiled and said, "You were right; that's *really* weird."

"Yep, weird," repeated Maria with a sigh. "And every time I think I might be starting to understand what's going on, it gets even weirder. Please don't say anything to the others about it though. We can talk about it again later if you like when we get home."

Lizzie nodded and said, "Sure, and we definitely need to talk more about it." She then walked out of the room.

Chapter 23

Everyone was pretty quiet at breakfast. The weekend had gone by so quickly, and now it felt like that all they had to look forward to was packing up their stuff, cleaning the house and then the long drive back to Sydney. Dad had some ideas about things they could do before they headed off, but even his almost unwavering enthusiasm was struggling to get people moving.

"C'mon guys, if we can get the car packed and the house sorted nice and quickly this morning, then we should have enough time to stop off at Fitzroy Falls on the way home. What do you say?"

"What's Fitzroy Falls?" said Bobby. "Can you swim there?"

"Well, umm ..." Dad was clearly doing his best to think up a positive response, or even a not-negative one, but in the end he couldn't. "Well, no, you can't swim there. *But*, there is an amazing waterfall. And there's also some great walks that you can do along the escarpments. The last time we went there, which admittedly was a quite a long time ago, we saw some lyre birds and an echidna."

"I don't remember that," said Mum not looking up from the magazine she was reading whilst eating her toast. However, the short period of silence that followed prompted her to look up and see that Dad was clearly not impressed with the level of support she was providing. "Ah, yes, actually, now that you mention it, I do remember that we saw some animals. In fact, quite a few if I recall correctly."

"You're just saying that to back-up Dad," said Lizzie. "I bet we won't see anything except maybe some flies."

Dad mouthed *thanks* at Mum.

And Mum mouthed *sorry* back.

"Well, if anyone has any better ideas feel free to let me know," said Dad with a tinge of frustration in his voice. And then after a few seconds he added, "I know you girls have some project work that needs to be done, so maybe we can just head back and you can spend some time on that this afternoon." As intended, this drew a response.

"I love waterfalls. That sounds like a great idea Dad," said Maria.

"I never said I didn't want to go there," added Lizzie.

"What's an 'achy-kid-knee'?" asked Bobby.

An hour later the house was cleaned, the car packed and they were all standing out on the deck taking in the view across the valley one last time. Mum insisted on taking some timed photos of the family on the basis that 'we hardly ever get ones with all five of us in'. But as usual it proved very difficult to get everyone looking at the camera and smiling at the same time. After four attempts everyone except Mum had lost interest and headed for the car.

As Dad drove the car out of the driveway and down to the main road, Maria was busy processing the events of the previous three days and nights. Especially the nights. In fact, she was actually looking forward to the prospect of a couple of hours in the car and an opportunity to try and get her thoughts in order. Consequently, she hadn't even entered into the discussion about which movie they'd watch on the way back. In the event it was Lizzie's turn to have the final say and she chose *Finding Nemo*, which Dad said was very apt because it was all about a Dad travelling to Sydney. Bobby wondered, probably innocently, if that meant that Mum was the Dory character. Mum groaned, "Thank you very much, Bobby." Dad, Lizzie and Maria burst out laughing. Bobby kept repeating, "What did I say? What did I say?"

As they approached the place where the road started to climb out of the valley, Maria suddenly remembered what had happened to Bobby on the way down. "Hey Mum, is Bobby going to be okay going round all these bends? You remember what happened on the way down."

"How could I forget?" Mum replied with a grimace. "Remember it was me who had to clean it out of the car. Phew, that was not pleasant. But don't worry. Bobby had a travel sickness tablet with his breakfast, so I'm hoping he won't be having a repeat performance going back."

Thinking about Bobby's vomiting episode prompted Maria to think back to their arrival in Kangaroo Valley. Was it really only three days ago? It seemed so much longer. Well I suppose I have fitted quite a lot in given how active I've been during the nights, Maria thought to herself, and smiled. It was just after Bobby was sick that I got that strange feeling on my arms and neck for the first time.

She then remembered the question that had started to form in her mind the previous night. Was that feeling somehow related to her seeing the aboriginal man? She focussed hard on her encounters with him, and was pretty sure that she had got the feeling on both the nights she'd seen him. And now that she thought about it, it had probably been him outside the window on the first night and she'd had the feeling that night too. So that was three times. But what about the other times she'd felt it? On the way into the valley, in the general store, and the mega one she'd experienced in the garden of the hotel. She hadn't seen him around any of those times. Then she had a thought which surprised her, and made her feel a bit like one of those clever TV detectives. Just because I didn't see him doesn't necessarily mean that he wasn't around somewhere, somewhere close by. But just say that it is somehow related to him. What could he possibly be doing that would cause the hairs on my arms and neck to stand up? Was he sending out some sort of signal, maybe something electrical, or something mystical? Maria smiled and shook her head. That's just daft, I've read too many fantasy books.

Trying to clear her mind a bit, she turned to look out of the window. They were about half way up the road that led out of the valley. It was yet another very sunny and hence very clear day, and in between the trees that bordered the road there were some amazing views of the valley. Maria remembered that it had been almost dark when they'd arrived and so they hadn't seen these views before. She pressed her nose against the window and tried to take in as much of it as she could.

And then she was suddenly hit by the strongest feeling, so strong that it was almost physical. She was going to have to come back. And it wasn't to do with finding out what had been happening to her for the past few days. It was because she was needed here. It was almost like someone was calling out to her. Maria closed her eyes and did her best to clear her mind. Tell me what it is you need me to do. And much to her surprise almost immediately an image popped into her brain. But it wasn't the old aboriginal man, instead it was the face of the young girl she'd seen standing on the other side of the river the night before. Even though she'd never been closer than 25 or 20 metres to her, Maria felt like she could now see right into her eyes. And her eyes indicated that she was sad, very sad. But she was also very strong. For a split second Maria felt like that she was somehow connected to her, almost like they were having a video phone call. Even though she didn't move her lips Maria was sure the girl spoke to her. "Please help me."

The car suddenly took a sharp turn to the right around one of the many hairpin bends, and the connection, or whatever it was, disappeared from Maria's mind. Maria quickly turned her head to the right so that she could look out over the valley again, but the car was now passing through a heavily wooded area and all she could see were occasional glimpses of the escarpments that surrounded the valley. *Wow*, she thought to herself, that was … Well, actually, she wasn't sure what it was. Other than, of course, being another very weird event in a weekend of total weirdness.

But the message had been very clear. It was the girl who needed her help. And, as far as she could see, the only way she'd be able to provide that help would be to come back to the valley.

***

A few minutes later the car completed the last of the hairpin bends and accelerated along the straight piece of road that took them out of the valley. And just a few kilometres later Dad turned right into the car park for the Fitzroy Falls visitor centre.

The car park was full of cars, with people moving between the cars and the visitor centre, either arriving like them or returning. As they walked away from their car Maria thought that it felt like they were now back in the real world. They'd spent the last three days and nights in the valley, and somehow they'd been protected – no, more like separated – by its walls. Separated from the rest of the world. She could see why some people would really like living there and having that feeling all of the time. And that others, and she glanced at Lizzie, wouldn't like it all.

Dad suggested that they bypass the café and shop that made-up the visitor centre and head straight for the waterfall. Bobby reluctantly agreed, but only after he'd managed to secure a promise of hot chips on their return. As soon as the negotiations with Dad and Mum were over, he ran to catch-up with Maria and Lizzie, who had gone on ahead. He couldn't let them get wherever it was they were going before him.

Dad had been right, Maria thought, the waterfall and the view from the platform at the top were both amazing. And even though the car park had been very busy there didn't seem to be that many people around. They even had to wait for a couple of minutes for someone to come who could take a photo of the five of them standing on the viewing platform. After that they followed the path round to another platform that sat – rather dangerously in Maria's mind – on top of a part of the cliffs that seemed to jut out into the canyon. She did have to admit though that it gave you a really spectacular view back towards the waterfall.

Maria looked at the water falling into the canyon for ages, and every so often she thought she could see a rainbow flash into existence in the water, and then equally quickly disappear.

"I love waterfalls," said her dad, who Maria hadn't realised was standing beside her.

"Me too," said Maria. "I don't know if I'm imagining it, but sometimes I'm sure I can see a rainbow in the water as it's falling down to the bottom. Do you think that's possible?"

"Sure" replied her dad. "It's something to do with how the sunlight hits the water. Just like how a prism splits up a beam of light. Have they taught you anything about that at school yet?"

"Not that I can remember," replied Maria as she turned to look at her dad, and then had to shield her eyes from the sun.

"Well I'm sure it'll come up when you get to high school and start doing a subject called 'physics'. Which I was terrible at by the way, and probably won't be able to help with you at all." Dad chuckled to himself, no doubt remembering his school days thought Maria.

Neither of them spoke for a while and then Dad pointed out towards the waterfall and exclaimed, "Look, there, did you see that one?"

"Yes!" responded Maria laughing. "Wow that one lasted for ages."

They were silent again for a moment. "So, did you enjoy the weekend?" asked Dad. "I know you weren't that keen on coming to begin with, and having to miss your dance classes."

That's a very interesting question thought Maria, and I'm not sure how I should answer it. I have enjoyed some parts of it for sure. But other parts have been a bit too weird to call enjoyable. After a few moments she decided to go for, "Dad, I've had a really amazing weekend."

"That's good," said Dad. But then he looked down at Maria and added, "Isn't it?"

Maria decided it was time to change the subject. "Dad, I've been wondering, is this canyon that the waterfall is dropping into part of Kangaroo Valley?" and she put her arm over the railing to indicate the canyon that was laid out in front of them.

"Hmm, I don't think it is," said her dad. "Though you see that mountain over there?" and he pointed way out into the distance. "I'm pretty sure you can see that from where we were staying, and so that's inside the valley."

"Yes, I see it," responded Maria.

"But I think this canyon, this river," and this time he pointed straight down and then out to their right, "goes around the valley."

Maria looked down at the canyon for a while and then said, "Dad, this might seem like a bit of an odd question …" She paused.

"So, are you going to ask it or not?" said her dad smiling.

"Do you think there's any chance at all that there might be some aboriginal people living in the valley, or somewhere nearby, who are …" she struggled to find the right word. "Well, I guess *living* like they used to do? You know, like they were before the white settlers came?"

"I think I'd call that an interesting question rather than an odd question." Her dad thought for a moment and then went on, "I don't think there are because if there were I think they'd be quite well known."

"What about though if they were doing it, you know, secretly?" Maria asked even though she knew it was pretty unlikely.

"Well I obviously I can't say a definite *no* to that, because if they were very clever and doing it very secretly then no one would know about them? But I'd have to say that I think it's very unlikely." Maria's dad turned to look at her. "I get the feeling that coming to the valley has sparked a bit of interest in the aboriginals who lived here before the white settlers, am I right?"

Maria smiled at him and said, "Yep, it sure has." And then to herself she said, *you have no idea.*

Her dad looked around the viewing platform and saw that they were only people left on it. "Oops, it looks like we've been left behind. Mum and the others must have gone on to the next one. Come on let's catch them up." And he offered his hand to Maria as he started walking towards the steps that led back to the path. Maria smiled and grabbed it, and then was half-pulled or half-carried to the top of the steps.

After they'd finished their walk they went into the visitor centre for lunch, which included some hot chips, and a quick look round the national park shop. Maria decided that she'd like to bring a present back for Liv, and when she went to the checkout to pay for it she saw some maps stacked on the counter. Out of nowhere she had the idea that it might be a good idea to have one of Kangaroo Valley, and she also thought she'd like to try and work out where she'd walked to the night before. When her mum asked why she was getting it Maria told her that it would be a good reminder of their trip, and she'd be able to look up all the places they'd been to. Her mum hadn't looked that convinced, but she had long since given up trying to understand all of her daughter's purchases.

The drive back to Sydney was long and hot. It seemed to Maria that everyone in Sydney had decided to go away for the long weekend, and they had also decided to travel back at exactly the same time.

One *interesting* thing had happened though. (Maria had decided to try and not use the word 'weird' for a while.) She had only been vaguely aware of the movie that Lizzie and Bobby were watching, when suddenly she heard the tune that she'd been trying to think of in bed that morning. Dory, the character who Mum wasn't at all like, was singing 'just keep swimming, just keep swimming.' That was definitely the tune and the rhythm that she had been trying to remember, but the words didn't seem quite right. And then Maria remembered why it had been in her head. That's what I was singing to myself last night as I crawled back to my bed. But I sang 'just keep moving, just keep moving' instead. How *wei* … interesting is that, Maria thought to herself. This morning I was trying to remember a tune and just a few hours later I hear it in a movie.

She was just about to announce to everyone that she'd experienced a white witch type moment when she thought better of it. Probably best not to go anywhere near that

223

Chapter 24

Maria couldn't remember ever sleeping as deeply as she did that night and as far she was aware she didn't dream at all. One second she felt her eyes getting extremely heavy and then, what seemed to her to be just a few moments later, she opened them again. She moved her head very slightly so that she could see the clock on the wall of her room and realised that nine hours had gone by.

She was pleased to have slept so well, but a part of her was also a bit disappointed about what it might mean. That whatever had been happening to her over the weekend was probably completely related to her being in the valley. And so she may never get to know what it was all about. Unless, of course, she was able to go back there sometime. But Maria didn't think there was much chance of that, not for a good while anyway.

Her mum walked into the room and came over to open the blinds, just like she did every morning. "Morning gorgeous girl," she said with a big smile on her face. "I didn't think I'd find you awake yet, not after all those lie-ins you had over the weekend. How did you sleep?"

"Really good, I think," responded Maria rubbing her eyes. "It was like I closed my eyes and then just opened them again, and I couldn't tell if I'd been asleep for one minute or one hour or all night. But I checked the clock when I woke up and so it was all night."

"That's good, Maria, really good. You needed it." Mum started to rummage through the clothes that lay in pile on the chair at the end of Maria's bed. "Now then, which uniform do you need to wear today? When I woke up I thought it was Monday, but of course it's not Monday, it's Tuesday. Long weekends always throw me. Maria, you really have to put your dirty clothes in the laundry. Just look at the stain on this sport top," she said holding it up to the light. "I hope you've got a clean one somewhere. Do you have any sports today?"

Wow, Maria thought, it doesn't take very long to get back into our normal routine. It already feels like we never went away.

"Maria, do you have any sport today?" repeated her mum.

"Err, no I don't think we do."

"That's good. You can wear a dress, and I'm pretty sure we've got a clean one of those. Now come on, it's time to get up." With that Mum left the room taking a bundle of clothes with her.

As soon as she had Maria rolled over, just five more minutes more should be okay she thought. She wasn't really looking forward to going to school, Tuesdays were normally pretty dull. But she was very much looking forward to seeing Liv. She'd being going over and over in her mind what to tell her about the weekend. Where should she start, and what she should include. She wondered what Liv would make of it all. Although they spent most of their time joking around, they did occasionally have quite serious chats about things. And Maria thought that Liv was good at making sense of things, putting them into order. Do or decide this thing first, and then the rest will fall into place – that sort of thing.

Her thoughts were interrupted by a shout from downstairs. "Time to get up guys! Don't make me come up there again," called out her mum. Maria rolled over, threw back the quilt and sheet, and swung her legs out of the bed. That seemed very easy she thought to herself. And then immediately thought that's a bit of a strange thought. But then she remembered how it hadn't always been quite so easy over the weekend, during the night at least. Just one of the many *weird* – oops I mean interesting – things that she'd experienced.

Maria wasn't the only one moving slowly this morning, and in the end Mum dropped them at school just as the first bell was sounding. As she walked across the playground Liv walked over to meet her.

"Hi Maria, how was Kangaroo Valley?" she asked, "Did you see any kangaroos?"

"Hi. Yeah it was good. Really good. Didn't see any kangaroos, but I'm pretty sure I saw a wombat. How about you? How was your weekend?"

"Yeah, okay. Well, pretty quiet actually. Dad had to do work stuff for most of it so we didn't get to go the cinema."

They were approaching the end of the line for their class, and so Maria took hold of Liv's arm to indicate that she wanted them to hang back a bit. She also had a quick look round to make sure that no-one was within earshot. Liv immediately knew that Maria had something important to say.

"I need to tell you about something very weird (she'd decided that was the best word for it and so she should probably just keep on using it) that happened to me over the weekend. So can we try and find somewhere quiet to talk at the lunchbreak."

"Sure. But what sort of weird thing?" asked Liv.

"I'll tell you at lunchtime. I don't want to risk anyone else overhearing us."

"Ooh sounds very mysterious." Liv thought for a moment, "Does it involve a boy?"

"OMG, you're as bad as my mum. No, it's nothing to do with boys," Maria said indignantly. She realised that she wasn't being entirely fair to Liv, and so smiling said, "It's just something a bit strange that happened to me, but I really don't want anyone else to hear about it. So can you please wait until lunchtime?"

"No, not really," said Liv, "but I don't suppose I have any choice, do I?" And she smiled back.

"No you don't," said Maria as she started to move towards the rest of their classmates as they were now entering the classroom.

As Maria had feared the morning passed excruciatingly slowly, but eventually it was time for the long break, and Maria signalled to Liv to stay in the classroom as the others made their way out. When all the other kids were gone she went over to Mr A's desk. "Excuse me Mr Andrews. I'm not feeling very well at the moment and I was wondering if it would it be okay if I stayed in the classroom during the lunchbreak, and if Liv could keep me company?"

"Oh, I'm sorry to hear that Maria. What's the matter?" he said with a concerned look on his face.

"I've got a bit of a headache, and I think it would be better if I could just sit quietly in the classroom," she paused for a second, "and out of the sun."

"Yes, that's no problem. Are you okay to stay with her Liv?" Liv nodded. Maria saw that she had put her best concerned face on, and Maria had to stop a smile from appearing on her own face.

"I just have to go and heat up my lunch," said Mr Andrews, "but if you need me I'll be in the staff room, or alternatively you can just go to the office. Okay?"

"Yes Mr Andrews," said Maria and Liv at the same time. And then Liv added, "Don't worry I'll make sure she's okay sir."

Mr A nodded, picked up a couple of folders and walked quickly out of the room.

"Good thinking," said Liv when she was sure he was far enough away.

"Thanks. I don't really like lying to Mr A, but I just couldn't think of where we could go outside and be sure of being on our own."

"So then, what's this strange mysterious thing that happened to you? Did you meet some vampires and werewolves like in Twilight?"

"Wow, how did you guess?" said Maria with an astonished look on her face. "Did you talk to Lizzie at recess?" And for a split second she could see that Liv had been taken in. But she quickly followed it up with, "Just joking. I'm afraid it doesn't involve hot boys of any sort." She thought for a second and remembering the face of the old aboriginal man she added, "In fact, it's pretty much the opposite of that."

As she spoke, Maria walked over to her hook to get her lunch box out of her backpack. She came back to sit at one of the desks. It was only as she took out her sandwich that she decided to tell Liv everything she could remember about the weekend that was at all weird. She couldn't really think of a reason why she shouldn't disclose it all, other than running the risk that Liv would conclude she was going nuts. She also felt it would be good for her to tell the whole story as it happened, and that maybe doing so would help her make a bit better sense of it all.

And so she started from the beginning. How the hairs on her arms and neck had stood up and tingled as they'd arrived in the valley, just after Bobby had thrown up. Of course, Liv thought that sitting in a car full of vomit was enough to give anyone a weird feeling.

But Maria told her that it was only the first of many times that it had happened and, "By the way, if you make a smart comment after every little thing I tell you about then this is going to take a *very* long time."

"Ooh, no need to get a strop on," said Liv. But then she saw something in Maria's eyes, and got a sense of how important it was to her. "Okay, okay I won't interrupt again," using her right thumb and forefinger to zip up her lips.

Maria nodded and went on. She described the first night, the tapping on the window and then not being able to wake her dad. And how afterwards she wasn't even certain that it had actually happened, and wondered if it could have been a dream. Or that maybe just some of it was real and the rest a dream.

But then there was the second night, seeing the old aboriginal man on the porch outside her window. How he'd spoken to her, and she'd eventually realised that he wanted her to come outside with him. Maria paused for a second to see Liv's reaction, and saw that her eyes and mouth were all wide open in a look of wonder. Maria couldn't help but smile.

"What? What?" asked Liv. "Have I got something on my face?" she asked, and put down her sandwich so that she could use her hands to rub around her mouth.

"No. No, there's no food on your face. It was your expression," said Maria, doing her best to impersonate it.

"Oh, okay then," said Liv, picking up her sandwich again. "Well what do you expect? What on earth did you do? You didn't go with him, did you? Please tell me you didn't."

"Yes. No. Well, yes and no actually." Maria noticed the look re-appear on Liv's face. She told her about deciding to follow him, going to the front of the house and opening the front door, then being unable to open the screen door and realising he'd suddenly vanished. She recalled all the things she couldn't do or feel or hear. She described how hard it was to move or turn the door handles, how the quilt had felt so heavy, and how quiet it had been.

When Maria had finished, Liv raised her hand like they did in class when they wanted to ask a question.

Maria smiled, "Yes Olivia, do you have a question?"

"Yes miss," replied Liv demurely. And then as the normal Liv. "All those things you've just mentioned, don't they mean it was definitely a dream? Those are the kind of things that happen in my dreams, things that don't happen or you can't do in real life. I sometimes have dreams where I'm flying." She put her arms out to the side to indicate how she did it. However, this caused a piece of cucumber to fly out of the sandwich she was holding and land with a splat on one of the desks. They looked at one another for a moment and then burst out laughing.

A moment later a figure appeared in the doorway. It was one of the boys in their class.

"Hey, what are you two doing in here?" he asked. "You're not supposed to be inside during lunch break."

"So what are you doing here?" Maria responded quickly.

This caused him to hesitate to for a second, but then he decided to ignore the question and continue with, "What were you laughing about? I could hear you all the way down the corridor."

Liv stepped in. "Well not that it's any of your business Ben, but ... Maria is sick, which is why she's inside, and I'm here looking after her. She did a huge sneeze, and that huge green bogey flew out of her nose and landed on Daniel's desk," she said pointing at the piece of cucumber. "And we were just wondering which one of us was going to get rid of it, which is why we were laughing. But now you're here maybe you could do it for us?" And finally pausing to take a breath, she took a napkin from her lunchbox and offered it to him.

The girls could see Ben staring at the cucumber bogey, partly horrified and partly fascinated by the size of it. And probably just a little concerned by the amount of mayo mucus that appeared to cover it. He took a small step forward to try and get a better view of it, but then thought better of it.

"You two are gross," he said, and turned away and walked back down the corridor.

The girls knew that they shouldn't laugh out loud again, but they almost fell off their seats as they rolled from side to side with their hands over their mouths.

Maria finally recovered enough to say, "So, where were we?"

"Umm ... bogey, cucumber, flying, dreaming," replied Liz working backwards. "Yep, that was it. All that weird stuff that you told me about, that must mean it was all a dream."

"Well I must admit that's what I first thought. Then some things happened that made me think it wasn't all a dream," Maria said, thinking of all that had occurred the following day and on the last night.

She told Liv about how dad found the door open when he got up, and how Lizzie had been woken up by the curtains being open in the morning and the sun shining on her. And so she was as certain as she could be that she had actually done those things during the night, which meant those parts at least she didn't dream.

Liv nodded but didn't say anything. Maria moved on to the events of the following day. How she got the really strong tingly feeling all over her body in the garden at the hotel. And about going to the Pioneer Museum and seeing the old man in a photo taken in 1860. At this point Liv brought both her hands up to her cheeks, clearly a bit surprised or shocked by what she'd heard.

"Are you absolutely certain it was him in the photo?" she asked, her voice now much quieter and less sure than it had been earlier.

"Pretty certain," said Maria.

"But if he was in a photo that was taken in 1860 then he couldn't possibly be alive today, which would make him a …" Liv seemed reluctant to say the word, or perhaps she was scared to say it.

"I know. A ghost," said Maria finishing the sentence for her. "I've thought a lot about that. Some of things that happened were, you know, kind of spooky. Like how sometimes he'd seem to appear or vanish really suddenly. But then there was the way he tapped on the window to get my attention and to get me to come outside. If he was really a ghost why didn't he just walk through the wall or, even easier, just appear in my room? And the way he spoke to me, that just felt so real, so …" Maria struggled to think of the right word and then settled for, "oh I don't know, so non-ghost like."

"Well, if he's not a ghost, and you're sure, well pretty sure at least that it wasn't a dream, then what on earth is going on?"

"I really don't know. And you know what, I haven't even got to the weirdest stuff yet," Maria said, putting both her hands out in front of her. Liv's eyes opened even wider, and for a second her shoulders sagged. Almost like she was beginning to find all the information that Maria was passing on to her a bit too heavy to bear.

Maria noticed and asked, "Have you had enough? We could always stop and carry on tomorrow."

"No, no, definitely not. I'm good. Carry on," said Liv. She glanced at her watch. "We've got another 15 minutes before the lunch break is over. Do you think that'll be long enough?"

"Should be," said Maria. "I'll try and be quick." And she proceeded to take Liv through the events of the third night. If Liv's face had a look of wonder before, it soon became one of amazement as Maria told her about leaving the house and walking to the river with the old man and then seeing the young girl. And as she heard about Maria's run back to the house and then her encounter with Lizzie, it was replaced by a look of complete bewilderment.

Maria finished off by telling Liv about seeing the little girl's face in her mind when they'd been driving out of the valley.

"It was such a clear image," she said, like a TV signal had been beamed into my head.

"And you're sure that she said, 'please help me'?" asked Liv.

"Well, as certain as I can be, given everything that's happened," responded Maria with a sigh. Neither of them spoke for a few seconds. "So, what do you think?" asked Maria.

Liv shook her head very slowly and then let out a big breath, which almost whistled between her teeth. "That was, is, such an amazing story." She shook her head again. "I really don't know what to say. In fact, I do believe I'm speechless." And they both burst out laughing. Liv was renowned for always having something to say about any topic that was brought up.

At that moment the bell announced the end of the lunch break was over. They started to tidy up their lunch things. As they walked over to the hooks where their backpacks were Liv said, "You know, even though I have no idea what was going on, I am pretty sure about one thing."

"What's that?" asked Maria.

"If we're ever going to find out then we need to find some way of getting you back down there. Back down to the valley," said Liv waving her arm in what she thought was the vague direction of Kangaroo Valley.

"Yeah, I know what you mean," said Maria. "I've been thinking the same thing myself." And she was pleased that Liv had said 'if *we*'re ever ...' and '*we* need'. It made her feel a lot less alone in dealing with it.

The first of the other kids in their class had started to form a line just outside the door. And so Maria indicated to Liv to stop discussing it and Liv nodded and mouthed the words, *let's talk more tonight*. And this time Maria nodded.

Mr A walked briskly back into the room, and the kids followed him in to take their seats.

As Daniel approached his desk he let out a loud urggghh sound, and then said, "What's that on my desk? It looks like a ... urgh, yuk. Who put that there? Who was it?"

Ben, who wasn't actually anywhere near the desk called out. "It's a bogey. Maria did a big sneeze and it landed there. Liv told me," and he pointed to where Maria and Liv were still standing at the back of the class.

"Sugar, I completely forgot about that," Liv muttered to herself. She thought for a second and then marched over to Daniel's desk, pushing aside the group of kids who'd gathered around to see what all the fuss was about. She paused for a second for dramatic effect, and then stepped forward picked up the cucumber bogey and made a show of placing it on her tongue and taking it into her mouth. "Hmm, *crunchy*," she said looking directly at Maria, who was almost doubled up at the back of the class.

Calls of 'she's gross' and 'disgusting' followed Liv as she walked to her desk.

Chapter 25

Over the next few days Maria and Liv talked of nothing else. Maria reckoned that she must have retold the Kangaroo Valley story in its entirety to Liv three, possibly four, times – though not always in a chronological order.

Liv would ask "tell me again about how hard it was to move the quilt and turn the door handles," and Maria would try to remember each instance from her three nights in the house. Or, "what were you doing when you had the hair standing on end feelings?" and Maria would try to recall what she'd been doing, and if she'd been excited or out of breath, or stressed in any way. However, no matter how she retold the events, they were at a loss to come up with any reasonable explanation to account for everything. Extremely vivid dreams could explain some of it, maybe even most of it, but certainly not all of it. But if none of it was a dream, then there were so many weird things that were impossible to explain in a rational way.

And much to Maria's amusement, Liv had made a remark about them needing to find a better word than *weird* to describe everything. "I'm definitely with you on that," Maria had responded, and had offered her hand to Liv for a high five.

The one thing that they did make a decision about was that the events Maria had experienced – be it the hair-standing feelings during the day or the visits of the old man

236

at night – were somehow linked. They had no idea why or how, but the fact that since returning to Sydney Maria hadn't had any further hair-standing episodes or nocturnal visits supported this view. In fact, Maria had been sleeping so deeply that on waking she couldn't even remember dreaming during the night.

On Friday afternoon after school Liv came to Maria's house for a couple of hours. Once called play dates, the visits had now been renamed screen dates by their mums. However, this time Maria's mum was surprised and quite happy to see that the girls were spending most of their time looking at the map of Kangaroo Valley, laid out on the floor of Maria's bedroom.

"Has Maria been telling you about our weekend away Liv?" asked Maria's mum as she folded a towel while standing outside Maria's room.

"Oh yes, she has," replied Liv excitedly. And then a little more reservedly. "Well, just a few things that you did while you were there actually. Sounds like a good place to go for a weekend."

"It is. Maybe your mum and dad could take you there sometime?" She paused to put the towel away and pick up another one, and then added, "Get them to call me if they are interested, because we can get Maria's dad to ask his friend at work about you staying at his place. Do you think they would like the house Maria?"

"Uh huh," was all Maria could manage as she attempted to work out something on the map.

"Mariaaa," said Mum. But it was the elbow that Liv dug into her leg that actually caught her attention.

"Hey, watch it," said Maria, before she realised that both Liv and her mum were looking at her expectantly. "Oops sorry, were you talking to me?"

"I was trying to," replied her mum. "I suppose it's better to see you plugged into a map instead of some sort of screen. Anyway, I was just asking if you think Liv and her family would like Pete's house. Because if they were interested in going to the valley one day, then Dad could speak to Pete about them booking it."

"Oh yes, definitely, you would love it there. It's a great house. And it's got amazing views of the valley." It suddenly dawned on Maria that she'd been so keen to talk to Liv about all the things that had happened to her that she hadn't actually told her about anything else. About the house or the valley or the things they'd done, unless they'd been things or places related to her story that is. "Actually, I think you'd really love it there." Maria paused for a second and then more to herself than to her mum or Liv she added, "I'd really like to go back sometime."

"Not much chance of that I'm afraid my love," replied her mum thinking that the statement was aimed at her. "Well not any time soon, anyway. Not with your dancing and Lizzie's netball and Bobby's soccer at the weekends. And I'm pretty sure Pete's place gets pretty booked out in the school holidays and ..."

Maria stopped listening to her mum and looked back down at the map. She'd put small crosses next to all the places they'd visited, and circles around the crosses at the places where anything *weird* had happened, such as the house, the bush walk behind the Pioneer Museum and the garden of the hotel. However, it didn't really seem to indicate very much other than weird things had happened to her all over the valley. She was pondering the significance of this, if any, when she felt Liv touching her arm, which she eventually realised was a sign for her to re-join the conversation.

"That's great Mrs H," she heard Liv saying. "I will definitely talk to my mum and dad about it. One other thing, I was wondering, if we were to go down there for a weekend, do you think it would be okay for Maria to come with us? Only I know I'd enjoy it a lot more if I had someone my own age there. And, of course, Maria would know all the best places to go to. What do you think? Would that be okay?"

"Hmm, I'm not sure," said Maria's mum as she put the last towel into the cupboard. She turned and saw the disappointment in the girls' faces. "What I meant to say was, of course it would be okay for her to go with you, assuming your parents are okay with it, Liv." Smiles immediately appeared on their faces. "The reason I'm not sure is because it would depend on when it was, on whether there was a dance show or dance exam coming up. I think Miss Leora would have a fit if Maria missed any more practice this term."

"How about early next term mum?" asked Maria, feeling a bit bad that she hadn't seen earlier where Liv was going with this line of conversation, or even thought of it herself. "I don't have any shows or exams until the end of term and so I think it would be okay then, wouldn't it?"

"Maybe," said her mum. She was quite interested to see how different Maria's response to missing dance classes was now compared to a couple of weeks ago when her dad first raised the idea of going away for a weekend. But she decided not to say anything about that now, and settled for, "Let me talk to your dad about it, and I'll check the calendar too."

"Great, thanks," said Liv.

"Thanks Mum," said Maria.

Maria's mum smiled, and turned to go down the stairs.

Maria waited until she was sure her mum was out of earshot and turned towards Liv. "That was good thinking, Liv. I'm sorry I was a bit slow to catch on."

"That's okay," said Liv sitting back down beside the map. "Now all I have to do is convince my mum and dad that they would like to go away for a weekend, and sooner rather than later."

"Do you think they will?" asked Maria.

"I'm not sure. I think they used to go away and travel quite a bit before I was born. And they were just trying to get back into it when Rory was born. But ever since then we've hardly ever gone away at weekends, unless it's a family thing like a wedding or birthday. And then we usually stay with a relative, or maybe just one night in a motel."

Maria nodded. Rory, Liv's little brother, was a couple of years younger than Bobby, and a real handful at the best of times. She could understand why her mum and dad might be a bit reluctant to let him loose in a nice hotel or someone else's holiday house.

"Well, all you can do is try." Maria suddenly felt excitement mixed with relief at the possibility of going back to the valley in the near future. So much so that she couldn't stop a huge grin appearing on her face.

"What?" said Liv.

"I can't help it. I know it's just an idea at the moment but even the thought there's a chance I might be able to go back to the valley, and with you, well it's just … just too exciting."

Liv smiled back, pleased to see Maria looking so happy. But she was also concerned that she might be getting ahead of herself. "Don't get too excited," she said, "I have no idea what my mum and dad will say about it. And even if they do think it's a good idea to go there, it might not be straight away."

"I know, I know," said Maria. "Don't worry, I do realise that it's a long shot." And as she said it the grin disappeared from her face.

Liv noticed it and thought it was time to change the subject. She leaned forward so that she could get a good view of the map, then asked, "So, do you think the crosses and circles tell us anything?"

***

On Monday morning in the playground Liv delivered the bad news to Maria. Even though they would definitely like to go one day, and they thought the house sounded fantastic, Liv's parents felt they already had too much planned for the rest of the year.

"Never mind, thanks anyway for trying," said Maria with a small sigh. They were both silent for a few seconds and then Maria added, "So what do you have planned?"

"Oh yeah, most of it was news to me actually," said Liv with a slightly sheepish look on her face. "There are a few family things, you know a wedding, and a big family get-together for my gran's 80th birthday, things like that. But the big thing is that they really want to go on a cruise in the Christmas holidays." Maria oohed. "Yeah, I know, pretty cool huh? They weren't going to tell me about it because they haven't booked it yet, and they didn't want Rory getting excited and then being disappointed if we end up not going. Anyway I nagged them so much they agreed to tell me, as long as I don't say anything to Rory. And they said if we do go on the cruise then we won't be able to afford any other trips away, even if it's just for a weekend. I'm really sorry about that, I know you were very excited about the possibility of going back to the valley."

"Nah, don't worry," responded Maria forcing a smile on to her face. "It's completely fine. I knew that there was only a small chance of it happening. And anyway, why should I be relying on you to get me there?"

"I know but ..." Liv started to say.

"No, no buts. It's my ... my *thing*, and so I need to sort it out." Liv tried to open her mouth, but Maria put her finger on her lips. "Now tell me about the cruise, where are your mum and dad thinking of going?"

241

Maria did her best to listen to Liv, and be excited for her, but after a few minutes her mind started to return to her disappointment. She was surprised about how disappointed she felt. And as the day went on, it began to dawn on her that not going back wasn't really an option. She needed to go back, or at least know that she would be returning sometime, ideally sooner rather than later.

And she also understood that going back wasn't just about helping the girl or the old man. She realised that it was very important for her too. Having concluded that everything she'd experienced over that weekend was most likely linked in some way, she had the strongest sense that she would discover something, possibly about herself, and possibly something very important. But how was she going to get there? She didn't think there was any chance her family would be returning in the foreseeable future, and now she knew that Liv's family wouldn't be going until the following year at the earliest.

Maria thought for a moment about explaining to her mum and dad why it was so important for her to go back to the valley. But although she knew they would listen to her, she couldn't think of an acceptable explanation of how and why she had left the house in the middle of night with a strange and very old aboriginal man and ended up meeting an aboriginal girl who desperately needed her help. On the other hand, if she made out that it wasn't real, that it was just a series of very weird dreams, then she felt certain that they'd see it as some sort of physical or medical issue, anxiety or puberty or something like that. And anyway, if it was just dreams and they've stopped happening now, then why on earth would you want to go back? She could almost hear them saying it.

For the next week or so, Maria let the whole thing churn around in the back of her mind, doing her best to concentrate at school and dance. Then one evening while she and Lizzie were watching an old episode of Dance

Academy, a thought suddenly struck her. Why not go to Kangaroo Valley by herself? She could do it on a Saturday instead of going to dance. And if she was able to get there and back in a day, then Mum and Dad wouldn't even know she'd been. But would that give her enough time to find the old man and the young girl and to work out what it was they needed her help with? Well it would just have to be enough she thought, and a brief time there would have to be better than no time.

Maria jumped off of the lounge and raced upstairs to find her iPod. She eventually found it under a pile of clothes at the end of her bed. She quickly accessed Google and searched for 'public transport Sydney to kangaroo valley'. Twenty minutes later she dejectedly put the iPod down. It seemed almost impossible to get to Kangaroo Valley at all on Saturday using trains and buses, let alone there and back inside eight hours. No wonder people relied so much on cars nowadays.

Maria wandered into her mum and dad's bedroom to get the phone, and then walked back to her bedroom as she dialled in Liv's number. As usual it was Liv who answered, she loved talking on the phone and always tried to pick it up before their answering machine kicked in.

"Hi Liv, Maria," said Maria.

"Hi Maria, what's up?"

"I'm a bit upset actually. I was watching TV when I suddenly had the idea that I could go to Kangaroo Valley by myself on a Saturday, instead of going to dance."

"Wow, that's a big call," interjected Liv.

"Yeah, I know, but I figured it was probably the only way that I'm ever going to get there. But then I looked at the timetables on the internet, and there's just no way of doing it in one day, in fact on a Saturday it's almost impossible to even get there."

"That's a bummer," said Liv, "but would you really want to go there on your own, and without letting your mum and dad know? That sounds a bit, you know, not right to me."

"I know," said Maria, "but I don't feel like I can tell them why I'm so desperate to go back."

Liv was a bit taken aback both by the tone of Maria's voice and her use of the word 'desperate'. "Are you really desperate? What I mean is, I know you really wanted to try and get back sometime, hopefully sometime quite soon. But I didn't realise that you were *desperate* to do it." Maria didn't respond, and Liv had the sense that she was fighting to hold back tears. "Are you okay Maria?" she asked quietly.

"Yep, I'm alright," replied Maria taking a deep breath. And neither of them spoke for a few seconds.

"Look," said Liv in a very serious voice, "I'm going to give this problem of ours some serious thinking tonight, and I'll let you know what the plan is tomorrow morning at school. Does that sound okay to you, missy?"

"You're crazy," laughed Maria, "but yes, if you really can think of anything then that will be very okay."

"Very good," said Liv, still using her serious voice, "and make sure you don't lie awake worrying about it and get lots of sleep. That's an order."

"Yes, yes, okay, I get it. And thanks."

"No worries mate," said Liv, this time in her normal voice. "See ya tomorrow."

"Yep, see you then," said Maria, feeling a lot better than she had a few minutes before.

***

Much to Maria's delight and appreciation Liv was true to her word. By the time they met in the playground the next day, Liv had come up with a great sounding plan.

"So after you hung up I had a big think about what was required," explained Liv. "Given what you said about the trains and buses it seemed to me we were definitely going to need someone to drive you, I mean us, there. As it didn't look like it would be your parents or mine I thought about who else might do it. And that's when I thought about my uncle John."

Maria had met John quite a few times. He was Liv's mum's youngest brother. In fact, he was much younger, and was only just doing his last year at university. Maria knew that Liv thought the world of him, and she herself had always found him to be very warm and friendly.

"He always seems to be on holiday," Liv went on, "and so I thought he might be able to spend a day taking us to Kangaroo Valley. Mum said it was alright to call him, so I did. And you know how he can never say no to me. Well, he's agreed to do it in the school holidays."

"Wow, that's amazing Liv. Thank you *so* much," said Maria, and she leaned over to give Liv a big hug. She thought for a second before asking, "Didn't he ask you why you – we – wanted to go there? Or why we weren't going with our parents?"

"Yes, he did actually. I told him that your family was too busy, and mine couldn't afford it because we're saving for a cruise. Hmm, now that I think about it, I probably shouldn't have done that because it's supposed to be a secret. I should let him know not to mention it in front of my parents or Rory," said Liv, the last bit mostly to herself.

"Okay, but what did you say about why we wanted to go? You didn't mention anything about what happened to me over the weekend, did you?" Maria asked with an anxious look on her face.

"Oh yeah right, I told him we needed to go there so that you could find a long lost tribe of aboriginal people who have been living there in secret for the last 100 years, but that have now decided to reveal themselves to you, and only you, because they need your help with some very mysterious quest or adventure." Liv paused for breath, and then they both burst out laughing.

"Actually, he did ask me why and that caught me a bit by surprise, and so I had to think of something on the spur of the moment. But in the end I think I did okay, because I told him that we want to go so we can visit the museum you told me about. To help out with a project we're doing this year at school. Do you think that was alright?"

Maria nodded and beamed a smile at Liv. She never ceased to be amazed at how resourceful Liv was. For a moment she wondered what would have happened if it had been Liv rather than her sleeping in that bed in that house on those nights? How would she have handled it? Maria was sure that she would have got to the bottom of what the old man and the young girl wanted much better and quicker than she had done. But there was little point in dwelling on that. She pushed the thought out of her head, and said to Liv, "That's very alright. Thank you so, *so* much." Maria paused and then added, "Now all I have to do is convince my parents to let me go. When do you think we'd actually do it?"

"Well I thought you'd want to go as soon as possible, so I've already suggested to John going on the first Monday of the holidays, which is only two weeks away. He'd said that was probably okay but that he'd double check and call me back tonight."

"Wow, that is soon," said Maria with excitement, "I really hope my parents are okay with it."

"Why wouldn't they be?" asked Liv. She thought for a second and then continued, "Remember you don't have to tell *them* it's for a school project. You can just say that I really wanted to go to see what you've been making all the fuss about. And that my Uncle John has agreed to take me and one of my friends for the day. And that I've asked you because you're my BFF, and because you know all the best places to go, blah, blah, blah."

"God I wish it was you asking them! They'd be sure to say yes," said Maria rubbing her temples with her fingertips.

At that moment the bell sounded. As Maria and Liv walked towards their classroom, Maria's mind was racing. She felt excited and apprehensive all at once. What if this time she went and nothing happened at all? After all they were only going for a day, and most of what had happened on her last visit had happened at night. But deep inside she also had a feeling that they – the old man and the girl – were so keen to get her help with whatever it was they needed help with that they would find a way to contact her. And, well, if they didn't, or if it really had just been a series of very weird and vivid dreams that she'd had over a particular weekend, then at least she would know that she'd tried. And surely they couldn't ask any more of her than that.

Chapter 26

Much to Maria's relief her parents had agreed to her going away on a day trip to Kangaroo Valley with Liv and her Uncle John.

Maria had repeated the explanation Liv had suggested, adding that Liv's family couldn't go there for a weekend because they were saving for a big holiday at the end of the year. Maria's mum seemed genuinely pleased that Liv was getting a chance to visit, and thought it was very kind of her and her uncle to invite Maria as well.

Unbeknown to Maria her mum had, of course, immediately called Liv's mum to confirm everything was as it seemed and that Uncle John was a suitably responsible person to take two eleven year old girls away on such a trip. And despite some confusion about whether it was Liv accompanying Maria, or the other way around, everything else was good. They both knew that the two girls had spoken of little else since Maria's family had returned from their weekend there, and so it would be great for them to go there together.

Normally Maria would be caught up by all the end-of-term at school. But this time she was completely distracted by the impending trip back to the valley. She spent hours looking at her map of the valley and searching on Google for anything she could find out about aboriginal people and the valley. Maria couldn't find any reference to aborigines currently living in the valley. As far as she could make out the Wodi-Wodi tribe, who had lived there before the white settlers arrived, had all moved on by the end of the 1800s. And so as the day approached for her return trip, she had pretty much given up on the idea that a tribe or group of aboriginals could possibly be living in the valley dressing as their ancestors had done without anyone else knowing about it.

Maria had never been that interested in history at school, but now she couldn't get enough of it. When Liv asked her why she was spending so much time reading about the Kangaroo Valley and its history, she'd replied that it was partly because she felt a connection to the place, and partly because she thought that she might find out something that would help her understand what had been happening to her. Liv had just nodded, "Hmm, that makes sense ... I think."

Maria learned that the first settlers to live in the valley had gone there to cut down cedar trees, which were used to build houses and furniture for the ever increasing number of people arriving from Britain and Europe. And then later, once the land had been cleared, other settlers arrived to establish dairy farms. She couldn't believe how quickly things had changed after that. She read that in 1841 it was thought that there were between 10 and 20 whites living in the valley; by 1860 it was 200, and by 1880 it was 1400. She was sure that was a lot more people than lived there today. No wonder the aborigines moved out.

Finally the day arrived and Maria's dad agreed to drop her at Liv's house on his way to work. Given that they were only going for a day trip both Maria and Liv wanted to get away as early as possible. However, when Maria arrived Uncle John had already called to say that he was running a bit late. Maria couldn't help but let the frustration show on her face.

"What time does he think he'll get here?"

"He said he'd do his best to be here by eight o'clock," replied Liv looking at her watch, "which is only 15 minutes away."

They sat on a lounge in Liv's front room that afforded them a view of the road, so that they would know the moment he arrived. And whilst they tried their best to make small talk they were both a bit too anxious and excited for it. Fortunately for them, a few minutes later Liv's brother Rory walked into the room. He was still dressed in his pyjamas, carrying a very scruffy teddy bear under his arm. Without even so much as glancing at the girls he marched straight over to the television, picked up the remote and switched it on.

"Hey Rory, have you asked Mum if you can watch TV?" asked Liv in a voice that would have left no one in any doubt that she was this boy's older sister.

"Don't need to. It's the holidays," he replied sharply and without taking his eyes off of the screen.

Liv looked over at Maria and raised her eyebrows. Maria smiled and mouthed *boys* back to her. On other days Liv might have responded to Rory, but she was actually quite happy to have the distraction provided by the TV. In the end they didn't notice John parking his car and then walking up the path to the front door. And so when the door bell sounded they both jumped. Liv ran to let John in, and then led him into the room where Maria and Rory were.

"Hi Rory," said John as he entered the room.

"Hi," said Rory, his eyes firmly on the TV.

He walked to where Rory was lying on the carpet and knelt down to ruffle his hair. "How are you going my little man?"

"Good."

"Okay. Are you pleased it's the holidays?"

"Yes."

"Well that's good," said John smiling. "Let's talk again real soon." He turned towards where Liv had sat back down and noticed Maria for the first time. "Oh, hi Maria, I didn't see you there. How are you?"

"Hi John, I'm really good thank you." Maria paused for a second, "and thank you very much for taking us today, it's really good of you." Maria had received strict instructions from her mum to say a big thank-you to John, and had decided to do it straight away in case she forgot later. But as soon as she'd done it she thought it was a bit too soon and felt her face starting to blush a little.

"Oh, that's fine. No worries at all." John leaned forward and added in a quiet conspiratorial voice, "Liv doesn't know it yet but she's going to owe me some big favours in the future."

"What's that? What did he say Maria?" asked Liv.

Maria was saved from responding by Liv's mum entering the room. She came straight over to John with her arms open. "Hey little brother you're here, it's good to see you."

"Hi big sis, it's good to see you too," he said as he stood to return the hug.

Maria smiled at the scene. Big sis was quite a bit shorter than little brother. In fact, it was hard to see any physical resemblance at all. Liv's mum was – how should she put it – quite round, and had short dark hair. While John was tall and very thin, and had long wavy blonde hair which he usually had in a ponytail. But one thing they definitely had in common was their happy personalities. Maria rarely saw either of them without a big warm smile on their face.

"Have you had breakfast yet?" asked Liv's mum. "Because if you haven't I'm very happy to make you something."

"Nah, I'm fine I had some fruit in the car on the way over," John glanced at Liv and Maria, and then added, "and I get the sense that the girls are keen to be on their way."

Maria wondered what made him say that as she couldn't recall anything being said, but she looked at Liv and saw that she was blushing. Ah, she must've said something to him at the front door about being late, Maria thought.

"Well okay," said Liv's mum, "but make sure you get a proper lunch. For you and them." Maria saw her pass John some money.

"Sure, sure," said John. "C'mon girls, let's get going. Bye Ror, have a good day."

John made a show of waiting for a response, but when none was forthcoming he started to turn towards the door.

"Rory, say goodbye to your Uncle John," said Liv's mum. "*Rory*. If you don't …" and she started to make a move towards the TV.

"Bye Uncle John," said Rory raising his right hand into the air, but still not taking his eyes off the screen.

"Hmm," said Liv's mum.

"Don't worry about it," said John smiling. "He's on holiday. Let him chill a bit."

"Hmm," said Liv's mum again.

Soon the three of them were in John's car and driving out of Liv's street. Liv was sat in the front alongside John, and Maria was sat directly behind her. Liv offered to take turns in the back, but Maria replied that she'd be very happy to sit there. While they'd been waiting in Liv's front room she'd started to get a strange feeling in her stomach, which she guessed was a mixture of nerves and excitement. Whatever it was she didn't feel much like making small talk right now, and anyway she knew that Liv and John would have lots to catch up on. Every so often Liv or John would ask her a question which of course she'd do her best to answer. But mostly she sat back and half-listened to the music that was playing quietly in the background, and thought again about how they should best use the day.

After they'd been driving for about an hour and a half John saw a sign for a service station and decided to pull in for a quick break. Maria didn't need the bathroom and so she walked over to the shop and went in to take a look around. A few minutes later John came in and asked Maria if she wanted a coffee – thought about it for a moment – and then asked if she wanted a hot chocolate. She thanked him but said she was fine.

While he was waiting for his coffee John came over to where Maria was standing and saw that she was checking out the maps.

"Hey, a map, now that would be a good idea. I was thinking about what I could do while you guys are in the museum, and was thinking about doing a bush walk, or maybe a cycle. Do you know if there's anywhere where you can hire a bike there?"

For a moment Maria was a little taken aback by John's assumption that they would be in the museum, but then remembered that Liv had told him that the main reason they wanted to go to Kangaroo Valley was to do some research for a school project. "Actually there is. In fact, I seem to remember there's one pretty much right beside the museum."

"Wow, that's handy," said John, smiling an even wider smile than he normally did.

Maria thought for a second, and then said, "You know, I'm pretty sure that you can also hire canoes there to go down the river. We didn't do it when we were there, but my dad has done it before and he said it's fantastic."

"Really, that sounds great. But I wonder how long it takes?" said John rubbing his chin. "I'm not sure how long I should leave you guys on your own."

Maria was about to say that they'd be fine when John heard his name called out indicating that his coffee was ready. As he walked over to get it, Liv came into the shop. Maria went over to meet her.

"Hey Liv, I was wondering, what you've said to John about what we'll be doing while we're in the valley?"

Liv thought for a second and then said, "Only what I told you before about us going to the museum to do some work on a school project. Why do you ask?"

"Well, he was talking just now about maybe hiring a bike to go for a ride while we're in the museum. Or maybe a canoe."

"Ahh," said Liv, "that could make things *interesting*."

Once Maria had realised that she wouldn't be looking for the location of a secret tribe or group of aborigines, she had thought a lot about what they should do while they were in the valley. She had wondered about going back to Pete's house to see if the old man would come to her there. But given it was the school holidays she felt certain that someone would be staying there. In the end she thought the best thing to do was to try and get to the place by the river that the old man had taken her to where she'd seen the girl. She'd discussed it with Liv, who had agreed that it was a good plan. But given that John was going to drop them at the museum they then had the problem of how to get there.

Maria had spent long hours looking at the map, and she was fairly certain that she knew where the spot was, well within a few hundred metres anyway. Unfortunately it was a long way from the museum, much too far to walk to and back in the couple of hours they would have on their own. And then Maria remembered that there were bikes for hire right beside the museum.

"Brilliant," said Liv. "We can easily get there and back on bikes."

"Hopefully," said Maria. She thought for a second and then said, "Do you think they'll let kids rent them without an adult there?"

"Hmm, good point, I don't know." Liv thought for a moment and then added, "But if we dress like we're proper cyclists, and I use my EFTPOS card then maybe they won't notice how young we are."

Maria nodded, "That might work." And then quietly added to herself, "It better work, otherwise we could be making a long trip for nothing."

Now in the service station shop Maria's mind raced as she thought about how John's plan might impact theirs. She'd just assumed that he'd go off somewhere in the car, maybe to a café or the pub. She wished now that she'd thought that through a bit more. But her thoughts were cut short when John re-joined them gingerly holding what was clearly a very hot coffee.

"Okay, everyone ready to get going?" he said opening the shop door. Maria and Liv nodded and followed him out. "I reckon it should be about another hour from here, so hopefully we'll be there around 11.00. Does that sound okay?"

"That's great," said Liv and Maria almost at the same time.

As they started driving along the highway again Maria felt a quite noticeable rise in the level of excitement and nerves flowing around her body. She realised that it had dissipated a bit whilst they were stopped at the service station and she'd been talking to John and Liv, but now it was back and stronger than ever. The only time she could recall feeling anything else like it was when she was warming up and waiting to go into her ballet exam. But, she thought, in that instance I knew that there was going to be an examiner waiting for me when I walked through the door. This time I can't be certain who or what will be waiting for me when I get into the valley.

About 45 minutes later they reached a T-junction which indicated that Kangaroo Valley was 17km to the left. As John made the turn Liv turned round and looked at Maria. She smiled kindly and mouthed, "You okay?"

Maria nodded uncertainly, mouthing back, "Kind of."

Liv then pulled a face at Maria, which caused Maria to let out a snort of laughter, which mostly came out through her nose. This caused Liv to burst out laughing, and a few moments later both of them were laughing uncontrollably.

"What is it? What is it?" asked John. "Did I miss something?"

But neither of the girls could respond. As soon as one of them seemed to be gaining some level of control, the other one would laugh and it would start all over again. After a few minutes they both had tears in their eyes, and were holding their stomachs.

"Stop it, stop it," pleaded Maria.

"It's not me, it's you," gasped Liv.

"It's clearly both of you," interjected John in a slightly exasperated voice, "and if you ask me, you're both nuts."

There was a very brief moment of silence as Maria and Liv looked each other and considered John's statement, and then they both let out a huge laugh and it started all over again.

Maria was so distracted by all this that she didn't notice at all when they started the long winding descent into the valley. During the laughing fit she had brought her feet up on to the seat and put her forehead on her knees, and so she wasn't really aware at all of what was going on outside of the car. And so it was almost with a jolt that she realised that the hairs on her arms were standing up and tingling, just as they had done when she'd arrived in the valley the previous time. And as if someone had flicked a switch all of the laughter instantaneously left her body.

It took a few seconds for Liv to notice that she was laughing on her own. She turned to look at Maria to see what was up with her, and could tell immediately from the look on her face that *it* was happening. She looked down towards Maria's lap and saw that she was gently stroking her right forearm. Liv looked back up into Maria's face and although Maria appeared to be looking straight at her, Liv realised that she was deep in thought and focused on a spot far off in the distance. She brought up her left hand up to get Maria's attention, and when she saw that Maria was looking at her she smiled and used her head to gesture at Maria's arms. Maria half-smiled back and nodded.

Chapter 27

As it had done before, the hair-standing sensation on Maria's arm only lasted for a short time, maybe 30 or 40 seconds. And a few minutes later they came to the end of the windy part of road and started the drive through the valley.

"Wow, it's amazing," said John. "No wonder you were so happy to come back Maria."

"Yeah, really amazing," said Liv as she swivelled in her seat trying to take it all in. "Where was it that you stayed Maria?"

Maria leaned forward and pointed between them. "The turn off is just up here on the left. Once you go past it you can see the house up on the hill. It's got the most fantastic views of the valley."

Liv sensed that Maria was a little nervous, but also quite excited about the prospect of seeing the house again. She leaned as far as she could round the seat and cupped her hand around the side of her mouth and then half-mouthed half-whispered, "Are you sure that you don't want to go up and take a look around?"

Maria shrugged her shoulders. Now that they were here she really wasn't certain what she should do. She briefly weighed up the options. Just as they passed the turn-off she decided that they should stick to their plan, and she smiled at Liv and nodded. She turned and looked out of the window to their left, but the car was now passing through a small patch of trees. Once it emerged Maria scanned the hills, and then pointed up and to her left. "That's the house up there."

Liv turned in her seat and looked out over the fields, but it took her a few seconds to see it. "I can't see ..." she started to say, but then changed it to, "Oh yes, I see it. Wow, it's bigger than I imagined it."

Maria didn't respond. She was looking out over the fields trying to see if she could recognise any part of the route that she'd walked with the old aboriginal man on her last night in the house. But everything looked so different in the daylight, and then the road veered to the right and took them away from fields that surrounded the house.

After a few minutes they came to a spot that Maria recognised very well, the sign outside the Barrengarry Store: 'The World's Best Pies'.

"Look at that," exclaimed John "this shop sells the world's best pies, and I'm as hungry as a very hungry man from Hungary. Are you two okay if we get an early lunch?" And before either Maria or Liv could reply he pulled the car over to the left and came to a stop.

"Did you come here before, Maria? Are the pies really that good?" John asked excitedly looking up into the rear view mirror so that he could see Maria's face. But without waiting for a reply John had opened the door to get out of the car.

John was already halfway across the road by the time Maria finally managed to say in a slow and very controlled manner, "Actually we did come here, John, and yes, the pies are pretty good." This caused Liv to burst out laughing. Maria felt that she was having a type of déjà vu as she remembered that her dad and Bobby had done almost exactly the same thing when they'd seen the sign.

259

"What is it with boys and pies?" she added, mostly to herself.

"I know what you mean. My dad loves them too," said Liv still chuckling at what Maria had said before. "Actually it would probably be a good idea to go and get something to eat too, that way we won't have to worry about it later."

"Good thinking," said Maria, and she opened the car door.

"I take it you got one of those feelings, you know on your arms, as we're coming into the valley?" asked Liv as they checked the road for traffic.

"Yep," said Maria with just a hint of a sigh as they started to cross.

"Oh, I thought you'd be pleased," said Liv. "Doesn't it mean that whatever happened to you before is going to happen to you again? Or at least there's a chance that it might? Which means that there's a chance you might find out what it's all about?"

They reached the steps leading up to the front door of the store, and Maria reached for the rail and then paused to look at Liv. "You're right, absolutely right. But …" she paused and looked up at the sky. After a moment she looked down again into Liv's eyes. "A big part of me is desperate to know what was happening to me. But there is also a small part that's not so keen. Or maybe it's a bit scared of what I, we, might find."

"I'm very pleased you changed that to 'we'," said Liv. "*We* are doing this together, and don't you forget it."

Maria leaned over to give Liv a hug and whispered, "Thank you, Liv, for being such a fantastic friend."

Just as she did John came back through the door of the store and called out, "Come on up you two. You've got to see these pies." And then, when he saw what it was they were doing, "And tell me, what *is* it with girls and hugging?" The girls laughed and turned to climb the stairs.

Twenty minutes later they were back in the car, and five minutes after that they slowed to turn into the car park of the Pioneer Museum. As they did Maria pointed out the bike and canoe hire place which was, as she'd remembered, pretty much next door to the museum. After John had parked they began to walk over to the office. They were about to go in when Maria suddenly stopped and turned to John.

"You know, John, I was thinking maybe it would be better if we came with you to the bike hire place first. That way we'll know what you're going to do, and … and maybe we could even get some bikes as well and, you know, meet you somewhere after we've finished doing our school stuff. Maybe we could even ride somewhere with you later on?"

John thought for a second, "Hmm, I don't see why not? Okay, let's do that." As he turned to head out of the car park Maria and Liv exchanged an excited look, and Liv lifted the thumb of her right hand to indicate that she liked Maria's work.

It was pretty busy in the hire shop, which Maria surmised was because of the school holidays. As they waited to be served John looked around the shop at all the bike and canoe equipment, pointing out what he thought was the good stuff. He was clearly looking forward to doing something active while they were in the museum, which Maria felt good about. It was so nice of him to bring them here, she thought, I really hope he has a good time.

John decided to join in with a group who were just leaving to canoe down the Kangaroo River. Initially he was a bit unsure about being away for four hours but the girls assured him that they would be fine. They would probably be in the museum for a couple of hours, then could either walk or cycle into the village and look around the shops while they waited for John to return. The person serving them helped the girl's cause no end by informing John that there was a cycle track that ran from where they were all the way into the village, and so they wouldn't have to go on the main road at all. As Liv pointed out with a big grin on her face, that would also mean that they could spend less time walking and more time in the shops. On that basis John used a credit card to pay for his canoe trip and two half-day bike hires for the girls. The three of them then moved outside, and John double checked the plan with the girls.

"So, girls, they reckon my canoe trip will last about four hours and it'll take about fifteen minutes to get back here in the van. Which means I should be back here at the shop at around four thirty," he added looking at his watch. "And so that means you need to start cycling back from the village at about four o'clock, okay?" Both of the girls nodded furiously.

"Yes, yes, no problem," said Liv.

"We'll definitely be back here by four thirty," said Maria looking at her own watch.

John looked at them a little uncertainly, but he could see how excited they were at having the afternoon to themselves. After a moment he nodded, then went over to join his group to help them load their canoes on to the trailer. The girls looked at each other, their eyes wide with excitement. They both knew that things couldn't possibly have worked out any better than this. Without saying anything they turned and started to wheel their bikes towards the museum. Once they got to the office they leaned their bikes against the wall close to the door and took off their helmets.

"So, how long do you think it'll be before they're on their way?" asked Liv using her thumb to indicate that she was referring to John and the rest of the canoeists.

"Oh, just a few minutes, I think they were almost ready to go before John decided to join them. But that's okay, because there's something I want to do before we get going. Come on, we're going in here." Maria turned to walk into the office. Liv wasn't expecting this at all and it took a moment for her to register that Maria had literally disappeared from in front of her. But she quickly hung her helmet on the handlebars of her bike and hurried to catch up with her.

Maria walked into the office hoping to see the same person she had talked to on her last visit a few weeks before. That way he might recognise her, which would maybe make this a bit easier to explain. But instead of the man there was a woman, who looked about the same age as her mum. In fact, she even looked a bit like her mum. Maria suddenly felt quite nervous about what she was about to do.

When she realised that Maria was there she looked up and immediately gave Maria a big smile. "Hi there, what can I do for you?" she asked in a helpful voice.

She seems very nice thought Maria relaxing a bit. "Ah yes, hello, my name is Maria. And this is my friend Olivia," who had just arrived by Maria's side. "The thing is, a few weeks ago my family came to see the museum, and the man who was in the office then let me and my dad go into one of the rooms down there to look at the collection of photographs that you have. I, actually we, have been doing a project at school about what it was like for the aboriginals when the white settlers arrived." The women nodded. And she was still smiling, and so Maria decided to press on. "Anyway, there were some really amazing photographs, some of them taken way back in the 1800s, and so I was

263

hoping it would be okay for me to show them to Liv? It'll only take a few minutes."

"Of course, of course," said the woman standing up and opening a drawer. "You know, I loved history at school, but I don't think it gets much of a look in nowadays, what with all the science and computers and technical stuff that they do." She turned and held up a bunch of keys, "Here they are." She started to walk around the counter, "It's so good to come across some young people who have an interest in their history … their heritage. Come on follow me. It's this way." She'd only made it as far as the doorway when she paused and then stopped to turn and face Maria and Liv, "But of course you already knew that, didn't you?"

Her sudden stop and turn meant that Maria also had to come to a sudden halt, and Liv ended up walking into the back of her. Maria just smiled and nodded back at the woman. She's nice, thought Maria, but also a little odd.

When they reached the room the woman unlocked the door holding it open for Maria and Liv. They both said thank you as they went passed her, and Maria headed straight for the corner of the table where she'd found the oldest photos on her previous visit.

"Well, you seem to know what you're doing," said the woman smiling again. "I think I can hear someone else coming into the office, so do you mind if I leave you to it?"

"No, of course not, that would be fine" said Maria immediately. "We will only be a few minutes. Would you like us to close or lock the door when we're finished?"

"Oh that's so nice of you to ask. But don't worry, I can do all that later. Have fun," and with that she turned and headed back up the corridor to the office.

"I don't remember you mentioning this part of the plan to me before," said Liv as soon as she was sure that the woman was out of earshot.

"Well that's because it's only been part of the plan for about five minutes," replied Maria as she turned to look at Liv. "I was thinking that we should at least appear to come into the office in case for some reason John didn't leave straight away. And then I just had the idea of showing you the photo with the old man on it."

"Wow, yes, good idea," said Liv, clearly pretty excited at seeing one of the key elements in Maria's mysterious weekend. "Which box was it in? Can you remember?"

"I'm pretty sure it was this one," answered Maria, tapping the box right in front of her. And she started to flick through the photos. She got about half-way through them without finding the one she was looking for when a thought started to form and then nag away in her brain. All of a sudden she stopped and said, "Hang on, I think I might be looking in the wrong place."

To Liv's surprise she moved back and got down on to her knees. And then she put her head on the ground so that she could see under the shelf that was attached to the legs of the table.

"Aha, when I said it's in that box, what I obviously meant to say was it's under the table," and Maria reached an arm out under the table and very carefully brought out the photograph. She passed it up to Liv to take while she stood up, and then stood beside her as they both examined it in silence.

Maria looked into the face of the old man furthest to the right of the group in the photograph, and remembered how shocked she'd been the first time she'd seen it. For an instant she thought that her knees were going to start buckling again, but then Liv raised her hand and pointed at him, "Is that the man you saw at the house?" Maria was just about to respond when Liv added, "And then went for a midnight stroll with?"

Maria couldn't help but laugh and suddenly her knees felt a lot stronger. Not for the first time today she was *very* pleased that Liv was here with her. "Yes, that's him," she said with a chuckle.

Liv scanned the photo for a few seconds longer and then said, "Well, if we're going to find him, whoever, or whatever he is, we'd better get going, eh?"

"You're right," replied Maria. "John should be well on his way by now." She took the photo off Liv and went to take her back pack off her shoulder, but then stopped.

"What are you thinking?" asked Liv. But then she guessed. "You're wondering about taking it, aren't you?"

"Hmm," was all Maria could manage in response.

"Why on earth do you need to do that? You did bring your iPod with you, didn't you?"

"Umm, yes, yes of course I did, why?" said Maria still not catching on.

"Well, why don't you, we, just take a photo of the photo? Here, let me help you get that off," and she slipped the bag off of Maria's shoulder.

Two minutes later they were walking back along the corridor towards the office, with Maria feeling a lot less guilty than she had expected to be. The woman who'd helped them earlier wasn't anywhere to be seen, and so Maria scribbled a quick, 'Thank you from Maria and Olivia' on the back of a brochure and left it on the counter, and the two of them headed for their bikes.

***

After spending so many hours studying the map, Maria had developed a pretty good knowledge of the layout of the valley. And so she instinctively knew that they should turn left out of the gate of the museum and follow the main road back the way they had come into the valley for about half a kilometre. And she also knew that there was a bike path on the other side of the road that would take them all the way to the turn-off they would need to take. They pushed their bikes across the main road, put on their helmets and started off along the path.

They both had bikes of their own at home, so it didn't take them long to feel comfortable on the hire bikes, and they covered the distance to the turn-off very quickly. As they approached it Maria shouted over her shoulder that this is where they would turn right, and she heard Liv shout back, "Okay!"

The bike path carried on along the main road but not along this side road and so Maria headed over to the left side of the road and then stopped to make sure that Liv was right behind her. She looked out along the road, and couldn't see any cars or other cyclists. It seemed very quiet which she was happy about. Maria was pretty sure that this road didn't join up with any other main road, and guessed that the only people driving along it would be people who lived here or were staying in the farms and houses in this part of the valley.

She turned round and saw that Liv was right behind her, and that she had a big smile on her face. "You ready to go?" asked Maria.

"Girl, I was born ready," said Liv in the best American accent that she could manage.

Maria laughed and responded with, "Okay then, let's *go.*" And she pushed off and started to pedal. However, the road very quickly started to slope downwards and after a few pedals she allowed herself to coast down the hill. It seemed like the valley walls were all around her, and that they were approaching the very centre of the valley. Maria didn't know if that was true or not, but it somehow made the valley look and feel even more special.

The road flattened out and they had to start pedalling again. After they'd gone about another kilometre Maria noticed that they were approaching a bridge across a river. Maria was pretty sure that this was the river that she'd refused to cross *that* night, though the actual point was some way upstream to the left. She hoped that soon after the bridge the road would turn quite sharply to the left, and then they'd come to the start of a track or path that would allow them to get pretty close to the actual spot. As they crossed the bridge Maria looked down at the water. It didn't seem that deep or wide and she wondered why she'd been so reluctant to cross it; but then again it had been the middle of the night and very difficult to gauge the depth. *And* she'd only been wearing her pyjamas.

As these thoughts bounced around in her brain, Maria started to feel the hairs on her arms and the back of her neck stand-up and tingle. By the time she reached the road on the other side of the bridge it was already way past what she usually experienced and she could feel a shiver developing in her lower back. This was different … No, she had experienced this before, in the garden at the pub in the village. She quickly brought her bike to a stop and half-stepped, half-leapt off it. Liv wasn't expecting this at all and slammed on her brakes, which caused her to skid in the loose gravel that lay on the side of the road and then into the back of Maria's bike. She opened her mouth, about to request a bit more notice of Maria's intention to stop, but when she saw what was happening to Maria she quickly closed it again.

Maria was kneeling and the top half of her body, her arms, shoulders and head were all shaking uncontrollably. It was as if she'd suddenly been caught in severe blizzard and was very cold. But there was no way she could be cold. It was a beautifully sunny day, and there wasn't a cloud in the sky. In fact, even after the few kilometres they'd cycled to get here, Liv was already feeling quite hot and a bit sweaty.

"Hey, Maria, what's going on? Are you okay?" shouted Liv, and she rushed over and placed her hand on Maria's shoulder.

"Yes, yes," replied Maria as she fell forward and placed her hands on the ground in front of her, "or at least I will be when this has passed. Shouldn't be too long now."

Liv scanned her brain trying to remember everything that Maria had told her about what happened to her before. Then it came to her, "Aha, is this the same thing that happened to you in the pub garden?"

"Very similar," said Maria. And after a few seconds she added, "I think it's starting to ease a bit." She pushed herself back up into kneeling position and looked at Liv.

To Liv's surprise a smile had formed on Maria's face, and she asked, "Why are you smiling? That didn't look at all nice."

"Well, for one it doesn't actually hurt at all. And, as well as that, I think that it means that we're heading in the right direction. And so I'm taking it as a good sign." Maria paused for a second and looked back over her left shoulder. "You see that river we just crossed? I'm certain it's the one that I wouldn't go across for the old man that night." She looked back at Liv and saw that she was nodding. "The more I think about it the more sure I am that all these strange feelings I'm getting, in my arms and neck and my back, are somehow connected to him and the girl. I just don't know how or why."

"Well, that's what we're here to find out," said Liv in her most positive voice. "Do you think you're okay to get back on the bike?"

"Yes, I think so," replied Maria, and she got up and walked over to her bike. As she picked it up she realised that the sensation hadn't completely left the hairs on her arms or the back of her neck. That's a bit different from what normally happens, she thought to herself, whatever normal is. They started along the road again, and after they'd gone up a small hill the road turned to the left, just as Maria had hoped it would. "Not too much further to go now," she called over her right shoulder. And she heard Liv shout out "okay" from behind her.

Two or three minutes later Maria saw a turn off to the left up ahead of them. As they approached she saw that it wasn't a proper road, it was a dirt one, and pretty bumpy looking too.

Maria stopped and waited for Liv to come up beside her. "This is it. We go up there, and over that hill," and she pointed out to her left.

"Cool, looks like a fun ride too," said Liv excitedly. And she pushed off so that she was now in front of Maria. "Race you to the top of the hill," she said grinning back at Maria.

By the time they'd gone over the brow of the hill they were breathing a lot more heavily and were red in the face. As a result, it was a relief to be able to coast down the other side. After about 300 metres the road turned sharply to the right and Maria realised that this was probably the closest to the river they'd be able to get on their bikes.

Maria slowed down as she reached the point of the bend and put one foot on the ground. "I'm pretty sure that's where we need to go," she said pointing across and down a large field to a group of trees. "We should get off here and leave the bikes by the fence."

"Are you sure that's the place?" asked Liv.

"Pretty sure, but I'll have a quick look at the map." Maria had studied the map so closely that she could probably draw it from memory, but she thought it wouldn't hurt to double check. She took it out of her backpack and opened it on the grass beside the road. She traced the route they'd taken from the Pioneer Museum to where they now were with her finger, and it ended up very close to the boldest cross and circle on the map.

"Well, if I'm right about where the old man took me, then we've got about one centimetre left to go," she said folding up the map, and then pointing again at the trees across the field.

"Okay, let's do it," said Liv, and she wheeled her bike over to the fence and leant it against a post.

Maria did the same, and then they walked to the gate and climbed over together. As they walked across the field Maria gently rubbed the hairs on her forearm. The sensation normally went away completely, but this time it was definitely lingering and, if anything, Maria thought it was very gradually getting stronger. Surely it had to mean something, but what?

After walking for about five minutes they reached the edge of the trees. They were quite thick and underneath their branches and leaves the air immediately felt a lot cooler. The ground also changed, the lush grass of the field becoming a mix of leaves, twigs and ferns. And every so often there were rocky patches. As the ground started to slope slightly downwards they both heard the sound of running water, and within thirty seconds they could see the river passing by in front of them at the bottom of a much steeper slope.

"Well," said Liv, "does this look like the spot?"

"Um, it certainly looks and feels very familiar. But I don't think it's the actual spot." Maria closed her eyes and did her best to recall some details that would help her recognise the place again. "I would have been on the other side, of course, because we came from the house, which is up over there somewhere," and she pointed vaguely up and to her left. "And when I looked across the river and saw the girl she was standing on this side in some bushes on what looked like quite a flat bit of ground." Both Maria and Liv looked down and along their side of the river.

"Not much flat stuff along this stretch," said Liv, and Maria nodded.

"Let's walk along this way," said Maria, and she started to walk to their right. After about 75 metres the bank on their side of the river did seem to flatten out a bit, and so they headed down to it.

As they did Maria felt the tingle in the hairs on her arm and on the back of her neck grow in intensity very slightly. She wondered for the first time if it was some sort of indicator, or sonar mechanism a bit like the one bats used to fly at night. But once again she just felt as if a possible answer only seemed to lead to another question, an indicator of what?

When they reached the bank Maria stopped and looked around. "I think this is the spot," she said. "Yes, I'm sure of it. That's where I stood with the old man." She pointed to a spot about 15 metres away across the river, "And this is where the girl was, standing in these bushes here." Maria walked over to a waist high clump of bushes. Liv came across and they both had a look around and under them, but neither of them found anything to indicate that anyone had been in or near them anytime recently.

After they'd stopped looking, they stood in silence for a while. They were both thinking the same thing, but it was Liv who finally voiced the thought.

"So, *what* do we do now?"

"I don't know," Maria responded a little despondently. "I guess … I guess I thought that if we made the effort to get here then they, or one of them at least, would come to meet us. So maybe we should just wait here a while and see what happens."

"That sounds good to me," said Liv, as she sat down on a mossy patch of ground. "I'm actually feeling pretty tired after that ride. And we did get up very early considering it's the first day of the holidays." She paused for a while and then asked, "How do you think they'd know that you're here?"

"Hmm, I don't really know how. And don't ask me why, but I'm actually really sure that somehow they do know." Maria decided that she was feeling pretty tired too and sat down on another mossy patch a couple of metres away from Liv. "After all," she went on "*he* came to me last time, and that was after I'd had the hair-standing feeling on the way into the valley, just like I did today."

"Well, I'm very happy to wait a while," said Liv. "In fact I might even close my eyes. I'm suddenly feeling *very* tired," and she laid back and put her head on her hands. She was silent for a few seconds, and then added, "You know, when you think about it, every time the old aboriginal man came to see you it was after you'd been asleep. Maybe you should give that a try now."

Maria thought about it. There was still a small part of her that wondered if it could all have been a dream, and that she'd never woken up at all. But a much bigger part didn't think that and, if it was the case that she'd been asleep before each occasion that the man had visited her, then what Liv had just suggested actually made a lot of sense.

"You know what Liv, I think that's one of your better ideas, I'm going to give it a go."

"Hmm, thanks for that," said Liv in a very drowsy voice.

"But I am bit worried about us sleeping for too long." Maria looked at her watch and more to herself than to Liv, who was clearly nearly asleep already, she said, "It's just gone half past one, so I'm going to set the alarm on my iPod for two thirty." That will give us some time to decide what we do next, she thought to herself, and still get back to the shop by four thirty.

"Sounds good," said Liv very quietly.

Maria finished setting the alarm and placed the iPod on a small rock just beside her. Then she laid back, putting her head on her back pack. I am feeling quite tired, she thought, and so I should be able to go to sleep pretty quickly. Five minutes later she decided that her water bottle was making the backpack very uncomfortable and so she sat up to take it out. She lay back down and convinced herself that it was much better now and that she would be asleep in a few moments. Ten minutes later she still wasn't asleep. To make matters worse Liv had started to make a sort of purring noise. She considered getting up to give her a little shake, but then decided that wasn't very fair, she'd obviously been very tired and needed to sleep for a while.

The more she thought about trying to get to sleep the more anxious she became, and in the end she felt like she was more awake than she had been when she'd sat down. At two fifteen Maria knew that it just wasn't going to happen, and so she decided to get up and take a better look around before the alarm went off.

Maria walked past the bushes where the girl had stood glancing at the ground as she went to see if they'd missed anything during their earlier search. But she saw nothing new, and so continued on and started to walk up a small bank. At the top she looked down into a small gulley that was filled with bushes. She was about to turn and go back when she thought she saw what appeared to be a greyish brown rock move ever so slightly. She blinked and refocussed on it. It shuddered, and she was so surprised that she let out a short sharp shriek. This caused the rock to unfurl itself, and Maria realised that she'd disturbed a large kangaroo sleeping in the leaves under one of the bushes. It quickly got up on to its feet and stared up at Maria.

Maria had never been this close to a kangaroo before, and she couldn't believe how big this one was. For a few moments the two of them just stared at each other. Maria could feel her heart thumping in her chest. Then the kangaroo gave the very slightest impression that it was going to move to its left and Maria decided that if it was going to go that way she would give it plenty of space, and so she started to take a pace to her left. The kangaroo immediately started to bounce up the hill out of the gulley, but not as far to her right as Maria was expecting or hoping. She took a couple of very quick steps further to her left, but on the second one Maria felt her left foot come down on a hard curved surface, which immediately rolled away from under her. She could do nothing to stop herself falling, and the combination of her momentum and the slope caused her to roll over several times. She realised that she was about to roll under one of the bushes when she felt the back of her head hit something solid. She was just vaguely aware of a piercing pain in her head and a flash of light passing it front of her eyes, and then everything went black.

Chapter 28

Liv woke up but didn't open her eyes. She could hear someone saying, no singing, "get up, get up, get up" over and over again. Is that Maria she thought to herself? But after a few seconds she decided that it was a song from an iPod, and when the get ups changed to 'put your hands up to the sound' she realised that she was listening to 'Party Rock Anthem'. Why on earth has she put that on? Not very appropriate for the surroundings, not at all.

"Maria, what are you doing? Turn that music off," she said without opening her eyes.

As the music didn't turn off, and she didn't hear any response from Maria, Liv decided it was time to open her eyes. She turned her head to the left and saw Maria's backpack, and her iPod sitting on a rock, but no Maria. Great, she thought to herself, she's gone off for a wee and left the music for me. Liv pushed herself up so that her head was resting on her hand and her elbow was on the mossy patch that her head had been on. For a while she stared out across the river and eventually started to sing along to the song.

When it finished she got up, turned the iPod off and then did a quick scan around to see if she could see where Maria had gone. She couldn't see her anywhere and so called out, "Maria, Mariaaa, where are you?" She did a complete 360 degree turn to see if her call had caused

Maria to stand up or start heading back, but again there was no sign of her. Liv walked over to the river and looked up and down the bank, nothing. Maybe she decided to go across the river to have a look around on the other side, Liv thought. She looked down, the river didn't look that deep here, maybe thirty centimetres here on the side, possibly fifty centimetres at some points in the middle. She could have done it, but she would've taken her runners off and I can't see them ... But maybe she carried them over to put on when she got to the other side. Liv walked along the bank to her left and called out, "Maria, are you there? Maria, *Mariaaaa*."

After walking up and down the bank and calling out for a minute or so, Liv suddenly experienced that feeling you get when curiosity and mild annoyance turn into a bit of panic. She stood still and listened, but apart from the sound of the water and the odd bird chirp she couldn't hear anything. What's going on, she thought? And then she had it, she's hiding and is going to jump out any second. She's definitely watched too many prank shows. "Okay, Maria, that's enough. You got me, I'm freaked. Maria, Maria, you win, I'm officially freaked. Come out now. Pleeease, come out now."

Liv turned and ran up the bank that Maria had gone up about twenty or so minutes earlier. From the top she looked into and around the gulley. She saw lots of bushes and rocks, and without knowing it her line of sight passed right over the bush under which Maria was lying. From there she moved along the top of the bank to her right, peering between the trees and hoping that she would spot Maria walking around somewhere out there. Through the trees she could now see the grass of the field that they'd walked across to get to the river. I wonder if she's gone back to the bikes for some reason, Liv thought to herself. Liv couldn't think of a reason why she would do that, but she was beginning to feel a bit desperate, and decided that she would go back through the trees to the edge of the field if only to rule it out. She started to walk away from the river, and after a few metres her brisk walk changed into a jog, and so it only took her a couple of minutes to reach the field. As she emerged from the dark of the trees into the sunlight she momentarily couldn't see anything and had to bring up her hand to shield her eyes. Once her eyes had adjusted she looked out across the field, and was able to just make out the saddles and handlebars of the two bikes still leaning against the fence. But that was all.

She stood silently for a few moments wondering what she should do next. Eventually she decided that she should go back and wait at the spot beside the river. Maria's probably gone off for a walk and just lost track of time. When she realises what the time is, she'll come straight back to there. And anyway both of the backpacks are there, and so I need to get them before I think about doing anything else.

She walked slowly back to the river, constantly scanning to her right and left, hoping she would catch sight of Maria returning from wherever she'd been. Once she reached the backpacks, she immediately picked-up the iPod and put it in Maria's backpack. And then she walked over to her backpack and sat down. She glanced at her watch, it was almost three o'clock. She reckoned that it had taken them about forty minutes to get from the Museum to here, cycling then walking. And so, she calculated, Maria would need to get back by quarter to four if they were going to make it back to the shop in time to meet John.

Liv leaned forward and put her forehead on her knees. She realised that she was breathing very fast and that her heart was racing. She took a few deep breaths to try and calm herself. That helped a lot, and she tried to think more rationally about what was happening, and what she should do if Maria didn't come back. Quite suddenly she had the thought that maybe her suggestion had worked, and after she'd fallen asleep the old man or the girl, or both of them, had come to Maria. And then they had gone off somewhere. Yes, that's probably what's happened. Though, if that was the case, I'd have expected Maria to wake me up, or at least find a way to let me know what was going on. This caused her to look around to see if there was something obvious that she'd missed, like a note stuck to a tree, but as before she saw nothing unusual.

For the next thirty minutes Liv's thoughts raced exploring lots of similar 'what if' questions. Unfortunately, all of the answers led to more questions. She stood up a few times to walk about in an attempt to control the nerves that were slowly but surely building inside her. When she looked at her watch and saw that it was now past three thirty she started to feel really anxious, and to wonder about what was the absolute latest time she could leave and still get back to meet John. And then what could she possibly to say to John?

"Hey John, hope you had a good canoe?" she said out loud in the general direction of the river. "Me and Liv decided to go out into the fields instead of the village and, what do you know, while we were there I lost Maria. But I'm sure she's okay because I'm pretty certain she's hanging out with a two hundred year old aboriginal man and a small aboriginal girl that she met in one of her dreams." Liv half smiled to herself, thinking about how Maria would have responded if she'd been around to hear her speech.

A few minutes later Liv stood up again having decided that she would take one more look around before heading back to the bikes. She picked up her backpack, and then wondered about what she should do with Maria's. Her first instinct was to take it with her, but then she wondered what Maria might need if she came back say a few minutes after Liv had gone. She looked in the backpack and decided that she would transfer the valuable stuff, the iPod and Maria's purse, to her backpack, and then leave Maria's backpack with the bottle of water and the rest of her stuff here. She walked one more time along the river bank, about fifty metres to the left and then the same to the right before clambering up the bank for one more look around the gulley. As she feared would be the case she saw nothing new, and dejectedly turned and headed back towards the fields and the bikes.

As she climbed back on to her bike Liv took one more look across the field towards the trees hoping desperately that she'd suddenly see Maria running across the grass towards her. When she didn't appear Liv felt tears form in her eyes. Although extremely worried about leaving Maria behind, if she was completely honest with herself she knew it was probably more to do with the fact she was going to have to face John and explain what had happened all by herself. And that thought was making her feel very anxious, possibly more anxious than she'd been about anything in her whole life.

Liv had very little awareness of the cycle back to the shop and museum. One part of her brain had switched her auto-pilot on, and all the other parts kept going over and over what she'd say to John when she saw him. However, as she approached the shop she did look up and she was shocked to see the van and the trailer with all the canoes loaded on it was already back in front of the shop. She twisted her wrist to see what time it was on her watch, and saw that it was four twenty.

"Damn, they're back early," she said to herself. But then, as she came to a halt and got off the bike, she did think that in the circumstances it was probably better that they had arrived early rather than been delayed for some reason. She knew that they were going to have to go back out to the field and the river, and she could sense that the sun was starting to get pretty low in the sky, which meant it would be dark in an hour or so. She used her sleeve to wipe the tears away from her eyes and then pushed the bike across the road. Just as she got to the other side she spotted John coming out of the shop.

He had a huge smile on his face, and he came straight over to Liv and said, "Wow, that was so great. I'm so glad I did the long one, thanks for talking me into it."

"Hey, no worries, I'm really pleased you enjoyed it," said Liv, doing her very best to keep her voice steady.

"So, how was your afternoon? Did you manage to get all your school stuff done? And how were the shops?" John paused and looked over and behind Liv and then added, "By the way, where's Maria?"

Liv opened her mouth to reply, but was sure that the words weren't going to come out in anything like a steady way. She felt huge tears form in her eyes and her shoulders heave upwards, and from that point she knew wasn't going to be able to control it any longer. She let go of the bike, which fell sideways to the ground, and then ran forward and put her arms around John's waist and buried her face into his chest.

John hugged her back for a few seconds and then he put his hands on Liv's shoulders and pushed her back a bit so that he could look at her face. He was already starting to have one of those terrible feelings you get inside when you know you're about to be told something really bad.

"Hey Liv, what is it? What's the matter?"

But Liv was sobbing so hugely that she couldn't catch enough breath to get any words out. John put his arm around her shoulder and led her away from the roadside, and sat her down on a bench outside the shop.

"Okay Liv, try and take some deep breaths and calm down a bit," he said and showed her what he wanted her to do. Liv did her best to copy him, and she did start to get her sobbing under control. "That's good Liv, really good. Now try and tell me about what's happened. Is it something to do with Maria?"

Liv nodded.

"Is she hurt?" asked John.

Liv thought for a second and then shook her head. She took one more really deep breath in, and once she'd exhaled she said, "Actually I don't know if she's hurt, because I don't know where she is."

"*What?*" exclaimed John. "What do you mean by that?"

Liv took another couple of deep breaths and then said, "Look, I know you're going to be really angry with us, I would be if I was you." She paused, no matter how upset she was right now, she knew how important it was to get the next few sentences right. "After we went to the museum, instead of going to the village, it was such a nice day, that we decided to go for a cycle out into the valley." Liv looked at John hoping he would nod or give her some positive energy, but he stayed completely still with a very serious look on his face. She looked down again and went on, "Anyway we cycled for about half an hour over that way, and we found this beautiful spot beside a river. And it was hot, and we were both tired, and so we decided to have a little sleep. Maria was worried that we wouldn't wake up in time to get back to meet with you and so she set the alarm on her iPod. When it went off I woke up, but Maria wasn't there." Liv shook her head and looked back up at John. "Her backpack and her iPod were there, but she wasn't. I looked all around but I couldn't find her anywhere. I waited as long as I could to see if she came back, but she didn't." As she said this, tears welled up in her eyes again. "I'm so sorry John, I really am." And she used her sleeve to wipe away the tears. Then she sat silently with her head down looking at her knees.

John was also silent for a few seconds, obviously thinking about what they should do next. He wondered if they should call the police straight away, but if all that Maria had done was go for a walk and lost track of time, and was cycling back at this very moment, then it'd cause an awful lot of fuss for nothing.

"Look, Liv, I'm going to ask you some questions, and you need to be completely honest with me, alright?" Liv nodded. "Do you know how deep the water was in the river where you were?"

Liv felt very comfortable answering this one, "Oh, I checked that, because I thought she might have gone across to the other side to …" She paused thinking about what she ought to say and what she ought not. "To look around," she added. "And the water was only this deep," putting her hand out about thirty to forty centimetres above the ground.

"And was it moving very fast?" John asked. "What I mean is, if she had tried to go across do you think she could have been knocked over or anything like that?"

"No, no, definitely not. It was hardly moving it all. Honestly." Liv said nodding.

"Okay, well that's one good thing at least," said John trying to smile but not really managing it. "The other thing I want to know is did you see anyone while you were going there, or when you were coming back that looked at all … you know, odd, or somehow out of place?"

For a second Liv was taken aback wondering if John had somehow known or worked out something about the old aboriginal man or the aboriginal girl. She was almost certain that he couldn't know, but she thought she should try to check. "Why do you ask that? What do you mean by odd or … out of place?"

A very serious look came on to John's face, "Well Liv, as awful as it is to contemplate, and I'm sure you know this by now, there are some not very nice people in this world, and I'm just hoping that Maria hasn't been, you know, taken away by one of them."

"Oh, I see," said Liv, partly relieved, but suddenly quite scared for Maria.

Her thoughts started to race, and John could see it in her eyes. He put his hand on her shoulder and asked her again, "Well, did you see anyone or anything unusual?"

"Oh, um, er, actually now that you mention it, it was really quiet. We hardly saw anyone at all. Maybe just one, no two cars passed us when we cycled out, and they were both driving towards us. Away from where we were going," Liv clarified, a bit unnecessarily.

"And how about on the way back?" John asked, "Did you see anything then?"

"Hmm, I don't think so, but …" she said and then paused.

"But?"

"Well, to be honest, I was so upset that I don't really remember much about the cycle back at all."

John nodded and put his hand on his chin, and then rubbed it anxiously. And then he sighed and stood up. "I'm really not sure what I should be doing here. I probably should be calling the police, or maybe even letting Maria's parents know what's going on. But if Maria comes cycling down the road in five minutes I will have caused an enormous amount of fuss for nothing. And your mum would probably never let me near you or Rory ever again." He looked down at Liv, "What I'm going to suggest we do first is drive out to the spot and take a good look around together. We've probably got about an hour of daylight left – if we don't find her in that time then we will definitely have to report it to someone."

He paused as if to let Liv respond, but before she could he said, "Okay, let's get going, we've got no time to waste. You take the bike back in the shop and tell them we'll be bringing the other one back very soon. Say … say the chain came off and we're just going to pick it up. And I'll go and get the car and I'll pick you up right here, okay?" and he pointed down to the spot at his feet in a manner which suggested Liv should be standing exactly there when the car stopped, or he would not be best pleased.

"Yes," said Liv quickly, and she jumped up and went over to get the bike.

Three minutes later they were driving out along the main road. Liv could see that John was extremely tense, as he was holding the wheel very tightly and sitting very upright in his seat, looking left and right as they went. When they got to the turn-off Liv indicated that they should turn right, and after that she didn't speak again until they got to the turn-off to the track. When she said that they needed to go left she saw John glance at her as if to say why on earth did you go down here, but he said nothing. A minute or so later they reached the turn in the road and they saw Maria's bike still leaning against the fence just as it had been when Liv had headed back.

They got out and Liv pointed out across the field to the trees and said, "That's where we went, over to those trees."

John nodded and said, "Okay, let's go." As they walked he looked to his left and saw that Liv's eyes were full of tears, and he realised that his anxiety and silence was probably not helping her very much. He thought about what he could say, what he should say, and ended up with, "You know, I'm sure everything will be fine, she probably just went for a walk and got lost." He tried smiling as he said it, but he really wasn't up to that.

But Liv really appreciated the effort and took hold of his hand, "I am so glad you're here Uncle John. I mean I know you probably would rather be anywhere else right now, but I'm really glad that it's you here with me." She smiled at him, and this time he was able to smile back and he gave her hand a big squeeze.

285

Once they'd crossed the field Liv led John through the trees and along the side of the river until they reached the spot where she and Liv had last seen each other. Maria's backpack was still sitting where Liv had put it down after removing Maria's purse and iPod. John asked Liv to show him exactly where the two of them had slept, and then where she'd already looked for Maria. All this took about fifteen minutes, and at the end of it John stood beside Maria's backpack and scratched his head.

"This is very odd," he said looking down at the backpack. "The fact that her bag and her bike are still here suggest that she's not come back from wherever she went." He looked up and out over the river, "And I agree with you, even if she had crossed the river I don't think she could have got into any trouble in the water. It's just not deep or fast enough. And I really don't see how she could have got so lost around here that she wouldn't have found her way back by now." He paused and put his hands on his head.

"So what do you think might have happened?" asked Liv as she sat down on a rock.

John let out a long breath though his teeth and then said, "Well, I can think of two possible things, but unfortunately neither of them is very good. Either she's headed off somewhere and got into trouble, maybe twisted her ankle, or worse. Or … or she's been taken away by someone," John said in a very grave voice. He paused for a moment as if to compose himself and then went on.

"And so given that I don't think we should spend any more time here, we need to go and report this. *And* we need to let Maria's parents and your parents know what's happened." He glanced at his watch, it was five twenty. "I told your mum that we'd call her when we started back, and so they're probably already wondering why they haven't heard from us." He took his mobile phone out of his pocket, "Damn, no signal. We need to go back to the shop."

"Oh, do you think we have to? I mean can't we wait a bit longer?" asked Liv. "She might still come back before it gets dark. And then we can call my mum to tell her that we're on our way." Although she was obviously worried about what might have happened to Maria, Liv was beginning to feel very anxious about the prospect of talking to the police and, even worse, their parents. In her mind there was a very real alternative explanation for what had happened to Maria, but how much of that should she or, indeed, could she tell John or any of them about? At best they'd probably think she was losing it because her best friend was missing.

And then again how could she be sure that it was in some way related to what had happened to Maria before? Maybe John was right. What if Maria was in trouble and they just sat around here doing nothing. How bad would she feel then knowing that she hadn't done something quicker?

Liv looked up at John and saw that he was reconsidering what they should do, and at that moment she decided that it was time to help him out. "Forget what I just said John," she said as she stood up. "You're right, we should go now." And then she went over to Maria's backpack, picked it up and without turning she started to walk purposefully away from the river.

Chapter 29

At about the time Liv and John were getting into the car to drive back to the village, Maria opened her eyes and stared at a large leaf that was on the ground about twenty centimetres away from her nose. She was lying on her side with her head half-resting on the upper part of her left arm. After a few seconds she realised that the leaf was only one of many, in fact hundreds that were strewn all around her, and she thought this is not my bedroom.

Maria tried hard to remember where she was and how she'd got here. When nothing was immediately forthcoming she rolled her eyes around to her right and saw that there were more leaves, and twigs, above her, and through them she could see the sky. So I'm outside she thought to herself. And judging by the colour of the sky, which was blue and red, it's late in the day, almost sunset. This helped jog her memory and a series of images appeared in her brain – the drive down to the valley, the museum, the bike ride, walking across the field, the kangaroo. Yes, the kangaroo, that's how I got here, and she remembered slipping on a branch or log and then falling and rolling and then … She very slowly moved her right hand up to the back of her head. She felt a large lump, but to her surprise it didn't feel painful at all. Her hair felt a bit strange though, like it was sticky. She brought her hand back in front of her face and looked at her fingertips. They were smeared with red.

"It won't hurt, at least not until you go back," said a voice from behind her.

Maria didn't recognise the voice, so she knew it wasn't Liv. But it did sound like the voice of a girl, and so as she rolled over she had a pretty good idea of who she would see. And she was right.

"Hello, my name is Leena. What's yours?" said the aboriginal girl who she'd seen standing in the bushes across the river on the night of her midnight stroll. She was sitting cross-legged about three metres away from where Maria was lying. As far as Maria could tell she was dressed the same as she had been that night, because all she appeared to be wearing was a cloth or skirt around her middle. For a second, looking at her made Maria feel a bit odd, but then she realised that it was because Leena was sitting on the bank that she'd rolled down, and so she was actually looking slightly up at her.

"Umm, hi, I'm Maria. You speak, um, English?" she asked in a surprised voice.

"Yes, I do," responded Leena nodding. "Thank you for coming back. You're the first, you know. None of the others have ever come back."

Maria had lined up loads of questions for the old man or the girl, if she ever saw them again, but what Leena had just said caused her to forget them all. "What others?"

"The others like you. The ones who can walk with us."

"The others like me? What do you mean by that?" asked Maria as she brought her legs round in front of her and got herself into a sitting position. "And who is *us*, the rest of your tribe?"

Leena smiled and stared at Maria for a second. "I guessed that you didn't know when I saw you with my grandfather that night, on the other side of the river," and Leena moved her head to the left to indicate where she

289

meant. "But I did wonder if you might have worked it out since then."

"Worked out what?" asked Maria. She was beginning to feel quite anxious about what the answer might be, but she'd come so far she knew that she had to find out.

The smile on Leena's face disappeared and was replaced by a serious but kindly one. She leaned forward slightly, "Maria, I am what I think you would call a spirit or a ghost. I died here in this valley a very long time ago. I have no idea how long, as time is almost meaningless to me and my grandfather." She saw that Maria's eyes had opened very wide and her mouth had fallen open, and so she stopped for a moment to let her digest what she'd just said.

For a few seconds Maria felt her mind race in a hundred directions at once, but then she realised that she really wasn't that surprised and she suddenly felt quite calm. "So, the old man who came for me, is he your grandfather? And is he …"

"Yes," said Leena smiling, very impressed by how readily Maria had accepted what she'd just been told. "And, yes, he is a spirit too. He died many years ago as well, though some time after me." Maria nodded, and so Leena went on.

"There are a very small number of people who have the ability to walk with us, with the spirits, and Maria you are one of those people. In all my time here I have only come across four others, but none of them were able or willing to help us move on. We are hoping that you will be the one who will help us do that." Leena could see that Maria was about to ask another question, so she raised her hand and said, "I understand that you will have many questions, but just let me explain what I can, what I know, and then I will answer as many of your questions as I can."

Even though inside she was feeling a great mix of emotions – excitement, disbelief, and wild curiosity – at what she'd just been told, Maria nodded and said, "Yes, yes, of course, you go on."

Leena smiled, knowing how hard it must be for Maria to just listen at this point in time. "Many people, alive people that is, claim that they are able to speak to spirits. And a few of them can. However, there are a very small number who can transfer themselves into our world, the world of the spirits. Of course, I didn't know any of this when I was alive. I have only found out about it since I entered the spirit world. From what I understand most of the people who are able to make the transfer do so when they are asleep." Leena could see that Maria was thinking very hard about what she'd just said, and again she paused to give her time to consider it.

In her mind Maria did a lightning tour of her previous trip to the valley, and what Leena had just said seemed to make sense. Then she remembered what Liv had said earlier that afternoon about sleeping, and she smiled to herself. Maria suddenly realised that Leena was waiting for some signal from her that she should continue and so Maria said, "Okay, I think I understand. Please go on."

"In a sense, when you and the others like you make the transfer, you leave the alive world behind. To the other alive people it's as if you have disappeared from view. Even if you were standing right beside them, they would not be able to see you."

Maria immediately thought about her final night in the house when she stood right in front of Lizzie but Lizzie couldn't see her. She was desperate to ask a question, but she managed to restrain herself and instead just nodded and said, "Yes, I have experienced that."

Leena smiled again and then said, "For what I have to tell you next, it is perhaps best if I draw you a picture."

She raised her right hand so that it was out in front of her about level with her nose, and then she waved it gently from side-to-side. The leaves on the bank in front of her started to rustle and then move as if a very focussed breeze had just blown in. However, no breeze could ever have moved them so cleanly and accurately, for a few moments later an almost perfect oval of earth had been exposed in front of Maria. She then pointed her right index finger at the oval and started to move it, immediately a line started to appear in the earth. The line eventually formed a circle, and shortly afterwards there were three equal sized circles drawn in the earth.

"Put very simply there are three stages of being. The first is life itself," and as she said this Leena used her index finger to start drawing a picture in the circle to Maria's left as she looked. To Maria's amazement, within what could only have been two or three seconds, a line image of what was unmistakeably Maria's face had appeared.

"The second or middle stage is the world of the spirits," said Leena, "in which grandfather and I now reside." And this time Maria was not anywhere near as surprised when an image of Leena's grandfather, the old man who'd she'd taken the midnight stroll with, appeared in the middle circle. "It is a very difficult thing to explain, but let me try this. The world of the spirits exists around the world of the living, but slightly to the side." Leena used her hands to try and describe what she meant, and then looked at Maria to see if she understood. She saw that Maria was nodding, but the look in her eyes suggested that she wasn't completely certain about what Leena had said. However, Leena decided to press on.

"The third stage is the final one, and it has nothing to do with this physical world." Leena raised her arms to indicate everything around them. "Different peoples have different names for it. I think most pale people refer to it as 'heaven'. It is where you eventually meet up with those who have gone before you, your ancestors." And as Leena said this, the image of a face appeared in the final circle. This time Maria didn't recognise it and she wondered who it might be. But almost as soon as Maria had the thought, Leena said, "My mother." Maria was quite startled and looked up at Leena, and thought to herself, does she know what I'm thinking?

However, Leena gave no outward sign of hearing that thought and instead went on with her explanation. "For most spirits the middle stage is nothing more than a stepping stone to the final one, and they spend very little time there. However, for a few the stay there is longer, sometimes unimaginably long. There can be many reasons for this, but usually it is because something about their time in the first stage remains unresolved." Leena paused for just a moment, and then added more to herself than to Maria, "But as I know only too well, it can also be because something is unresolved in the middle one."

Maria looked up and saw a very sad look on Leena's face. Leena didn't say anything for a few seconds, and so Maria thought it would be okay to ask a question. "So that's what you need my help with, moving to the final stage? You and your grandfather?"

Leena raised her eyes and looked towards Maria and said, "Yes, that's right." To Maria it felt as if she was refocussing, not just on Maria but on this moment in time, as if she'd been thinking about something that had happened long ago. Leena paused for a moment and then went on, "But what I'm going to ask of you, it's … it's not an *easy* thing. And I won't be at all surprised if you decide that you cannot do it."

Maria felt her heart start to beat faster. She was anxious, maybe even scared about what it was Leena wanted her to do. But at the same she was intrigued. And for a reason that she couldn't really put her finger on she also had a feeling that she was meant to help. She took a deep breath, "Tell me what it is you need me to do. I promise I will help you if I think I am able to."

Leena smiled, and Maria saw a sparkle in her eye. "Thank you," said Leena. "For some reason, ever since I first felt your presence in the valley I have thought that you would be the one." She stood up and beckoned Maria with her hand, "Come, let me tell you what it is while we walk."

Maria started to get-up, and she did so quite slowly worried that she might be a bit groggy from the bang on her head. But when she got to her feet she felt fine. Then she remembered the first words that Leena had spoken to her a few minutes before, and wondered if she still had that feeling to look forward to when she got back to the *real* world, along with a very sore head. She walked slowly up the bank until she was about a metre away from Leena.

For a moment the girls stood looking at each other. Maria saw that Leena was a very similar height and build to her, and that her hair was about the same length, though it was much curlier. However, whilst there were similarities, there were also differences. Maria couldn't believe how dark Leena's skin was and her eyes too. And her hands, and her feet too now that she saw them, were rough, a bit like an adult's might be. Of course, Maria realised, Leena had probably never worn a pair of shoes, or a pair of gloves, let alone used sunscreen. What different lives we have she thought. And then Maria remembered that Leena's life was over, and cursed herself for forgetting that fact so quickly. For the second time she hoped that Leena couldn't read her thoughts.

But Leena simply smiled and turned. "We need to follow the path of the river and back up into the mountain," she said pointing in the direction they needed to go. "I am going to be honest with you Maria, what I'm about to ask you to do for me, I do not know that it will definitely fix what needs to be fixed in order for me, us, to move to the final stage. But in my heart I am as sure as I can be." Leena saw Maria nod to indicate that she understood. "When I left the alive world ..." She paused, and then started again. "When I died, I was trying to retrieve something that was very important to me, something that I had said I would treasure forever. As hard as I tried I couldn't quite reach it, and so it didn't come with me into the spirit world." She stopped and laughed a little. "It's a good job I wasn't swimming alone, otherwise I might not even have brought this skin with me," and looked down at the material that wrapped around her waist.

Maria smiled back at Leena, and as they started to walk again a thought occurred to her. "So, when you come into the spirit world, you come with whatever you're wearing at the time that you, um, you know, um ...?"

"Die like I did, or when you transfer like you have?" said Leena helpfully.

"Er yes, that," said Maria, feeling a little embarrassed at her reluctance to say it.

"I think that must be the case," said Leena moving straight on. "It was the case for me and grandfather, and it appears to be the case for you and the others who have visited our world. In fact, I'm depending on it being the case, because what I'm going to ask of you is to retrieve what I couldn't retrieve, and bring it to me in this world."

Maria nodded, "I see." And then, "So where is this ... *thing* you'd like me to retrieve for you?"

Leena stopped again and said, "It's a necklace, a necklace that my grandfather made and gave to me. And as for where it is?" She paused and looked up into the trees as if she was not just remembering something, but reliving it. "Well, that is the part that has caused the others who have visited not to return." She closed her eyes for a moment, and as she opened them she turned to look at Maria. Maria saw that the sad look from before had returned to her face.

Leena shrugged and tried to smile. "What's done is done." She started walking again and said, "Come on we better keep moving. We've got a way to go. And while we walk let me tell you a story."

Maria listened as intently as she ever had to anything as Leena told her about her family and her life in the valley, the coming of the white settlers and her friendship with Robert. What she heard evoked a huge range of feelings and emotions. In many ways the simplicity of Leena's life seemed very appealing, but Maria realised it could also be very hard. She wondered how her family would cope with walking as far as Leena's family did to reach the gatherings, or sleeping out in the open all the year around. And how amazing, but also how incredibly weird would it have been to come across white people – and a *horse* – for the first time in the way that Leena had.

As Leena started to tell her about the special day she planned to spend with Robert before heading off to the gathering, Maria felt a bad feeling forming in her stomach. She knew somehow that it was not going to have a good ending. But when Leena described what happened in the river it still came as a huge shock and large tears rolled down her cheeks. It all seemed so unfair. Leena's life was hard enough, how could it be that she died after saving the life of her friend? But Leena seemed to show absolutely no signs of regret or of being angry about it, which Maria thought was amazing. It made her wonder if she could ever be that strong if something similar ever happened to her. And it also made her even more determined to help Leena if she was possibly able to. Even though, despite being a very strong swimmer, she was very nervous about trying to retrieve the necklace from the river.

After Leena had finished describing her final moments with Robert, they walked in silence for a while. Then Leena turned to Maria and said, "Now it's your turn. Have you got any questions for me? I can't promise I will be able to answer all of them."

Maria took a deep breath, and then as she let it out she said, "Phew, where do I start?" She knew she had loads of questions, but what she'd discovered and heard over the last – however long it was – had caused them to turn into a completely unordered jumble. After thinking for a few seconds, something that had been bothering her popped into her head. "Why is your grandfather's spirit still here, in the middle stage?" Having said it, she immediately thought of something else. "And come to that, where is he? I would have thought he'd want to be around for this moment."

"Ah, yes," said Leena with a sigh. "My grandfather was completely devastated when I never returned. He refused to join the rest of my family when they departed for the gathering, and instead stayed behind to search for me. And after he was convinced that there was no trace to be found in the valley, he would go off on long walks outside of the valley hoping to find some evidence of what had happened to me. The search consumed the rest of his life." Leena paused and closed her eyes for a moment. She opened them again and then went on. "When he eventually joined me here, in this world, he vowed that he would not leave it until we did so together. This is why, whenever someone comes into the valley with the ability to move between the worlds, he's so determined to bring us together."

Leena paused again, and Maria thought she'd forgotten the second part of her question, "So why isn't he here now?"

A stern look came onto Leena's face. "That is because – and I do not know why this is the case – spirits are not able to move about freely in this world. There are boundaries across which we cannot pass or even communicate. These can be obvious physical boundaries such as rivers or mountains, but they can also be seemingly invisible lines on the ground. My grandfather and I have been kept apart by this river ever since he joined me in this world." Leena pointed over to the river which was now about fifty metres to their left as they walked.

"That's terrible," said Maria shaking her head. She thought about it for a moment and then went on. "That's why he was so desperate for me to go across it when he brought me to meet you that night." One small piece of the puzzle finally falling into place.

"Yes, that's right," said Leena nodding.

"If only he could have explained it to me." Maria thought for a second and then said, "You know, before now, before *all* of this," and she raised her arms, "I would have guessed that spirits or ghosts would be able to communicate with anyone. You know, they'd be able to speak any language."

"I'm afraid that's not how it works," said Leena. "There's no magic in any of this. What you know in the alive world is what you know in this world."

Maria nodded, "That makes sense." But then she thought that it did, of course, kind of depend on you first making sense of there being such a thing as a spirit world, and that she was currently in it, going for a walk with a girl who was in fact a spirit, and having a very friendly chat, thank you very much. And she smiled to herself.

"What?" asked Leena.

"Oh nothing, just a thought I had," replied Maria. "Can I ask another question?"

"Of course," said Leena.

"If I have this thing, this ability to move myself into the spirit world, then I'm guessing that I've always had it. So my question is why has it happened to me now? Why not before?"

"That's a good question," replied Leena (which made Maria smile again, though Leena didn't notice this time). "I do not know everything about how your ability works. However, from my contact with the others like you, I think it is possible for you to move into our world when *you* want to. But usually it happens when you are called by a spirit. And that's what happened to you. As soon as you came into the valley, grandfather and I started to call out to you."

Maria's brow furrowed as she tried to recall, amongst everything that had happened to her on her last visit to the valley, if she'd heard any strange voices. But then it came to her, it wasn't voices. It was the feelings she'd had on her arms and on her neck.

"Ah yes, now I understand," Maria said nodding and grinning at the same time. "I did hear you, or I should say feel you. In fact, the first time was straight after we drove into the valley, though of course I had no idea what it was." She thought for a moment, and then added, "I told my mum about it and she thought that it might be a sign of that I was suffering from anxiety, which seems kind of funny now." She looked at Leena and saw that she had a confused look on her face.

"Who is 'Mum'? And what is 'an-zi-tee'?" she asked.

Maria laughed, "Oh sorry, Mum is my mother, and anxiety is … actually don't worry about that."

Suddenly it hit Maria that she was really enjoying speaking to Leena, really enjoying her company. She was becoming friends with a spirit who existed in a completely different world, a different reality. How weird was that?

"Actually it would it have been my grandfather who called out to you when you first came into the valley," said Leena, interrupting Maria's thoughts. "You were on his side of the river then. The first time I called out to you was when you were playing with a girl and a boy in the big grass field."

Maria thought for a second and then realised that Leena was referring to the time she, Lizzie and Bobby were playing in the pub garden. "Wow, that was you? That was a whole different level to what I felt when your grandfather called me. It was like a shiver travelled all around my body."

"That was probably because I was so close to you at the time. Actually about this close," and she indicated the couple of metres that separated them as they walked. "And maybe a little bit because I was so desperate for you to come into our world."

"I get it," said Maria. "You were shouting at me to come and visit."

"Yes, that's a good way of putting it," Leena said smiling, and they both started to laugh.

Maria had focussed so completely on their discussion that she had no idea about how far they had travelled on their walk, or how long it had taken them. She was vaguely aware that it had got darker as they walked, but somehow it didn't feel like the normal sort of dark. The sort of dark you got in the alive world, as Leena might have put it. So when Leena said that they were there, Maria wasn't expecting it at all.

Maria saw that they were standing on the edge of a clearing. But as she looked out and around it, she realised it wasn't a clearing of grass. A few steps in front of her started a large area of flat rocks, and beyond that she saw that the river formed a large bend just before it cascaded over the rocks. Even in the semi dark she could sense that it was a special place, a beautiful place.

Leena stepped out on to the rocks. "Follow me Maria, I'll show you where it is."

After feeling so good walking and talking with Leena, Maria suddenly felt quite nervous, scared even. And almost as soon as these thoughts came into her head she started to feel tired. In fact, now she thought about it she was feeling very tired and wondered whether she ought to have a little lie down before she went on with Leena. At that moment Leena realised that Maria wasn't following her and turned to see what she was doing.

Leena immediately called out, "No, not yet!" She ran back to where Maria was standing.

"What do you mean 'not yet'?" asked Maria, and she noticed that just the sound of Leena's voice somehow made her feel less tired.

"It looked like you were about to transfer back to your world," said Leena, "and I don't want you to do that until I've shown you what it is I need you to do."

"How could you tell? What did I do?" said Maria.

"Well, to me it looks a little like you're about to fall asleep standing up. As if all your energy is going to leave your body all at once. I remember that one of the others who came said it happens when your brain has decided that you don't want to be in this world anymore, and that after a certain point it's almost impossible to stop it from happening."

Maria thought about her previous visits to the spirit world, realising quickly that was pretty much exactly what she had experienced, even though she had no idea what was going on at the time. She closed her eyes and imagined clearly walking with Leena across the rocks to the river, and the tiredness – or whatever it was – disappeared. She opened her eyes and smiled at Leena. "Okay, let's do it. Show me what you need me to do."

Leena smiled back and then started walking back across the rocks. This time Maria followed close behind.

Chapter 30

Liv and John drove back to the bike shop in silence. As they parked opposite it looked as if the shop had already closed, but then noticed the front door still slightly open. John quickly jumped out of the car and took Maria's bike out of the back of the car. He wheeled it across the road and reached the shop door just as the shop assistant was approaching it, presumably to lock up.

"Just in time," he said in a friendly manner. He opened the door down, looked down at the bike and then added, "Looks like you managed to sort out the chain then?"

"What?" said John, and then he remembered what he'd told Liv to say earlier and added, "Oh, yes, yes we did."

The man took the bike from John. "Wait here a sec, I'll go and get your deposit." He came back after just a few seconds and handed John some notes, "There you go."

John said a quick thanks as he took the money, and without even looking at it pushed it into his back pocket. His mind was racing and he was beginning to feel very anxious about what they should do next. He was in the process of turning round to leave when he changed his mind and swung back around. As a result he almost bumped into the assistant who was following him to shut the door, "Sorry, ah, can I just ask you something before I go?"

The man pulled up sharply, "Sure, what is it?"

"Look, um, it's not anything to do with the bikes, but I need to, um, report something. And I was wondering, ah, where's the nearest police station?"

"Nothing serious, I hope?" said the assistant in a genuinely concerned voice.

"Me too," said John. "Me too."

The assistant waited for a second to see if John was going to expand on this at all, but when nothing more was forthcoming he shrugged slightly and said, "There's a police station in the village." He walked forward a couple of steps and pointed to his right. "Stay on this road and go across the bridge. The village is only about a kilometre along. And the station is just past the pub on the left hand side. I don't think ..."

Before he could finish the sentence John grabbed the man's hand and gave it a quick firm shake. "Thanks mate. I really appreciate it." Then he turned and ran out of the shop and across the road.

As he got back into the car he could see that Liv had tears running down her cheeks. "What do we do now?" she asked in a shaky voice.

"I don't think we have much choice, Liv, I think we need to go and report what's happened to the police. There's a station in the village just up the road," he said, starting the engine.

"And then we call my mum and Maria's mum?" she asked, even though she already knew what the answer would be.

"Again, I don't think we have much choice, do we? They have to be told about what's going on," and he glanced to his left and saw that Liv was nodding.

Neither of them said anything else on the short drive into the village. The moment of strength that Liv had experienced back beside the river had started to wane on their drive to the shop. And now, as they rapidly approached the moment when they'd have to face *other* people with their situation, it was all but gone. Liv guessed that they were going to be in a whole lot of trouble for not doing what they had agreed to do, while John was off canoeing. And so now she was apprehensive about holding back anything when they talked to the police and their parents. But then she was equally concerned over revealing the truth about why they had cycled into the valley. It wasn't exactly an easy thing to explain, or to believe. She'd also promised Maria that she wouldn't tell anyone else about it. What a mess it was. She considered closing her eyes and going to sleep, fantasising that by the time she woke up Maria would be back. Liv had just started to imagine how good that would be when John started to slow down. The momentary good feeling was quickly replaced by a tight knot in her stomach.

They got to the pub and, just as the man had described, only a little way up the road John saw the sign for the police station. He parked the car and as he started to get out said, "Come on Liv, it's not going to get any easier by waiting. The sooner we report it, the sooner they can get started on whatever is they do in these situations."

Liv knew that John was right. "Yes, I know. Let me just wipe my face a bit," she said and used the sleeve of her hoodie to wipe away the tears. As she got out of the car she tried to put on a brave face, "Okay, let's do it."

John attempted a smile in response but his face wasn't really up to it. So instead he walked over to Liv and took hold of her hand, and they walked the short distance up to the gate at the front of the police station. As they did Liv ran her eyes over the station building. Apart from the blue and white police sign in the front garden, it looked to her just like an ordinary house, and this made her feel a bit less anxious.

As John opened the gate a huge figure emerged from the station and stepped out on to the path. When the policeman caught sight of John and Liv, a big smile spread across his face, "G'day people, what can I do for you?"

John ushered Liv along the path until they were about three metres away from the policeman. "The thing is," said John, "my niece here went for a cycle with her best friend out in the middle of the valley this afternoon," and he pointed out over the head of the policeman, "and they decided to stop and have a rest by a river." John paused and put a hand on his forehead and rubbed it, and then continued. "My niece fell asleep, and when she woke up her friend wasn't there. Her backpack was, and her bike, but she wasn't." As he said this John let out a huge sigh. "Anyway, she came back to find me. And we both went back to the spot to look around, but there was absolutely no sign of her. And so then we decided that we should come and report it. So here we are …"

The smile disappeared from the policeman's face as John spoke, but while he looked serious he didn't look particularly worried. When John finished he leaned forward and looked at Liv, "Hello young lady. My name is Constable Matthews, though I prefer to be called Charlie. What's yours?"

"Olivia," said Liv. "But I prefer Liv," she added after a moment with a little smile. There was something about Constable Matthew's – Charlie's – manner that immediately put her at ease.

"And what's the name of your friend, the one who's gone walkabout?"

"Maria," said Liv.

Charlie stood up straight and turned to look at John. "And you're Liv's uncle …" and he held out his hand.

John stepped forward and shook the outstretched hand. "Yes I am. My name is John. Liv's mum is my sister."

"And is she here in the valley with you? Or any of Maria's family?" asked Charlie.

"No. No, it's just the three of us. I brought Liv and Maria down for the day so that they could visit the Pioneer Museum and do some stuff which they said would help them with a school project. And while they were doing that I went for a canoe along the river." John paused and shrugged his shoulders. "I also hired some bikes for them so that when they …"

Liv stepped between John and Charlie. "None of this is John's fault. We told him that if we got the bikes, then when we'd finished at the museum, we'd cycle into the village. But we decided to go out into the valley instead. And we found this beautiful spot beside the river, and it was so nice in the sun that we thought we'd have a little rest on the grass, and I fell asleep, and when I woke up Maria wasn't there. And so I looked and looked but I couldn't find her anywhere. And so then I decided to cycle back and get John and …" Tears started to form again in Liv's eyes.

Charlie brought his large hands up in front of him and then moved them up and down in a calming motion. "Hey Liv, it's okay. It's not John's fault, and it's not your fault either. In fact, whatever's happened it's almost certainly no-one's fault. This happens down here every so often. People go for a wander in the bush and can't remember their way back. It's not like being in the city where there are lots of people to ask directions, or where you can just jump in a taxi and ask to be taken somewhere. I'm sure that's what's happened to Maria and she's going to be fine." He smiled at Liv and she managed a sort of smile back. Even though he's a very big man, there's something very gentle about him Liv thought to herself.

"However, even though that is almost certainly the case, there are still some things we need to do," said

Charlie and he turned his attention back to John. "Have you contacted anyone else yet, Liv's or Maria's folks?"

John shook his head, "No I haven't. And I said I'd call Liv's mum before we set off back to Sydney, which was going to be like," he glanced at his watch, "an hour ago. In fact, now that I think about it, I'm kind of surprised that I haven't had a call from her by now to see what's going on."

"Well, we definitely need to let them know what's going on. And I need to get some information from you. So why don't you come inside, we'll can get all that done as quickly as we can. And then we'll take a drive out to the spot you last saw Maria and have another look around."

John looked up at the sky and Charlie knew what he was thinking. "Yeah it'll be dark pretty soon, but there's a going to be a full moon tonight and so we'll still be able to see pretty well." Charlie turned and started to walk back towards the front door of the station.

Liv looked up at John. He managed a little smile and used his eyes to point at Charlie. Liv knew exactly what he meant by that. She nodded and whispered, "I like him too, and I'm very glad now that we decided to report it." She took hold of John's hand and then they followed Charlie along the path and into the station.

John was hugely relieved when Charlie indicated that he would make the call to Liv's mum, and very impressed about how he went about explaining to her what had happened, and what was going to happen next. Even though John couldn't hear what she was saying, the words Charlie used gave you a very clear sense of the shock and worry his sister – Liv's mum – was experiencing on the other end of the phone. After a few minutes, Charlie indicated that he needed to call Maria's parents now, and he jotted down some stuff, presumably names and numbers, on his notepad.

Charlie had barely started to tap the numbers into the phone when John's mobile rang and he saw that it was Liv's mum calling. He answered, and to his surprise, and again to his relief, he could tell immediately that she wasn't calling to give him a hard time. She just wanted to know how he and Liv were going. John told her that they were both okay, and that they were just worried about Maria, before passing the phone to Liv.

John then found himself listening to two phone calls at the same time. Not surprisingly the call to Maria's mum was a much harder one. John had huge respect for the people who had to make these calls as part of their jobs. How on earth do you go about telling a mother that her daughter is missing?

He heard sobbing coming from Liv's direction and looked over at her. She was sitting in a wooden chair with her legs brought up in front of her and her chin resting on her knees, and had tears streaming down her face. He heard her say, "Yes Mum, I love you too," and then she pressed the call finish button and held out the phone for John.

John took it and asked in a very quiet voice, "How are you doing?"

"Okay, I guess," said Liv. She looked past John at Charlie who was still talking to Maria's mum and then closed her eyes. "I just wish we hadn't gone out for that cycle on our own. But …"

"But what?" asked John.

Liv looked at John. Part of her was desperate to tell someone about the real reason why they had gone for that cycle, but … but this somehow didn't feel like the right time. She felt pretty sure that if she mentioned Maria's dreams and meeting the old man and all that now, then it would just make things more difficult and very likely more upsetting for everyone. No, it's not the time for that thought

Liv. Just try to stay as calm as possible, and let things run their course.

She refocussed on John and said, "But … you know, you never think that things are going to end up like this. This is the sort of thing that you just hear about in the news that happens to other people."

"You're dead right there," agreed John. He thought for a second, "How did your mum sound? What did she say?"

"She was concerned about how we were doing," Maria replied, wiping her eyes with her sleeve. "But she was even more worried about how Maria's family were going to be about it all."

John rubbed his eyes with the thumb and forefinger of his right hand, "I can't imagine what it must be like for them getting this sort of news."

Liv nodded. "Mum's sure that Maria's mum and dad will want to come straight down here. She's going to call them to see what help they need. Maybe drive them if they're not feeling up to it, or see if they need someone to look after Maria's brother and sister."

John sighed and sat on the floor beside Liv. Neither of them said anything. Liv put her forehead on her knees and closed her eyes, whilst John stared straight ahead and unconsciously twirled his phone in his hand.

After a few minutes Charlie came over to them. "As you know I've spoken to your mother, Liv, and also Maria's parents. They're going to come down as quickly as they can. I've suggested that they come with your mum or dad, Liv. I think it'll be good for you to have a member of your family here too, and it'll be some support for Maria's parents." Liv nodded and Charlie glanced at his watch. "They'll probably get here around nine o'clock, and so that gives us some time to go and look around the place you last saw Maria. I've called a couple of the families that have properties in that area, and they're going to start looking for her as well. Sound okay?"

Liv and John said "yes" and "that's fine" at the same time.

Charlie looked at them and scratched his goatee beard. "I'm just wondering, when was the last time you two had something to eat?"

Liv looked at John, and then they both looked up at Charlie. "We had some pies at the old store when we got to the valley," said John, "but I haven't had anything since then, and I'm guessing that you haven't either Liv." Liv shook her head.

"Okay, if you guys are going to keep going then you're going to need some fuel. So before we head off let's get some food, and you can eat as we drive out there."

Charlie turned away, "I'll just go and grab some stuff, torches and the like. I'll meet you in two minutes by the car, my car."

Liv slowly unfolded her legs and started to stand up. "Weird isn't it, by this time I would usually have eaten an afternoon snack and my dinner. But until Charlie mentioned it I hadn't even thought about food." She stretched her arms out to the sides, and added, "And I'm not even sure I feel like eating anything. My tummy feels really odd." And she brought her hands down and rubbed her stomach.

"Mine too," said John as he stood up. "That's all the worrying and stress. But we should probably try to eat something, I've got a feeling this is going to be a very long night."

Liv grimaced, "Oh, I hope not. It won't take that long to find Maria, will it? She can't have gone that far." They turned together and headed towards the front door. "I keep thinking about her being out there, in the dark," and after the briefest of pauses she added, "all alone." But privately

310

she thought, "I don't actually think you are alone, but I do hope they're looking after you."

They went out and saw that Charlie was already there loading some bags into the back of the huge police vehicle that was parked in the drive.

Chapter 31

Maria felt herself becoming awake. Her first thought was my bed is very hard. Her second was I don't feel very warm, in fact I'm pretty cold. And the third, which pushed the other two right out of the way, was my head is very sore.

Maria opened her eyes, bringing her right hand up to her head. As her hand passed in front of her eyes she noticed that there was something red on her fingertips. She stopped moving her hand and looked at her fingers. Suddenly she started to recall the events of the previous day and evening. The cycle. The kangaroo. Banging her head. Meeting Leena. The small matter of finding out that she was one of only a few people who could enter into the world of the spirits. And then the walk to this place.

Maria looked past her fingers out across the rocks to the river. She could see the water cascading over the rocks and, now she thought about it, she could also hear it. That was another one of the things she wanted to ask Leena – why was it that when she was in the spirit world she couldn't hear sounds being made in the alive world? She smiled at her own use of that term. Maria had thought that it had sounded odd when Leena first said it the night before, and here she was using it herself. She mouthed it again, the *alive* world. Actually it made perfect sense.

All at once Maria sensed that she shouldn't really be lying around thinking about things like that. She guessed from the colour of the sky that the sun was about to come up, which meant that she'd been away all night. She thought about Liv and John. What on earth had they done after she'd disappeared? For a moment she wondered if they might have gone on back to Sydney without her, then realised what a ridiculous thought that was. No, they would have stayed and tried to find me, and … And then, when they couldn't, they would've had to call our parents and let them know what was going on. Oh my god, how hard would that have been? I wonder what they said, and what they did? Knowing my mum she would have called the police straight away. Oh, I hope she didn't. Liv would have told them … And then she realised that Liv had no idea what had happened to her, and anyway what could she really have told them about Leena and her grandfather?

A mix of panic and urgency swept through her. I need to get back to them as soon as I can, she thought. But there is something I must try and do first. She brought her arm up so that she could start to push herself up into a sitting position. But as soon as she put weight on her arm she felt a sharp pain in the back of her head, which then travelled down the back of her neck like a jolt of electricity. Leena was right. The blow to the back of her head, which she'd got the previous day after the kangaroo had startled her, hadn't hurt at all in the spirit world. But now she was back in the alive world, it hurt like hell.

Maria moved her body so that she could bring her other arm around under her, and then gritted her teeth and started to push herself up. As she got to her feet she could feel a throbbing sensation around the lump on the back of her head, but thankfully once she was standing it subsided. Unfortunately it was almost immediately replaced with a feeling of dizziness, and instinctively Maria raised her arms to help keep her balance. After a few seconds she started to feel a little steadier and she tried a step forward. As she did she felt a throb in the back of her head. "Great," she murmured to herself, "if I stand still I feel dizzy, and if I move my head feels like it's going to explode."

Maria realised that this was all related to the bang on her head, and she knew that the sensible thing – indeed the *easy* thing – to do would be to lie down and rest. But after meeting Leena, and hearing her story, Maria felt that sensible or easy weren't options she could consider. She took another step forward, and then another, and almost dared the throbbing or dizziness to try and stop her.

As she reached the platform of rocks that bordered the river, the light around her suddenly changed, and looking to her right she saw that the sun had risen above the escarpments out to the east. That's good, she thought, I could do with some warmth. And she realised that her sore head and the dizziness had distracted her from the fact that she was actually pretty cold. Well, I have just slept outside she thought. But how much of that sleep was in this world? This is definitely going to take some getting used to, she thought, and tried to clear her mind by shaking her head. She immediately regretted it, the throbbing and dizziness returned at the same time.

Maria closed her eyes and did her best to forget the pain and focus on what Leena had told her just a few hours before. As she looked out over the water and her eyes adjusted, she realised that the water was incredibly clear, and she could actually see the ledge where ... Where ... It was all she could do to stop tears forming in her eyes again. Even though Leena had already told her the story whilst they'd been walking together, when she had pointed out over the water to indicate the spot where Robert had fallen into the river, Maria hadn't been able to stop tears from streaming down her cheeks. And now there it was. And it was there that she had to go now.

She pushed away thoughts that the water was probably pretty cold. Worrying about a little cold water was pretty pathetic when you lined it up against what Leena had been prepared to do all those years ago. And then it suddenly hit her. Leena was almost certainly here now watching her. Wow, how weird was that? Maria wondered if Leena would hear her if she said something, but remembered the night she'd been in the hallway with Lizzie, who hadn't been able to hear what she'd been saying. Probably not then, she thought. But somehow the idea of Leena being somewhere close by, watching over her, made Maria feel much better. And maybe also just a little bit nervous.

Maria refocussed on what she had to do, and decided she couldn't do it with all these clothes on. And so she carefully sat down and removed her runners and socks. Then she equally carefully stood up again, and took off her hoodie, jeans and t-shirt. She wondered about whether she should take off her crop top and undies too, but even though no-one alive was around, it didn't feel quite right.

Right. This was it. Maria very gingerly stepped into the water. It was cold enough for her to let out a little squeal but after a second or two she decided it wasn't actually as bad as she had feared. Maybe it was a good thing that she hadn't had a chance to warm up yet, otherwise it might've felt a lot colder. The ledge was about five, maybe seven metres away from her, and as she walked slowly out towards it the water got steadily deeper. As it passed her knees and started to wash against her thighs she instinctively started to walk on her toes trying to keep as much of herself as she could out of the water for as long as possible. But after a few steps she realised that this was a pretty useless thing to be doing, and she took the last few steps on the soles of her feet. By the time she reached the ledge the water came up to her belly button, and although it was cold she didn't feel too bad. In fact, the throbbing and dizziness that had been on the edge of returning now seemed to have eased considerably.

Maria peered down into the deeper water beyond the ledge. It was lot darker than the water around her but she was able to make out some boulders down on the river bed. That must be where it happened. And again she felt a huge pang of sadness about what had happened to Leena. She looked up and around her wondering if she might somehow catch a glimpse of Leena, or maybe at least get a sense of where her spirit was. But then that other part of her stepped in and said that isn't how it works.

With that Maria decided that she should just get on with it, but felt that she shouldn't try to dive down straight away, she would have a look around first. She took a small step forward so that her toes were over the edge of the rocks, and in a single smooth movement she let herself sink into the water and then pushed herself forward. The water felt very cold but also very refreshing as it flowed over her body. Maria kept her eyes shut as she took one big stroke, and then opened them whilst her head was under the water and facing downwards. After a couple of blinks she could make out the bottom more clearly than when she'd been standing on the ledge. She could see the two large rocks that Leena had told her about and the crevice between them. A terrible image started to form in Maria's head, but bringing all of her consciousness to bear on it she managed to force it away. Just think about what I have to do, just think about what I have to do …

Maria took a second stroke and came up for a breath. Then, as she put her face under the water again, she started to turn sharply to her left so that she could swim back over the rocks again. This time she tried to gauge the depth. It looked deeper than most pools she'd been in, but then she thought about the time she'd gone to the Sydney Olympic pool and jumped off the diving boards. The water there was about five metres deep, and she thought it looked very similar to this. That made her feel a little uneasy as she'd never even thought that she could touch the bottom of that pool. But then again she hadn't actually tried to, so how did she know what she could do? After a few more strokes she got back to the ledge and stood up on it.

Maria rubbed her eyes, taking in some big breaths to fill her lungs with as much air as possible. She was just about to drop back into the water when she thought of Leena, and gave a thumbs-up sign, just in case she was looking on. And then she let herself sink again. But this time instead of pushing out in front of her, she leaned forward and down, and then kicked her legs up behind her. She took a couple of big strokes with her arms, and found herself very quickly just above the crevice between the two boulders. She stopped her stroking for a second, and there between the boulders she could see the smaller rock that had trapped Leena's hand all those years ago. It's kind of amazing that it's still there thought Maria, but then again it is protected from the flow of the water by the boulders.

Her thoughts were quickly halted by the first messages being sent from her lungs to her brain that the air in them wasn't going to last forever. She immediately stroked forward and brought herself down so that she could use her left hand to grasp a jagged bit on the left hand boulder. Once she'd done that she brought her right hand down and pushed against the rock in the crevice. It didn't budge at all. She tried again, this time taking her hand back a few inches and bumping the rock with the palm of her hand. Again it didn't show even the slightest sign of moving, and by the third bump her palm felt pretty sore. The messages to her brain then jumped up a few panic levels, and so she decided to go back to the surface and have a think about what she should do next. And so she brought her legs round underneath her, put her feet on the boulders, and pushed up.

By the time she got to the surface she was ready for air, and treaded water for a few seconds while sucking in a few big breaths. A little despondently she swam back to the ledge and then splashed her way back to the spot where she'd left her clothes. Maria didn't really want to get her hoodie wet as she thought she'd use it as a towel when she was finished, but now she was out of the water she was feeling very cold. And so she quickly pulled it on, zipped it up and tugged the hood over her head. The sun was higher in the sky now and noticing a few patches of sun on the rocks, she moved over to stand in one of them while she considered how to move the rock.

Maria's eyes scanned the immediate area hoping to spot something that might help her. After a few seconds she noticed a broken off branch sitting in the water that cascaded over the rocks. She walked over to it and picked it up, wondering if she could somehow use it to knock the rock loose. It's heavy enough, she thought, but I don't see how I could swing it while I'm underwater. Then she remembered her dad moving a large rock in their back yard using an iron bar and some bricks. She looked around to see if there was anything that could give the branch some leverage, but didn't spot anything. Maria put the branch down and turned to walk back to the sunny spot. As she did she remembered that her dad had also given the rock in the back yard a few hefty kicks with his foot. Maybe I could try that she thought, using my legs will definitely be easier than trying to do something with a big branch. And so she walked straight past the sunny spot and over to where she'd left her clothes and runners. She picked up one of the shoes and felt the bottom. Definitely worth a try she thought and she sat down and pulled on both of the shoes.

Once that was done she got up and pulled the hoodie off over her head, and then walked purposefully over to the water. Maria was surprised but not at all upset to find that it didn't feel quite as cold this time, and she waded straight out to the edge of the rock ledge. She took a couple of deep breaths in and dropped down into the water. It was a little harder to swim with her runners on, but she was soon back down above the boulders. This time she made straight for the handhold and after grasping it she brought her legs down beneath her so that she ended up in what was almost a sitting position. She took a moment to get herself ready and then kicked out at the rock with the sole of her right shoe. The impact caused her to lose her grip on the boulder and, as the rock didn't budge at all, she ended up floating backwards away from it. Damn, that wasn't very clever. She momentarily thought about swimming back to the boulders to have another go, but didn't think she'd have enough air, and so let herself float back up to the surface.

As she treaded water and took some breaths, Maria racked her brains to come up with something else to try on the rock. But absolutely nothing else came to her. A shiver suddenly swept through her body, and her teeth started to chatter. She'd been trying not to think about how cold the water was, but knew that she couldn't stay in it for much longer. This is the only plan I've got, she thought, so I'd better give it one more try before I get too cold to do even that.

Maria swam over to the ledge and turned so that her feet were on the edge. And then for the third time she dived down to the boulders. Whilst the repeated attempts were making her colder, they did mean she knew exactly what she had to do, and she was soon in position to kick the rock lodged in the crevice. This time she took a fraction of a second longer to make sure she had the best possible grip on the boulder and then she kicked out with her right foot. This time it had the desired effect, well at least partially, as the rock moved back and up a couple of centimetres.

Maria allowed herself a little *yesss* in her head, but she knew that it hadn't moved far enough. As she retook her grip on the boulder her lungs sent messages to her brain along the lines of "you've only got a few seconds more ..." She did her best to ignore them, getting herself ready to take another kick at the rock. This time she leaned back a bit further, hoping to force the rock up as well as back. She summoned up all her remaining energy and did her best to direct it through her thigh and along her leg into her foot. She brought her right foot back and then kicked out. All at once the rock came free, but rather than moving back it rotated through ninety degrees, and the front edge came up and caught the back of Maria's calf as her leg passed over it. She instantly felt a sharp pain travel up her right leg and she had to fight the urge to open her mouth and cry out. Instead she twisted her body and used her arms to push herself off the boulders and up to the surface. The instant her mouth was free of the water she opened it and sucked in a huge breath of air. But it wasn't nearly enough and her chest heaved as she tried desperately to get more and more air into her lungs.

For a few seconds Maria concentrated only on getting air into her lungs, but soon realised that her right leg wasn't contributing much to her effort to tread water, and so she was running the very real risk of sinking below the water again. For the second time in a matter of minutes she felt as if she was drawing on the very last reserves of her energy, and somehow managed to get herself into a swimming position and then to take the few strokes required to get her back over the ledge of rocks. She decided against trying to stand up until she could see how her leg looked, instead she half swum half crawled until she was in shallow enough water to twist herself into a sitting position.

For a few moments she sat there with her eyes closed. Her leg felt really bad and she was more than a little afraid about what she would find when she looked at it. But she knew she couldn't put it off forever, and she had to get out of this cold water very soon. At the same time she opened her eyes and twisted her leg to give her a better view of her calf. A long wide graze ran from just above her heel to the top of her calf. And whilst it looked pretty awful, particularly as the red and blue contrasted very starkly against her now very white skin, she was relieved to see that there were only a few tiny drops of blood sitting on top of the wound.

For just an instant Maria thought that she'd achieved what she'd set out to do, and she could now get herself out of the water and start the process of sorting herself out, and best of all getting warm again. But then she remembered that she hadn't completed the task at all. The main thing was still to be done. Her shoulders sunk, and she felt tears form in her eyes. "I'm sorry Leena," she whispered. "I don't think I can do it."

Almost as soon as she finished saying the words she felt a tickle on the back of her neck. Maria raised her head and spoke to the air. "Is that you? Are you there?" The tickle thing happened again. Maria managed a half-smile. "You are there. I knew you would be." Just the thought that she wasn't completely alone here in this place made her feel better, and a bit stronger. She closed her eyes again and tried to think as positively as she could about what she still had to do. It's just one more dive, one more very quick dive. I don't have to move anything now. Just go down there, find it and then come back up. I'm already as cold as I've ever been, and so how much colder can I actually get? Maria smiled inside as she wondered how positive that last thought actually was. And even that made her feel better too.

And then Maria knew she was going to do it. And she was going to do it right now, before she had a chance to think about how sore her leg was or how her teeth were chattering incessantly. She used her arms to push herself forward, and then she carefully brought her legs round behind her. She took a couple of long slow strokes to take her out past the ledge. When she thought she was in the right spot she lifted her head high out of the water to take one last deep breath in, and dived down.

As she approached the boulders she saw that moving the rock had disturbed the sand and sediment on the bottom and so it wasn't as clear as it had been on her previous dives. But she knew where she had to look, and she continued down until her head was only about fifty centimetres above where the bottom of the rock had rested. She blinked and stared at the patch of river bed that had been revealed, but there was no obvious sign of a necklace. She scanned the stones that lay there, and at the same time gently kicked her legs to stop her from floating away from the spot. Her lungs started to send the messages again, and she knew she only had a few more seconds. She also knew that she wasn't going to be able to come back down again, this was it. As these thoughts flashed around her brain, she continued to scan for anything that looked like … And then she saw it. A large red stone with a hole in it. Despite the increasing complaints being made by her right leg, she kicked harder to bring herself lower and closer. Her shoulders were almost in the crevice now and so she twisted slightly to let herself get even closer and to reach out, and she felt her fingertips touch the bottom. She gave one more kick and at the same time she dug her fingers into the sand and around the red stone. And then, just as the messages from her lungs started to resemble a fire alarm, she used her left hand to push away from the boulders.

Holding on very tightly to the collection of stones and sand in her right hand, Maria used her left arm and legs to drag and push her way to the surface. Thankfully she made it a bit more comfortably this time, and after reaching the surface was able to continue straight over to the ledge. When the water was shallow enough she got herself into a kneeling position, and finally allowed herself a few moments to catch her breath. She wondered about what anyone who happened to come upon this scene would make of it. An exhausted and half drowned eleven year old girl kneeling in the river, her chin on her chest. With a lump the size of an egg on the back of her head, and a massive graze on her leg. Not your normal everyday sight, she thought, and had a little chuckle to herself.

After maybe thirty more seconds she felt that she had enough energy to make it to her clothes, and so used her left hand to help push herself up into a standing position. Her right leg felt very sore, but to her surprise she was able to put her weight on it okay, and wondered if the cold water had helped numb it a bit. Whatever, Maria was just very happy to be able to finally get out of the river without too much difficulty. Her first instinct was to go over and get her clothes on as quickly as possible, but then she realised she still had the stones in her right hand. She'd kind of forgotten they were there, which was a bit weird when you thought about it. They were the whole reason for what she'd just put herself through. Well, at least she hoped they were.

She decided to put them very carefully down in a sunny spot on the rocks, then get dressed as quickly as she could, before looking at them to see what she'd managed to recover. Not surprisingly it was quite difficult not to check them out straight away, but she was so cold that the pull of her clothes was actually greater.

She used her hoodie as a towel to get her body as dry as possible. And then, after very quickly slipping off her undies and crop top, she pulled on her t-shirt, jeans and socks at lightning speed. Once this was done she felt much better, though still extremely cold. As Maria walked over to the small pile of stones she alternately blew on her hands and hugged herself. When she got there the warmth of the sun was very welcome, and she let the rays shine on her face for a few seconds. In the back of her mind she could almost hear her mum asking if she'd put on any sunscreen yet today? She smiled and bent down to examine what she'd recovered from the river.

The red stone with the hole was the first thing she picked up. Although it had been in the water for well over a hundred years, it still looked shiny and special. It must have been part of Leena's necklace, Maria thought. However, whatever string or twine had been used to connect the stones and shells was nowhere to be seen. And as Maria moved the other stones and pebbles around it became clear that there wasn't anything else there that looked like it had once been part of a necklace. That's a little disappointing she thought, I don't think this is what Leena was hoping for. Then she spotted something else stuck to the back of one of the bigger pebbles. She turned the pebble over and saw what looked like … As she realised what it most likely was, a strange feeling passed through her mind and on through her whole body. It was a tiny white bone. That until a few minutes ago had sat in the stones and sand under the rock that had trapped Leena's hand all those years ago.

For a moment Maria thought, no, that's not right. How could it possibly be one of Leena's? I saw her as clear as day, and as whole as – well, a whole person – only a few hours ago. But then she realised that what she'd seen then was just Leena's spirit, not her physical body. Leena's physical body had been trapped under the water just over there, and Maria looked up at the river, still not quite believing what she was experiencing and thinking, but also not able to deny the growing evidence. And then over the years her physical body had … Maria could hardly bring herself to think about it. But she was old enough to know that that was the nature of life. When you died your physical body eventually withered away one way or another, whether that was in the ground, or under the water.

Maria's thoughts were suddenly interrupted by a sound she wasn't expecting at all. It was a car, and the sound was coming from the trees high up on the side of the slopes that surrounded this bend in the river. Maria stood up and realised that the sound was getting louder very quickly, which meant that the car was heading this way. She stared in the direction of the sound and was amazed when she caught sight of a large white car through the trees. She had absolutely no idea that she was so close to a road. The car took a left turn and then travelled down a steep part of the road that ran parallel to the river. As it got to the bottom of the slope, which was only a few metres higher than the ground where Maria was standing, the car slowed and then stopped. It was only about 80 or 90 metres away from her now. Through the trees she could see that the car had some blue markings and words on it, and realised that it was a police car. Maria watched as a man got out of the car, walked over to a gap in the trees and then started to scramble down a short slope. She could see that he had a uniform on, and felt a huge sense of relief that she wouldn't have to find her own way back to wherever it was she would have gone on her own.

She bent down and put her wet undies in one of her runners and the wet crop top in the other, and then gathered all the laces up in her left hand. She put her hoodie under her left arm and then picked up the red stone and the small bone in her right hand. And then she stood up to see where the policeman was. He had just made it to the bottom of the slope, and so was about forty metres away from her. She could see that he was a very large man, that he had a goatee beard, and had a concerned but friendly look on his face.

He stopped when he made it on to the edge of the flat rocks. "Your name wouldn't be Maria by any chance, would it?"

Maria couldn't help but smile at the way he said it. "Yes, my name is Maria. Have you been looking for me?"

The policeman smiled back and replied, "Yes I have. Though to be completely accurate, I'd have to say it's been me and a few dozen other people."

Maria's smile disappeared. She'd been so preoccupied with her *stuff* that she'd not really given thought to how people would have reacted and what they would have gone through during her absence. Maria suddenly felt very empty, exhausted, and worried, and she could feel tears start to roll down her cheeks. "Did my parents come to look for me? Were they very worried about me?" she asked, though she already knew the answer to both of the questions.

"Yes," the policeman said nodding. "They came last night, and they spent the whole night searching the fields around where Liv last saw you. And you don't really need me to answer that second question, do you?"

Maria shook her head, and then looked down partly so that she could pick her way across the rocks and partly to avoid having to have eye contact with the policeman while she did it.

When she reached him he put an arm around her shoulder and said in a very kindly voice, "C'mon Maria, let's get you back to them as quick as we can."

Chapter 32

The policeman helped Maria clamber up the slope to the road, and then to climb up into the car. As she got in Maria was struck immediately by how warm it was. It felt to her like she was getting into an oven, and it was very welcome.

After helping Maria into the car, the policeman walked to a spot in front of the car and made a call on his mobile phone. Maria couldn't hear what he was saying but by the way he was nodding and smiling she guessed that he was letting people know that he'd found her. After he finished he came round the car and got into the driver's seat. As he pulled his seat belt across and clipped it in he said, "Well, I know who you are, so I think it's only proper that I let you know who I am. I'm Constable Matthews" he said holding out his huge right hand. "Though everyone round here calls me Charlie," he added, and gave Maria a little wink.

Maria took his hand. "I'm very pleased to meet you Charlie, very pleased indeed."

Charlie smiled and nodded, and then started the engine. As he started to turn the car around he asked very casually, "That's a nasty looking bump that you have on the back of your head. How did you get that?"

After scraping her leg on the rock and getting so cold in the water, Maria had pretty much forgotten about her head. "Oh, that happened yesterday," she replied. "I went for a little walk after Liv fell asleep, and a big kangaroo jumped up and surprised me. And as I tried to get out of its way I slipped and rolled down a hill and hit my head on a log. I think I must have been, what do you call it, oh yeah, knocked out. And when I woke up, or you know, whatever you call it …"

"Came to?" suggested Charlie.

"Yeah that, I …" Maria paused, she really had no idea what to say next.

"Yes?" prompted Charlie.

"Umm, well, I didn't see Liv or John." Maria knew that the next words she was supposed to say were "and so I", but she absolutely couldn't tell him what had actually happened then. But on the other hand she didn't want to lie about anything, and so far she hadn't. Though, deep down, she knew that not saying anything wasn't that much better. Even so she was very relieved when Charlie didn't push her on it.

As they started to drive back up the slope he glanced at his watch. "It'll take about fifteen minutes to get to where your parents are. That is if we don't meet them somewhere half way, speeding towards us." He paused and then added, "I hope they're not speeding so much that I have to issue them with a ticket." He turned his head and Maria could see that he was smiling.

They drove for a couple of minutes in silence before Charlie said, "That swim hole where I found you is quite a way from where you and Liv were yesterday afternoon, around twelve kilometres, maybe a bit more. How did you get there?"

Maria was shocked to find out that was how far she and Leena had walked. It hadn't seemed anything like that distance. Or maybe it was more that it hadn't seemed to take that long. She immediately knew that her response wasn't going to sound that convincing, but at least it was the truth she thought. "Oh, ah, I walked."

Charlie nodded and just said, "Okay, I see."

For the next ten minutes they sat in silence, until they rounded a bend and they saw two cars heading towards them, and Maria said, "I think they might be speeding."

Charlie chuckled. "I think you're right, but I might let them off just this once."

As soon as the cars realised that it was Charlie's police car that was approaching them they slowed and pulled over to the side of the road. Maria could see that Liv's mum was driving the first car, and her mum and dad were in it as well, along with Liv. And she saw that John was in the second car with some people that she didn't recognise. Her mum was waving wildly at her and trying to open the door at the same time. Charlie got out of the car and then walked round to open Maria's door. Maria was still holding on to her runners in her left hand and the stone and bone in her right, so she sidled to the edge of the seat, and was very happy when Charlie offered to help her down on to the ground. Despite this, when her right foot made contact with the ground she felt a sharp pain in her calf and her face briefly contorted in response. This just happened to be the exact moment that her mum and dad appeared around the front of the car.

"My god Maria, are you okay?" exclaimed her mum as she came towards her.

"Yes, I'm okay, I just scraped my leg on rock," said Maria, and then she started to move forward to meet her mum. As she did she saw that her mum's eyes were very red, and just the thought that she had been crying caused tears to start rolling down Maria's cheeks. As they hugged Maria whispered into her mum's ear, "I'm so sorry Mum. I really didn't want anything like this to happen."

"Maria, Maria, I'm just so happy that we've got you back," said her mum squeezing her tightly.

Maria's dad came over and took the runners out of her hand, and then wrapped his arms around both of them. After a few moments he stepped back slightly and put his hand on the back of Maria's head. Maria immediately let out a squeal and jerked back sharply.

"What did I do? What's the matter?" exclaimed her dad.

And at the same time Maria closed her eyes and grabbed the back of her head and cried out, "Ooh, that's sore, very sore."

"Have you hit your head, Maria? How did that happen?" asked her mum in a very concerned voice. She moved round and tried to see the back of Maria's head. Maria's hand was still there but she saw that her hair was matted with dried blood. And now she looked she realised that her hair was very wet as well. "What on earth happened to you, Maria?

But Maria was clearly in too much pain to answer and so Charlie stepped forward. "Maria told me what happened. She was out walking when she was surprised by, of all things, a kangaroo. She fell and hit her head on something, a log she thinks. She was knocked out for, well she doesn't really know for how long. Only, that when she came to, there was no sign of Liv or John." Charlie looked over at Maria and saw that she had opened her eyes. "That's right, isn't it Maria?"

Maria nodded. Charlie mentioning Liv had triggered a thought that she desperately wanted to see her. "Where is Liv?" she asked.

"She's over by the other cars," said her dad. And then he called out for Liv and everyone else to come over.

Maria started walking out past the front of the car to meet her. She really didn't want to appear hurt, but each time her right foot touched the ground she felt a pain in her calf, and she couldn't help but limp a bit. And each step also caused the lump on the back of her head to throb, making her wince. However, Liv didn't seem to notice any of this and came rushing up and gave Maria a big hug. Neither of them said anything for quite a while and then they each took step back and looked into each other's eyes. Liv's eyes widened just a fraction, so little in fact that none of the people standing around would even have noticed. But Maria knew exactly what it meant, what she was asking. And she responded by raising her eyebrows a tiny amount. A big smile appeared on Liv's face and she gave Maria another hug. And despite her leg and her head and everything Maria couldn't help but smile too.

Maria looked out past Liv and noticed John was standing there. Liv didn't seem in a rush to end her hug, and so she held out her left hand in his direction. He came forward and took it. His hand felt a lot colder than hers, which caught her by surprise. Maria looked up into his face, and although he was smiling she could see that he had big shadows round his eyes. Clearly he'd had very little sleep, and he's probably been outside most of the night helping to look for me she thought.

"I'm so sorry about all of this John," Maria said, and she felt tears forming in her eyes again.

John smiled and shook his head. "You didn't mean for it to happen," he said kindly.

Maria's mum and dad came over to where Maria, Liv and John were standing. Her dad said, "We've been talking to Charlie and he's happy for us to take you now, Maria. Though given the size of that bump on your head he suggests we should take you straight to a hospital or doctor to get you checked out. Just in case you've got any concussion. He mentioned that you walked a very long way after you came to, which might be a sign of you being disorientated."

Maria nodded, she was very happy indeed to go along with all of that.

Then her mum asked, "When was the last time you had anything to eat or drink, Maria? There's a flask of hot chocolate in the car. Would you like some of that?"

Maria smiled, that was so like her mum. But then again, when was the last time she'd had anything to eat or drink? "Yesterday," she said "when we had a pie at the old store. That does seem a long time ago now, a very long time ago," looking at Liv and John as she said it. They both nodded back at her. "And I would absolutely love some hot chocolate."

Her dad came over and very gently put his arm round her shoulder, and then everyone except Charlie started to cross over the road to the two cars. When Maria realised he wasn't coming with them she stopped and looked back at him. "Thank you Charlie," she called out.

"You're very welcome Maria," he responded, and winked.

Maria made a mental note to send him a card when she got back to Sydney, to say thank you properly.

By the time she got to the car Liv's mum was waiting for her with a cup of hot chocolate. "Thank you," said Maria to her, "and thank you for coming and …"

"Don't say another word Maria, I'm just so happy that you're okay." She looked Maria up and down and then added, "Well, mostly okay." And they both smiled. That's another card Maria thought to herself.

After she'd had a few sips of the hot chocolate, Maria's dad suggested that she bring it with her into the car so they could make a start on their drive. She got into the back of Liv's mum's car, and Liv sat in the middle beside her. As the car started up Liv put her left hand on top of Maria's right hand. It was only then that Maria realised that her hand was still in a fist, tightly holding on to the stone and the bone.

Oh no, she thought, the stone, what am I going to do about the stone? Leena had been certain that being reunited with the necklace was the thing would let her and her grandfather move on from the spirit world. Maria didn't know if just a part of it, a single stone, would be enough, but she knew she couldn't make that call. She had to try and get it to Leena, somehow. But now they were just about to drive away. How far would they go?

Maria tried her best to keep the anxiety she was starting to feel out of her voice. "Where is the nearest doctor or hospital?" she asked.

"We're going to go straight to the hospital in Berry," said her dad from the front passenger seat. "Charlie reckons it should take us about 30 minutes to get there."

Maria suddenly felt very anxious indeed. And this wasn't helped when she realised that they were already passing the turn off that she and Liv had taken on their bikes to reach the river. Oh my god, she thought, in a minute or two we'll go over the river and I won't … And even as this thought started to form in her head she started to feel a tingle on her arms and on the back of her neck. She looked down and she could see that the hairs on her forearms were definitely beginning to stand up. It's Leena, she's calling out to me. And no wonder. She doesn't want me to leave when she's so close to maybe moving on, or at least knowing if she can or not.

Maria felt the sensation grow in intensity, just like it had yesterday when she was on the bike, and when she'd been in the garden of the pub. She looked up and out of the front window of the car, and up ahead she saw the bridge over the river. All at once the tingling changed into a shiver. It started at the top of her back and then began to work its way down her spine.

Liv was suddenly aware of it. "What's the matter Maria? Are you okay?"

Maria was not sure what to say. But as the shiver began to turn into shake, and she sensed everyone in the car was turning to look at her, she finally said, "I'm feeling a bit strange. Can we please stop the car so I can get some air?"

Liv's mum quickly slowed and pulled over. Maria immediately opened the door and thrust herself out of the car, throwing the cup of hot chocolate to one side. By now her whole body was shaking and, after taking a few big but clumsy steps away from the car, she fell forward on to her hand and knees.

"Maria!" screamed her mum and dad at the same time. However, they were so taken aback by what was happening that they didn't actually move. It was Liv who was first to get out of the car and go after Maria. But then she did have a bit of an advantage over the grown-ups, as she had seen this happen before, yesterday afternoon in fact. And since they'd had their eyes-only conversation a few minutes before, Liv also suspected that Maria would have a lot better idea of why it was happening. She moved forward so that she was directly between Maria and the car and then whispered, "Maria, do you know what's going on? Is there anything you need me to do?"

It was the strongest that Maria had ever felt it, and she knew that Leena was calling out to her very loudly and probably from very close by. But now it was starting to ease off, and as everyone else got out of the car, she was able to first kneel up, and then with Liv's help stand up. "Sorry about that," she called out, "I'm fine, really I'm fine."

Suddenly she made up her mind. It was a mad thing to do, and probably a very bad thing too, given what she'd already put everyone through. But she knew she couldn't possibly explain it here and now, they'd definitely think she was concussed and babbling. She looked at Liv and said very quietly, "This is too much to ask, I know. But please do your best to keep them here for as long as you can. There's something I just have to try and do. I promise that I'll explain it all to you as soon as I can."

Liv nodded. "Go."

Maria smiled at her, and then turned and ran as fast as she could towards a gate to a field that was about 20 metres from her.

"*Maria!*" called out her mum and dad at the same time. "What *are* you doing?" shouted her dad, and he started to jog after her.

"She's fine, really she is," said Liv as he passed her. "She just needs a little bit of time on her own."

This caused him to stop, and he turned to look at Liv. He could see in her face that she was being absolutely honest and sincere with him. He opened his mouth to say something to her, but just as he did Charlie's police car skidded to a halt directly behind the car they'd been in. Charlie jumped out and ran over to where Maria's dad was standing. "What's going on? Where's Maria going?"

Maria's dad shook his head and in a despairing voice answered, "I don't know, I really don't know. Maria started to shiver in the car, and said she wasn't feeling very well. So we pulled over and she got out, and had … what looked like … a kind of fit." He opened his arms to re-enforce that he was just guessing. "And then she ran off," and he looked over towards the gate to see that Maria was already over it and running further away. He turned back and looked directly at Liv, "But Liv thinks she is fine and needs some time on her own."

"Liv, do you know what's going on here?" asked Charlie.

Liv shrugged, and opened her mouth as if she was about to say something, but then closed it and looked down at the ground.

"Liv, if you know something you really need to tell us," said her mum, who had come over to where they were standing along with Maria's mum. The tone of her voice indicated that she wasn't going to stand for anything other than the truth.

Liv looked up at her, she had tears in her eyes. She took a deep breath. "Look, I do know something, but it's not anything that you're going to understand or probably even believe. But I really don't think anything bad is going to happen to Maria. She said to me that she needed some time to try and do something. But I have no idea what it is, and that's the truth."

Her mum nodded, and then walked over to her and put her arm around her shoulder.

"Be that as it may," said Charlie, "we are talking about an eleven year old girl here, who may well be suffering from a concussion. And so I think we have a responsibility to get her to someone who can give her a medical check-up as soon as possible. And we definitely can't let her out of our sight again."

At which point all of them turned to look in the direction that Maria had headed in after climbing over the gate. She was already well over a hundred metres away from them, and due to the undulating shape of the field even Charlie could only see her head and shoulders. "Come on," he said "we need to get her back." He started to run over to the gate closely followed by Maria's dad.

Maria, meanwhile, had stopped running and had started to call out to Leena.

"Leena, are you there? I've got your necklace, well part of it anyway. And they want to take me away from the valley, like now." She paused waiting, hoping for some sort

336

of sign. But there was nothing, even the tingling sensation of her arms and neck had all but gone. "Leena," she called out again, but this time much louder. "Leena, I really want to help you, but now I really need your help. *Leeennaa*."

Whilst she was doing this Maria was facing away from the gate. Suddenly she heard Dad calling out her name. She swung round and saw that her dad and Charlie had climbed over the gate and were running towards her, and that Liv was a little way behind them. She started to walk backwards away from them and called out, "Leena, Leena, where are you?" She turned and started to jog, and then run. She could hear her dad and Charlie coming up behind her.

Her dad called out, "Maria, please stop, we just want to talk to you."

She knew that in a few seconds they would catch-up with her.

Maria focussed all her thoughts on sending a message to Leena. The previous night she'd worried about whether Leena could read her mind, now she really hoped that she could. As she ran up a small slope she concentrated as hard as she ever had on a single thought; Leena please help me get to you. Just as one part of her brain registered that the small up slope was followed by a much steeper and longer down slope, the rest of it started to experience the strangest sensation. As her physical body realised that it was going to have to jump on to the downward slope, she began to feel as if the world around her was starting to shrink. It was like the world that she was aware of, the one formed by the ground and the horizon and the sky, was half of a ball, and someone was squashing it in from the outside. No, that wasn't it, it was more like she was pulling it inwards towards her. And the thing doing the pulling was her mind. Even though the whole experience took less than the time it took her to jump through the air, it felt as if it started quite slowly and then got quicker and quicker and quicker, until in an amazing rush the whole of the world she knew was pulled into a single spot inside her brain. And then, even before her right foot hit the ground, the whole process started to happen in reverse, and it seemed as if the world was exploding outwards.

As it did her right foot hit the ground and Maria felt a pain surge up her leg. Her knee buckled and she fell forward, rolling over two or three times before finally coming to a rest about ten metres down the slope.

As one part of her mind did its best to make sense of what she'd just experienced, another one thought, "Well that's that." She waited to see her dad and Charlie appear at the top of the slope. But it took them longer than she thought it would, and when they did it seemed as if they were looking around rather than down the slope where they'd surely seen her go. And then Liv appeared beside them, and she too seemed to be searching for something. Maria saw that Liv's lips were moving and she was calling out. No, she's not calling, she's shouting. Then Maria realised what she had experienced, what had just happened. She carefully started to push herself up into a sitting position, but quickly realised that her leg no longer hurt. Now she was sure, and she looked around, and at the same time called out, "Leena, Leena, are you there?"

"Yes, I'm here," said Leena.

Maria twisted around to see that Leena was standing directly behind her about 15 metres away. Forgetting momentarily where she now was, she spun round again wondering if her dad and the others had heard or seen Leena, but she saw that they were still on the top of the slope looking all around and calling out. Maria breathed a sigh of relief, comfortable with the fact she was now in a version of the world that they couldn't see. She stood up and walked over to Leena.

"Thank you Leena. There was no way I was going to have the time to come to you by falling asleep. We were just about to cross the river and drive out of the valley. I really didn't know what to do, so thank you for helping me."

"There is no need to thank me," said Leena smiling, "because I didn't give you any help. There is nothing I can do to help you, or anyone else, make their way into this world. That was all your own work. It is I who needs to thank you for everything that you have done for me. For what you have put yourself through, and for what you have put others through in order to help me." And Leena glanced up towards where her dad and the others were. Or at least where they had been.

Maria saw that only Liv was left standing there, her dad and Charlie had moved away, presumably to try and solve the mystery of where she had gone. She knew that she really should get back to them as quickly as she could, but first she just had to do this.

Maria turned and faced Leena again, and at the same time she opened up her right hand to reveal the red stone and the small white bone. She'd been holding on to them for so long and so tightly that they had left clear impressions in her skin.

"I'm sorry Leena. I wasn't able to find the necklace, but I think, I hope that this stone was part of it." She looked up into Leena's face and saw that there were tears in her eyes. It was the first time that she had seen Leena show any emotion.

Leena reached over and picked the stone out of Maria's hand, and then brought it back and held it to her chest. She nodded, and as she did a tear rolled down her cheek. "This was part of it," she said simply.

When she didn't go on Maria felt compelled to ask, "Do you think it's enough for you and your grandfather to move on, you know, to the next world?"

Leena didn't say anything for a few seconds and seemed to be staring out at a point on the others side of the valley. And then she said, "I feel that we are able to move on." On hearing this Maria smiled excitedly. "But, I'm not as certain as I was that it is because of the necklace," added Leena, "or at least it's not only because of that. I think it's as much to do with you being the one who helped me. Helped us," she said, correcting herself.

"What do you mean by that?" asked Maria.

"I don't know for sure," replied Leena, "but I just have a feeling that it needed to be you who did this for us." Maria nodded but she didn't really understand what Leena was suggesting.

Leena then looked down at Maria's hand again, and moved as if to pick-up the bone, but at the last second she didn't. "Hmm, that's a bit too strange," she said, with a half-frown and a half-smile on her face.

"I know what you mean," agreed Maria. And they both laughed.

"You can keep that," said Leena. And she used her left hand to close Maria's fingers around it.

They were silent for a few seconds, before Maria asked. "When will it happen?"

"Soon, I think. Now we are free to go there, I have a strong sense that we should be there. It's almost like I'm being called or pulled. I can already feel it." She closed her eyes and then said, "It will be good to sit beside my grandfather again."

Maria felt happy but very sad at the same time. She was happy that Leena was going where she wanted to be, and that she would soon be with her grandfather again, but … but even though she'd only been in her company for what, one night and a bit of morning, she felt like she was saying goodbye to someone very special. Someone who she could easily spend a lot more time with. Someone she could easily imagine becoming a very close friend.

Maria looked at Leena and tried to smile while tears rolled down her cheeks. She wanted to say something, something meaningful, but she couldn't think of the right words. She looked down at the ground. "I don't really know what to say, but I just want you to know ..." As she did she looked up and saw that Leena was no longer standing in front of her. Maria looked quickly to her left and right, but she already knew that she wouldn't see her. Momentarily she thought that meant ever again, and felt a huge empty feeling inside her. But she soon realised that her experiences over the last 24 hours were pretty strong evidence that this wasn't necessarily going to be the case. And this very quickly made her feel better.

Maria was immediately overcome by a sudden feeling of extreme tiredness. Straight away she thought of the discussion that she'd had with Leena beside the swim hole the previous night. Whilst she hadn't consciously thought it was time to leave this world, Maria was very aware that part of her brain was telling her that she should really return as quickly as she could to the alive world, as everyone would obviously be worried about her. Again.

Maria sat down, and lowered herself to the left so that she was lying on the ground with her head resting on her left arm. She very carefully put the little bone into the pocket of her hoodie and pulled up the zip. And then she closed her eyes and within seconds was asleep.

Chapter 33

Maria woke up and immediately opened her eyes. She very quickly closed them again. She was lying on her left side facing a window through which very bright sunlight was shining, and her wide open pupils just weren't able to cope with it.

So I'm not in the field anymore, she thought. And that's not my bedroom window, or any other window I recognise, and so where am I? She didn't move for a few seconds trying to listen out for any sounds that would give her a clue. She thought she could hear some people talking, but she couldn't make out any of the words or who was speaking them.

Maria tried opening her eyes again, but this time much more gradually. That was definitely better, and once she was comfortable with the light she moved her eyes around to check out what she could see of the room. There really wasn't very much to see. A picture of some flowers on the wall, a bedside table, and a chair. Not very homely she thought. And then she noticed the sheet, which was very thick and crisp, just like the sheets you got in a hotel ... no, a hospital. I'm in a hospital.

At this thought she decided it was time to roll over, and immediately came face to face with Liv.

"You're awake," said Liv with a beaming smile on her face, "and about time too. I know you have reputation for sleeping in, but 24 hours non-stop is a bit much."

"What?" said Maria "I've been asleep for how long?"

"Well actually, now that you ask, it's probably more than twenty-four hours. I guess it was about eight thirty when Charlie and your dad carried you out of the field, and it's now just before ten o'clock," said Liv looking up at a clock that was on the wall above Liv's head. "And that's ten a.m. the following day," she added.

Maria shook her head not quite believing what she was being told. "So what day is it?"

"It's Wednesday." Liv could see that Maria was having trouble processing it and so added, "We came down to the valley on Monday morning. We lost you on Monday afternoon, and spent all Monday night looking for you. We found you on Tuesday morning, but then we lost you again. That was only for a few minutes, but what a few minutes they were," said Liv with a look which was both excited and questioning. "When we found you, you were asleep, well at least it looked like you were. And then we brought you here, and they cleaned you up and put some bandages on you."

"Wow," was all Maria could think to say. They were both quiet for a few seconds, and then they both started to speak at the same time.

"You first," said Liv smiling.

"Where are my folks?" asked Maria.

"Well your dad went back to Sydney yesterday afternoon to look after Lizzie and Bobby. And your mum has just popped out for a coffee. She was in here all night." Liv turned her head to the left to indicate a chair that had a pillow and blanket draped over it. "And so I said I'd wait here with you while she was out. She'll be back very soon I think."

Maria smiled, thinking about how her mum always said that she needed a coffee before she could really face the day. Ten o'clock was actually a bit late for it.

Maria nodded. "And what about your mum and John? Did they go back to Sydney too?"

"Actually it was my mum who took your dad back. But she's planning to come back down as soon as we know that you're okay to travel. And as for John, he went back yesterday morning. We were all worried about him driving after having so little sleep, but he just wanted to get back. I think it was all a bit too much for him."

Maria nodded again, thought for a moment, and then asked, "So what was it you were going to say?"

"What do you reckon I was going to say?" Liv said laughing. "What on earth happened to you? Tell me everything. But especially the bit about how my best friend has somehow developed the ability to disappear into thin air right in front of my eyes?"

Maria blinked a few times. "Of course I'll tell you everything. But you know, I think it's time for me to tell my mum as well. Including all the stuff you already know about, from the weekend. So if it's okay I'm going to wait until she comes in. Okay?"

"Of course that's okay," said Liv. "Actually it'll be a big relief for me. When you ran away from the car, and into that field, in order to convince everyone that I thought you were going to be fine I um …"

"Yes," prompted Maria.

"Well … I ended up admitting that I did know something about what was going on. I got some pretty stern looks, I can tell you, especially from my mum. But thankfully Charlie was so concerned about not letting you get out of sight that I didn't have to say anything else." At that point a smile started to form on Liv's face.

Maria raised her eyebrows and said, "What's funny about that?"

"Well, we were chasing after you in order to not let you out of our sight, and just when we thought we'd caught up with you, you quite literally disappeared out of sight. Just like that." She clicked her fingers to emphasise how sudden it was.

"Really," said Maria excitedly. "Tell me exactly what happened, what it looked like to you?"

Liv settled herself in her chair. "Well, your dad and Charlie were running across the field trying to catch up with you, and I was a bit behind them."

"I remember that," said Maria.

Liv nodded and then continued. "Anyway, they were getting pretty close to you, maybe twenty five or thirty metres away. And then you started to go up a bit of a slope, and I thought they were sure to catch up with you very quickly, so I stopped and just watched." Liv leaned forward and lowered her voice. "You got to the top of the slope and then jumped – though from where I was I couldn't see that there was a drop on the other side. And then you were gone, just like that. There wasn't a flash or anything like that, you know like you get in the movies," she said with a smile.

Maria shook her head in disbelief, she could hardly believe that what Liv was describing was about her, about something she had done. "What happened then?" she asked.

"Well, your dad and Charlie stopped running, and just walked slowly up to the place where you'd jumped from. Obviously they were pretty, you know, freaked out by it. For a few seconds they didn't say anything, they just stood there and looked at the air where they'd last seen you. I remember that Charlie was scratching his head. It was like they couldn't believe what they'd seen. No, that's not it; I mean I found it pretty hard to believe myself. It was more that they couldn't even accept the possibility of it. I guess, maybe, knowing what I knew, what you'd already told me about, I was a bit more prepared for the possibility of something *weird* happening."

They both smiled when Liv used the word 'weird'. "Anyway, then I walked up to join them, and just as I did they both started shouting out your name, and I joined in. I'm not really sure why we did that, but I guess we didn't know what else to do."

"You know, *I* could see *you,*" said Maria very quietly. "I could see all of you calling and shouting out to me. But I couldn't hear you. That's not the way it works."

Liv's eyes opened so wide that for a second Maria thought that her eyeballs might pop out of her head. "Not the way *what* works?" she eventually managed to get out.

Liv thought for a second, and then said, "I will tell you, but please let me do it when my mum gets here."

Liv slumped back in her chair. "Ah that's so cruel. You can't do that." Then she smiled and nodded, and said, "Okay, okay, I can wait."

"Thanks," said Maria. "I really appreciate it. Now tell me, before my mum gets here, how did you find me? How long was I away for?"

Liv leaned forward again. Even though she was desperate to hear Maria's story, she was really enjoying telling her bit. "Well, I think it must have been about twenty minutes after you, you know, so mysteriously *disappeared,*" and she put her hands in the air and made some 'oooh wooh' sounds. Maria laughed; she was enjoying listening to Liv tell her bit of the story almost as much as Liv was in telling it.

Liv went on. "When we couldn't find you right where we thought you should be, we started to spread out. Your dad and Charlie walked over to some trees that were at the

346

bottom of the field, thinking that somehow you'd managed to make it down there. It was actually quite a long time before our mums came across the field and joined in with the search. I think that was because they couldn't really see what was going on beyond the little hill. When they did get to us your dad ran back up and tried to tell them what had happened, though I remember he said something like 'we lost sight of her', rather than she disappeared into thin air right in front of our eyes. Anyway, your mum still said, 'I can't believe it' and 'How could that happen with you being so close'?

"And then your mum and my mum said they'd start looking, and about two minutes later your mum shouted out that she'd found you. We all ran over to where she was and saw that you sleeping very peacefully on the grass." Liv rested her head on her left arm to show Maria what she'd looked like. "Your dad and Charlie were very confused by it all because where you were lying was kind of over to the side of where we'd last seen you, and not at all in the direction that you'd been running." Maria nodded and smiled ever so slightly but said nothing. "Your mum said your name a few times, and even gave you a little shake, but you wouldn't wake up. And so your dad and Charlie carried you over to the car, and then we came straight here."

Liv sat back in her chair, just as the door to the room swung open and Maria's mum came in with someone who Maria guessed was a nurse.

"*Mariaaa,*" said her mum very excitedly, "you're awake."

"Yep, I'm awake," replied Maria, confirming the obvious.

"How are you feeling?" her mum said as she put her arms around Maria in a big hug.

"I'm feeling okay," said Maria. Though the question did make her wonder about her head and her leg. She'd been so wrapped up in the conversation with Liv that she hadn't given her injuries a single thought. She lifted her hand up and very carefully touched the back of her head. There was a bandage or dressing there.

"That was a pretty big bump you got there," said the nurse. "There was a small cut as well, and so we put some glue on it, which is why you have that dressing on it. Don't worry, your hair will grow back in no time." Maria frowned, but didn't say anything. "You also had a very nasty graze on your leg which we've cleaned and bandaged. I reckon that might be a bit stiff for a few days. I've told your mum how to take the bandage and dressing off, and put new ones on, if that's required." She came over to the side of the bed. "Just let me check a few things and, if everything's okay, you'll be able to get out of here in a few hours."

"That would be good," said Maria. "I'm really looking forward to getting home."

"Me too," echoed Liv.

The nurse did her checks and indicated that everything looked fine, but they wanted to wait a little while longer before discharging her just to make sure that Maria wasn't suffering from any concussion. As she was heading out of the room she stopped and turned. "By the way, are you feeling hungry? Do you feel like you can eat anything yet?"

Maria thought for a second and realised that she was very hungry. She tried to remember when she'd last had anything to eat, but was beaten to it by Liv who said, "I don't think you've eaten anything since Monday morning, you must be starving."

"Actually, I am. Yes, please can I get something to eat?" she said in the direction of the nurse. The nurse smiled and then turned round and went out of the room.

Maria turned to look at her mum. She had a big beaming smile on her face. "Mum ..." Maria said, then stopped. Ever since she'd woken up she'd been thinking how she should say what she was about to say, but now the time had come she couldn't think of the right way to start it. What the heck, Maria, just get it out. Good idea she thought. She reached out for her mum's hand and then started again.

"Mum, I want to tell you about everything that's happened to me, not just over the last few days but also some stuff that happened when we visited Kangaroo Valley and stayed in Pete's house." Maria saw her mum's eyes widen a bit, she clearly hadn't been expecting that Maria's disappearance over the last few days had anything to do with their previous visit.

But Maria's mum simply said, "Okay, I'd very much like to hear it."

"If it's okay with you I'd really like Liv to stay as well."

Her mum nodded. "Of course, that's completely fine."

"Okay, great," said Maria, and she breathed in a slightly larger breath as if to signify it'd already gone better than she thought it might. "But just before I start I do need to tell you a couple of things. First, you don't how many times I thought about telling you, or Dad, or both of you about what's been happening. And I can't really tell you why I didn't – I guess it just never felt like the right moment, or probably, more likely, I really didn't know what to tell you it was all just so *weird*."

Maria's mum shook her head and said, "Don't worry about that Maria, not at all. I completely understand."

"Thanks Mum," said Maria.

"What's the second thing?" said Liv, eager to get past the intro and into the story.

Chapter 34

It was about six hours later, and Maria was sitting in the back of Liv's mum's car, along with Liv. They were on the highway, coming into the outskirts of Sydney, and Maria had just finished re-telling her story in its entirety for the second time that day.

Liv's mum's reaction had been very similar to that of her own mum. They had both listened intently, and had asked a few questions, but not too many. And when Maria had told them about her first proper meeting with Leena, and how Leena had explained to her that she had a special ability, the ability to transfer herself into the spirit world, they had both gone very quiet. And it wasn't just that they hadn't said anything, they both seemed to withdraw into themselves, as if their body language had gone quiet too.

When she'd been telling her mum and Liv earlier that morning, Maria had paused at that point to see if they wanted to ask any questions about it, but neither of them did. Eventually her mum had just said, "Okay, go on." The next time either of them said anything was after Maria had told them about her final meeting with Leena, and Liv had asked, "Can I see the bone?"

"Sure," said Maria pointing. "Can you please pass me my hoodie?" She'd seen that her clothes were folded over the arm of a chair in the corner of the room. Liv passed it over to her, and Maria opened up the pocket, took out the tiny bone and held it out for them to see.

Liv leaned forward over the bed to look at it. "Can I hold it?"

"Of course," said Maria. "Just don't drop it or lose it," and she tipped it into Liv's hand. Maria turned to look at her mum and saw that she had tears in her eyes. "What are you thinking Mum?" she asked in a quiet voice.

Her mum sighed deeply and then said, "Phew, a hundred things all at once." She reached over and took Maria's left hand in her right hand and gave it a squeeze. "To be honest I think I'm going to need some time to work out what I do think about it all." And she smiled as a tear rolled down her cheek. "Obviously you need to tell all this to your dad, and then the three of us should have a chat about it together. And I think that's all I can say about it right at this moment." She paused again for a few moments, and then added, "Except of course that I think you are a very brave girl for doing what you did to help Leena. *But* if you ever do anything like that again without telling ..."

Maria smiled and nodded, "I understand. And don't worry, I definitely won't. I promise."

No one in the car said anything for quite a while. Then her mum had suggested that until she, Maria and Maria's dad had had a chance to talk about it, and to decide what if anything they should *do* about it, none of them should say anything about it to anyone else. Liv's mum had very quickly agreed with that, and then immediately checked that Liv understood what that meant. And also that she understood how much trouble she'd be in if she so much as hinted at anything about it to anyone.

Liv had said, "Yes, yes, yes Mum, I understand."

But her mum had continued, "Not your dad, not Uncle John, and not Rory, especially not Rory."

"Yes Mum, I get it. Don't tell anyone anything about it." Liv turned and smiled at Maria and then said, "Hey Mum, is it okay if I talk about it to ..."

Her mum said, "No," at the same time as Liv said, "Maria."

Her mum let out an exasperated sigh as she glanced to her left to look at Maria's mum's face. She received a knowing look in return, and a little nod. Then she said, "Yes, that's okay. But only when you're sure no-one else is around."

After that, for the rest of the journey, it was not talked about again. At about five o'clock Liv's mum dropped Maria and her mum at home, and there was lots of hugging and thank-yous on the pavement, before Maria walked back into her house. She'd only been away for two nights, but it seemed like she'd been gone for weeks. She found herself looking around the house to see if anything had changed, like she did when she came back from a long holiday.

Lizzie and Bobby were still at their vacation care place – her dad was going to collect them on his way home from work – and so fortunately she was able to go up into her room and generally settle herself back into the house without any distraction. After a while she came back downstairs and sat with her mum at the breakfast bar and drank hot chocolates. Her mum suggested that she didn't say anything yet to Lizzie or Bobby about Leena or the spirit world thing, and Maria agreed. They decided that the story she would tell them was that she'd been knocked out, got concussed and disorientated, and so had not been able to find her way back to the village, and ended up sleeping outside for the night.

When Lizzie and Bobby did eventually arrive with her dad, Maria got lots of practice telling that version of the story, as they both wanted to hear about it over and over again. And Bobby, in particular, was fascinated with

Maria's injuries and how she'd got them, and asked when he'd be able to see them without the bandages, "Can I now, can I now, please, please."

"No," Maria and Mum had said together. "I'll make sure you're around when we change the bandages, but that won't be for a couple of days, alright?" added Mum. Bobby decided to settle for this, and then went on to ask a whole load of questions about the kangaroo.

Maria was allowed to stay up after Lizzie and Bobby had gone to bed. Initially Lizzie wasn't too impressed by this, but her mum explained that given how long Maria had slept for over the last couple of days she probably wasn't going to feel that tired for quite a while yet. And then Maria retold her story for the third time that day, to her dad and her mum together. Maria wondered how much he'd already been told by Mum, because Dad didn't seem to be anywhere near as shocked by it, and he asked a lot more questions about things along the way. As a result it took far longer to get to the end. By then Maria was actually starting to feel pretty tired again.

When she had finished her dad leaned back in his chair and stared at his hands for what seemed like ages, but it was probably only a few minutes. Eventually he said, "Hmm, I really don't know what to say or suggest we do. Actually I think I need some time to think about it properly."

Both Maria and Mum laughed at this, and Mum said, "That was exactly my response as well."

Dad smiled. "Well I guess that's pretty understandable. I mean, it's not something that you hear about or confront every day, is it?" He paused, "It's not like you're ever going to get called by the school and have them say 'by the way, I just need to let you know, we've just discovered that your daughter has a special ability in the subject of walking with spirits and ghosts, and we'd like her to represent the school in the upcoming spirit meeting championships'." All three of them burst out laughing, and Mum eventually had to 'Sshh' them in case they woke up Lizzie and Bobby.

Once they had settled down again Dad did say one more thing. "Maria, please promise me that if you ever feel that anything like this is starting to happen or even about to start, then please tell us straight away."

Maria said, "Yes, of course I will Dad," and went over and gave him a big hug.

That was pretty much how it got left. Maria spent the next couple of days at home with her mum, Lizzie and Bobby, and spent some time writing thank-you cards to Charlie, Liv's mum and John. And then the following week she went to vacation care with Lizzie and Bobby and Liv. To start with, whenever they were alone together, all Maria and Liv talked about was Leena and her life in the valley, and Maria's time in the spirit world and what that was like, and would she ever be able to go there again. But by the end of the week they didn't talk about it as much, and their attention turned increasingly to the upcoming term, which was going to be their second last together at primary school.

If Maria's mum and dad ever spent time thinking or talking about what had happened to her, Maria wasn't aware of it. And the three of them never did sit down together again to discuss it, or to work out what, if anything, they should do. The only time Maria ever thought it might get discussed was when she did something and Lizzie made a remark about her being the daughter of a white witch. In the past everyone would have commented on it and had a bit of a laugh, but this time there was just a series of knowing glances shared between Maria and her mum and dad.

Weeks went by, and then months, and Maria never got even the slightest sense that either she was about to be contacted by a spirit, or that she was suddenly going to be catapulted into that world. Sometimes she wondered about how it was *supposed* to work. She and Liv loved superhero movies like *Spiderman* and *The Fantastic Four*, and in those stories as soon as someone found out that they had special powers or abilities they always put them to use straight away, mostly to do good, or defeat evil.

Maria felt like her special ability was a bit of a disappointment, and said to Liv on more than one occasion, "I mean, what's the point of having it if you never get to use it?"

But then, on her thirteenth birthday …

Epilogue

It was quite a while before Robert had any sense of what had happened behind him in the water.

After inadvertently kicking the rock he had a throbbing pain in his left foot, and he could feel grazes forming on his knee caps as he crawled across the rocks and out of the water. Once he was clear of the water he slumped on to his right side and took a few deep breaths. He closed his eyes and moved his foot from side to side. It hurt a lot. He opened his eyes, and was a little surprised to see that Leena wasn't already out of the water, or at least on the ledge. He figured she must be doing something in the water.

As his breathing started to settle down he listened out for any sign that she was moving around in the water. When he didn't hear anything he experienced his first feeling of uneasiness. He called out. "Leena. *Leena.* Are you okay?" Nothing. He pushed himself up into a sitting position and scanned the top of the water and the surrounding rocks. Still nothing. He got quickly to his feet and waded back into the water, all the way calling out to Leena. He slowed when he thought he was getting close to the ledge; he certainly didn't want to make that mistake again. He stood and looked out across the water. All of a sudden, about four to five metres in front of him, there was a sudden eruption of bubbles. And then the water was still. It took him a moment to realise what this might signify, and when it did he felt a sharp pain inside his chest. Surely it couldn't be that, Leena was the best swimmer he'd ever seen.

He leaned forward and looked into the water. The surface was still slightly agitated by the ripples he'd caused when he'd waded out. But after a few seconds, as it started to calm, he thought he could make out the outline of a … of a person. For some reason that he couldn't work out, the person seemed to be stuck to the bottom of the river, and *she* wasn't moving.

The truth, the terrible truth suddenly hit home. "*Noooo*," he shouted at the top of his voice. He desperately racked his brain for something that he might do. For a second he considered jumping in, but just the thought of getting back into the water made him gag. What else, what else, and he looked around for any inspiration, anything that might help. He caught sight of a branch on the rocks, and half-ran half-hobbled over to it. No, that wouldn't do, it was way too short. He looked over into the trees, and saw a branch hanging down that looked like it was a lot longer. He went over and grabbed it, only to find it was still attached to the tree. He pulled at it, but it wouldn't come free. He lifted his legs off the ground, hoping his body weight might help to dislodge it. But after four or five bounces he accepted that it wasn't going to break off. Holding on to the branch he allowed himself to slide down to the ground and into a sitting position. He started to cry uncontrollably and huge tears rolled down his cheeks.

Even after he'd stopped crying and the tears had dried up, he just continued to sit and stare out into the trees. He had no sense at all of how long he sat there. Then, without really knowing why, he decided it was time to stand up and to leave this place. Without even a single glance behind, Robert walked away from the river and up into the trees. For quite some time he walked through the bush without the slightest thought about which direction he was heading.

However, eventually he realised that he was beginning to head up quite a steep slope, and it hit him that he had no idea where he was. The thought of being lost combined with the huge feeling of grief was almost too much to bear and he literally fell to the ground in a heap. And for a second time he cried uncontrollably.

By the time Robert felt able to get up again the sun was just about to disappear behind the cliffs. However, this did give him a very good means of working out in which direction he needed to head. He walked that way for a couple of hours, but after darkness had fully taken hold he found it impossible to gauge where he was going, strongly suspecting he was going round in circles. Eventually he opted to give up and get some rest, finding a sheltered spot under a large tree.

It took him nearly all of the following day to finally make it back to his family's camp. Not surprisingly his mother and father had been very concerned about him, and were overjoyed when he walked in. However, their joy was short lived because Robert was completely inconsolable over what had happened to Leena, especially as had it happened straight after *she* had saved *his* life. The next day his father went with Robert to find Leena's family to tell them the terrible news, but they didn't find them, that day or any other. Unbeknown to them her family didn't return directly to the valley after the gathering, and instead spent a period of time living to the east, closer to the sea.

A few months after Leena's death Robert and his family moved away from the valley up into to the highlands to the west. Over the next few years they combined stints back in the now rapidly growing town of Sydney with surveying trips out to the southern highlands. After finishing his schooling, and much to his father's delight, Robert trained as an engineer in Sydney. But despite proving to be very accomplished at it, he never really took to it, and in his late thirties Robert decided to take up a teaching post back in the southern highlands.

It was soon clear that teaching was Robert's true vocation and he became very highly regarded, not only by the children, but within the local community. Not just with the white settlers, though. Wherever and whenever it was possible Robert sought to engage the local aboriginal people about how best to combine their respective approaches to teaching.

It was here that he met Elizabeth, and although he was some way past forty when they eventually married and started a family, they ended up having five children, the oldest of whom was named Robert. When he, in turn, named his oldest son Robert, a tradition was started that lasted through the next three generations. The great- great-grandson of Robert – Leena's Robert – was born in Sydney in 1966. He married Janet, and they had three children together. There was never any doubt that they would name their oldest son Robert, though just like his dad he was known as Bobby.

But Bobby wasn't the oldest sibling, he had two older sisters. One named Elizabeth, known to everyone as Lizzie, and the other, the eldest, was named Maria.